Politicians And Kings

Part II Libertas

Book 8

Of The Warrior Series

By

Sandra J Yearman

Seraphim Publishing LLC

We Will Bring Light To All The Dark Places

Registered trademark-Sandra J Yearman

Seraphim Publishing
438 Water St
Cambridge, WI 53523
sandrajyearman@gmail.com

Library of Congress Catalog Number: 2015904985

ISBN: 978-0-9890263-6-9

First Edition

About The Author

Sandra J Yearman is a native of Wisconsin, where she currently resides. She graduated from the University of Wisconsin with a Bachelor of Arts degree in Journalism. Sandra was a member of the United States Army Reserves for over twenty years. She retired from the Dane County Sheriff's Office in Madison Wisconsin as a sergeant.

Sandra is a cancer survivor. And it is on this journey that she says she found her voice and began to write. She established Seraphim Publishing LLC in 2008. Sandra has spent decades supporting and working with rescued domestic animals.

Books written by Sandra:

Novels

Brother Kings
The Scroll And The Sword
Song Of The Second Son
The Faces Of The Damned
A Single Lion Roars
Stand Before The Children
Tyrants, Dictators And Kings

Politicians And Kings
Armada Of The Dead

Poetry

A Gathering Of Angels
I AM Who You Seek
A Celebration Of Angels
The Time Of Angels Is At Hand
The Warrior On Bended Knees
Celebration of God
On His Wings
The Voice Of An Angel
If I Had Wings
Souls On Fire
As Angels Hover Over
From The Mist The Angels Came
You Are The Song
Be Still
Walking With Angels
When Angels Smile
Angel Dreams
An Angel's Touch
Dancing With Angels

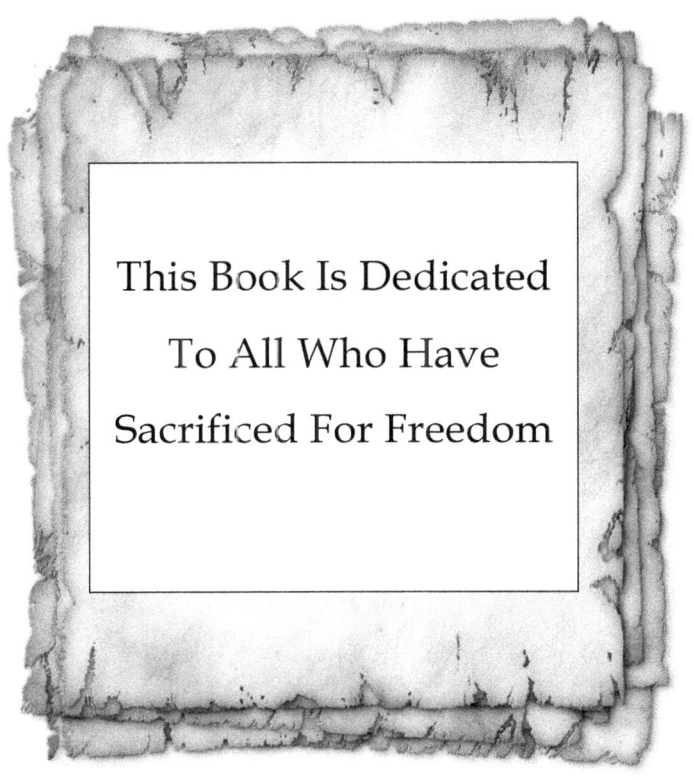

This Book Is Dedicated
To All Who Have
Sacrificed For Freedom

Contents

Contents

Chapter I
The Scroll

Whenever Gabriel was gone from home Nicholas and Cerey would sleep with Hannah. Although the children greatly missed their father, sleeping in bed with their mother was a treat for them.

"Nicholas are you awake?" Hannah asked as pain surged through her body. "Nicholas."

"Yes Mama."

"Nicholas get grandma Emeral and tell her that Daniel is coming."

"Daniel!" Nicholas yelled excitedly. "Cerey come on; our brother is coming." Nicholas jumped out of bed and grabbed his little sister's hand. Both children were yelling before they opened the bedroom door. "Grandma, Daniel is coming," Nicholas yelled as he and Cerey ran down the hallway.

Hannah laughed as she got out of bed and moved to a smaller bed that had been put into the bedroom chambers for the birth of her son.

"Hannah," Iris said excitedly as she ran into the bedroom.

"Did the children wake you?" Hannah asked as she gritted her teeth.

"No, I couldn't sleep so I was in the kitchen baking cookies. I will stay with you until someone else gets here then I will start making tonics. Would you like some tea?"

"Yes, perhaps you should send someone for Gala."

Within minutes Hannah's bedroom chambers were filling with people. "I am sorry the children woke all of you up," Hannah said apologetically.

"Nonsense," Emeral said. "Of course we all want to be up. Luca already left for the castle to get Gala."

"Ella is getting towels and Vivian is starting tonics. But I dare say, I wouldn't be surprised if she didn't give birth soon."

"I know," Iris said excitedly. "I thought Vivian would go before Hannah because of the way her stomach has dropped."

"I wish Gabriel was here," Hannah said sadly. "He so wanted to be home for the birth."

"I know dear," Emeral said and put her arm around Hannah and kissed her on the forehead.

On the other side of the Continent of Opots in the dark Kingdom of Ryed, Gabriel was leading a rescue mission in the City of Teivel. The lives of thousands of political prisoners depended on the skills of Gabriel and his small army of freedom fighters.

The city was shaken before dawn by the explosives that Ruala warriors dropped upon the castle of Teivel, buildings that housed both demons and Teivel's troops and the building that Gabriel had bought which was filled with Teivel's soldiers. Soldiers that Teivel had planned to use for an ambush against the freedom fighters.

But on this night the explosives of the freedom fighters were not the only things that shook the city. Monsters of incredible proportions were released from the dungeons below Teivel's castle. Monsters that were deformed by the rage that consumed them. The Kembutos were monsters like no other. They towered above mortal men. Kembutos were twenty feet tall. They walked on two legs but also had wings. Kembutos were distinguished from other hell beasts by their four sets of eyes that surrounded their bald heads.

The massive arms of the Kembutos could tear trees from their roots and their hands could crush a human body. Buildings shook in the large City of Teivel as an army of Kembutos ravaged the streets; destroying everything in their path.

"Mother! Mother!" Adrone screamed as he beat on the door to Hannah's bedroom chambers. "Mother!"

Ella was the closest to the door and quickly opened it. "Is someone hurt?" Ella asked as she saw the look of terror on the small boy's face.

"Honey what is it?" Iris asked as she ran to her son.

"Something is wrong with Vivian; you have to come now," Adrone cried.

"If she is going into labor," Hannah said as the sweat poured down her face. "Bring another bed in here, it will be easier for everyone that way." Iris did not hear Hannah's words since she was running to the kitchen.

"Ella stay with Hannah," Emeral said and quickly left the room.

"Her water broke," Zelda said as she was helping Vivian out of the kitchen which was filled with children.

"Boys get Maxwell and Sam and bring them here," Emeral said as Iris hugged and kissed her daughter. Emeral turned to Vivian and asked, "Hannah wants us to put another bed in her chambers for you. Is that alright with you?"

"Yes," Vivian said then she turned to her little brothers. "I am alright, really. My baby is coming."

Maxwell and Sam ran into the kitchen with looks of fear on their faces. "Don't look so worried," Emeral said with a grin. "We have two grandbabies coming this night. I need you to move another small bed into Hannah's chambers."

"Gala's here," Luca yelled nervously as he and Gala entered the house.

"Vivian's having a baby too," Christopher said as he ran up to Luca.

"Well, we are going to have a busy night," Gala said with a smile. "Take me to them."

Simon was leading the attack on auction house number three, Matthew was leading the attack on auction house number four and Gabriel was leading the attack on auction house number two. These buildings were located in distinctly different locations of the large City of Teivel. Each building contained hundreds of political prisoners who Teivel planned to execute as soon as the sun rose in the sky. Teivel planned the executions as a means to force the freedom fighters to expose themselves and to surrender. Teivel did not expect to have a war within his city.

Simon, Matthew and Gabriel and crocks of a chemical smoke thrown through the windows of the auction houses to blind the soldiers inside. The first warriors to run into the auction houses were Gabriel's large team, soldiers from the kingdoms of Lentz and Wetpr, warriors of the Nordes and Ruala tribes and citizens of Ryed who had joined the doomed freedom fighters.

"Something isn't right here," Prince Simon yelled to Dominic and Jared as they fought with Teivel's soldiers in the smoke filled auction house. "There are too few soldiers here. This must be a trap." The rescuers who were not fighting with Teivel's men were freeing the prisoners of their ropes and helping them to escape the building.

"What the hell!" Jared yelled. "Is that an earthquake?" The auction house shook violently.

"I have a really bad feeling about this," Simon yelled and ran out of the building and onto a sidewalk. Simon stared in disbelief as he saw a group of Kembutos coming towards the auction house. The Kembutos were not flying but were deliberately stomping on everything in their path. "Miranda!" Simon yelled. "How do we stop them?"

Prince Matthew, Fennel and Archetenus were leading the attack on auction house number four. The Enrops had previously told Gabriel's team that this auction house contained many prisoners who looked gravely injured. Matthew commanded the battle as Archetenus and Fennel led the rescue of the prisoners.

Many Ruala warriors were assigned to this auction house to carry the injured to the castle of Nehmota, where High Priest Raphael was making preparations for retribution by Teivel and his armies.

Matthew heard a woman scream and ran towards the sound. In the thick smoke he saw the outline of a soldier preparing to plunge his sword into a person on the floor. Matthew grabbed one of his knives and hurled it at the soldier of Ryed. Matthew ran, following his knife which had struck the soldier in the right side of his neck.

"Go, run to the others," Matthew said as he helped the terrified woman up to a standing position. He turned to the soldier and knelt down to retrieve his knife. Blood was running from the soldier's mouth. He looked at Matthew and laughed. The soldier choked on his own blood as he laughed.

"You fools," the soldier said condescendingly. "You walked right..." the soldier died before he could complete his sentence.

In the midst of the chaos Gabriel heard Edward screaming his name. But Gabriel could not respond as he was fighting with two of Teivel's men. Gabriel was moving in an effort to keep both of his attackers in front of him. When one of the men lunged at Gabriel the second man did a forward roll and came to a standing position behind Gabriel. "Gabriel look out!" screamed Chaez as he plunged his sword into the back of the soldier who was behind Gabriel with a knife.

Gabriel bent down and ran forward ramming the other soldier in the chest with his head. Gabriel's attack momentarily knocked the wind out of the soldier giving Gabriel the time he needed to kill his opponent.

Gabriel and Chaez now fought back to back as other soldiers charged towards them. Suddenly the building shook with such force that the ceiling above Gabriel and Chaez started to collapse.

"Miranda!" Simon yelled a second time but the Angel did not answer. Simon ran back into the auction house. "Get the prisoners out! Get the prisoners out!" He yelled. "There are demons coming for us." The auction house shook again as there were now sounds of explosions coming from the streets. Simon ran back outside and saw Prince Lakin leading a group of Ruala warriors who were flying over the Kembutos dropping crocks of explosives on the beasts.

Matthew's blood ran cold as he listened to the words of the dying soldier for Matthew's instincts were telling him something was very wrong. He stood up and looked around him as dozens of his warriors were carrying injured prisoners from the building. The prisoners who could walk were helping to carry their countrymen and women out of the collapsing building. "Matthew outside," Joao yelled as he ran up to the prince.

When Matthew got into the street he saw the small army of Kembutos descending upon them. Matthew knew the monsters would reach the building before all of the prisoners could be rescued. "Miranda have we come this far not to save them?" Matthew yelled in frustration.

Gabriel and Chaez both leaped to their right as a huge beam and plaster fell onto the spot where they had been standing. "Gabriel this is a trap," Edward yelled. "Come." Edward turned and ran towards the front door of the auction house. Gabriel and Chaez stood in momentary disbelief when they saw the Kembutos marching towards them. Ruala warriors were flying over the monsters, shooting them with arrows as Enrops attacked the eyes of the beasts.

"The Lion said the Sanuri would give us a diversion," Gabriel said to his friends. Then Gabriel said to the heavens, "We could use that diversion now."

The Sanuri, Michael and Raul were still trying to escape the hordes of demons and men who were chasing them.

The Scroll of Imari that was inside of one of the Sanuri's saddlebags illuminated the darkness of the night thus exposing the three men to their enemies. Fifty Gants were fighting at the side of these three men to protect the scroll and thus fulfill their covenant with The Great Ruler.

"The sun is coming up," the Sanuri yelled as he rode in the lead.

"Is that going to help us?" Raul asked as an arrow sped past his right shoulder.

"It is going to change everything," the Sanuri said.

"Dominic get them out of here," Simon screamed referring to the prisoners.

"They will fight with us," Dominic said proudly as he readied his sword. "We have given them weapons."

"They aren't warriors," Simon yelled. "They will be killed."

"We have bowed down to these demons long enough," a voice rang out from the crowd that was forming around Simon. "Tonight we stand up to our fears." Simon turned and saw an old man walking towards him. The man held a sword with the expertise of a trained fighter. "Tonight we say no," the man said and stood next to Simon.

"Archers ready!" Matthew yelled to his meager army of warriors on the ground. The ground was shaking from both the powerful steps of the Kembutos and the explosives that Ruala warriors were hurling onto the monsters.

"Those who can will fight with us," Fennel announced as he ran up to Matthew. "We have been distributing the weapons."

"Release!" Matthew ordered but the volley of arrows did little to deter the Kembutos.

"Release!"

"We have to keep them distracted until the Rualas can get all of the prisoners out of here," Edward said.

"No need," Dack said as he ran up to Gabriel, Chaez and Edward. "The prisoners will fight with us."

"If this is to be our last fight then let it be one hell of a fight," Gabriel said. "Dack have some Rualas grab the rest of those crocks of smoke and be ready for my signal. Chaez have the archers fire up their arrows and prepare for my signal. Edward we need to get some rope."

"Dagon what is happening?" Raphael yelled as he ran up to his friend. Dagon had carried an injured prisoner to the safety of the castle of Nehmota and was preparing to return to the City of Teivel.

"It was a trap. There are giant demons attacking; I have to get back," Dagon said and quickly ascended into the air.

"Miranda, Daniel, Ruth, anyone we could use some help down here," Raphael prayed as he ran to the front wall that surrounded the castle.

"We have to get these ropes tied before the sun comes up," Gabriel yelled as he and Edward worked quickly to tie off ropes intended to trip the Kembutos.

"Done!" Edward yelled and ran towards Gabriel. Both men ran back towards the auction house and faced the oncoming demons.

"Archers ready!" Edward yelled.

"Rualas now!" yelled Gabriel. Twenty Ruala warriors who were already in the air now sped towards the Kembutos and dropped crocks of the chemical smoke on the demons. The Rualas then quickly ascended higher into the air so as not to be struck by arrows.

"Release!" Edward ordered.

"Release!"

"Release!"

The Kembutos were blinded by the smoke and were not impervious to the fire that was being shot into them. The Kembuto in the lead tripped over one of the ropes that had been stretched across the road. This monster fell and tripped the two Kembutos closest to him thus causing a chain reaction. The archers kept shooting flaming arrows into the demons that were falling upon each other. When the archers ran out of arrows the small army ran forward and started to hack the demons with swords and axes.

Simon and many of his warriors were literally running between the legs of the Kembutos. The demons were clumsy because of their size and did not move quickly. As Simon and some of his warriors sought to distract the Kembutos others ran up to the monsters and struck them in the back of their legs and ankles, trying to sever their tendons.

Some of the warriors were climbing up the monsters; stabbing the beasts as they ascended.

Matthew and his warriors were trying to turn the attention of the Kembutos away from the auction house, where the Rualas were helping the injured prisoners to escape. Matthew divided his men into smaller groups and they all ran in different directions in an effort to get the Kembutos to follow them.

Archetenus was inside of the auction house helping to evacuate the injured when the front wall of the building collapsed as a Kembuto kicked it. As the demon bent down to peer inside of the building Archetenus ran forward and thrust his sword into the left eye of the demon. The Kembuto screamed in pain and quickly pulled back. Archetenus knew the creature would strike again and quickly jumped backwards.

The enraged Kembuto violently kicked the auction house a second time causing the roof to collapse on those still inside.

All Archetenus could see was darkness as he tried to crawl out from the mountain of debris that covered his body. He felt great pain in his left leg as he pulled himself forward.

Archetenus started to see a little light through the rubble as the first rays of dawn illuminated the city. Suddenly he felt nauseous. Archetenus' head was spinning and he felt as if he would pass out. "Miranda, where are you?" He called and collapsed onto the floor.

The air pressure in the City of Teivel shifted so drastically that it caused many people to become sick and disoriented. People and demons felt as if they were moving in slow motion, their limbs feeling huge and heavy. "What deviltry is this?" Matthew yelled.

"Deviltry it is not," the Sanuri said as he appeared next to Matthew. "Get those prisoners and return to the castle, this is our fight now."

Matthew was so shocked to see the Sanuri that he did not initially see the Gants that were attacking the Kembutos and the Blue Hengers that now filled the sky. "Everyone back to the castle," Matthew yelled and ran back into the auction house.

Simultaneously, Raul appeared next to Simon and Michael next to Gabriel.

"What is going on?" yelled Gabriel.

"I can't explain it," Michael said. "But the Sanuri is using The Scroll of Imari. I am not sure what he is doing but we have to get all of you out of here now."

As Simon and Raul were getting the last of the prisoners from auction house number three they saw the Sanuri appear on top of one of the buildings. He was holding The Scroll of Imari which shone with great light. The Sanuri looked around and when he saw the last of Gabriel's small army leaving the city the Sanuri turned his attention to the castle of Teivel.

Soldiers and demons were leaving the castle for the city. The light of the scroll had attracted the attention of Teivel as well as Emeric and Banaka.

"Thank you friends," the Sanuri said as he looked down at the Gants. With his words the Gants were instantly transported from the City of Teivel to the Caves of Muldun.

The legions of soldiers and demons that had been chasing the Sanuri, Michael and Raul all night thought they were still after their prey. Their amazement slowed their reactions when they suddenly appeared in front of Teivel's armies.

These armies that fought for different dark masters all wanted the same prize. Collaboration never entered the minds of any of these soldiers as they now battled each other.

Chapter II
Horace

"Open the gates!" yelled Ruala warriors who were flying ahead of the army of freedom fighters.

"Open the gates, they are coming!" yelled Wetprian soldiers who were standing guard on top of the wall that surrounded the castle of Nehmota.

Soldiers and citizens of Ryed now ran to the front gates to help with the wounded. Rachel had stayed at the castle to help care for the injured. Her heart leaped within her chest every time a Ruala warrior landed with a prisoner. But so many of the prisoners bore incredible wounds that fear also consumed her.

Rachel pushed her way through the crowd that was forming around the front gates. "Rachel, Rachel," Dagon yelled as Rachel looked to the sky where dozens of Ruala warriors were flying into the front courtyard of the castle. Rachel strained to recognize her husband among the Ruala warriors who were all dressed identically.

"Dagon," Rachel yelled and walked away from the crowd.

"Rachel, Dack has your father," Dagon yelled as he descended towards the ground with a woman who was weak from starvation.

"Dack!" Rachel screamed as she ran towards the landing Ruala warriors. "Dack!"

"Rachel behind you," Dack yelled as he landed.

"Father!" Rachel screamed and ran towards Horace as Dack helped the older man to stand. "Father," Rachel was crying so hard she could barely speak. "Father what have they done to you?" Rachel cried as she threw her arms around a now weak and frail man.

"Honey all of these people have been starved and tortured," Dagon said as he landed next to Rachel, still holding the woman in his arms. "We need to get them inside."

"Father can you walk?" Rachel asked as tears ran down her cheeks.

Before Horace could answer Dack said, "I will carry him. Let go of him Rachel."

Dagon gently set the woman he was carrying on a mattress that was in the huge parlor of the castle. "This woman needs some food," Dagon called out.

"I will be right there," a woman's voice called, as one of the women from Ryed was walking towards Dagon with a bowl of soup and a cup of water.

"I will stay with you until she gets here," Dagon said to the woman he had been carrying.

The woman grabbed Dagon's hand and kissed it. "Thank you so much. When I first saw you I thought I was dead. I thought you were an Angel."

"No, we are Rualas," Dagon said with a warm smile.

"That's what the others said," the woman said weakly. Then she smiled. "Well, young man you are my Angel."

Rachel ran to get soup and water for her father as Dack helped Horace onto a mattress in the parlor. Dagon joined the two men. Horace looked at Dagon and grasped his hand. "You called my daughter Honey; why?"

Dagon knelt down near the older man. "Rachel is my wife."

"Your wife," Horace repeated in disbelief. "How long have I been gone? Where are Zelda and Zack?"

"They are safe. They are with my family in the Kingdom of Wetpr. I will take you to them. I wanted Rachel to leave also but she wouldn't. Rachel has been searching for you for months."

"Father here, try and eat this," Rachel said as she quickly ran to Horace with a bowl of soup, some bread and a cup of water. "I just can't believe you are alive."

Horace stared at Rachel. "Dagon tells me that he is your husband."

Rachel glanced nervously at Dagon then said, "Yes Father. Dagon is a wonderful man and he has been taking very good care of our family. We married quickly because this war is just starting but we will have another ceremony. Are you angry?"

"Perhaps I should leave," Dack said as he was feeling uncomfortable.

"No Dack, stay. It sounds as if you and my daughter are friends also," Horace said.

"There is much to tell you," Dack said. "But we came here to save all of you and Rachel joined us on this mission. She has been working with us and the freedom fighters."

"Dack is my friend and he is right there is so much to tell you," Rachel said. "Father I will not lie. I do not intend to keep anything from you but you look so weak. Please eat this food and I promise I will explain everything."

"Horace, Rachel wanted to wait for marriage so I could ask you for her hand. But I pushed her to marry me before the fighting began."

"Why?" Horace asked as he looked into Dagon's eyes.

"There are two reasons and I would make the same decisions again," Dagon said. "First I have been on many other missions and I know how badly they can turn out and I didn't want to lose Rachel and secondly." Dagon paused for a moment then looked at Rachel and smiled then Dagon looked back at Horace. "I am not telling you anything you don't know but both Rachel and Zelda are strong willed women. I wanted to get them to safety because this war will get much worse before it ends. Once I became the man in the family, Zelda finally agreed to leave Ryed with Zack."

Horace did not speak but stared intently at Dagon then to everyone's surprise Horace started to laugh. "Son you have no idea what you are in for being married to my Rachel."

"Dagon, Dack I could use some help," Lakin yelled as he walked into the parlor. Jared was helping Lakin carry Archetenus. "I need some boards and bandages," Lakin continued. "He has a broken leg."

When Dagon and Dack left Horace and Rachel, Horace put the palm of his hand on his daughter's cheek. "I never thought I would see you again. I am so relieved to hear all of you are alive and well."

Rachel kissed her father's hand. "They came for us. The demons burned our house and were carrying us away when members of Dagon's team saved us; then they hid us. I didn't trust them for a long time but I was wrong they are very good people. Father you will like them but you have to concentrate on getting better now. You must eat."

"I am not really sure what the Sanuri is doing," Gabriel said to Raphael as they were helping a wounded soldier inside of the castle. "All I know is that Michael said the Sanuri was using The Scroll of Imari and that The Lion had told us the Sanuri would create a diversion."

Raphael and Gabriel set the soldier on a mattress then turned to get more wounded from the courtyard. "Have you seen the Angels?" Raphael asked.

"No and I know many of us called to them," Gabriel said. "Something much worse must be happening."

"Michael your shoulder is bleeding again," Raul scolded. "Go inside and get some care. We can bring the rest of the wounded in."

"I can still walk; which is doing better than some of these poor bastards," Michael said.

"Can't tell he is our brother, as pigheaded as he is," Simon said with a grin.

"Open the gates," one of the Wetprian soldiers yelled from the top of the wall. "Thaos and Stephan are coming with a whole lot of people."

"Thaos and Stephan," Gabriel said as he looked at Raphael. "Where have they been?" Both Raphael and Gabriel now walked quickly to the front gates.

"I thought they were with you," Raphael said. "It's not like them to just disappear."

The gates were opened and Thaos and Stephan led a long caravan of bocas and people on horseback into the courtyard of the castle. "Where have you been?" Gabriel asked.

"Didn't Ruth tell you?" Thaos asked. "Well, from the looks on your faces I guess not. When we were in the barn saddling our horses Ruth appeared. She told us to go into the city and to get Clay and all of the people he had at the hotel."

"Yeah, it turns out Clay had called to Ruth yesterday and she had him gathering people and supplies," Stephan said as he dismounted in front of Raphael and Gabriel. "And there's about forty men here who Clay hired as fighters. Most of them aren't from Ryed so they aren't Teivel's spies. They will be of help."

"Thanks for getting us," Clay said as he walked up to the four men.

"Honestly it was Ruth," Gabriel said. "Raphael and I didn't know about this. But we are glad to have you here. What did Ruth tell you?"

"Raphael after you told me that I could call to Ruth, well the more I thought about it, the more it seemed like something I had to do," Clay explained. "I really didn't think she would come to me but no sooner did I say her name than she appeared in my office and she had a list of things for me to do."

"I have bocas full of food and medical supplies," Clay continued. "And Ruth had me going into neighborhoods and get people. I don't think any of these people know that Ruth is an Angel but they know her."

"As soon as I said Ruth wanted them to pack their things and come to the hotel, well it was the damndest thing. Everyone just did it, they didn't argue or even ask why. I already had the body guards to help when your mission started but I didn't think it was going to be like this."

"Actually we didn't either," Raphael said. "We're expecting an attack here soon."

"That might be a while," Thaos said. "We saw the Sanuri on top of a building. He was glowing like he was on fire. He must have brought the Gants that were fighting with those giant demons. All of a sudden the Gants just disappear then armies of demons and men appeared where the Gants had been. As soon as Teivel's men see these new guys the fight is on."

"Raul, Michael and the Sanuri were being chased by armies," Gabriel said with a smile. "The Sanuri must have pitted them all against each other."

"Mama is he here yet?" Nicholas asked as he ran into the bedroom chambers where both Hannah and Vivian were visiting with their company. Both women laughed.

"No Honey, it might be a while yet," Hannah said.

"Why? Doesn't he want to come out?" Nicholas asked. Everyone in the room started to grin.

"I am not even sure how to answer that," Hannah said as she looked at Emeral.

Emeral looked at Maxwell, who was sitting in the chair next to her. "Don't look at me; you're the one who always knows what to say," Maxwell said with a grin.

"Honey it's kind of hard to explain," Emeral said as she pulled Nicholas onto her lap. "But babies come when they are ready."

Nicholas stared at Emeral with a confused look on his face. "Well what does he have to do to get ready?" Everyone in the room was grinning.

Emeral was trying hard not to grin. "I really don't know but when Daniel is big enough to talk we should ask him."

"Ok Grandma," Nicholas said and jumped down from Emeral's lap. No one said anything until Nicholas left the room. Gala shut the door and everyone broke into laughter.

"It was late afternoon by time the Sanuri appeared within the walls of the castle of Nehmota. He was surprised to see all of the people who were now taking shelter behind the walls of the castle. The Sanuri walked through the castle until he found the areas where the wounded and injured were being cared for. He said a prayer then started to place his hands upon the injured to help them heal.

"Sanuri when did you get here?" Raul asked as he walked up to the holy man.

"Moments ago. Raul tell me how did all of these people know to come here," the Sanuri asked."

"The prisoners?"

"No, all of the people of Ryed who are on the walls and in the courtyards."

"Raphael told me that Ruth had Clay gather the people and hide them in his hotel. Then she sent Thaos and Stephan to bring everyone here. This happened while we were rescuing the prisoners so no one knew about it until later. Why?"

The Sanuri moved to another patient as Raul spoke. "You know how I see fragments of visions. I have seen some things I don't yet understand. But if Ruth had these people brought here then they must not be spies," the Sanuri said.

"Sanuri do you know where the Angels are?"

"No, why?"

"Many people said they called to them when we were in the city and the Angels did not respond."

"Everyone is wondering if something worse is happening that we don't know about," Raul said.

"That is always a possibility. I am sure the Angels were with all of us whether they responded or not. Raul, I will be with the wounded for a while. Will you gather the main people for a meeting in the Great Hall in, say, two hours?"

"Dagon where have you been?" Rachel asked. "I have been looking for you for a while."

"I was helping Lakin then Joao and I moved a small bed into our chambers for Horace. I was just coming to get you and him."

"You are the sweetest man. I just love you so much," Rachel said and stretched up and kissed Dagon on the lips. She stepped back so she could look him in the eyes then asked, "Dagon why did you tell Father right away that we were married? I wasn't sure he was up for the shock."

"He heard me call you Honey and asked me about us as soon as you left for food. He looks bad and I wasn't going to lie to him but I was concerned about giving him the news too."

"Well he says he likes you and Dack. He is overwhelmed with gratitude that we are all alive and safe. Father said over and over that he never thought he would see any of us again. It means a lot to him that you have been taking care of all of us."

"I told him I was taking him to Wetpr. Did he say anything to you about whether he might want to stay there?"

"No, I think he is still too emotional and trying to take all of this in."

"When we get Horace up to our chambers why don't you stay there with him and start some letters to our parents. I am going to help with more patients then the Sanuri is calling a meeting."

"You can all go in now," Iris said with a proud smile as she walked into the parlor.

"Both babies are boys and wait until you see them. Raphael and Gabriel look like brothers and so do these babies."

As the adults were walking out of the parlor, Emeral was leading the children from the playroom. Nicholas and Cerey ran ahead of the other children and burst into the bedroom. Ella, Zelda and Gala were finishing cleaning up the room while Hannah and Vivian were both sitting up in their beds holding their sons.

As the room filled with people Gala said, "I am grateful for the help. Both babies were coming at the same time."

Nicholas and Cerey stood by the bed in awed silence and stared at their baby brother. "Daniel looks like the two of you," Hannah said warmly. "He has the same dark curly hair and brown eyes."

The children pushed through the group and ran from bed to bed to look at the babies. "Everyone this is Robert Joshua Gabriel," Vivian said proudly and handed the baby to her mother.

"And this is Daniel Isaiah Raphael," Hannah said as she handed her baby to Emeral.

"Iris was right," Sam said. "These babies could pass as brothers. I love it here with all these children."

Bekka smiled and hugged her father, "Yes you are a grandpa again."

"I'll bet you girls are starving," Zelda said. "I will make some trays."

"After everyone holds the babies Hannah and I want to be alone for a few minutes," Vivian said. "Raphael and Gabriel wanted us to call to the Angels right after the babies were born."

"Well then we will leave you," Emeral said then she turned to Gala. "Gala please join us for dinner."

Cassandra and Elan were the last two people to leave the bedroom and they shut the door behind them. "Do you want to call them?" Vivian asked.

"Daniel, Miranda would you like to see our babies?" Hannah asked as she looked around the room.

Both Angels materialized in the room instantly. "Here Daniel, we named him after you," Hannah said and handed the infant to the Angel."

"Miranda do you want to hold Robert?" asked Vivian. "We know we wouldn't have the babies if it wasn't for you. Thank you so much."

"They are beautiful," Miranda said as both Angels lovingly held the infants. The room seemed to warm and to become brighter.

"Miranda you kissed both our husbands on the forehead and that same night we got pregnant," Hannah said. "Does that mean these babies are special?"

"All babies are special," Miranda said with a warm smile. "Some perhaps more so than others."

"Will you see Raphael and Gabriel tonight?" Vivian asked. "If you do would you please tell them about the babies? Of course we will send letters but that will take longer."

"I believe a visit is in order," Daniel said then he kissed both babies on their foreheads. Miranda too kissed the babies.

"Perhaps you have something of the babies that you want to send along?" Miranda asked.

Both Hannah and Vivian smiled and reached for envelopes on the tables next to their beds. "They are small swatches of hair for their lockets," Hannah said as she handed her envelope to Miranda.

"I thought Lakin told you to stay in bed," Jared said as he helped Archetenus to the Great Hall.

"If I lay around I will go crazy," Archetenus said. "You should talk you are the same way."

Jared laughed. "When are you going to tell Delilah?"

"She has enough to worry about with the babies," Archetenus said. "Hopefully I will be healed by time we get home."

As soon as everyone was seated the Sanuri stood up in front of the room. "Gabriel, Raphael and I want to review the various aspects of the missions that we were on. I believe these different pieces will help form a picture and hopefully answer some of our questions."

"Simon why don't you start out by telling us what your team encountered," Gabriel said.

"After we threw the smoke into the auction house and ran in I knew it was a trap. There were too few guards for all of those prisoners. I ran outside and that is when I saw those ugly giants. We..." Simon stopped talking as Daniel, Miranda and Ruth appeared at the front of the room.

"We are glad to see you," Gabriel said to the Angels.

"Before we talk business we have something to give you," Daniel said with a smile and handed Gabriel an envelope. "A swatch of hair from Daniel Isaiah Raphael."

"What!" Gabriel said and jumped out of his chair. Tears came to Gabriel's eyes as he took the envelope.

"And for you Raphael," Miranda said as she walked around the table and handed him an envelope. "This is from Robert Joshua Gabriel." Raphael couldn't speak and his hands were shaking as he took the envelope. "Your sons were born this afternoon at the same time. Both babies are beautiful with black hair and brown eyes. They both look like their fathers and your families believe the babies could pass for brothers. Your wives are fine and miss you."

Raul started clapping and soon everyone in the room was applauding the birth of the two baby boys.

"Thank you so much," Gabriel said. "We so wanted to be home for the births."

"Hannah and Vivian are sharing a room and they were surrounded by loving family and friends," Daniel said. "Your wives called to us within minutes after the family saw the babies. Of course they will be sending you letters with all the details."

The three Angels now turned and addressed the entire group. "You did well today," Miranda said. "But much more was happening than you realized. As we told you before, the eyes of the underworlds knew that all of you were somewhere near Ryed. We blocked them from seeing your exact locations. Five of The Seven Sons, two powerful high priests and two men who turned hell upside down. Teivel set up the ambushes to stop the freedom fighters but all of darkness knew you would answer the call."

"Are you saying other demons besides Teivel were waiting for us?" Gabriel asked.

"Yes, but first lets step back and talk about the messages that Erebus sent to the underworlds," Daniel said. "Teivel's transformation was a closely guarded secret. Erebus did well and the news hit the hell regions like an explosion. You see the demons and dark lords understand that for Teivel to transform into a demon high prices had to be paid. Paranoia is out of control within the Insidiae and among many demons as they are trying to determine if they have been sold out by Teivel."

"At the last minute we asked Erebus to add one additional statement to his messages. A suggestion that Emeric and Banaka were helping Teivel transform as payment for his work in helping these two Grand Masters betray the Old Ones of this world. Now the demons are finding out that Emeric and Banaka are responsible for inciting many of the conflicts between the hell regions in an effort to keep the Old Ones distracted from invasions."

"Emeric and Banaka have left the World of Nunc and are being pursued by executioners of the Old Ones. They will have difficulty finding allies even among the Old Ones of different worlds. Without Emeric and Banaka, Teivel has been weakened but he still plans on going through the transformation. If he is successful he will have incredible powers," Daniel explained.

"But at the point that his body is physically transforming Teivel will be vulnerable. He now needs to find someone to protect him during this process. Teivel has few friends among the demons and dark lords so he will have to make many deals to get someone he can trust to protect him."

"Can he postpone the transformation?" asked Matthew.

"No," Ruth said. "The energies have already been put into motion."

"So chances are good that the other demons or dark lords will stop him?" Thaos asked.

"They will try," said Miranda.

"But then that opens up his territory to others," said Daniel.

"So are you saying that because of Erebus' messages the eyes of all kinds of demons are on us here?" Simon asked.

"They have already been watching you," Ruth said. "And this morning they saw you beating Teivel's forces without our assistance. They now understand how powerful humans are when they refuse to bow before darkness. Every time someone stands up to a demon and says 'no, I will not give you power' this world becomes a less desirable feeding ground. Mankind could rid this world of the demons without and the demons within if they just realized their own power."

"But when the Sanuri showed up, well wasn't that like help from you?" Jared asked.

"I am still a man," the Sanuri said. "And they could clearly see that the power I had was coming from The Scroll of Imari, a physical thing in this world that they covet. They will all be searching for me now."

"Sanuri do you have the scroll on you now?" asked Raul.

"Yes."

"Why did it stop glowing?"

"Because we don't need it as a distraction right now. All those armies that came after us would have been sent here to look for all of you."

"So we were the distraction?" Michael asked with a huge grin.

"Yes that dangerous journey we chose to take saved the lives of all within this castle. Not bad for a night's work," the Sanuri said with a grin.

"So what exactly does this mean for our mission?" Raphael asked.

"It means things are changing once again," Miranda said. "Teivel has to come up with new allies and new strategies but the energies are already tied to the transformation taking place on the thirteenth day of the Gefrey Games. The prisoners who you did not rescue today will be taken to the games but security will be very tight after today."

"But what of our people?" Dominic asked. "We were slaves to the Grand Masters and Teivel; now will there be wars among demons and dark lords for this kingdom?"

"Yes, there will be wars. But it was people who called the demons into this kingdom and people have the power to drive them out," Ruth said. "Every citizen of Ryed who came to this castle has made the decision to no longer let the darkness enslave them. Choices were made this morning. The prisoners made the same decisions and fought at your sides."

"Gabriel and Raphael you were at Fort Salar when five Old Ones were defeated," Miranda said. "Tell the others what you saw."

"There were demons as far as you could see," Raphael said. "Armies of them on the ground. Then the sky filled with all manner of flying monsters. Then the Rogetts appeared. Then the Old Ones took form. They wanted the Sanuri, who was not at the fort and they wanted King Sudfad to surrender."

"Gabriel what were the King's words?" Miranda asked.

"Sudfad asked the Old Ones why they didn't just attack since they were trying to intimidate everyone with the show of force. And when they didn't answer, Sudfad said the demons didn't attack because they knew for all their armies they had no power in Wetpr."

"Sudfad said, the kingdom, its people and its Royal Family had pledged their allegiance to The Great Ruler and darkness would never rule in Wetpr. Darkness had no power there. Then the army of Angels came."

"Dominic you and your brothers and that handful of fighters you lead have sacrificed greatly. You do not have to be a king or a high priest to call the Angels in. One child with faith in The Great Ruler can intimidate a powerful demon. Ask Simon, his wonderful wife did just that. You have been fighting as men without hope. You need to be fighting as men with faith."

Chapter III
Memories

"Misha will you button me?" Diana asked as she walked towards the evening campfire in a pink and white cotton dress.

"Well look at you," Joshua said. "You look very pretty."

"That leather dress is just getting too tight over my stomach. I could hardly breathe in it," Diana said.

"Where did you get this?" asked Misha. "You didn't go shopping in Teivel did you?"

"No, I thought I was pregnant when we left home so I bought a few things," Diana said.

"You and Ingr are about the same size," Sorren said as he stirred the fire. "She didn't look pregnant at all for months with the twins then in one week she looked really pregnant. It is good you are going home now."

"I don't want to scare you," Natasha said. "But Annabelle told me that when she was pregnant with the boys she couldn't do anything the last two weeks. She said Simon had to help her out of bed and dress her."

"I hope you two are home by then," Diana said to Misha and Thor.

"We do too," Joshua said. "But there are plenty of people in the house who will take care of you."

"We better be home," Thor said with a huge grin. "Misha we will have to drop things just to see if Diana can pick them up." Thor laughed and his laughter was infectious. The laughter around the campfire grew louder when Diana punched her brother's arm.

Sorren stopped laughing and looked at Diana then at Erebus. "Erebus would you do that magic thing with your map again?" Sorren asked.

"Last time you thought Morgan and Bruno were heading towards Nora. If they are still in that area I think we should let the girls go on a shopping trip. It might draw those bastards out."

"Oh this will be fun," Natasha said. "We can buy gifts and work at the same time."

"I don't know how this sell your soul to a demon thing works," Misha said. "But I do know Morgan and Bruno. Nora is full of women and whiskey, they will want to stop there."

"Would you rather have us wear our warrior's clothes or dress like the other women?" Bianca asked.

"Let me think about that," said Sorren. "You will stand out more if you wear your leather outfits but that might tip Morgan and Bruno off that this is a trap."

"You don't think those two would be intimidated by a group of women warriors?" Erebus asked as he spread a map on the ground near the campfire.

"No, it will probably be more exciting for them," Calen said.

Both Raphael and Gabriel had difficulty sleeping this night. After they wrote letters to their wives both men found themselves mesmerized by the tiny swatches of hair from their sons. Finally Gabriel left his room and knocked on the door to Raphael's room. Raphael opened the door immediately.

"I had a feeling you would be up too," Gabriel said with a grin. "I am just so excited I can't sleep." Raphael moved so Gabriel could enter the chambers.

"I am both excited and filled with guilt," Raphael said. "I didn't want Vivian to go through that alone."

"I know exactly how you feel," Gabriel said. "Hannah and Vivian know we can't be home now but I was thinking we should do something really special for them after we return. What would you think about taking them on a trip?"

"I like the idea but we might have to wait until the babies are older."

"Who knows how long we will be on this mission," Gabriel said with sadness in his voice. "Since it appears that demons watch our every move I was thinking we should go to the Ice Caves. Emeral and Maxwell built a house for Natasha and Calen with a wing for me. Calen and Natasha haven't even seen the house yet. But knowing Maxwell and Emeral I would imagine it is very nice. We could relax in the Ice Caves without fearing an attack."

"I like that idea," Raphael said. "Did you mention it in your letter to Hannah?"

"No, I wanted to discuss it with you first."

"I think we tell the girls now. It will be something to keep them excited. Do you think two letters or one?"

When Rachel awoke she was facing Dagon's back. She softly kissed his spine starting at the nape of his neck and working down to his waist. Dagon rolled over and took Rachel in his arms. "I love waking up with you," he said and kissed his wife.

Rachel crawled on top of Dagon's chest and kissed his face and neck. "I can't tell you how different I feel now that we found Father. I felt like I was dead before." Rachel moved so she could look into his eyes. "Now I feel like I can focus on us. Thank you for being so patient." Rachel kissed Dagon on the lips. "Let's start working on a family."

"Well if it isn't Tina and Charles," Bruno said with a grin as he and Morgan walked into the dining room of the Endleson Hotel in the City of Nora. "Still mooching off the good citizens here?"

"Keep your voice down," Tina snapped with embarrassment.

"Tina you never change," Morgan said as he and Bruno sat down at Tina's and Charles' table.

"Where have you been?" Charles asked in a lowered voice as he looked around the dining room. "The death squads broke into your room and said it smelled of demons. They stayed here for a couple of weeks then left. Are you alright?"

"You might say we made a deal with the devil to save us from the death squads," Morgan said. "But we may have been better off letting them kill us."

Both Tina and Charles stared at Morgan and Bruno with fear in their eyes. "Are you saying you sold your souls?" asked Charles.

"I guess it wasn't a far leap for us," Bruno said. "Actually it is the second time for us. The first demon was much better to work for. This one is married to Nada and wants Morgan and me to know he is the jealous type."

"Nada is married to a demon?" Tina gasped.

"I don't think she had a lot of choice in the matter," Morgan said. "But from the little we saw he treats her a whole lot better than he treats us."

"So what are you doing here?" asked Tina.

"We are headed for Ryed," Morgan said. "Can't really tell you but we are working." Morgan stopped talking as the waiter came to the table to take everyone's breakfast order. "So you heard any good gossip?" Morgan asked after the waiter left.

"Understandably we are trying to live quietly here," Charles said. "So we don't introduce ourselves to any Rualas in the city. But we have been hearing a lot about Ryed. Teivel is sponsoring two weeks of Gefrey Games that are open to the entire continent. Apparently there are big money prizes. All kinds of men and demons have been passing through Nora going to the City of Teivel."

"Why are they traveling through Nora when the City of Teivel is in northern Ryed?" Morgan asked.

"Can't give you an answer to that," Charles said. "Is that why you are going to Ryed?"

"Yep," Bruno said as he filled his cup with coffee.

37

"Then why are you in Nora?" Charles asked with a suspicious grin.

"We got some business here," Morgan said. "And besides we like this city."

"Is the business with us?" Tina asked fearfully.

"Now why would you think that?" Bruno asked and laughed. "Tina you always think the world revolves around you."

Sorren's group had arrived in the City of Nora before dawn. Just as they were entering the city the stones on their mystical necklaces started to glow, telling them that Morgan and Bruno were near.

Natasha, Bianca, Batina and Diana started walking up and down the streets looking in store windows. The women were supposed to make their presence known in an effort to draw Morgan and Bruno into the open.

Ratri, Calen, Misha and the other Rualas hid on roof tops to watch over the women and to search for Morgan and Bruno. Sorren and Erebus formed a group and walked in and out of hotels and restaurants thinking Morgan and Bruno might be having breakfast. Joshua, Thor and Micha formed a second group. They were walking into taverns looking for the two murderous Rualas.

"We really have to buy things or we will look suspicious," Natasha said to her friends. "If you need money, I have plenty with me." Natasha suspected that Bianca and Batina didn't have any money. "Speak up girls."

"We can't take your money," Batina said.

"Well think of it as getting paid for you work," Natasha said with a big smile. "Follow me." The women walked into a dress shop. Natasha led her friends to the back of the store where there were no customers or staff. "Here take these," Natasha said and handed Batina and Bianca each a leather pouch of gold coins. "Diana do you need some?"

"No. Misha gave me money but I didn't think to ask for some for the others. Now I feel bad," Diana said.

"We can't take this?" said Bianca.

"Until recently all of the team members were mostly Calen's family and you know they have lots of money. But with all of the new members Gabriel and Raphael are realizing they need to pay some kind of wages to the team. So think of this as part of your pay," Natasha said.

"But you already pay for everything for us," Bianca said.

"But you need spending money too. This is a wonderful city; buy some gifts for your families and some things for yourselves and that is an order," Natasha said and giggled. "If you need more just let me know."

"I didn't know they served breakfast in taverns," Micha said as he sat down at a table with Joshua and Thor.

"I'll get us something so we don't stick out," Thor said and stood up from the table. "On that mission in Salar they wouldn't let me work in the tavern because they said I didn't look like the kind of guy who went into taverns. I want to watch some of these men."

Joshua laughed. "I heard about that mission. That tavern was filled with criminals and mercenaries. You two boys will have to spend a lot of time in taverns to get anyone to believe you can fit in with that crowd."

"Well then this will be our first lesson," Micha said with enthusiasm.

"Ok, I don't really understand how magic works," Sorren said as he and Erebus were walking down a street. "Can you sense anything?"

Erebus laughed. "My senses are the same as yours with the exception that I can see auras. But that is not from magic."

"What do you mean?"

"You know when you look at the suns you see the ball then the light that surrounds them. Well when I look at people I see the person and the energy they give off. That energy field is called an aura and it is an extension of the person. Auras have different colors and that helps you read the person."

"What do you mean?"

"Well looking at the Sanuri is like looking at the sun. When I saw Nada's aura it was black as night and I suspect that Morgan and Bruno's will be the same. Now when demons take human form they can disguise their auras. Now I just gave you two very extreme examples. Most people are kind of a blend and the colors change."

"Do I want to ask what you see when you look at me?" Sorren asked and laughed.

"I see courage and passion and now that I am getting to know you I understand that these are very strong characteristics of yours."

"I guess I hadn't thought about it," Sorren said humbly. "Let's stop in here." Both men walked into the Lazy Cow Restaurant.

"Father what are you doing out of bed?" Rachel gasped as she returned to her chambers with a tray of breakfast food for Horace.

"Rachel I have company," Horace said. "I am fine."

"Company?"

"I was just opening the windows to let some fresh air in," the Sanuri said. "Horace and I have had a very interesting conversation."

"Sanuri I have extra cups, would you like some coffee?" Rachel asked as she set the tray on a small table.

"You know my weakness," the Sanuri said with a smile.

"When the Sanuri was healing me yesterday he saw some things," Horace said. "I am not sure how to explain it."

"I saw pieces of a vision," the Sanuri explained. "But I wanted to wait for Horace to heal a little before I spoke with him. Your father was a captive but not a victim. He has the mindset of a warrior and a freedom fighter. His mind contains a great deal of information which can help us. Now, understandably his mind has also been dulled from starvation and disease. But I gave him some more of my essence. I believe by lunch he will be strong enough to join us in the Great Hall and share the many things he heard and saw."

"Really," Rachel said with a proud smile.

"Horace your daughter is a talented artist and has used her talents to help us in a variety of ways," the Sanuri said. "Don't push yourself but if you are feeling up to it after breakfast perhaps you can describe some of the prisons, buildings and other things you have seen so she can draw them."

Sorren and Erebus walked into the dining room of the Endleson Hotel as Tina, Charles, Morgan and Bruno were finishing their breakfast. Neither Sorren nor Erebus had seen Morgan and Bruno before but Batina had drawn pictures of the men. Both Sorren and Erebus recognized Tina and Charles and were curious as to their association with Morgan and Bruno.

The dining room was crowded so Sorren and Erebus could not find a table near the Rualas but they found one that allowed them to watch the Rualas.

"Do you want to have some fun?" Erebus whispered to Sorren.

"Like what?"

"If I could get some of their hair or blood I could find out if their demon masters are giving them any extra power and perhaps sever it. But I might have to make a little noise to get the samples."

"I could use a good laugh," Sorren said.

"Just stay seated no matter what happens," Erebus said and began to softly mumble. Suddenly the table that the Rualas were seated at burst into flames. All four of the Rualas jumped up and when they did a small flock of ravens appeared and started attacking Morgan, Bruno, Tina and Charles. People in the dining room screamed at the sight. The four Rualas were batting at the ravens but the birds persisted. The Rualas ran out of the dining room and the ravens disappeared. Erebus opened his right hand which now contained four swatches of hair.

Tina and Charles did not stop running until they reached the safety of their hotel chambers. Unlike Morgan and Bruno, Tina and Charles were so frightened that they did not realize the ravens had disappeared.

"You can't tell me a demon isn't responsible for that," Tina shrieked. "We have to stay away from those two, they are dangerous."

"Oh and I suppose you are the one who is going to tell them to leave us alone," Charles said sarcastically. "Especially now that we know they sold their souls. Do you really want to piss them off?"

"You are right," Tina said as she sat down on the bed. "What are we going to do?"

"I honestly don't know. But we have to think very carefully about our next moves."

"What the hell just happened?" Bruno asked as he and Morgan stepped out onto the sidewalk in front of the Endleson Hotel.

"Maybe one of our bosses was telling us to get to work," Morgan said with disdain.

"Well screw them!" said Bruno.

"You do know there is a possibility one of them can hear us."

"You think so?" Bruno asked in a lowered voice.

"I really have no idea," Morgan said. "I say we have some fun here and if something like that happens again we will take it as a sign to get to Ryed. I could use a drink how about you?"

Sorren and Erebus walked out of the hotel and watched Morgan and Bruno walk into the Harvest Moon Tavern which was across the street. "You really should let me do a couple of spells before anyone tries to touch them," Erebus said.

"What do you need?" asked Sorren.

"I have my supplies in this bag," Erebus said. He was referring to a large leather bag that was slung over his shoulder by a thick leather strap. "But I need some place private. Stand guard on this alley and I will go to work." Erebus and Sorren walked into the alley to the left of the Endleson Hotel. Sorren was watching the front door of the Harvest Moon Tavern when an Enrop landed near him.

"Tell the others that Morgan and Bruno are in the Harvest Moon Tavern but Erebus needs to find out if the demons are giving them power before we can attack," Sorren said to the Enrop who immediately took to the air.

Morgan bought a bottle of whiskey and he and Bruno took seats at a table near the front window of the tavern. Neither Morgan nor Bruno saw Sorren standing in the street or the Enrops that were flying over the buildings.

"I don't care if they can hear me or not," Bruno said. "We've got to find a way to get free."

"I would like to find Hecate again," Morgan said. "As a boss she wasn't bad at all and we might need some protection from Visterle."

"Visterle was looking for her. Do you think he set us free to see if we would contact Hecate?"

"I wish we could."

"Well looky here," Bruno said and nodded at four women who were walking across the street. "Every one of them is a beauty; this may be our lucky day after all."

As Morgan and Bruno stared at Natasha, Diana, Bianca and Batina, Morgan said. "That one, isn't that Ratri's woman. The one with blue ribbons in her hair."

"Damn you're right. I get her first," Bruno said salaciously.

"If she is here, Ratri is too. Why?"

"They are probably headed to Ryed," said Bruno.

"That means Gabriel's team might be here," Morgan said. "Keep it in your pants this could be a problem."

"You worry too much," Bruno said as he watched the women.

"That woman in the blue dress is Calen's wife; I have seen her before. And what do you want to bet that little blonde is Misha's wife, the one who turned us in. I don't know who that other brunette is."

"That means we've got four beautiful warrior women; my blood is already boiling," Bruno said with a grin.

"That means we've got their husbands close at hand."

"Ok, so we just grab two of them and take off but it's going to be hard to choose."

Morgan and Bruno were searching the building tops and the streets for any sign of Gabriel's team. They paid no attention to the three Venatores who entered the tavern and sat at a table behind the two Rualas.

Sorren and Erebus entered the tavern and took seats at a table to the left of Morgan and Bruno. Natasha and the other women knew that Morgan and Bruno were sitting in the window of the Harvest Moon Tavern watching them. The women walked into a store then returned to the sidewalk a few moments later.

"I want to go in there," Diana said but smiled as she spoke to keep up appearances.

"I know but it should be Misha and Calen; you know that," Natasha said.

"Oh, I think Ratri wants them too," Batina said.

44

"Let's walk across the street," Natasha said as she pointed to a store next to the tavern.

"I don't know which one of them I want first," Bruno said as they watched the four women crossing the road and walking towards the tavern.

"Which one of our wives are you talking about?" Misha asked with a coldness that others had not heard in his voice before.

As Bruno and Morgan jumped from their chairs, Thor and Micha blocked the front door of the tavern. Joshua and Sorren stood up to keep the other patrons away from the Rualas. Bruno and Morgan turned and faced Misha, Calen and Ratri who had entered the tavern by the back door.

"These two Rualas are murderers and rapists," Sorren yelled. "We have been hunting them. The fight is theirs'."

Misha dove for Morgan's throat as Bruno threw a knife at Ratri. Calen kicked the side of Bruno's knee causing the huge Ruala to lose his balance. Ratri punched Bruno in the stomach as Calen grabbed Bruno's arms. Both Ratri and Calen were going to let Misha kill the monsters of his nightmares.

Morgan was a great fighter but Misha was consumed with rage and revenge. Misha tightened his grip on Morgan's throat as memories of Morgan and Bruno raping and beating him and his brothers and sisters exploded in Misha's head. Morgan tried to gouge Misha's eyes as Misha choked the life from him. The last thing that Morgan heard was Visterle's laughter in his head.

Diana, Batina, Bianca and Natasha ran into the tavern as Calen and Ratri were releasing their holds on Bruno. Misha jumped off from Morgan's body and attacked Bruno like a wild animal. Bruno was a much larger man than Misha but Misha was filled with the emotions of a lifetime. Bruno and Misha punched, kicked and gouged each other. Diana started to move towards them but Thor held her back. None of the patrons in the tavern wanted to get involved in the fight; they watched and placed bets.

Misha never pulled a weapon, he beat Bruno to death with his fists. Misha was exhausted both physically and emotionally when he stood up from Bruno's body. Diana ran to her husband. "Thor help me," Diana said as she felt Misha get weak in her arms.

Calen walked up to the bartender and handed him a pouch of gold coins. Those two were raping children," Calen said with disgust. Here's money for the damages do what you want with the bodies.

"We don't hold with no baby rapers," the bartender said. "We might just string those two up with signs on them."

"That's fine with us," Calen said and turned around and walked towards Natasha. Sorren and Joshua searched the bodies of Morgan and Bruno but all they found was money and a hotel key.

Chapter IV
Surprises

"I would like to wait a few moments before we start the meeting," the Sanuri said to the warriors in the Great Hall of the castle of Nehmota. "We have some more coming."

"Who?" Gabriel asked as he looked around the room and saw the usual faces of leaders and team members.

The doors to the Great Hall squeaked on their hinges as Rachel opened the door and helped her father to walk inside. "Rachel," Dagon said and jumped from his chair and quickly walked up to Rachel and Horace.

"Horace and Rachel, I would like you to sit up here with us," the Sanuri said and Raphael got up and put three mores chairs at the front table that was facing the group.

"I can make it," Horace said stubbornly as Dagon and Rachel both tried to hold his arms. Dagon and Rachel smiled at each other and slowly walked next to Horace in case he fell. Dagon also took a seat at the front table.

"Yesterday as I was giving Horace healing energy I started to see fragments of visions. He was so weak yesterday that I did not want to speak with him about them at the time. This morning I visited Horace and gave him more healing energy. I believe he has information that can help us," the Sanuri said. "Then he looked at Horace. "Tell them what you told me this morning."

Horace slowly stood up and addressed the group. "Eight months ago I was a strong and powerful man. My captors would take the strongest prisoners and have them work on special projects. One of my tasks was to help carry the dead and injured from the Gefrey Games. When I say dead and injured I am talking about all the combatants, the demons, animals and men. The Sanuri asked me to have Rachel make drawings of the things I saw. She has made drawings of all the entrances of that arena that I am aware of."

"I will make more," Rachel said. "I didn't have much time." Rachel circulated six pieces of paper. Each paper contained different drawings. "These are all different so you will have to pass them around," she added.

Horace now looked at his notes before he continued. "The drawing with the number one on it is a sketch of the floor of the arena from the combatants view. Rachel told me you had some sketches like this but I have to tell you about the doors. As you can see it appears that the floor of the arena is encompassed by dozens of doors. It is designed like this to confuse the fighters because not all of those gates open up. And some are used only for dragging out the dead and wounded. Rachel put an 'A' by every door that prisoners enter the arena through."

"She put a "B" by the only door that other human fighters enter the arena. There is a 'C' by every door that demon's use to enter the arena. I heard that some of the demons have to be separated or they would start fighting before they entered the arena. There is a 'D' by every door that is used to bring wild animals into the arena. All the other doors are false fronts."

"Sketch number two shows two back doors to the arena that are used for dragging the dead out. These doors are large because we are pulling demons and anything else through them. I have never seen guards on either sides of these doors and that is probably because they just pile the dead bodies outside of the doors. The smell alone is enough to keep others away. But anyone can walk up to the doors from the outside because the only obstacles are the dead," Horace continued.

"Picture number three shows the secret entrance that Teivel always uses to enter the arena. I don't know where he comes from or if that door opens to a tunnel. But Rachel also drew a picture of Teivel's seat in the arena stands and the area between the entrance and his seat."

"From this picture," Stephan said. "It looks like the entrance door is maybe only fifty feet from Teivel's seat. I assume that is also an escape route for him. Is this drawing accurate?"

"I don't know the exact distance but your estimate is very close," Horace said.

"Pictures four and five show the entrances that the prisoners are led in from the dungeons and they show the cells the prisoners are kept in until they are put onto the floor of the arena. Since they often use the strongest prisoners for the games; the soldiers chain these prisoners up when they transport them. The chains are taken off as soon as the prisoners are put into the cells. There are always a lot of soldiers transporting the prisoners but once the prisoners are in the cells all the soldiers go to the doors and watch the games."

"But are they still close enough to see the prisoners?" Dominic asked.

"They might not be able to actually see the prisoners but they can quickly run into the areas with the cells," Horace replied.

"Is anyone given medical care?" asked Lakin.

"No," Horace said. "The last picture shows the outside entrances where the demons enter their area of the arena to wait their turns to fight. I had to go in one of those areas to drag out a dead demon and all it is, is a long hallway that they stand in. There aren't any guards on either sides of those doors. Excuse me but I will have to sit down now."

"Horace where were you kept?" Gabriel asked.

"In dungeons in a building across the road from the arena."

"Was it an auction house?" asked Gabriel.

"No, I will have Rachel draw the location. Myself I can't draw at all. But you have to understand there was about ten of us and it was our job to carry out the dead so we were in the arena for every game. Sometimes people would get hurt by the demons or animals before the games even began so they usually moved us into the arena before the other prisoners."

"There are four entrances that are indicated as entrances for the prisoners," Raphael said. "Does that mean there are four buildings used as dungeons?"

"That I don't know. I was always brought in through this door," Horace said and pointed to a particular door on the drawing that Raphael was holding. "I found it curious that all the doors where men, demons and animals entered the floor of the area could be locked from the outside, although I never saw them locked."

"So then our people could possibly be locked between those doors and the gates," Archetenus said. "This isn't good."

"Horace do you know anything about the keys?" the Sanuri asked. "Because I saw keys in a vision."

"The soldiers kept us busy so we would be too exhausted to fight with them. There are statues and fancy metal in the arena that we had to polish and sometimes they made us polish the keys. The keys are kept in an office of sorts. The keys are on huge brass rings and each key ring is hung on a numbered hook. Whatever soldier is assigned to work in the arena is given a ring of keys by the sergeant, who writes down the key number and the soldier's name. If a soldier loses his keys they kill him on the spot."

Horace continued. "The keys all had symbols on them but I don't know what the symbols meant."

"Could you draw them?" Michael asked.

"Do they have a weapons room?" asked Raul.

"It is the same room where they keep the keys," Horace said. "I will have Rachel draw more pictures."

"Dagon you were in charge of our group of artists," Gabriel said. "Have them make lots of copies of these drawings." Gabriel turned to Horace. "Has Rachel and Dagon told you our complete mission."

"No," Dagon said then looked at Rachel who shook her head to indicate 'no'.

"Horace I know you have been through a lot and I don't want you to over exert yourself but I want you to sit in the rest of this meeting. You have such valuable information that you might be able to provide more insight for us."

"I am honored to help," Horace said proudly. "And if I get my strength back in time I would like to do more."

"I was thinking of sending you and Rachel to Wetpr to be with Zelda and Zack," Dagon said.

"Thanks to you my wife and child are safe," Horace said. "I want to see them dearly but I want to help you also and I am willing to bet there are others you saved who feel the same."

Misha had to sit down before the group left the Harvest Moon Tavern. He was both physically and emotionally exhausted from the attacks on Morgan and Bruno. Misha suddenly felt like crying but he would never do that in front of others. Calen saw the look on his brother's face and made an announcement.

"We could all use a break. When we get to the Endleson Hotel I am getting rooms for everyone. I think a day or two in the city might be what we all need. Does anyone think otherwise?"

"I don't," Sorren said with a grin then he turned to Misha. "Come on son, let's get out of here."

When they walked out of the tavern, Calen motioned for the rest of the Rualas who were on rooftops to join them. He also motioned to some Enrops. Calen sent the birds in different directions with the news that Morgan and Bruno were dead. A small flock flew to the Ice Caves, another to King Sudfad, a third flock flew to Calen's parents and the fourth to Ryed to tell Gabriel and Raphael.

Misha was covered with blood so Calen felt compelled to explain to the desk clerk that they had just killed two criminals; criminals who had a room at the hotel. The desk clerk got the manager who was familiar with Gabriel's team. While the rest of the group signed for rooms, the manager took Calen, Sorren and Erebus to the hotel room that Morgan and Bruno had rented.

"I knew the Rualas were looking for those two but none of us realized who Morgan and Bruno were. If we had we would have told someone," the manager said sincerely.

"You are just lucky they didn't hurt anyone here," Calen said but stopped talking as the manager opened the door to the room. All four men stood silent when they saw the dead body of a young woman lying on the floor of the parlor. The carpet was soaked with her blood.

"She hasn't been dead long," Sorren said as he examined the body. "Those bastards raped and killed this girl then went downstairs for breakfast. I wish I would have been the one to kill them."

"I know her," the manager said sadly. "I will have someone get her parents."

"We can't let her parents see her looking like this," Sorren said. "We need to get her dressed."

"I'll get Natasha," Calen said and left the room.

Erebus covered the girl's body with a blanket that he took off from the bed.

Sorren and Erebus started to search the room which contained little more than whiskey bottles and some small pouches of gold. "We will give the gold to the girl's family," Sorren said then he walked up to Erebus and whispered. "Are you detecting anything that I am not?"

"No, there weren't any demons in this room besides the two that Misha killed," Erebus said. As he completed his sentence the rest of their group now ran into the hotel room.

"Calen told us," Natasha said. "We will dress the poor thing."

"Her clothes are ripped apart," Batina said as she picked a blouse up from the floor.

"All of you men out," Natasha said. "We may have to buy the girl some clothes." Natasha looked at the manager. "We can't let her parents see all of this blood."

"I will have a room prepared," the manager said. "Her parents are good people, this will destroy them."

"What do you want us to do?" Ratri asked.

"You really can't do anything," Natasha said. "This all just makes me so damn mad."

"I know I should have killed them when I had the chance," Batina said guiltily.

"Batina stop that," Diana said. "You don't know if you could have killed them. You were fighting against three and your priority was to save Christopher, which you did. You have nothing to feel guilty about." Diana turned around and said. "Thor will you stay with Misha until I am done here?"

"I am alright," Misha said.

"Yes you are," Joshua said in a fatherly tone and took Misha's arm. Joshua, Thor and Micha escorted Misha to his hotel room.

Rachel was filled with pride that her father was asked to join Gabriel's mission. Although she was very concerned for her father's health she saw him come alive when he realized that the knowledge he gained during his months of torture could be used to save others.

During the meeting many of the warriors had questions for Horace. At the end of the meeting Gabriel had a question for Horace that greatly surprised both Rachel and her father.

"Horace you look exhausted; you need to rest," Gabriel said. "But I am going to ask you to think about something. You now know that we are trying to stop Teivel's transformation and save his prisoners. I am sure you have more information in the regions of your mind than you are aware of. So I am going to ask you to think about what you would do if you were leading this mission."

"Visterle where have you been?" Nada asked as he materialized in their chambers.

"My pet, you know I have to leave for business," Visterle said as he walked up to Nada and kissed her on the lips.

"Yes, but usually you tell me before you leave and, and," Nada stammered. "We need to talk."

"Alright but I have something important to tell you," Visterle said. While Visterle was pleased that Morgan and Bruno were dead and now being tortured in Dael's hell region, he knew the news would upset Nada.

"Alright," Nada said nervously. "You go first."

Visterle stared at her when he realized she was wringing her hands. "Nada are you alright?"

"No," she replied and started to cry.

"Nada what is the matter?"

"I think you are going to be really mad at what I have to tell you," she said. "Promise me you won't yell at me."

"Nada what did you do?" Visterle asked sternly.

"I didn't do anything, it's what we did."

"I don't understand what you are saying."

"Visterle," Nada paused and took a deep breath. "Visterle we are going to have a baby."

"Nada are you sure?"

"I've had ten children, yes I am sure," Nada said with annoyance. "Are you angry? You don't look angry."

"Why would you think I would be angry?" Visterle said as he pulled Nada close to him and kissed her on the lips.

"Well, because you have talked about other wives but you have never talked about children so I didn't know if you wanted children."

"I had a son once. He was very important to me but he was killed. I don't talk about him. I am actually very pleased by this news."

"Visterle I have to tell you that I am scared because I don't know what to expect. I have heard of demons and humans having babies but I am Ruala. And once the baby is born, I mean I know you take human form to please me. But what if the baby looks like a cloud of smoke or something; how do I take care of it?"

He started to laugh, "These are good questions. Why don't you change and we will go into the city and find a midwife. I will hire someone to help you through the pregnancy and afterwards."

"Oh, thank you Visterle," Nada said and kissed him. "This makes me feel so much better."

Nada turned to walk to her closet when the coldness of Visterle's voice made her stop in her tracts. "Nada don't think you will ever treat our child like you did your other children. I will not tolerate it."

Chapter V
Acts

"That was so sad," Batina said to Ratri as she entered their hotel room. "I felt so badly for those parents. We all started to cry too."

"Come here," Ratri said and hugged Batina tightly. "That was a good thing you girls did."

Batina was quiet for a few moments as they embraced then she pulled her head back so she could look into Ratri's eyes. "Did you open the packages?"

"You mean the things you bought? No."

"Here," Batina said as she reached into her pocket and pulled out a pouch of gold coins. "This is what is left. Natasha gave us each a pouch and ordered us to buy gifts. She said Gabriel and Raphael have decided they are going to start paying the team members."

"Why? They provide us with everything."

"Natasha said so we would have spending money. I bought gifts for our parents since they are doing all the planning for our wedding. I need you to tell me what you think," Batina said excitedly as she ran to a small table that was piled with packages. Batina sorted through the packages then turned around with a bright smile on her face. "First this is for you."

Ratri opened the pouch that Batina handed him and a golden necklace with a ruby pendant fell into his hand. "All of the men on the team wear such beautiful necklaces, I wanted you to have one too. Ratri do you like it?"

"Yes, I like if very much. Thank you," he said and kissed Batina.

"Put it on so I can see if it fits." Ratri put his precious gift on. "Oh, Ratri that looks so nice on you. Go look in the mirror."

"This means a lot to me Batina," he said sincerely and kissed her again.

56

"Now this is what I got for your parents, if you don't think they will like them tell me now. I know your father likes to smoke a pipe after dinner so I bought these," Batina said and handed Ratri a wooden box that contained four beautifully carved pipes. "And I got him some pouches of different kinds of tobacco. Do you think he will like these?"

"Father will love these, you did well."

"Your mother has the most beautiful hair so I bought her these combs. I don't know what jewels she likes but I bought her this silk blouse so I bought the emerald combs to match. They actually sell clothes for Rualas here so there are the openings for wings." Batina was so excited about the gifts that Ratri smiled.

"Mother will love these. But how do you know her size?"

"There was a woman in the store who looked like the same size as your mother so I asked her to help me. She was very nice. I bought my father something he has always wanted and I had it engraved." Batina handed Ratri a golden pocket watch with the inscription: *love Ratri and Batina*. And Mother has never had a store bought dress before so I bought her a fancy one so she can wear it for our ceremonies. Batina held up a light blue dress with lace trim.

"I think everyone is going to love the gifts you bought. But did you get yourself anything."

"No but I hope you don't mind I bought my brothers and sisters some clothes and toys."

"Why would I mind?" asked Ratri as he put his arms around Batina. "But I think we need to find something for you now."

"What do you mean you bought me some gifts?" Joshua asked as he followed Micha and Bianca into their hotel room.

"Natasha gave us a lot of money and ordered us to buy gifts. I am glad we are staying here today so I can return them if they don't fit. Now you two just sit down."

Joshua and Micha grinned at Bianca as she was sorting through her packages. I bought some things for my family too but I will show you those later. I liked these so much I bought you each one." Bianca turned around and handed Joshua and Micha each a leather jacket. "And look, that wool lining is buttoned on so you can take if off if you want."

"Bianca these are beautiful," Joshua said sincerely.

"Try them on because if I got the wrong sizes we will go back to the store. I hope you don't mind that they are identical."

"No," Micha said. "Mine fits me well. Thank you." Micha kissed Bianca on the cheek. He always felt uncomfortable kissing her on the lips in front of his parents.

"Mine is perfect," Joshua said. "That was very thoughtful of you. Thank you." Joshua too kissed Bianca on the cheek.

"Oh, there is more," Bianca said and handed each man three shirts and a bulky wool sweater.

"Why so much?" asked Joshua.

"I was just following orders," Bianca said with a grin. She turned back to the table then quickly turned around and threw the pouch of coins to Micha. "We still have that much left."

"I know Iris likes emeralds but I thought this dress would be so pretty on her and I got this shawl to go with it. What do you think?"

"She loves lavender and you are right she will look beautiful in that," Joshua said warmly.

"I bought Vivian these combs for her hair. Now Micha I hope you don't get mad but I couldn't very well buy toys for Adrone and Paul and not the other children too."

Both Joshua and Micha laughed as Bianca piled toys onto the bed. "Why would I get mad?" Micha asked. "This is very sweet."

"Bianca what did you get for yourself?" asked Joshua.

Bianca gave Joshua a surprised look. "We were all having so much fun buying gifts that none of us thought to buy things for ourselves."

"Come on children," Joshua said with a grin. "Let's get Thor and we will do a little shopping and see the city."

"I am glad you packed another robe," Diana said to Misha. "I don't think I can get the blood out of this one."

"Honey don't worry about that," Misha said and walked up to Diana and hugged her. "I am so glad you are here."

"Misha I was thinking. Killing Bruno and Morgan affects all the family. I know you and Calen were going to go back to Ryed but why don't you fly home with us and talk to Emeral and Maxwell about this. They have been so filled with guilt ever since you told them about your childhood."

Misha didn't say anything so Diana continued. "You would only be gone a few extra days and it's not like Gabriel thought we would find those two right away. If you don't want to do this for yourself I think you should do it for them."

"You make some good points. Let me talk to Calen about this."

"We need to decide on the baby's name," Calen said. "So I can have another disk made for our family necklaces. I told the jeweler that I would have him make all of our disks.

"There are jewelers in Salar you know," Natasha said with a laugh.

"I now but I want to make it a tradition. So Isaiah was your father's name but Gabriel is using it as the middle name for Daniel. What was your father's middle name?"

"Jonathan."

"That is a good name. How about Jonathan Gabriel Maxwell?"

"I think we are ready for the jewelers," Natasha said and laughed.

It wasn't until late that night that a small flock of Enrops arrived at the castle of Nehmota with the news that Bruno and Morgan were dead. The birds carried only the verbal message from Calen so they didn't have many details.

"How is Misha?" Gabriel asked.

"When I saw him he was covered in blood but I don't think it was his. But he was sitting in a chair and everyone was looking at him like they were worried," an Enrop explained.

"I am not sure we should expect them to return right away," Raphael said to Gabriel.

"Actually I wasn't," Gabriel said. "We should find Dagon and Lakin and tell them."

"I am sorry to knock on your door so late, but I did see a light," the Sanuri said as Dominic stood in the doorway of his room.

"No, please come in. I wasn't sleeping," Dominic said as he was greatly surprised by the visit from the Sanuri.

"I won't keep you long," the Sanuri said as he entered the room. "Gabriel and Raphael told me you are very interested in becoming a Patronus priest. Is that true?"

"Yes but I will be honest I don't know what my future holds."

"No man does. The reason I ask is to invite you to join Chaez and me. Every day the two of us meet to study The Holy Scrolls. You know that Chaez wants to become a priest."

"Why, thank you. I would very much like to join you."

"We try to meet right after breakfast every day. We usually sit in one of the gardens."

"Would it be alright to bring Fennel and Asher along?"

"Bring as many people as you want. The Great Ruler's Word is for everyone. I will see you in the morning." As the Sanuri was walking towards the door Dominic called out.

"Sanuri can I ask you something?"

"Of course."

"There are many who want me to lead this kingdom if we topple Teivel but I don't want that job. I truly want to become a Patronus priest but I am filled with guilt that I may be abandoning my people."

"You know I always find it interesting that when people talk to The Great Ruler they never believe that He talks back. What does that voice inside your heart tell you?"

"To become a priest."

"Then you have the answer that you seek. You have risked your life to protect and to serve your people. While those two issues should be on the forefront of a leader of a kingdom the roles are very different."

"I don't understand what you are saying."

"Being a politician and being a warrior are very different roles. Some people like King Sudfad can master them both but that is not often the case. These old bones are telling me that you will be able to protect and to serve more people by becoming a Patronus priest. I believe it is someone else's path to become king of this kingdom. But there is more on your mind."

"If I do not take that position, then Fennel or Asher might be forced to and I fear they will be killed. While we may win a few battles I think this war will be going on for a very long time because evil is too ingrained here."

"Do either of your brothers want to become king?"

"No but they feel the same as I, that we might be abandoning the people."

"Tomorrow after the class let me meet with the three of you."

"You must understand that the citizens of Ryed have always outnumbered the demons and dark lords. The citizens could have taken back this kingdom at any time. But they let a handful of people with the courage to say no to darkness do their fighting for them. I believe you and your men have played your parts. The people of Ryed have choices to make. Everyone has paths that they must walk; you cannot walk their paths for them," the Sanuri explained.

The Sanuri was pleased when Dominic brought all of his men to the morning lessons. Chaez too was glad to have company in the class. "Chaez I don't know if you are aware that Dominic is also considering becoming a Patronus priest; so he may be joining us on a regular basis. Perhaps you can share with him the information about the training sites, the requirements and the fees," the Sanuri said.

"Fees?" Dominic repeated. "I didn't consider that. I should have guessed there would be fees for the education."

Chaez heard the sadness in Dominic's voice. "My father is very wealthy and he was so overjoyed that I wanted to become a Patronus priest that he sent enough money along to pay for the educations of five men. I know he would be honored if you would allow our family to pay for your educations."

Dominic looked at Chaez then at the Sanuri then back at Chaez. "Are you serious?" Dominic asked. "But I could not accept such a gift."

"Perhaps you and Chaez could work out a trade of sorts," the Sanuri said. "Chaez is well educated as a nobleman but an event in his life has changed the path he was on. You may notice the boy is always covered with bruises that is because he is trying desperately to learn the skills of a warrior so he doesn't get eliminated from the training."

"I don't understand," said Dominic.

"As you know the Patronus priests are warrior priests," Chaez explained. "Only the best warriors are allowed to continue with training. They start competing with each other from day one."

"I had never even been in a fight until I decided to become a Patronus priest. Gabriel and Raphael have been afraid that I wouldn't make it through the first few months. But I have been working really hard."

"Dominic I believe that if you and your brothers would help Chaez with his training you would make both Chaez and his father very happy," said the Sanuri.

"Of course we will help you," Fennel said. "And I know it is not my business but you look awful why are you doing this?"

Chaez looked at the Sanuri who said, "You cannot hide what Timothy did."

"My parents are wonderful people," Chaez said. "My father is a great warrior and tried to protect us all from the things he had to endure. None of his children wanted to become warriors and I never realized how that broke his heart. My older brother became a monster and I am not just saying that to be unkind. He literally prayed to demons and became a monster. He raped and butchered women and children, including my little sister," Chaez paused as he composed himself. "And he wanted to kill my parents."

"I never knew monsters like that existed in this world. And Timothy's actions did so much damage to so many good people. I want to stop people like him and I want to help the victims."

"This kingdom is filled with monsters like your brother," Dominic said. "I do not speak lightly when I say we understand. Of course we will help you train."

"Then you will allow us to pay for your educations," Chaez said with determination. "If more than four of you want to become Patronus priests I will make sure the fees are paid. You are all good men who have had very difficult lives; allow me this."

Tina and Charles stopped abruptly as they were entering the dining room of the Endleson Hotel for breakfast. Sorren, Calen and their entire group were seated at a long table in the dining room and they all turned and stared at Charles and Tina.

Misha and Calen both got out of their chairs and walked up to Tina and Charles who did not know if they should run or stand their ground.

"We heard you were here," Calen said as he grasped Charles' arm.

"Please join us," Misha said as he took Tina's hand and pulled her towards the table.

Neither Charles nor Tina said a word but sat down at the table. Calen looked at the other Ruala warriors who were seated at the long table. Calen was directing his words to the Ruala warriors but he was speaking loud enough for everyone in the dining room to hear.

"I know you all know that Charles and Tina here were admonished for their treatment of their children and their threats to kill their children and grandchild. But did you know that King Sudfad banished them from his kingdom? I was there when King Sudfad ordered his troops to lock Tina and Charles in the dungeons if they did not leave."

"And Tina will you repeat the profanities you screamed at Queen Renya that night?" Natasha asked loudly.

"We heard you left the Ice Caves," Misha too spoke loudly. "And apparently you have been allowing the good people of Nora to pay for your lifestyle." Charles was sweating as he looked around the room and saw that all eyes were upon them.

"Tina it is not like you to be quiet," Diana said sarcastically. Then she looked at the other guests in the dining room and said, "This woman threatened to kill a five year old boy."

The manager of the hotel walked up to Charles and handed him a note. "This is your bill," the manager said. "I expect it to be paid in full. You no longer have lodging here." Then the manager looked at Calen and said, "They have arrived."

Calen motioned to the soldiers who were in the lobby of the hotel. "You can't do this!" Tina screamed. "Charles do something."

64

Charles looked at the soldiers, "Calen can't we work something out?"

"King Sudfad has an arrest order for you both if you ever enter his kingdom again. And that extends to the City of Nora. Are you asking me to disobey an order of the King?"

"But you are friends with him," Charles said.

"And we are family with your children and grandchildren," Misha said. "And not that you care but you have a granddaughter now also."

Two soldiers took Tina's arms and two took Charles' arms and escorted the couple out of the dining room. "Charles I told you they would find out but oh no you never listen to me," Tina screamed. "Now look at the mess we are in."

"It's your mouth that got us in this mess to begin with," Charles yelled back. Charles looked at one of the soldiers and said. "Don't put me in the same cell with her."

"Our things. What about our things?" Tina shrieked as they left the hotel.

There were no crutches at the castle of Nehmota for Archetenus to use so others had to help him walk. "Just leave me here," Archetenus said with frustration.

"Are you sure?" asked Simon.

"I am going to call to Miranda and ask her to help me," Archetenus said.

"Well, one of us will come back and check on you in half an hour," Jared said.

Simon and Jared left Archetenus sitting on a stone bench in one of the gardens that surrounded the castle. "Miranda please come so we can talk," Archetenus said. "What I am going to ask is for the others not for me."

"Tell me Archetenus, have you ever said those words before?" Miranda asked as she materialized in the garden.

Archetenus grinned. "You know I don't think I have. Miranda please help me to walk. I am the only one here who has fought in Gefrey Games like this. I have the experience and will know when things aren't right. I can't sit back here while the others are in so much danger. Please if this is some kind of punishment, well can you punish me later; after the mission."

Miranda laughed. "That broken leg is no punishment from the heavens it was an accident and you were lucky you weren't killed."

"Miranda the games are in a few days. We have a handful of warriors compared to Teivel's armies. Look around you; most of these people are farmers and tradesmen. They will be slaughtered. And the prisoners we saved want to help but they are half dead. Miranda I know I owe you a lot but please do me this favor."

"So the man who once walked with demons would risk his life because of compassion. You have come far," Miranda said and disappeared.

Archetenus did not feel any different so he didn't know if Miranda had healed his leg. He waited for a moment then said, "Well what the hell. Guess there is only one way to find out."

"Raphael, Gabriel can I speak with you in private?" Chaez asked.

"Certainly," Gabriel said and the three men left the Great Hall and walked into a small room of the castle.

"Dominic, Fennel and Asher are talking with their men right now. The eight of them are deciding if they want to become Patronus priests. You should expect them to speak with you shortly. They have no money and I told them that my father and I will pay for their educations. "Father sent enough money for four others besides me and I will pay for the other four men."

"First this news pleases me," Gabriel said. "They are all good men. And secondly this is a very charitable act Chaez. I didn't realize you were friends with them."

"I don't know then well. But they are good men and great warriors and they have joined the morning lessons that the Sanuri teaches me."

"Can I ask why you are doing this?" Raphael asked.

"I always knew I had a good life," Chaez said. "I just never realized what difficult and painful lives others had until I came here. I have the money and it will change their lives."

"I came from a poor family," Raphael said. "And Gabriel paid for my education so I could become a priest. I am touched by what you are doing."

Gabriel looked at Raphael and said, "Perhaps we should combine our ideas."

"Gabriel and I are starting a sort of fund. We are putting money aside to help men pay for their educations to become Patronus priests. We will help also with the costs for the freedom fighters."

"I promised them that I would pay for their educations and I would like to do so," Chaez said. "But you should tell others of this fund. I'll bet that my father, Mathas and Claudius would donate."

Chapter VI
News

"I'm back," Archetenus announced loudly as he walked into the Great Hall. "Miranda healed me so I could fight."

"Damn glad to hear it," Jared said kiddingly. "You're kinda heavy to carry around."

"Where's Gabriel and Raphael?" Archetenus asked.

"They are talking with Chaez," Lakin said. "I would not expect them to be gone long."

When Gabriel, Raphael and Chaez returned to the Great Hall, Dominic and his men were waiting for them. "Can we speak with you?" Dominic asked Gabriel.

"I get them first," Archetenus yelled with a grin. "Gabriel Miranda healed my leg so I want to be in charge of the games again."

"I think this is a day of good news," said Raphael.

"You have the assignment again," Gabriel said. "Rachel brought us some more drawings that I was going to pass out at the meeting. They are on the table. Why don't you pass them out and start the discussion while we speak with Dominic and his men."

"Look at him grin," Jared said teasingly of Archetenus. "He looks like a kid."

"I feel like one," Archetenus said as he walked up to the front table and grabbed a pile of drawings.

Chaez joined the large meeting as Gabriel and Raphael took Dominic and his men into a neighboring room.

"I suppose Chaez told you by the way you two are smiling," Asher said.

"Let's hear what you have to say," said Gabriel.

"Earlier today Asher, Fennel and I met with the Sanuri because none of us want to be leader of this kingdom and we all feel guilty about abandoning our people," Dominic explained. "All of us have prayed for guidance and the Sanuri made us realize that, that voice we hear inside is giving us our answers. So we talked with the rest of our men and all of us would like to become Patronus priests."

"Chaez said that he and his father would pay for our educations if we helped him train," Fennel said. "We aren't really sure if he was serious and if he isn't we will have to work something out with you."

"Oh, Chaez is very serious. In fact we offered to help but he wants to pay for all of you," Raphael said.

"We don't really know him," said Seth. "Why would he do such a thing?"

"I think he wants to make up for all the darkness that his brother brought to this world," Gabriel said. "But you will have to ask him about that."

"He already told us," Dominic said. "He carries a heavy burden."

"Chaez is a good man and will make a good priest," Gabriel said.

"There are two training sites," Raphael said. "One at the monastery in Philiste and the other in Salar, they are both in Wetpr. Gabriel and I spoke and we would like you to attend the training in Salar, which is where our home is."

"Our suggestion is somewhat selfish," Gabriel said with a grin. "We can help all of you with the training and perhaps you can help us occasionally with mission work."

Dominic looked at his men then at Gabriel and Raphael, "I believe that sounds good to all of us."

"King Sudfad is not like what you would expect of a king," Gabriel said. "Don't get me wrong he is a wise and great leader and a courageous warrior."

"But he and Queen Renya rather adopt everyone who enters their castle. They are very informal and treat everyone as family. They have built barracks for the students but I am sure they will ask you to stay in the castle. Just something for you to think about."

"Are those the parents of Raul, Simon, Michael and Matthew?" Asher asked.

"Yes but Matthew is their nephew who they also adopted as a son. Matthew's father is King Mathas of Lentz," Raphael said.

"I asked because we didn't believe they were princes at first," Asher said. "I mean because they work just as hard as everyone else."

"And they talk to everyone like regular people," Fennel said.

"So is it settled?" Gabriel asked. "After this mission you will return to Wetpr with us and all of you will start training."

"Do any of you have family members you want to bring along?" Raphael asked.

"We are the only family that any of us have," Dominic said. "But we would like to say goodbye to High Priest Othnial. He was like a father to us. I wish we could bring him with us."

"We can certainly ask him," Gabriel said.

"What is all of this?" Calen asked as a flock of Enrops flew into the hotel room through the patio doors. "Has something happened that there is so much mail?"

"Most of this is mail that has been piling up for all of you in Ryed," an Enrop answered. "Gabriel said that all of you probably don't know that Hannah and Vivian had boys."

"What!" Calen said and laughed. "I have got to get these letters to the others. Does your flock go to the Patronus Headquarters to eat and rest?"

"Yes."

"Before you leave the kingdom I will have some letters for Wetpr and the Ice Caves," Calen said and started to sort the envelopes into piles.

Calen walked into the hallway and knocked on a door. "Joshua open up, you're a grandfather."

"What?" Joshua asked as he opened the door to Sorren's room.

"I haven't read the letters yet but the Enrops said that Vivian and Hannah had baby boys," Calen said as he walked into Sorren's hotel room and started to hand out mail to the small group seated in the room. "I have to find Natasha," Calen said. "She will want to know right away."

"All the girls are shopping," said Micha. "They love this city."

"After I hand out the rest of the mail I am going looking for them if any of you want to come with me," Calen said.

"I'll go," Thor said. "Let me drag Misha out of his room. It will be good for him to get out."

"I think this took more out of Misha than anyone thought," Sorren said as he was opening an envelope. "We should all keep an eye on the boy."

Calen and Thor left the room as the others read their mail. "Rachel sent me a letter," Erebus said with surprise. Erebus read the letter then set it down. "They found her father, he was one of the prisoners who was going to be executed. She say's he used to be a big man and now he is thin and frail. But the Sanuri has been helping the prisoners to heal and even though Horace is still in bad shape he is helping with the mission."

"How?" Sorren asked.

"Apparently Horace had a work assignment where he had to carry the dead out of the arena so he knows a lot about the buildings, keys and things," Erebus explained.

"Are you alright?" asked Joshua.

"I know it sounds awful but I am both happy for Rachel and her family and a little sad too."

"That is understandable," Sorren said. "Rachel was treating you like a father. And Zelda and Zack both think a lot of you. You know just because they found Horace doesn't mean you can't still be a friend of the family. You did a lot for them."

"Erebus have you decided what you are going to do after this mission?" Joshua asked.

"What do you mean?"

"Are you planning on staying in Ryed?"

"My home is here."

"You are a wealthy man you can have a home anywhere you want," Joshua said. "Thor keeps telling you that you are part of the team and he means it. Why don't you come back to Wetpr with us? If nothing else you could get a second home there and visit often."

"You could always come to Lentz too," Sorren said. "You really seem to enjoy being with everyone. Do you really want to go back to that huge castle and live there alone?"

"Actually your suggestion for a second home does have merit. I will give it thought," Erebus said. "I will admit I have become attached to a lot of you. Isn't it strange how life works out? A year ago we could have considered ourselves enemies."

"Speaking of work," Joshua said with a grin. "If you do come to Wetpr or Lentz you know that Gabriel will probably put you to work."

"Actually that would be fine," Erebus said and smiled. "I would rather feel helpful."

"What are you buying now?" Calen asked with a big grin as he, Misha and Thor found Natasha, Diana, Batina and Bianca in a jewelry store.

The old clerk was showing Diana some necklaces when Misha and Thor walked up to her. "Well since you just ruined the surprise," Diana said and giggled. "I am having the jeweler make the same kind of family necklaces for us that Calen had made. The disks are engraved so Misha why don't you pick out the chain you like. And Thor I had disks with the babies names made for your necklace do you also want disks with my name and Misha's?"

"Sure," Thor said with a bright smile.

"Then why don't you pick out your chain," said Diana.

"Calen why are you grinning like that?" Natasha asked. "What are you up to?"

"Hannah and Vivian both had baby boys," Calen said and handed Natasha a letter. Natasha squealed with delight and tore the letter out of the envelope and read it. Then she handed the letter to Diana, who was standing the closest to her.

"I just can't believe Vivian is a mother," Diana said with excitement and handed the letter to Thor.

"Well you are going to be," Misha said with a grin.

"No, what I mean is all those years that we were growing up Vivian always said she would never marry or have a family because she wanted to devote her life to hunting. I guess I never really thought about getting married but I didn't say I wouldn't."

"We have to buy some baby gifts," Natasha said with excitement.

"Let's make family necklaces for them," said Calen.

"Everyone come over here," Bianca called. Batina and Bianca were standing at one of the counters together with a different clerk.

"Look at these," Batina said. "They are bracelets with disks and other jewels. Aren't they pretty."

"Oh Calen we have to make one for Emeral with all the names of her children and grandchildren," Natasha said.

"She might not be able to lift her arm it will be so heavy," Calen said kiddingly.

"I think we should make one for Iris too and Ella," Diana said. "Misha do you know the names of Bekka's sisters?"

"Yes and their husbands."

"We already ordered bracelets for our mothers," Bianca said.

"And I got one for Ratri's mother too," said Batina.

"Now just wait a minute," Misha said and laughed for the first time in days. "You know how all you girls are. You all like the exact same things. I think we should have one made up for every woman in the household."

Calen looked at the clerk and laughed, "You better get some paper this is going to be a big order." Then Calen looked at Natasha. "You know for everything Renya does for us, we should make ones for her, Vitomas, Annabelle and Laurel too."

"We might have to stay here an extra day or two until these are done," Natasha said. "I really like this city."

"I love it here," Ella said as the family was gathering around the dinner table in Gabriel's house. "All these babies just fills my heart with joy." Bekka kissed her mother on the head as she took her seat at the table.

"I know," Maxwell said as he was holding baby Daniel while Hannah brought food to the table.

"I love it too," Zelda said as she put two platters of meat on the table. "But I think Hannah and Vivian are overdoing it."

"Neither of us can stand to stay in bed," Vivian said and laughed.

"Besides Mother hasn't put Robert down since he was born. She is doing all the work except for feeding him."

"Look!" Cassandra said excitedly as she walked out of the kitchen with a large pile of envelopes. "Elan can you sort them while I finish in the kitchen?"

Zelda squealed and started to cry when Elan handed her two envelopes. "Mother what is the matter?" Zack asked as he ran to her.

"Look; that is your father's handwriting. Zack you open it; I can't stop crying," Zelda said. Emeral and Hannah both walked up to Zelda and hugged her. Zack took the letter from the envelope and handed it to his mother. Zack was now crying too. The tears poured down Zelda's cheeks as she read the letter from Horace. "Your father is alive," she gasped.

"What does it say Mother?" asked Zack.

"Honey the soldiers were very bad to your father. He is sick and weak but he is alive. Rachel and Dagon are taking care of him. He is so grateful that we are here in Wetpr and he will be joining us as soon as he can," Zelda paused and frowned. "Your father is helping with the mission so he won't be coming here right away."

"How is he helping?" Luca asked as Zelda handed him the letter.

"He has a lot of information that Gabriel and the others can use," Zelda said as she wiped the tears from her eyes. Then Zelda looked at Emeral and Maxwell. "You can read the letter for yourselves but Horace likes Dagon very much and is so grateful that he is taking care of us. I didn't know if Horace would be angry because we left Ryed."

"What are you doing here?" Gabriel asked with a grin as he stood up to shake hands with Koby who had just walked into the Great Hall at the castle of Nehmota.

"Guilt," Koby said as he took his large pack off his back.

"I was feeling guilty every time I read a letter from one of you. "And I did not come empty handed. Where is Simon?"

"I'll get him," Joao said and left the room.

"You are going to need to clear this table off because I have a lot of things to hand out. I need to see Archetenus, Jared, Raul and Michael too besides our team." Koby talked as he took items from his huge back pack and placed them on the table. Suddenly Koby paused and looked around the room. "Where is my new sister-in-law I haven't even met her yet?"

"What are we having a celebration?" Raul asked with a laugh as he entered the room with a small group of people. Raul, Simon, Raphael, Michael, Jared, Archetenus, Matthew, Thaos and Stephan all walked up to Koby and shook hands with him.

"If someone wants to get some glasses and plates I will finish putting all this stuff on the table before I hand out the mail and gifts," Koby said. "I only brought mail from Wetpr but you know how Renya and Sudfad are."

"Well if it isn't my misfit brother," Dagon said loudly. Koby turned around and saw Dagon, Rachel and Dack walking slowly with Horace. Koby walked up to them and hugged Dagon. "Rachel, Horace this is my brother Koby," Dagon said.

"Horace, Zelda and Zack are just fine and I have some letters for you in my pack," Koby said as he shook Horace's hand. "Dagon how did you ever get such a beautiful girl to marry you?" Koby said kiddingly and hugged Rachel."

"Is everyone from our team here now?" Koby asked as he saw Jasmine and Darla carry trays of plates and glasses into the room. "Jasmine, Darla do you want to help me?" Koby asked as he returned to the table in the front of the room and finished emptying his pack. "Good thing we Rualas carry these big packs or more of us would have had to come," Koby said and laughed. Then he looked around the room and said. "I can't believe I am saying this but I've really missed all of you."

"Sudfad sent cigars and good whiskey for everyone and Jasmine and Darla are unwrapping a bunch of treats."

"Our wives are all great cooks but now that Emeral, Iris, Ella and Zelda are at the house everyone is getting fat because those women bake every day and they sent along treats for you. You can help yourselves while I talk."

"First of all," Koby continued. "Renya had an idea for some gifts so she spoke with Mathas. Matthew, Thaos and Stephan before you go back to your seats I have these for you. Where is Sorren?"

"Some of them are on another mission," Raphael said. "We'll explain later."

Koby handed Matthew, Thaos and Stephan each an envelope. Each envelope contained a silk pouch that held drawings of their children. "Ingr drew the ones for you. Simon, Annabelle drew all the rest." Koby handed envelopes to Gabriel and Raphael first. "You get to see your sons," Koby said. "Archetenus, Jared, Michael, Raul and Simon I have drawings for you too." All of the men eagerly opened their gifts and every one of them was silent for a few moments.

"Horace do Zelda and Zack know you are safe now?" Koby asked as he walked up to the older man.

"I sent them a letter, I don't know if they have received it yet."

"Well, they both sent letters with me in case we found you," Koby said and handed Horace two envelopes. Horace's hands shook as he took the letters.

"For those of you who know Renya and Sudfad this isn't going to be a big surprise but they are throwing a huge celebration to honor all of you when we get home. Thedes, Ibula is working with Renya to get things prepared for the Rualas and Shettees so she has a list of things she wants from you." Koby laughed as he handed the envelope to Thedes.

"Darla and Jasmine I am going to put you in charge of the next thing. Renya and Shara have been writing to each other and the families of all of the warriors here will be at the celebration. I don't know if you have been to one of these celebrations before but they are very fancy."

"For your service, Renya and Sudfad will pay for gowns and suits for everyone who is here in Ryed and Mathas will pay for family members in Lentz. Here are several long lists of information that Renya wants. Do you mind doing this?"

"No," Darla said excitedly. "I've never had a gown before."

"I think Renya has it in her letter but if not she wants you to get that information from everyone here who would like a gown or suit," Koby said. "Now I have a project from King Sudfad and King Mathas. I don't think it's a surprise but heck I am telling you anyways. Each King has designed medals from their kingdom for your services and you will get them at the ceremony. But Stephan and Thaos your father had another idea which everyone liked. The leaders here are supposed to design a medal for those who serve on these special missions. Send your final drawings to Sudfad and he will have them made."

"I like that idea," Simon said. "But we should start working on that soon."

"Are Dominic and his men here?" Koby asked as he took some items off the table."

"Yes," Dominic said.

"Actually could you all come up here? Koby asked. "And to think of it, Raul, Simon, Michael, Matthew, Thaos and Stephan come here; you should be handing these things out." The six men joined Koby and smiled as they read the papers that King Sudfad and King Mathas had sent for the freedom fighters. "There is more," Koby said and handed envelopes and pouches to the men.

"Michael you're the oldest call them forward," Raul said with a grin. Michael called the names and Raul and Simon handed each of the eight freedom fighters a rolled parchment, an envelope and a pouch of gold coins.

"The parchment is a declaration that you are now citizens of Wetpr," Michael announced. "The letters are from Sudfad and Renya offering you jobs in the Army of Wetpr and other things. And the gold is for your service."

Dominic, Fennel, Asher, Seth, Noah, Martin, Oliver and Lawrence were speechless. "Stay right where you are," Matthew said with a grin and again announced the names of the freedom fighters as Thaos and Stephan handed out rolls of parchment, envelopes and pouches. "You are now also citizens of Lentz and have received the same offers from my father. Mathas and Sudfad are good men, they will not be angered because of the decisions you make. They want to offer you opportunities that you do not have here."

"They all look so in shock," Gabriel said with a grin. "Dominic and his men have already asked to become Patronus priests and Chaez is paying for their educations."

"Chaez, we may have to fight over that," Stephan said with a grin.

"We don't know what to say," Dominic stuttered. "We are truly in shock."

"How do your fathers even know about us?" asked Asher.

"We have all written about you in our letters home," Raul said.

"If you are going to be Patronus priests are you going to study in Salar?" Simon asked.

"Yes," Raphael said with a huge smile.

"Good, you can stay at the castle," said Simon. "Or Father built barracks."

"I was hoping they would help us on missions now and then," Gabriel said.

"Chaez come up here," Stephan said. Chaez looked embarrassed and reluctantly walked to the front of the room. Stephan spoke to the freedom fighters. "Matthew's father is King of Lentz but in his wisdom he has two other men who help him rule the kingdom."

"Mathias did this to keep stability in the kingdom if something should happen to him. Claudius is my and Thaos' father and Fahron is the father of Chaez. So Chaez should also be up here representing our kingdom."

79

Chaez didn't say anything but he was filled with pride at Stephan's words. For the first time Chaez felt accepted by Stephan, Thaos and Matthew.

Chapter VII
Strategizing

"Are you having a party and you didn't invite us?" Edward asked as he, Lakin and Clay walked into the Great Hall.

"No one ever sees you anymore. We forgot you were here," Jared said jokingly.

"My friends," Edward said sarcastically as the three men walked towards the front of the room. "Koby when did you get here?"

"Thirty minutes ago; have some treats."

"We think we've got some things," Edward said to Gabriel and Raphael as he grabbed a handful of cookies.

Gabriel stood up and addressed the group. "Edward and Lakin have been working on a special project which is why no one has seen them. For any of you who do not know Clay; he has grown up in Teivel and has kept records on many people. Clay owns several businesses including the Teivel Manor Hotel which allows him to see different sides of people shall I say."

"Gabriel is being kind," Clay said. "I got dirt on people and blackmailed them in order to protect my businesses and my employees. I own businesses that are frequented by the elite of the city. And anyone who is elite is working for Teivel. They have their secret meetings and their affairs in my businesses. I gave Gabriel my records and Edward and Prince Lakin have been trying to find ways you can use this information."

"Actually Clay has done more than that," Edward said. "Since we have been at this castle, Clay has been going to various businesses that he doesn't own and getting receipts and information."

"There were some things that Edward and I read in the records but did not understand the significance until Clay joined us," Lakin said. "I am going to repeat a little of this since Koby just joined us. The Gefrey Games will be held in three days."

81

"Thousands of prisoners will be forced to fight in those games and from what Ruth said we fear that Teivel will need to feed on the day of his transformation. Ruth believes Teivel plans to feed on the prisoners first. So our concerns are one, to save the prisoners and two to stop the transformation."

"Yesterday King Neputa, Thedes and the other Shettees went to the arena as a visiting delegation. They asked for a tour and received one immediately. Horace had already provided us with information about the building. Perhaps King Neputa and Thedes should tell you the rest."

"Thedes and I acted as more of a distraction," said Neputa, "While some of our warriors examined things more closely. We found the weapons room which also has the hooks containing the rings of keys. We replaced one set of keys with a ring from this castle. Horace was right in that the key rings are very similar. We also examined the doors. The areas where our warriors would enter the arena are set up to be a perfect trap. The warriors enter a really long hallway that is blocked on one end by the outside door which locks from the outside and a metal gate on the other side."

"Archetenus wants to sneak into the arena the night before the games begin and jam the locks on the doors but the metal gates are a different matter. The gates are raised by levers that are located inside of the arena itself. Horace said that a soldier stands next to every lever. So there are levers to the tunnels for warriors, prisoners, demons and wild animals. Since I am a visiting King, I am invited to sit in the private area that Teivel reserves for dignitaries. Teivel also sits in this area."

"Because of this invitation, Gabriel doesn't want me and Thedes to fight; he wants us close to Teivel. I will demand that several more of my men sit in that area as part of my court. That is all I have for now."

"Koby, we have stolen quite a number of uniforms and will replace the soldiers at the levers with our men," Raphael explained.

"Clay provided us with the names of several people who always sit in the dignitary section of the arena," Edward said.

"These men and women are well known to him. Tonight there is a large celebration at the Grand Ballroom. Clay is going to introduce some of us to these people. And we are going to try and make enough of an impression that we will be invited to sit in this section."

"Are ya gonna get them drunk?" Jared asked and laughed.

"Actually we are going to use Clays' information to blackmail them," Edward said. "Me, Gabriel, Raphael, Raul, Simon and Matthew are going to make contact with these people. Dagon, Joao and Dack are each leading security details to watch the building and to get us out of there if needed."

"I have two questions," Jasmine said and raised her hand which made many smile. "I thought all music was banned in this kingdom yet there was dancing at Clay's hotel and now this ball. Is this part of some special ceremony for Teivel's ascension?"

"Teivel is a hypocrite," Clay said. "He has outlawed music as a way to control the masses but the elite of this city are not governed under these laws. Teivel feels that by giving the elite these special privileges he garners their devotion. You would be surprised at what the elite get away with."

"Thank you for explaining that," Jasmine said. "Then my second question is can Darla and I come along as your escorts? Usually its couples going to balls isn't it? I am afraid you will stand out."

"Do you have dresses?" asked Raphael.

"Natasha gave us all kinds of things for disguises," Jasmine said. "We can look the part but neither Darla or I know that fancy dancing."

"We can teach you enough," Dack said. "We will start right after the meeting."

Rachel and Dagon whispered to each other for a few moments. Then Horace, who was sitting between them said loudly, "I will be alright. Go."

"Rachel would like to go along too," Dagon said. "She still has her outfits."

"Very good," Gabriel said. "We will meet with you girls after the meeting."

Edward once again spoke. "Gabriel wanted us to try and locate the spot where the transformation would take place. Now we all know that when Roch was going to transform into a demon the Insidiae built a huge tub to put him in. Clay was not able to get any information from the various businesses about anything like a tub or really anything highly unusual. But we did find a couple of things that may be of interest."

"Teivel is a butcher and orders a great deal of shackles and weapons designed for pure torture. But one of the blacksmiths told Clay that Teivel placed an order for knives, which was not unusual. But Teivel wanted a unique design carved into the knives and the entire time the blacksmith was making the knives a man wearing a long robe was standing in the blacksmith shop and chanting. This man also prevented any other customers from coming into the shop. We have a copy of the design and are trying to research it."

"The other thing may be nothing but yesterday the cooks went into the city because it was market day. When they returned all of the women were in a tizzy because two of the herbs they use most were sold out of the entire city. I didn't think anything of it until one of the women is accusing witches of buying all the herbs. I started asking questions and was told that these two herbs were used for food and medicines but also by witches and warlocks. None of the cooks understood the reason the herbs were used in black magics."

"The herbs are schumack roots and the leaves of the talamar plant," Gabriel said. "The Sanuri is researching these herbs and I sent a letter to Erebus asking him to return to the castle." Gabriel now looked at Koby. "I don't know if you received any letters before you left Wetpr but the Angels told us that Morgan and Bruno were working for a demon and coming here. Many members of our household intercepted them and Misha killed Morgan and Bruno."

"Apparently Misha was having some issues afterwards and the group decided to stay in Nora a couple of days. Erebus is with them."

"Well I must say you girls look very beautiful," Gabriel said as Rachel, Jasmine and Darla entered the Great Hall with Dack, Joao and Dagon later that evening.

"We have never dressed like this before," Darla said and giggled. "Jasmine and I feel like princesses."

"Dack and Joao had to show us how to dance in these shoes and dresses," Jasmine said. "I think this is going to be fun."

"The way they look I might stop thinking of Jasmine and Darla as sisters," Joao said with a grin and Jasmine punched him on the arm which caused the others to laugh.

"The girls all have scarves tied to their wrists," Dagon explained. "If one of them needs rescuing they will drop the scarf on the floor."

"Good thinking," Raphael said. "We don't want anyone taking chances because we can't afford to have our disguises exposed."

"We know," said Jasmine. "But you should know too that we are all carrying weapons on us." Gabriel and Raphael grinned. Darla and Jasmine looked at each other then Jasmine spoke. "This may not be the right time but Darla and I want you to know that after this mission, well; if you ever need help again we would like you to consider us. We are learning so much and enjoying this."

"They just want to be near us," Dack said kiddingly. Both Darla and Jasmine rolled their eyes.

"You two have done well," Gabriel said. "I can certainly see us calling upon you again. But I think this is something you should talk over with your parents first. All of our team members have the blessings of their parents to be on the team." Both Jasmine and Darla looked confused by Gabriel's words so he continued.

"We try to minimize distractions so the members can be focused on the missions. Family issues can cause a great deal of distractions."

"Our parents wrote letters to Gabriel requesting him to consider us for the team," Joao said.

"I would not require letters but I would like to know how your parents feel about your participation," Gabriel said.

Darla looked at Jasmine and said, "Maybe we should send letters home soon and ask them."

"Will I need to get permission?" asked Rachel. "Since I am married to Dagon?"

"Have you and Dagon talked about this?" Raphael asked.

"A little," Rachel said and looked at Dagon who was smiling. "Perhaps we should discuss this."

"If you want to work on the missions that is great with me," Dagon said. "But I would prefer you not when you are pregnant. Now don't give me that look. Raphael's wife is a Venator and an incredible warrior but she was so sick when she was pregnant that she had great difficulty on one of the missions."

"Vivian almost had to compromise her disguise on that mission," Raphael said. "We were all concerned for her. Dagon is also thinking of the mission and other members when he said that."

"I understand," Rachel said. "I would like to work on other missions if you can use me. I too have learned a great deal and it is kind of fun."

"As long as you and Dagon have an agreement that is fine with the rest of us," said Gabriel.

"We are ready," Edward announced as he, Clay, Matthew, Raul and Simon entered the Great Hall. "Clay had three carriages brought here from his hotel. Our men are driving them and we just filled them with weapons."

"Oh my god!" Darla gasped. "I can't believe how different you all look. I hardly recognize you."

"Gabriel and Raphael want us all to be in disguise," Raul said. "I don't know how they wear these beards, mine itches." Everyone laughed.

"Of course Clay is playing himself," Edward said and laughed loudly.

"Attendance at this ball is by invitation only," Raphael said. "Clay got us all invitations. Since Rachel and Gabriel have been seen in public together before, they will again pretend to be a married couple." Raphael was handing out the invitations as he spoke. "Please memorize your new names on these."

"Matthew and Jasmine will play brother and sister but she will also be dating Simon," Gabriel said. "So the three of you will stay together. Edward, Darla will be your date for the evening. We did not want to disguise all the women as wives in case we need them to flirt with someone."

The Teivel Ballroom displayed an opulence and splendor to be rivaled in any other city in the Continent of Opots. While many of his people starved, Teivel and the politicians of the city invested in grand buildings that fed their egos.

Only the society's most elite and powerful people were ever invited to a grand event at the Teivel Ballroom. All in attendance wore their finest clothing and most expensive jewels. And this night there was an excited energy flowing through the guests as there were rumors that the dictator Teivel himself would make an appearance.

"I think I am going to leave most of the talking to you two," Jasmine said as she was intimidated by the wealth she saw around her. "I don't think I know how to speak to rich people."

"Simon and I are rich," Matthew said with a grin. "And you speak to us just fine."

"Well, you are different; you seem so normal."

"Matthew I believe that was a compliment," Simon said kiddingly.

"Oh, you know what I mean," Jasmine said as she blushed deeply. "You are warriors and you are so nice."

"A lot of rich people are nice," Matthew said and winked at Simon.

"I think I better stop talking now," Jasmine said with embarrassment.

Gabriel, Rachel and Raphael stayed together as a team while Raul, Edward and Darla made up the third team inside of the ballroom. Clay arrived at the event alone as was his normal behavior. The plan was for Clay to introduce the three teams to powerful politicians during the dance.

"I thought I was ready for this," Darla whispered to Edward but I grew up poor. I don't know if I can carry on a conversation with these people."

"Is something the matter?" asked Raul.

"Darla is intimidated by the wealth here," Edward said as he squeezed Darla's hand.

"You will do just fine," Raul said. "Just follow our lead and remember your stories."

Simon was dancing with Jasmine, as he took her around the large dance floor he nodded to both Gabriel and Edward, who in turn asked their partners to dance. "The rumor is that Teivel will come here tonight," Simon whispered to Gabriel as they danced near each other. Gabriel and Rachel left the dance floor as Simon gave the same message to Edward and Darla.

"Is this going to change anything?" asked Rachel.

"It might," Gabriel said. "I think we might need to wait a while before we make contact with anyone."

Clay was well known by the people in the ballroom and was working his way through the crowd.

Clay was a shrewd man and was identifying the most dangerous men as he greeted everyone in the room. He found that working with Gabriel and his team gave him a sense of purpose and freedom. As Clay worked his way around the ballroom he felt like he was seeing everything with new eyes.

An hour into the festivities the ballroom suddenly filled with soldiers who were not guests. The soldiers surrounded the interior of the ballroom by lining up against the walls.

Everyone stopped dancing and watched the soldiers. Trumpets started to blow as a military honor guard entered the ballroom. Gabriel's pulse quickened as Cedrick Teivel entered the room surrounded by bodyguards.

Teivel was a large and stocky man with dark wavy hair and a mustache. His thick eyebrows seemed to connect to form one large dark line across his face. His eyes were dark and piercing. Everyone in the room clapped as the dictator walked up to the platform that held the musicians and addressed the crowd. Teivel feasted on attention and it was obvious to all that he enjoyed the loud applause in the room.

"My good friends," Teivel said pleasantly. "I am pleased to join you at this event. As you know the Gefrey Games will start in three days' time. These games will be as none other ever held in our world. I hope you all attend; trust me you will not be disappointed." There was loud applause again that continued for several minutes.

Teivel held up his hands for the applause to stop. "Many of you may have heard the rumors about the freedom fighters attacking the games. I must assure you these are nothing more than wild stories. But to ease any apprehension you may have; please know that there will be a heavy military presence at the games."

"Is it true that freedom fighters attacked the city and helped prisoners to escape?" a man asked from the crowd.

"I am glad you brought that up," Teivel said. "That never happened. It is just another wild rumor that the rebels are circulating to enhance the illusion that they have some type of power."

"Do not worry, your families will be safe at the games. Are there any more questions?"

Clay now spoke loudly from the crowd, "Then the stories we have heard about retribution because of the prison breaks are still just wild stories? I have many employees who have said they are fearful of getting caught between the forces." Clay was making this up, he was fishing for information from Teivel.

"Put the minds of your people at ease. Nothing is going to happen within the city," as Teivel said these words a look came across his face that caused the entire room of people to pause. It happened so quickly that most did not understand what they saw but they remembered how they felt when for a moment in time, Teivel's human mask was removed. No one in the room spoke for several moments. "Please return to the dance," Teivel said and walked off the stage.

Jasmine suddenly swung around and grabbed the hands of both Simon and Matthew. "Tell me the truth, am I pretty enough to attract that monster?" Jasmine asked with such earnestness that both Simon and Matthew were taken back.

"Jasmine you are a very beautiful woman but what are you talking about?" asked Simon.

"I just have an overwhelming feeling, I can't explain it. I know he is planning something awful. Perhaps if I become friendly with him I can find out some information."

"That is a very dangerous thing you are proposing," Matthew said. "Ruth told us he was a notorious rapist but stopped after he was told that his seed would come back to destroy him. Since it is so close to his transformation he may have changed his attitude."

"I can at least try," Jasmine said. "I don't know how to explain it." Jasmine took a long stemmed rose out of a large flower arrangement behind Matthew and turned and walked towards Teivel.

"You stay here and watch her," Simon said. "I am telling Gabriel."

90

"Miranda if any of you are listening please watch over Jasmine," Matthew said softly.

"What is she doing?" Darla whispered as she watched Jasmine walk up to the bodyguards that circled Teivel. The guards moved and Jasmine walked close to Teivel and curtsied then she handed him a long stemmed rose. Jasmine's friends watched with trepidation as she smiled and flirted with the dictator. Teivel was smiling and talking with Jasmine when she turned and motioned for Matthew to join them.

"I am sorry I am just so excited," Jasmine gushed. "This is my brother Matthew and this is…"

Teivel interrupted Jasmine and said, "You can call me Cedrick." Teivel shook hands with Matthew.

"Well this has taken a new turn," Gabriel said as he watched Teivel invite Jasmine and Matthew to join him at a large table.

"Are you mad at her?" Rachel asked in a whisper.

"I am not sure yet," Gabriel said. "It is not safe for the team members to act too spontaneously but she may have jumped at an opening that we did not see."

"Should I join them?" Simon asked. "The invitation merely says my name not my relationship to them."

"Let's wait a little bit," Gabriel said. "This might be interesting." Gabriel turned to Rachel, "Let's dance towards that table." Raul took Darla's hand and walked onto the dance floor when he saw Gabriel gliding across the floor towards Teivel's table.

"Are you ready for some introductions?" Clay asked Edward. Then Clay whispered, "I hope that girl knows what she is doing?"

"So do I," Edward said sincerely and followed Clay to a small group of people.

Chapter VIII
Without Honor

Edward was an incredibly intelligent man with many talents; one being his ability to memorize anything he once read. Gabriel was aware of Edward's ability which is why Gabriel had Edward read the piles upon piles of extortion records that Clay kept. Edward smiled inwardly as Clay introduced him to six people sitting at a table near the dance floor.

Barnabas was an exceptionally wealthy man but his wealth came to him because of his marriage to Lucile. Barnabas and Lucile enjoyed a comfortable but loveless marriage. But that was not how their marriage started. Lucile believed that she and Barnabas were very much in love. It took her several years to realize that Barnabas had created an elaborate façade that tricked Lucile and her family into making him the executor of the family fortune.

But Lucile's late father put one clause in the contract that would haunt Barnabas the rest of his life. To maintain power over the money and real estate Barnabas had to remain married to Lucile.

Barnabas and Lucile cared greatly about how others viewed them; this was one of the few things the couple shared in common. Because their images were so important to them, Lucile never made public disturbances about Barnabas' many affairs. Instead she let the pain and anger harden her heart until it could feel nothing at all.

Next to Barnabas and Lucile sat Colonel Charter and his wife Nadene. Charter was an extremely jealous man almost twice the age of his beautiful wife.

The third couple sitting at the table was Patrick and Felistine. Patrick liked to refer to himself as a private contractor but he ran a company of mercenaries. A company that had a great deal of business in a kingdom as dark as Ryed. Felistine was a beautiful young woman who was attracted to money.

Charter asked Clay and Edward to join them for a drink. Edward was amused with the deceptions at the table; for Barnabas was having affairs with both Nadene and Felistine. Neither Charter nor Patrick knew of the affairs although Lucile suspected. And Nadene and Felistine both believed they were the only woman that Barnabas was having an affair with.

Clay bought the second round of drinks and Edward bought the third. The group laughed and talked for several hours. Meanwhile, Jasmine and Matthew remained the table guests of Cedrick Teivel. Matthew engaged Teivel in many subjects of conversation while Jasmine spoke little but flirted with Teivel, who was charmed that such a young and beautiful woman seemed so enamored with him.

Matthew was surprised that his conversation with Teivel was so interesting. Matthew had so looked upon Teivel as a monster that he failed to realize Teivel was an intelligent and surprisingly charming human being.

Although Raul and Simon were disguised with wigs and facial hair, Gabriel and Raphael did not want the two young Princes speaking with Teivel for fear he would recognize them. It was Raphael who eventually approached the table. Two of Teivel's body guards stood up and blocked Raphael before he could reach the table.

"Oh, he is our cousin," Jasmine said to Teivel then she turned to Raphael and said in a scolding manner. "Raphael where have you been? We were looking for you." Teivel nodded to his guards and Raphael was allowed to take a seat at the table.

Raphael shook hands with Teivel, "It is an honor to meet you," Raphael said.

"Where were you?" Jasmine scolded again.

Raphael grinned. "I was checking out the scenery." Jasmine gave Raphael a confused look.

"He was with a girl," Matthew said with a grin.

"Raphael," Jasmine scolded and everyone at the table laughed.

Raul and Darla and Gabriel and Rachel spent the night on the dance floor so they could be close to Teivel's table. Simon joined Edward and Clay.

Teivel did not act as if he recognized either Matthew or Raphael. Both men wore disguises but they did not know if Teivel had some dark powers to see through their disguises. Teivel bought round after round of drinks. Matthew and Raphael were careful not to get drunk and Jasmine sipped one glass of wine. Teivel on the other hand was drinking great quantities of whiskey. He was in a festive almost elated mood because his transformation was just days away. Teivel had been planning for this event for centuries.

The more that Teivel drank the more flirtatious he became with Jasmine who acted attracted to the murderous dictator. Teivel was in the middle of telling a story when a young officer quickly approached the table and motioned to one of the bodyguards. The guard walked away from the table and whispered with the soldier for a moment then allowed the officer to approach Teivel. The officer whispered into Teivel's ear and Teivel's demeanor quickly changed. "I will be right there," he said gruffly to the officer.

Teivel turned to Jasmine and took her hand and kissed it. "I would very much like to see you again." Then he turned to Matthew and Raphael. "Would the three of you be my guests tomorrow for lunch at The Wild Rose Restaurant?"

"We would be honored," said Raphael.

"Should I send a carriage for you?" Teivel asked.

"That won't be necessary," said Matthew.

Teivel snapped his fingers and one of his bodyguards handed Teivel a piece of paper and a pen. Teivel wrote a few words and handed the paper to Matthew. "That restaurant is exclusive. You will need to show them this to get through the door," Teivel said then turned to Jasmine and kissed her hand again. "Tomorrow at eleven," Teivel said and quickly walked out of the room. All of the soldiers and bodyguards left with their leader.

94

"We will be watched now," Raphael said. "We cannot return to the castle."

"Raphael I know I should have asked permission but I can't even explain it; I had this overwhelming feeling, well to do exactly as I did." Jasmine said. "I hope you aren't angry with me."

"Gabriel stresses the safety of the team which is why he doesn't want people acting independently," Raphael said. "You are well trained; I believe you understand that. But that being said, as any warrior you have to look for an opening in your opponent. Honestly Gabriel and I had considered asking one of you girls to meet Teivel but we decided it was too dangerous. I think we ride this out and see where it goes."

"Jasmine, Archetenus once told me that many times when he was overwhelmed with a feeling to do something, especially when it was something he didn't want to do it was Miranda communicating with him. Now I am not saying that is what is happening here but perhaps you should call to her later and find out," Matthew said.

Clay strategically left the table because he knew that Edward and Simon were planning to confront Barnabas soon. Edward and Simon were going to blackmail Barnabas into getting them special seats in the arena for the Gefrey Games. Clay knew that it would not be suspicious if he walked up to Raphael, Matthew and Jasmine as he was talking with everyone in the room. "You know Teivel will be having you watched now," Clay said he joined the three at their table.

"We figured that," Raphael said. "He invited us to join him for lunch tomorrow. Can we get rooms at your hotel so we can keep up appearances?"

"Of course. I will back date the register so it appears you have signed in days ago. Just tell me a date," Clay said.

"Last Tuesday," Raphael said. "He wants us to meet him at the Wild Rose Restaurant at eleven tomorrow. Do you believe it to be safe?"

"It is a very exclusive restaurant," Clay said. "It has a great reputation but it is not opened to most of the public which means it could be a trap. And not to insult you but you have to be a member to get in."

"He gave us a note," Matthew said. "Can you draw us a map and we will have the place watched?"

"Of course but we should wait until we return to the hotel," Clay said. "Do you know why Teivel left so quickly?"

"No and that concerns me," Raphael said. "Will you tell Gabriel what we told you? He can decide if the others should be seen with us now."

Within the hour, Gabriel, Raul, Darla and Rachel met Simon and Edward outside of the ballroom.

"That was like shooting fish in a barrel," Edward said and laughed. "Barnabas has six seats for us and will do just about anything we ask."

"So where are Matthew, Jasmine and Raphael?" asked Simon.

"The Teivel Manor Hotel," Gabriel replied. "They will be staying there for a few days. Clay is with them. Teivel wants to see Jasmine again and has invited them to lunch tomorrow but we will need to get some things to them tonight. We should return to the castle.

Raphael, Matthew and Jasmine registered for three chambers but they decided to all stay in the same one. Both Raphael and Matthew were concerned about leaving Jasmine alone. They did not trust Teivel and worried that he would send his men after her.

Raphael had requested that all three of the chambers have balconies that faced the back of the hotel so that Ruala warriors and Enrops could enter the rooms. The chambers assigned to Raphael were the largest and contained two bedrooms.

96

Jasmine had just gone to bed and Raphael and Matthew were finishing their glasses of whiskey in the parlor when they heard noise at the balcony. Both men pulled their swords.

"It's Koby, Dack and Joao," Koby called out as the three Rualas entered the parlor. "We have clothes and money for you and Gabriel wants us to stay with you in case you need to leave quickly."

"Where is Jasmine?" Dack asked.

"She just went to bed," said Matthew.

"You should probably get her," Koby said.

"Is something wrong?" asked Raphael.

"We will tell you all at the same time," Koby said.

Matthew got out of his chair and was walking towards Jasmine's door when she opened it. "I heard," she said. "I just needed to get dressed."

"We all left the ballroom about an hour after you did," Joao said. "When we got back to the castle, Calen, Misha and most of the others were back. They sent Natasha, Diana and fifteen Rualas to Wetpr." Joao paused. "After Erebus got Gabriel's letter he wanted to go back to his castle and get some books and things that would be of use."

"As they were all flying to Erebus' castle they saw big plumes of smoke coming from both the villages of Benjem and Marlas," Joao continued. "Teivel's soldiers attacked these villages because they thought freedom fighters were there." Joao paused again.

"They killed all the children," Dack said in a hoarse voice. "They only killed the children. We think it was retaliation because we freed the prisoners."

"They killed children!" Matthew said through gritted teeth. "Are there no warriors left?" Matthew pounded his fist on the arm of the chair he was sitting in. "What kind of monsters kill children?"

"It wasn't even the monsters it was the men," Koby said. "Teivel didn't send his demons to the villages he sent his troops. Calen sent six Rualas back to Erebus' castle to guard Erebus while he got his things. Then the rest of the group went looking for the soldiers. The soldiers did not attack the Village of Gesmal but they did attack the Village of Tara which is just south of the castle of Nehmota. The soldiers were burning the village when Calen and Misha and the others found them. Our men killed the soldiers and dropped all of the bodies in the courtyard of Teivel's castle."

"That must be why he ran out of the ballroom," Raphael said.

"None of our warriors are dead but every one of them is wounded and some pretty bad. Joshua and Micha ran into a burning house to save a family. They both have such bad burns that the Sanuri is trying to heal them," Koby said and paused. "Raphael, Joshua is in really bad shape. We have not sent any letters home about this, so Vivian and Iris don't know."

"Calen was stabbed in the stomach and Misha stabbed in the back. Bianca was shot with an arrow in her thigh and another in her arm. Thor jumped out of Misha's arms and jumped onto a soldier. Thor isn't cut but he hurt his back again. Batina and Ratri both have multiple knife wounds. And there are others with minor wounds."

"Our friends are hurt and all those children are murdered," Jasmine said loudly as tears ran down her cheeks. "This has to stop! Miranda!"

"This has to stop!" Gabriel yelled and pounded his fist on the table in the Great Hall. "Miranda!"

"Miranda how do I kill that monster?" Jasmine yelled as she looked around the room for an Angel to appear.

"Miranda were those children killed because of us?" Gabriel yelled. "Were they butchered because of our actions? God forgive us."

"Miranda how do we save them all?" Raphael whispered.

"Ruth, Miranda, somebody," yelled Michael as he, Archetenus and Jared burst into the Great Hall. "What is this? What is happening? Answer me! I am the one who can destroy him. We have been doing everything you said. That's enough! I am doing it my way." Michael kicked a chair and turned to leave the Great Hall.

"Miranda!" Jasmine screamed. "Why aren't you..."

"Where the hell are we?" Archetenus asked as he looked around the dark cavern. "Miranda did you do this?" Suddenly torches came alive with fire and the large man-made cavern was filled with light.

"How did we get here?" asked Dack as he looked through the crowd. "Joao are you here?"

"Yeah, I'm with Jasmine," said Joao as he pushed through the crowd. "Is everyone from the castle here?"

"Daniel, Miranda, Ruth," Gabriel called. "Why are we here?"

Everyone grew quiet as the three Angels materialized in the cavern. Before anyone could speak Miranda stepped forward. "You are all so filled with guilt and pain and we understand that."

"We are damn angry," Michael said. "How could you let those children be slaughtered? Aren't we here to stop these things?"

"Michael let us speak," Daniel said. "The atrocities committed against those villages were not the retribution Teivel has planned for the prison breaks."

99

"Members of two of those villages schemed against their neighbors and told Teivel's soldiers that the people of Benjem and Marlas were hiding freedom fighters. The soldiers reported this to their commander; a man named Barush. Major Barush ordered the attacks as a means to garner the favor of Teivel. The soldiers were in such a frenzied blood lust that they took it upon themselves to attack the Village of Tara."

"Teivel did not know of the attacks. He was informed of the bodies of soldiers in his courtyard. He is now meeting with many of his commanders to find out what happened. And when he does his retribution will be swift and brutal."

"Retribution against who?" Gabriel asked.

"His people," Ruth said. "He will not punish Barush for the massacres. We know you have many questions but first you must understand that the actions taken by Calen and the members of your team have greatly changed what will be happening here."

"We hear the cries of your hearts," Miranda said. "You cannot save everyone."

"I don't mean to be disrespectful," Chaez said. "But can't you?"

"Our hearts too cry out for those children. We would have been there but no one called us in," Miranda said.

"What about the men who told the lies to the soldiers?" Dominic asked as anger welled within him.

"They were exposed and hacked to pieces by the parents of the slain children," Daniel said. "News of the massacres are racing throughout this kingdom causing panic. People who were already paranoid of their neighbors and living in fear are now past the breaking point. And it will only get worse."

"How can it get worse if we are here?" Matthew asked. "Didn't we come here to help?"

"You came here for many reasons," Miranda said. "And you have called us in."

"Miranda where are we?" Gabriel asked.

"We are in the chambers underneath Teivel's castle. To the right is the room where the transformation will take place. Now set aside your anger and tell us what you are willing to do," Miranda said.

"Can Teivel be killed before he transforms?" Michael asked.

"By you he can be killed any time," Ruth said.

"How do I kill him?" As Michael asked these words The Scroll of Imari appeared in his right hand.

"Even with the scroll you will need the power of The Seven Sons," Ruth said. "Tell me Raul, Simon and Matthew will you stand with Michael?"

"Of course. How can you even ask?" asked Raul as he, Simon and Matthew all gathered around Michael.

"How do I use this?" Michael asked about the scroll.

"The scroll has many powers," Daniel said. "It effects time and matter. Remember when the Sanuri had the armies of demons that had been chasing him, Raul and Michael appear in the city and fight with Teivel's troops?"

"Wait a minute, just wait a minute," Sorren said. "The way you have been phrasing your words. Everyone this isn't what we think. Archetenus what did you say that Miranda used to tell you all of the time?"

Archetenus started to grin. "Miranda always made me specifically ask questions so that I could control the information I received. I didn't really understand it but it had to do with my choices."

"Can we use the scroll to stop the massacres?" Sorren asked. "And to help our wounded friends?"

Miranda, Daniel and Ruth looked at each other and smiled. "Keep asking your questions," Daniel said.

"You wouldn't have us in this cavern if you didn't want us to stop Teivel," said Simon.

"But during all the planning for this mission the concern has always been how do we destroy Teivel without endangering his prisoners. Now you are telling us that perhaps we can go back in time and stop those massacres. There is more that you aren't telling us. What is it?"

"Perhaps I can help with that," said Erebus as he stepped forward. "I have been doing research about the herbs that Gabriel requested. Those particular herbs are used in black magic to alter people's senses and to create illusions of the mind. And that is in small quantities. In the enormous amounts that we were informed about, I believe they can affect time itself. Is Teivel changing the date of his transformation?"

"Ok Miranda what questions should we be asking?" Archetenus asked impatiently. "Just tell us what we need to do to get the job done."

"If we affect time here will it also be affected in other kingdoms?" asked Gabriel.

"Can we use the scroll to go forward in time too?" Raul asked.

"You are asking questions about concepts that normally would be beyond your imaginations. You have reached beyond the limitations you have put upon your own minds. Do these things scare you?" Daniel asked.

"I am going with Archetenus," Thaos said. "It seems like this entire mission is nothing but a cat and mouse game. We do a lot of planning without actually accomplishing a lot. I don't think I am the only one getting frustrated. What exactly do you need us to do?"

Chapter IX
Prophesies

"We aren't playing games with you," Ruth said. "You are all angry, frustrated and wanting to go home. We understand that. But do you understand that the choices you make here will affect the history of your world? Every decision in every war has consequences that can affect generations. You are at war. Only the decisions you must make now have repercussions that are beyond your understanding. The stakes are higher in this mission than in any other you have worked before."

"Archetenus you said that Miranda made you ask specific questions, thus making you think things through before you made choices. Look at all of you here. You all have choices to make and there are many more beings who are making choices this night besides your group."

"You want us to make your decisions for you but we cannot. You must make the decisions. We are trying to make you really think about the issues and not just decide on what seems fast or easy. Now that you understand the enormity of what you are doing," Ruth continued. "Gabriel and Raphael you have both read the Prophesy of The Seven Sons have you not?"

"Yes, but it has been a while," Raphael said.

"It amazes me that more of you don't read this prophesy since you play such major roles in it," Ruth said. "Gabriel do you remember what you read?"

"It is written in very ornate and wordy language but it tells of The Seven Sons finding each other then leading battles against the dark lords and demons."

"And does it say that The Seven Sons win all of their battles?" asked Ruth.

"Actually it says they incur severe losses but persevere," Gabriel said as his eyes widened. "It says that the powerful demons unit to defeat The Seven Sons and great plagues and massacres occur. Many people turn away from The Seven Sons because it appears the demons have more power."

"I guess we should be reading that," said Raul.

"The prophesy is playing out as we speak," Ruth said.

"Can we change the prophesy?" Raphael asked.

"How else would you ask that question?" asked Ruth.

"Would you help us change the prophesy?" Sorren yelled out as Gabriel was asking the same question.

"Now my children you are asking the right questions," Ruth said. "You keep forgetting that we cannot just come in and take over. Since you have started this mission many powerful people and demons have been working on changing The prophesy of The Seven Sons among others. After the Sanuri, Michael and Raul escaped from the Caves of Muldun, the information that some of The Seven Sons had The Scroll of Imari was broadcasted throughout hell dimensions of many worlds. The Insidiae, the Grand Masters, the demons and many of your everyday criminals are searching for you."

"You are here because an attack was launched upon the castle you were in," Daniel said.

"The wounded?" Koby asked fearfully.

"They are with the Sanuri and Lakin; the choices you make tonight will determine whether they join us or we send them to their homes," Daniel said. "Not only are all of you being watched but so is Teivel. There are many who do not want him to become a powerful demon. Teivel is aware of this and is going to great lengths to protect his destiny. Erebus was correct, Teivel is changing the date and time of his transformation."

"If we use The Scroll of Imari to go back in time and prevent the massacres will they still count for fulfilling the prophesy?" Stephan asked.

"Yes," Daniel said. "But changing time here will affect time everywhere so you will have to choose a time that will have the minimal amount of damage to your world."

"And you will help us with that?" Matthew asked.

"Yes." Daniel said. "As we speak the warlock who is working for Teivel will soon tell him that the potions are ready to alter time. Teivel will order all of his prisoners brought to these chambers for both sacrifice and for him to consume after the transformation."

"Can we go back in time and stop the massacres then go forward so that all of the prisoners are brought here?" Gabriel asked.

"That sounds like a good plan," Ruth said.

"So I should kill Teivel between the time the prisoners are transported here and the time he starts his transformation?" Michael asked.

"You will not have much time," Daniel said. "You will need to plan well."

"So how do we use this scroll?" asked Michael.

"Michael hold the scroll and concentrate on only it. Empty your mind of other thoughts. Remember when you were being tortured as a boy, you would mentally remove yourself from your body. What you need to do now is similar. When you feel the connection with the scroll then concentrate on the massacres and ask to erase them from time," Miranda said.

"What about the men who sold out their neighbors and caused the massacres, won't they still do the same thing?" asked Raul.

"Since you asked us to help you; those men will now have a delay in their plans which will prevent those ideas from taking form," Ruth said.

"I am going to need everyone to be quiet," Michael said then he closed his eyes and tried to concentrate on The Scroll of Imari. Everyone quietly stared at Michael for five, ten, fifteen minutes. "Nothing is happening," Michael said with frustration.

"Harness the power of your mind, Michael," Daniel said. "Put all of your focus there."

Michael again closed his eyes and tried to focus his thoughts but his fears of failing were causing chaos in his mind.

Michael was also aware that hundreds of people were watching him which added to his anxiety. The sweat started to run down Michael's face as the minutes ticked by. Michael was just about to open his eyes again when he heard Ruth's voice in his head."

"Michael if you need help, ask for it."

Even though Michael was fulfilling a holy destiny he was not a praying man. After Ruth said those words, Michael was momentarily confused as to who he should ask help from. After thinking about his options Michael prayed, "Great Ruler help me to save those people."

"What happened? Where are we?" Calen asked loudly as he suddenly appeared in the chamber.

The Sanuri and Lakin stepped forward with broad smiles on their faces. "You saved more than the people in those villages," the Sanuri said.

"Your burns are gone," Koby said with amazement as he saw Joshua pushing through the crowd. "You were covered with them."

"What are you talking about?" asked Joshua.

"Miranda how can they have no memory of what happened yet we do?" asked Gabriel.

"Because those of you in this cavern need to remember that we are helping you," Miranda said. "Sanuri you will need to join the rest of The Seven Sons in order to change the future."

The Sanuri joined Michael, Raul, Simon and Matthew. "Stand in a semi-circle," Daniel said. "And each of you touch the scroll, even if it is just a fingertip."

"Maybe you should hold it," Michael said and handed the scroll to the Sanuri.

"What exactly do we ask for?" asked Simon.

"I will tell you," said the Sanuri. "Mentally repeat the thoughts I send you."

106

Everyone in the cavern stood in silence and watched five of The Seven Sons concentrating on The Scroll of Imari. Time seemed to pass slowly but after a few minutes the five men opened their eyes. "I may be a fool," Simon said. "But I didn't really understand what we said. What exactly did we ask for?"

"None of us understood," Raul said.

"This was very complicated, which is why I took the lead," the Sanuri said. "In exactly five minutes Teivel will order his soldiers to gather the political prisoners from all the various prisons and bring them here. We are allowing that to happen so we can save those people. But as soon as the last prisoner is brought to this cavern time will reverse for one hour. Michael that is the time frame you have to kill Teivel."

"How will I know where he is? That isn't much time," Michael said. "And how do I kill him?"

"The massacres were erased from history but not any of the events last night," Miranda said. "Some of you still have a luncheon engagement with Teivel."

"And you believe he will still show up?" Raphael asked.

"Teivel desires Jasmine greatly," Daniel said. "He will show up. But now that he is expediting the time of his transformation he may try to separate Jasmine from Matthew and Raphael."

"Will he hurt her?" Matthew asked.

"He wants to make her his queen," said Daniel.

"Can I kill him?" Jasmine asked.

"You can injure him but only Michael can kill him." Daniel answered.

"So I just need to keep him distracted until Michael joins me?" asked Jasmine.

"Jasmine you do have a choice in this," Miranda said. "You are well trained but this is a very dangerous thing you propose. You don't have to do it."

"How can I not?" Jasmine asked. "I could never live with myself if I allowed that monster to continue in this world. Just tell me what I need to know. Do I need special weapons or anything?"

"While I agree with Jasmine's words and she makes me proud," Sorren said. "I did promise her parents I would watch out for her. Is there any way I could go with her? I understand she may have to distract him alone for a while but at least I could be close to her."

"Be a bodyguard," Stephan said. "Everyone with wealth here has bodyguards. In fact several of us should be guards like we played with Gabriel. One of us drive the carriage and three or four others be bodyguards. That would allow Michael to be close too."

"Would that work for you?" Gabriel asked the Angels.

"That is a very good plan but you will need to have more than four or five men at that restaurant. And while you are distracting Teivel, you will be waging a battle here," Daniel said.

"Should Simon, Matthew and I go with Michael or how will that effect the prophesy?" Raul asked.

"I am proud that you are thinking as one of The Seven Sons," Miranda said. "The energies for Teivel's transformation have been in motion for some time. He is no longer a normal man. It would be wise to have you there but the Sanuri should stay back here. It would also be wise for Gabriel to remain here since Raphael will be at the restaurant."

"Dominic it would probably be better to have your men here with the prisoners," Gabriel said. "Thaos and Stephan choose your men and lead two teams to attack the restaurant. Archetenus, Jared, you and I will lead the attacks on the soldiers and demons in this castle. Sanuri and Dominic you will lead the rescue missions for the prisoners. And Lakin we will need your warriors at both sites; I will let you organize that."

"Might I say something?" Erebus asked.

"Of course," said Gabriel.

"I don't believe any of you have an idea of the powerful magics that are being put into place to help Teivel. The warlock working for Teivel must be very powerful. I should battle with him."

"Are you sure?" Gabriel asked.

"Trust me when I say this. The Sanuri could battle him but no one else here. And I agree the Sanuri is needed with the prisoners."

"You know Diana would kill me if I let something happen to her friend," Thor said with a grin. "I will go with you."

"So will I," said Misha but you might need to give us some tips if he hurts you."

"That warlock may be protected by soldiers," Joshua said. "Micha, Bianca and I are coming too."

"Add Rachel and me," Dagon said. "Unless Gabriel thinks Rachel will be needed with the prisoners."

"No, I think Joshua is right, that warlock probably is protected. Perhaps you should take a few others with you," Gabriel said then he turned back towards the Angels. "We should assume that these prisoners are in the same shape as the ones we rescued before. Can we take them to the castle?"

"There will not be time," The Lion said as he suddenly materialized in the cavern. "The warlock who works for Teivel was just given orders to open a door into this world. Teivel knows that he will be under attack by other demons and dark lords and he knows that he will be weakened during the transformation. He has spent centuries putting energies into motion to allow him to open a portal into this world. Emeric and Banaka have been helping Teivel. Even though these two Grand Masters are on the run from the death squads that the Old Ones of this world have sent after them; they have maintained contact with Teivel."

"Emeric and Banaka are calling in powerful demons from other worlds to attack the Old Ones here. And these two traitors are receiving wealth and power beyond your imaginations for their devious acts." The cavern was silent as The Lion paused and looked at the faces before him. "We will heal the prisoners but Sanuri and Lakin give them a choice to fight with us."

"So you are in this fight too?" Matthew asked.

"Why would you think otherwise?" asked The Lion.

"We have thousands of weapons at the castle can we still get them to the prisoners?" Archetenus asked.

"They were transported here when you were," Daniel said.

"What is the name of this warlock?" Erebus asked.

"Rybkin," The Lion replied.

"How can he be that powerful and I have never heard of him?" Erebus asked.

"Because he is not from this world," The Lion said. "And the answer to the question in your mind; no you are not powerful enough to stop him. Erebus you can back out of this and we will understand."

"I may be many things but I am not a coward," Erebus said angrily. "And you know as well as I that the people here are not prepared to go against a warlock of that magnitude."

"You have wanted to commit suicide for a very long time," The Lion said. "Going against Rybkin is a suicide mission and what would you gain? You would lead your friends to their deaths."

"If I can't stop him many will die," Erebus said. His face was turning red from anger. "I know what you are doing. This is a trick!"

110

"It is no trick," The Lion said. "But in your heart you know it is the right answer or you would not have said it. We will not force you. Erebus it is your choice to make." Erebus turned and marched out of the cavern.

"What are they talking about?" Darla whispered to Dack.

"He will have to call upon The Great Ruler to give him the help he needs," Raphael said.

There was silence then Joshua spoke. "I would consider Erebus a friend but for him this is a heavy decision he must make. I believe we should prepare for anything he may decide."

"I agree with Joshua," Sorren said. "This entire mission has been nothing but working on plans and now at the final hour we don't have time. What are we going to do about the portal?"

"You have The Scroll of Imari," The Lion said. "But you will need to know the location of the portal."

"That is the information I need to find out, isn't it?" Jasmine asked as she stepped forward.

"I don't like this at all," Raul said. "It is too dangerous for her."

"And who else here can get that information?" Jasmine asked then she turned and looked at the Angels. "During this entire mission I felt like I was trying to see something that was just before me. Now I understand that this is why I am here. I remind Teivel of someone don't I?"

"You favor greatly someone he once had feelings for," Ruth said. "But now that you understand the danger, it is still your choice."

"Will you give me what I need to get this information and to help stop Teivel?"

Ruth walked forward and kissed Jasmine on the forehead and said, "You have what you need."

"I will not be bullied!" Erebus yelled with such force that lightening shot from his fingertips and crumbled a small amount of the stone wall in front of him. When Erebus saw this he realized he had to get control of himself for he did not intentionally produce the lightning strikes.

Erebus tried to calm himself but the rage rose within him. "They are just trying to trick me," he spat. "Who the hell do they think they are?"

"Why are you so angry?" Ruth asked as she appeared in the small chamber where Erebus was standing.

"You know very well why I am angry. I am a warlock. That is who I am and you are asking me to give it up."

"I haven't asked you to do anything," Ruth said. "Nor have the others. And we don't force people to do things. You are filled with many emotions because you care about the people you have been working with. And you perhaps more than the others understand what they face."

Erebus stared angrily at Ruth without speaking so she continued. "How do you plan to get enough power to fight Rybkin? And are you sure you even want to? This really isn't your fight."

"You know you are just insulting me with your words," Erebus yelled. "My friends are going to get themselves killed for your mission. They are fools. Hell I am a fool!"

"Your friends," Ruth repeated. "When was the last time you said those words? While many of them don't really understand what you are they have taken you into their group and they would die to protect you as any other member of their team."

"I know," Erebus said in a whisper.

"So are you this angry because you have developed feelings for these people and because of that you are putting yourself in danger?"

"I am not concerned for my safety."

"Then why are you so angry?"

"Because you expect me to start worshipping The Great Ruler to save my friends."

"I find that statement so curious. First The Great Ruler never forces anyone to worship Him. That is something men made up to empower their false gods. But you make it sound that you believe He has the power to save your friends."

"I have always viewed The Great Ruler as somewhat of an opponent. I know He exists and I know He is very powerful but that doesn't mean that I worship Him."

"Do you know how many people question whether He exists?"

"That is really beside the point; don't you agree?" Erebus yelled as he paced back and forth in the small cavern.

"So tell me Erebus, if you were to pray to The Great Ruler to help you fight Rybkin and help to save all those lives. What would you say? You know He isn't going to help you with black magics. Is that what scares you?"

Erebus stopped pacing and stared at Ruth. "You are right. He couldn't help me. I will have to think about something else."

"I didn't say He couldn't help you. I said He would not help you with black magics."

"But that is all I know. How else would I fight that warlock?"

"Let's look at this situation. You could just walk away from all of this or you could try to help as you are. But you know that would be suicide and your death would not save your friends. You don't have the time or the means to increase your power in the way you are used to. Or you could try talking with The Great Ruler. Really what could it hurt?"

"You make it sound so easy."

"Do you fear The Great Ruler?"

"Well I haven't exactly been playing on His team. I can't imagine He is pleased with me. In fact why would He help me anyways?"

"Erebus you are so filled with anger. Why are you considering any of this?"

"To help save innocent people and to stop the demons," Erebus said after a lengthy pause.

"And you are afraid that if you ask for guidance with this that The Great Ruler will punish you?"

"I really don't know."

"You know Erebus unlike your human friends, The Great Ruler knows who you are. As do I and the other Angels. And as does the Sanuri. Have you had any reason to fear us?"

"None of this makes any sense," Erebus spat.

Chapter X
Screams

"I am glad you came back here to help me get ready," Jasmine said to Darla. Jasmine, Darla, Matthew and Raphael had been transported by the Angels back to Raphael's chambers in the Teivel Manor Hotel. "I can't believe how nervous I am."

"I am nervous for you," Darla said. "I wish I could go in there with you."

"I do too but I think it would look suspicious. Help me, which jewelry should I wear?"

"I hear voices, I think the others are here."

"I will never get used to this," Sorren said as the Angels transported him, Raul, Simon, Michael and Edward into the parlor of Raphael's chambers.

"Simon and I will get the carriage," Raul said. "The rest of you stay here. I don't trust Teivel not to try and grab Jasmine."

"We're ready," Matthew said as he and Raphael walked out of one of the bedrooms into the parlor.

"I'll be right there," Jasmine yelled through the closed door of her bedroom.

"Well don't you look pretty," Sorren said as Jasmine and Darla entered the parlor.

"I wasn't sure what to wear," Jasmine said. "I was going to wear one of the jackets with the knife sheaths but Darla said that if Teivel put his arm around me he would feel the knives."

"You do have weapons on you?" Edward asked.

"Of course," Jasmine said. "But I am so nervous."

"I went down to the lobby earlier," Raphael said as he walked towards Jasmine. "Clay gave me this rose. I thought you could put it in your hair. Then if you need to signal us for help, take the flower out of your hair and smell it."

"Oh, I like that idea," Jasmine said and took the rose.

"I wish I could go in there with you," Darla said.

"Gabriel wants you to stay with Clay," said Edward. "There are Enrops here. If you need to get messages to us or to Gabriel give them to the Enrops and the Angels will somehow get them to us. I have to admit I don't understand how they are going to do it."

"Michael you are so quiet," said Raphael.

"I am a fighter; that is what I know. This clearing my mind to connect with The Scroll of Imari is a lot harder than you might guess. I'm kind of worried that I will get distracted."

"You just take care of the scroll and Teivel and we'll take care of the rest," Sorren said. "What I am concerned about is just how Jasmine is going to let us know when she finds out the location of the portal because we can't kill Teivel until then."

"Jasmine, you know that Teivel will probably separate you from the rest of us. He wants you for his queen so I would imagine he will try to charm you, at least at first. I am not sure if this will work on Teivel but here is a vial of that truth potion," Raphael said.

"Thanks this makes me feel better," Jasmine said as she took the vial.

"Remember it takes a few minutes to work," Edward explained. "He will act drunk when it takes hold."

"We still have to figure out a signal," Sorren said. "Hell, if nothing else scream."

While Michael, Jasmine and their small group prepared for the meeting with Teivel, those remaining in the caverns below Teivel's castle hastily developed plans. Centuries before this day, Teivel had constructed an elaborate system of caverns and tunnels that ran underneath his castle. Some of these tunnels ran to the City of Teivel itself, others ran underneath the castle of King Nehmota.

A third set of tunnels ran westward to the shores of the Sea of Talmont. This third set of tunnels were designed solely as an escape route.

Teivel was a brilliant man and designed the caverns and tunnels to form a labyrinth to slow down and confuse any invading armies. This system did confuse Gabriel and his army until the Angels provided the rescuers with a map. The room where the transformation was to take place was surrounded by four large caverns. Gabriel and his team speculated the prisoners would be housed in these caverns. They followed the entwined tunnels on the map and found that all of these caverns were connect to tunnels that led to the City of Teivel.

Dagon was still in charge of the group of artists. He quickly put these men and women to work making copies of the map. The Angels promised Gabriel's army that they would provide the rescuers with what they needed, then the Angels disappeared. Now minutes later, piles of food, water, medical supplies, paper, weapons, torches and other items were appearing inside of the cavern in the areas where the Angels had appeared.

The Angels had provided light within the cavern where they gathered Gabriel's team but the tunnels and other caverns were dark. Gabriel's army was still assembled in this cavern when the torches suddenly extinguished. The Sanuri's voice was heard inside of the minds of all. "Quiet, soldiers are down here lighting all the torches."

Joshua, Thor and Micha led three groups through the blackness of the tunnels to spy on the soldiers. These soldiers had no reason to believe they had enemies in the tunnels, so they talked loudly as they lit thousands of torches.

"What do you think the old man has planned?" a soldier asked his group of companions.

"Hell if any of us know," another soldier replied. "I had no idea there were so many tunnels down here. Wait! You have to come in here," the soldier yelled as he entered the cavern where the transformation was to take place. The soldiers lit the many torches in the cavern designated for Teivel's transformation.

They stared in awe at the rich carpets and expensive furniture that were displayed in front of a huge unholy altar. In the center of the room was a pool surrounded with a small wall of rocks.

"That damn water is bubbling. There's something in there," yelled one of the soldiers.

"What the hell!"

Suddenly the cavern was filled with blood curdling screams then silence. Thor slowly led his group forward and they peered inside of the cavern. The stone floor surrounding the pool was covered with blood but no bodies were present. The water of the pool appeared calm. Thor's group backed out of the chamber.

"Do you think that smoke is coming from Nehmota's castle?" Edward asked as he drove the carriage towards the Wild Rose Restaurant. Michael was sitting next to Edward. Raul and Simon were sitting in the rear bodyguard seats of the carriage while Sorren was inside of the carriage with Raphael, Matthew and Jasmine. Now this entire team looked at the huge black plumes of smoke that filled the sky southeast of the city.

"Not that it probably makes any difference," Raul said. "But I was confused by what the Angels said. Who exactly led the attack on that castle?"

"I think it was a group effort," Simon said sarcastically.

"Does that mean that group knows they didn't get us?" Michael asked. "Because we could be fighting a lot more than Teivel today."

"You are probably right," Raphael called out from the carriage. "But for now we must all focus on Teivel."

Erebus found the Sanuri and Dominic in one of the caverns where they planned to put the wounded. No torches were lit but the end of the Sanuri's staff was glowing and providing some light for the men.

"Sanuri can I speak with you for a moment?" Erebus asked.

"Certainly but know that Teivel's soldiers are in the area," whispered the Sanuri.

"I do not have the power to defeat Rybkin," Erebus said solemnly. "You will need to confront him and I will help with the wounded."

"I would not have picked you for one to give up so easily," the Sanuri said. "You have already defeated yourself. Is it Rybkin you fear or talking to The Great Ruler?"

"I don't fear Rybkin," Erebus said angrily.

"You fear praying?" Dominic asked incredulously. "Why? You've spoken to Angels."

"I don't have to explain myself to you," snapped Erebus.

"Many men are afraid to pray to The Great Ruler," the Sanuri said to Dominic. "That is a lesson you must learn if you are to become a priest. Sometimes the fear is because of shame or guilt and sometimes they fear punishment." The Sanuri now turned to Erebus. "I have looked into your mind; I know you fear little in this world. You are angry at yourself because you are experiencing this fear and not conquering it. But you fear something different, don't you?"

Erebus stared angrily at the Sanuri. "Erebus your fear is not uncommon. But for all that you have faced in your life; this is the fear you are allowing to cripple you?"

Dominic looked back and forth at Erebus and the Sanuri because the tension was great. "Erebus every one of us is here for a reason; we all have our roles to play. I truly believe that although I can't explain it. I don't know what your fear is and it is probably none of my business but can I help you or can you show me what needs to be done?" asked Dominic.

"You can't go against that warlock," Erebus said through clenched teeth.

"One of us has to," Dominic said. "I don't have the powers that either of you do but I have not come this far in this fight to quit now."

"So one of you is going to have to teach me or you are going to have to get your head in the game. You heard what the Angels said; the decisions we make this day will affect the future of our world. I would fear shame if I didn't make a decision."

Neither the Sanuri nor Erebus spoke; they continued to stare at each other and now at Dominic also. Erebus turned and marched out of the cavern.

"What is he so afraid of?" Dominic asked. "Because he looked terrified."

"Change."

"I don't understand."

"He is afraid that contacting The Great Ruler will change him forever."

When the Angels transported supplies to Gabriel's army they also transported the hundreds of uniforms that had been taken from Clay's laundry service. Thaos and Stephan hand-picked the men they took to the Wild Rose Restaurant and these men dressed in the military uniforms of the Army of Ryed.

Before Natasha left for Wetpr she had forged dozens of papers for members of Gabriel's army. Thaos and Stephan now carried papers which identified them as officers in Teivel's military. Stephan played the role of a colonel and Thaos a captain.

The Angels transported these men out of the caverns and to an area between Teivel's castle and the city. This area was a small valley which now held all of the horses that the Angel's had transported from Nehmota's castle. Thaos, Stephan and their troops saw the black plumes of smoke that filled the sky.

"I don't have a good feeling about any of this," Stephan said to Thaos as they rode towards the City of Teivel.

"Calen, Misha promise me that you will take care of Rachel and Horace if something happens to me," Dagon said to his brothers.

"Of course, they are family," Calen said. "Where are they?"

"She is making more maps and apparently the Angels healed all of the wounded from the castle, so Horace is going to help the Sanuri and Dominic with the wounded."

"They are starting to bring the prisoners in," Koby whispered as he ran up to his brothers.

"Are you ready for this?" Sorren asked as the carriage stopped in front of the Wild Rose Restaurant.

"Right now I wish I had one of those poison darts that Vivian carries in her hair. If I live through this I will have some for the next mission," Jasmine said as she tried to joke.

Sorren got out of the carriage first and looked up and down the busy street. Raphael and Matthew exited the carriage next then Matthew turned and helped Jasmine out. Edward, Michael, Raul, Simon and Sorren were all acting as bodyguards as they escorted Raphael, Matthew and Jasmine into the restaurant.

As soon the group entered the building they were met by two well-dressed men who looked like hired fighters. Raphael handed Teivel's note to one of the men, who read it, returned it then moved so the group could walk into the dining room. A host who was wearing more jewels than Jasmine greeted the group. Raphael handed this man the note.

"He did not tell us he was having guests," the host said nervously. "Lord Teivel always has a private room. I will move him to a large room. Please have a drink on the house as you wait."

"So he isn't here yet?" Matthew asked.

"No," the host replied then he stepped forward and whispered. "Lord Teivel is a very busy man; he is often late."

"I would like a couple of my men to check out the new room," Raphael said. "You understand; one can never be too careful these days."

"But of course My Lord. Your men may follow me." The host turned and walked to the right side of the restaurant and disappeared inside of a private dining room; Michael and Simon walked with him.

"There aren't many people here," Sorren said in a low voice. "I hope that isn't a bad sign."

The group sat down at a table in the front of the restaurant and ordered drinks. Within moments a waiter brought their drinks to the table.

"Careful there," Matthew said as he saw how quickly Jasmine was drinking her glass of wine.

"I am just trying to calm my nerves," Jasmine said with a smile. "But you are right."

Michael, Simon and the host returned to the others. "Please you may follow me now," the host said and motioned to a waiter to carry the drinks. The private dining room was decorated as a garden with small statues and a fountain in the room. The entire right wall was windows with a view of a wooded area. As soon as the host left the room, Raphael walked to the window and motioned to a small group of Enrops. The Enrops flew to Thaos and Stephan with the information about the location of Raphael's group.

"As paranoid as Teivel is, I am surprised he would dine in a room with all of these windows," said Raul.

"He probably has someone watching this room," said Simon as he searched the room.

"If he wants to get Jasmine alone he will have to take her into the main dining room," Sorren said as he checked the walls for hidden doors.

Teivel's soldiers were emptying all of the prisons in the city and transporting the political prisoners to the chambers beneath Teivel's castle. Many of the soldiers questioned these moves but they voiced their questions to no one.

The soldiers believed that the prisoners were acquired for entertainment in the Gefrey Games. The prisons themselves were located closer to the arena than to Teivel's castle. The officers too wondered about the moves since Teivel had not shared his reasoning with any of his subordinates.

Gabriel's army was not alone in spying on the prisoner movement. Teivel had many enemies among the Masters of the Insidiae and demons. Rumors had spread through the undergrounds about Teivel's manipulations of the demon wars as well as his unholy covenant with the Grand Masters Emeric and Banaka. These rumors which were initiated by Erebus turned the eyes of many of the dark ones on the Kingdom of Ryed.

Gabriel and his army were watching for signs of the Insidiae or demons interfering with their plans to rescue the prisoners. Unknown to Gabriel and his men, some of the transporting soldiers worked for the demon Chaladrone. Chaladrone was an Old One, one of the first group of thirteen to enter the World of Nunc. Chaladrone had learned that Teivel spread false rumors stating that Chaladrone was planning to attack Nieatzae and Maligma, both Old Ones. Because of these rumors; these two powerful demons united and attacked Chaladrone.

Chaladrone was greatly weakened but not defeated in his war with Nieatzae and Maligma. Erebus' rumors exposed Teivel's treachery gaining him enemies among these three Old Ones. Chaladrone wanted revenge and he wanted to attack Teivel before he transformed into a powerful demon.

Chaladrone was literally looking through the eyes of the soldiers who worked for him. He saw the underground caverns where the prisoners were being transported to. Chaladrone understood the significance of this; what he wanted was to find the room prepared for the transformation. Although Teivel was a human, Chaladrone knew Teivel had powerful beings and energies protecting him. Chaladrone planned to attack Teivel when he was most vulnerable; during the transformation. The Angels were aware of this and shielded Gabriel and his army from the eyes of the Old Ones.

"Show time," Raphael said as trumpets announced the arrival of Teivel to the Wild Rose Restaurant. Teivel enjoyed grand entrances. The people in the restaurant stood and applauded when Teivel walked through the door. Raphael and the others did the same when Teivel entered the private dining room.

Six soldiers entered the small room with Teivel and took their places along the wall of the dining room. Teivel was not surprised that Raphael, Matthew and Jasmine also had bodyguards standing in the room.

"This time I bring you flowers," Teivel said and handed a bouquet of red roses to Jasmine. Jasmine was standing and now leaned upwards and kissed Teivel on the cheek.

"Thank you so much; they are beautiful," she said excitedly.

"Please everyone be seated," Teivel said as he sat down at the head of the table. Jasmine was sitting to the left of Teivel; she had her back to the windows and was facing the door to the main dining room. Matthew sat next to her. Raphael sat to the right of Teivel. Raphael faced the windows and had his back to the door to the main dining room. Sorren and Simon were standing with their backs to the windows and Raul, Edward and Michael were standing along the wall.

Jasmine was wearing her long curly dark hair up with ringlets on one side. She was wearing a pale yellow dress that was cut low in the front. Teivel could not keep his eyes off from her.

"This is a beautiful restaurant," Raphael said. "But I am a little surprised at how exposed this dining room is." He was referring to the wall of windows.

"Don't worry I have men surrounding the building," Teivel said as he stared at Jasmine.

"Well that makes me feel better," said Matthew.

Several waiters entered the dining room carrying trays of wine and whiskey.

"I hope you don't mind that I took the liberty of ordering," Teivel said. "We are celebrating today."

"What are we celebrating?" Jasmine asked with a flirtatious smile.

"A venture I have been working on for a very long time is coming to fruition soon," Teivel said as he poured more wine into Jasmine's glass.

"What sort of venture?" asked Raphael. "You have my curiosity peaked."

"You would never believe me if I told you," Teivel said and laughed.

"Try me," Raphael said and took a sip of his whiskey.

"Sanuri, the caverns are filling," Gabriel whispered. "How will we know when the last prisoner has been brought here?"

"We have a while yet. I expect that the Angels will tell us. I also suspect that some of these soldiers are vessels for powerful demons. We may not be the only ones attacking Teivel's castle. If other demons attack, we need to concentrate on getting the prisoners out of here."

"Can't the demons see us then?"

"Our presence is being masked."

"I feel guilty listening to those prisoners cry and scream."

"We can't expose ourselves yet."

Chapter XI
The Face of the Demon

Teivel was highly energized, which was noticed by all at the table. He was talking rapidly and drinking large quantities of whiskey. Although Teivel said he was excited about his upcoming venture, the members of Gabriel's team wondered if they were seeing some of the effects of the transformation. The Sanuri had explained that Teivel had been undergoing a variety of rituals for years to prepare for the transformation.

All of the members of Gabriel's team who were in that small dining room knew that time was important. Jasmine in particular was feeling anxious because she couldn't pour the truth potion in Teivel's drink with his bodyguards in the room. Teivel rambled on for an hour without giving anyone else a chance to talk. Sorren and the others knew they needed a diversion.

A soldier quickly walked into the dining room and whispered to Teivel. "I will be right back my dear," Teivel said and kissed Jasmine's hand. Teivel and his body guards walked out of the room. Edward watched them from the doorway as Jasmine poured the vial of truth potion into Teivel's whiskey.

"Is anything the matter?" Raphael asked when Teivel and his men returned to the dining room.

"Unfortunately something has come up and I must leave," Teivel said and gulped his glass of whiskey. "Perhaps we can all meet later."

"Do you have to go?" Jasmine asked as she took Teivel's hand and pretended to pout.

Teivel stared at her for a few moments then said, "I do have to return to my castle but perhaps all of you can join me. I still owe you lunch."

"We would be honored," said Raphael.

"Splendid. Just follow my men," Teivel said then turned to Jasmine. "Perhaps you would honor me by riding in my carriage."

While Jasmine was scared she knew this might be her only chance to get information. "I would love to," she said breathlessly. "But my brother never lets me go anywhere without a bodyguard."

"By all means bring one along, he can ride on the outside seats," Teivel said. Sorren quickly moved forward before the other men could move. Jasmine took Teivel's arm and they walked out of the restaurant, followed by Teivel's bodyguards and Sorren.

"This could be a gift or a trap," Raphael said as he and the members of his team walked out of the restaurant and to the carriage. Raphael looked up and saw Enrops flying overhead as he got into the carriage.

Both Stephan and Thaos became concerned when they saw Jasmine get into Teivel's carriage and Raphael and the others following. What Teivel did not know was that Thaos' and Stephan's troops killed Teivel's soldiers who were hiding around the restaurant. Stephan, Thaos and their men now fell in behind Teivel's and Raphael's carriages. Teivel thought it was his troops who were escorting them.

An Enrop suddenly appeared before Gabriel, who was meeting with many of his leaders including the Sanuri. "They have all left the restaurant and appear to be coming here," the Enrop said. "Jasmine is in Teivel's carriage and Raphael and the others are riding in their carriage behind Teivel's. Stephan and Thaos are leading our men and they are acting as a protection detail for the carriages."

"Do you know why there was a change in plans?" asked Gabriel.

"No," the Enrop replied. "All I know is that a lone soldier entered the restaurant and left after a few minutes. Then Teivel and the others left."

"How long before they get here?" asked the Sanuri.

"Maybe twenty minutes unless they make a stop," the great bird replied.

"This could go two ways," the Sanuri said. "I doubt if Teivel's men are aware of our presence, so perhaps they have discovered the spies for the demons or they are setting a trap for Raphael and the others. And if they are setting a trap we will be prepared."

"Hannah this is a surprise," Maxwell said as he looked up from his desk at Fort Salar. "Is something the matter?"

"Oh, Maxwell I am sorry to bother you but with Gabriel gone, well, I was wondering if you could help me with something," said Hannah.

"Of course dear," Maxwell said as he moved a chair to his desk for Hannah to sit in. "What do you need?"

"This morning I went to check on one of my patients. Ike Ferguson is an elderly man who recently broke his hip. He and his wife Wanda are neighbors of ours. They own the property just north of us. Well, Wanda tells me that they decided to move in with their daughter and they are selling their land. They have an interested buyer coming in less than three hours. Maxwell, we could really use extra pasture land for our horses and ponies. And the house is very nice; I thought we could offer it to Zelda and Horace. So what do you think? I feel guilty doing this without talking to Gabriel first."

"First of all I think that buying that land is a very smart idea and giving the house to Zelda is most gracious of you. And I believe Gabriel will feel the same way. How would you like me to help?"

"Would you come with me and look at the land, then help me draw up the papers if we decide to buy?"

"Certainly. Just let me tell Luca where I will be."

"Clay, I think you should come out here now," Darla said as she ran into his office in the Teivel Manor Hotel. "Something is not right, the streets are filling up with soldiers."

"Are they coming in the restaurant?" Clay asked as he jumped up from the chair behind his desk.

"No, they are just filling the streets. They don't seem to be fighting with anyone."

"Darla if they come in here, we will tell them you are my new office assistant. That way I can keep you with me if something happens."

Clay and Darla walked out of his office and through the front foyer of the hotel, where Clay looked outside through the glass front doors. Hundreds of soldiers wearing the uniforms of the Military of Ryed were standing in formations on the streets that were visible to Clay. Clay turned and walked up to the desk clerk and asked, "Do you know anything about all of the soldiers in the street?"

"Only what I have heard from customers," the older man said nervously. "Nehmota's castle was attacked last night and is in flames and it sounds like there are soldiers everywhere in the city. Why would anyone attack the King's castle?" the man asked then said in a whisper, "We thought Teivel killed the King and Queen long ago."

"I don't know," Clay said then turned and walked into the dining room where all the customers were out of their seats and looking out of the windows at the soldiers.

"Do you always carry wine in your carriage?" Jasmine asked as Teivel poured them both drinks.

"I was rather hoping we could be alone for a few minutes," he said with a grin. Fear consumed Jasmine as she realized she may have been tricked.

"I don't understand; did you plan for us to leave the restaurant like that?" Jasmine asked as she took her wine.

"Actually no. I was planning on taking all of you to the castle after our meal but something came up." Teivel said and held up his glass. "To us," he said and took a drink of the wine.

Jasmine smiled and sipped her wine. "I must admit that I am very flattered but you have taken me quite by surprise. I mean why would a man like you be interested in someone like me?"

"I don't understand what you mean Jasmine. You are a breathtakingly beautiful and charming woman."

"You think I am beautiful?" Jasmine asked shyly.

"Very much so and there are many things I would like to talk about with you," Teivel paused and took Jasmine's hand. "I am not sure how to explain this. I have many things going on in my life right now which demand my attention. Many extremely important things. I certainly wasn't planning on meeting someone like you, not now. But I want you to be part of my life too. Jasmine how do you feel about me?"

Jasmine drew on everything inside of her to try and sound sincere. "I like you very much and I too would like to spend time with you. But..."

"But what Jasmine?"

"I know we don't know each other very well but the way you are saying your words; you sound so, oh I don't know how to explain it. Is something awful going to happen? Are we going to war?"

Teivel laughed loudly. "You are brilliant as well as beautiful my dear. I have many enemies and I was informed that my men found some spies within my military. I know who sent the spies and I am preparing for an attack. You and your family will be safe at my castle."

"Oh my," Jasmine said with a worried look on her face. "Thank you so much for protecting us."

"Something is wrong; I can feel it," Archetenus said as he returned to Gabriel, Dominic and the Sanuri.

"This place is lit up now like it's daylight but...I don't know how to put my finger on it. The soldiers are still brining in prisoners and so far that part seems normal. But I am telling you something isn't right."

"You are sensing the energies that Rybkin is putting into motion," Erebus said as he walked up to the group. Erebus' eyes were red and swollen. The Sanuri gave Erebus a knowing smile. "Yes I did," Erebus said irritably. "And I will admit it wasn't anything like I expected. But I will also tell you I honestly don't know if I have any more power to stop Rybkin but I am going to give it my best shot."

"I believe that Rybkin is upstairs in the castle because of the intensity of the energies. But if Teivel is going to transform today, Rybkin will need to come down here to the cavern set up for the transformation. And as strong as he is I suspect he will detect our presence."

"Chaladrone, one of the Old Ones was seeing through the eyes of some of Teivel's men earlier. The Angels were masking our presence. They may continue to do that," the Sanuri said.

"That might explain some of the things I am sensing," Erebus said.

"What do you mean?" asked Gabriel.

"I will bet you that Teivel is moving up his transformation even sooner because he believes he will be attacked by the Old Ones," said Erebus.

"But won't he be weakened during the transformation and for a while afterwards?" Dominic asked.

"Yes, but I am sure he has some protective measures in place," said Erebus.

"How long will he be weakened?" Archetenus asked.

"Mind you I am not an expert on this but I believe for a couple of days," Erebus said. "That is why he needs so many victims to eat; it will hasten him in getting his full powers."

"Clay," Darla yelled as she ran into the kitchen of the Teivel Manor Hotel. "People are running in here saying the soldiers are grabbing people off the street and arresting them."

"Darla you gather all of my employees and customers and take them to the wine cellar below my office," Clay said as he ran out of the kitchen and into his office.

"Ruth, please, I don't know what is happening but tell me how do I save these people?"

As Edward drove the carriage through the streets of Teivel all of his team saw the thousands of soldiers who were filling the streets. Since Edward was following Teivel's carriage the soldiers moved for Teivel's caravan.

"This is looking real bad," Edward yelled down to Raphael.

"I know, something has gone wrong," Raphael said to his men. Then Raphael called out, "Miranda, Ruth, Daniel we might need some help."

Jasmine was wondering why Teivel was not showing the effects of the truth potion and her fears increased when she saw the crowds of soldiers that were filling the streets.

"Why are the streets filled with soldiers? Are we coming under attack now?" Jasmine asked with genuine fear.

"I expect an attack very soon which is why I want to get you to the safety of my castle. Jasmine I want you to know that I will protect you and your family but once the attacks start you must do as I say."

"Of course, but I don't really understand."

"It is complicated; I am not saying that you can't understand what I need to tell you I am saying that I don't have enough time to explain everything now."

132

Jasmine heard Ruth's voice in her head, "Ask him where he believes the attacks will come from."

"Who do you believe will attack us and where will they come from?" Jasmine asked. "I have many friends and while I am so grateful for your protection I now fear for others."

"I am expecting attacks on multiple fronts," Teivel said with his speech slurring.

Jasmine now realized the truth potion was affecting Teivel. "Who is attacking you?"

"I have many enemies among demons and men. My men found spies that work for the demon Chaladrone in my castle this morning. I expect that Chaladrone will attack me...Teivel started to shake his head back and forth and as he did the appearance of his face was changing. Teivel kept losing his human mask and exposing the demon inside.

Jasmine knew she had little time to get the information she needed. She mustered all of her courage and grasped both of Teivel's hands with hers. "Help me," Jasmine prayed silently. "The portal, where is the portal?" she asked Teivel. Jasmine could feel his body shaking and he was shaking his head back and forth with more rapid movements.

"Cedrick where is the portal for the invading demons?"

Teivel was starting to drool and foam appeared around his mouth. His body started to shake spasmodically. "Cedrick where is the portal?"

"In Emeric's and Banaka's temple," Teivel said in a whisper.

"Where? I didn't hear you."

"In Emeric's and Banaka's temple," Teivel said as blood started to drip from his nose and eyes.

"Cedrick where is this temple?"

"In the mountains of Rihlet."

"Where in the mountains?"

"The highest peak of course." As Teivel said these words he doubled over and grabbed his stomach. Blood ran from his mouth.

"Jasmine get out of there now," Ruth said.

"Can I kill him?" Jasmine cried as she grabbed for one of her knives.

"No, get out of there."

"Can I hurt him?"

"Yes."

Jasmine grabbed Teivel's hair and pulled his head back with her left hand. With her right hand she quickly stabbed Teivel in his left eye then his right eye. Teivel screamed in pain and grabbed for Jasmine as she opened the door to the carriage. Jasmine screamed the Nordes war cry as she jumped out of the carriage and rolled down a small embankment. Sorren too screamed the Nordes war cry as he impaled his knife into the soldier sitting next to him; then Sorren jumped from the moving carriage.

The driver of Teivel's carriage stopped but Teivel screamed for him to keep driving to the castle. Edward sped up to the location where he saw Jasmine and Sorren jump and stopped the carriage. Neither Jasmine nor Sorren were visible from the road because they had both rolled down an embankment of long grasses.

"Stay here," Raul said as he and Simon jumped from the back outside seats of the carriage and ran down the embankment. Within moments they saw Sorren stand up; he was holding Jasmine. "I'm alright but she hit rocks," Sorren said as Simon and Raul ran up to him. "I think she broke her leg and some ribs. I'm not sure about that shoulder."

"You are bleeding," said Simon.

"I stabbed him in the eyes before I jumped out. He is already transforming. The portal is in the highest peak of the Rihlet Mountains; in the temple of Emeric and Banaka."

"That's near Erebus' castle," Sorren said.

Thaos and Stephan did not stop to help Sorren and the others for Daniel's voice told them to keep following Teivel's carriage. Jasmine was in severe pain but her adrenalin was running wild within her.

"Teivel said his men found some spies of the demon Chaladrone in his castle this morning. That is why he was returning to the castle because he expects to be attacked by demons," said Jasmine.

"Miranda," Raul yelled. "Where do you need us?"

"We are returning you to the cavern," Ruth's voice said for all to hear. But Jasmine has seen enough horror this day; she will heal in the house of Gabriel."

"I can't leave," Jasmine gasped.

"Child you are too injured," Sorren said. "Have Hannah call Sudfad to the house and tell him all you know." Jasmine disappeared from Sorren's arms.

Chapter XII
Hell Beasts

"I am so sorry we are late," Hannah said as she and Maxwell entered their dining room. "How is Daniel?"

"He is sleeping and Vivian fed him," Iris said. "And you aren't late, lunch will be ready in a few minutes."

Emeral walked into the dining room carrying two bowls of mashed potatoes. She set the dishes on the table and walked up to Maxwell and kissed him on the cheek. Then Emeral stepped back and looked at both Hannah and Maxwell. "You two are up to something, I can tell from the looks on your faces; what have you been doing?"

"Hannah has a surprise," Maxwell said with a grin. "Is everyone home?"

"I will gather everyone," Iris said. As she spoke Luca walked into the dining room.

"So what was your secret errand?" Luca asked Maxwell with a grin.

"We are just about to tell everyone," said Maxwell.

Within moments the entire household was gathered in the dining room. "I'm just so excited I can hardly talk," Hannah said. "Maxwell do you want to start?"

"One of Hannah's patients is the elderly man who owns thirty acres of land to the north of us. He and his wife decided to sell their property and move in with their daughter but they already had a buyer lined up and he was coming to look at the land today."

"It is beautiful property. Twenty acres of pasture land for our horses and ponies and ten acres of woods and it all backs up to the river," Maxwell continued.

"So you bought it?" asked Vivian.

"Yes," Hannah said then she looked at Zelda. "The house is really cute and Maxwell said it is in good shape but it needs a few repairs. We were wondering if you and Horace would like to live in that house?"

All the adults in the house started to smile when they saw the look of shock then joy on Zelda's face. "Hannah, I just don't know what to say. This is so wonderful, but, but, I can't let you buy us a house."

"Zelda we needed the land for the animals, the house is sort of a gift." Zelda started to cry and hugged Hannah.

"Does Zack have to move?" Paul asked with concern.

"Honey he will be living on our property," Emeral said. "All of you can still play and go to school together."

"And as well as all of you are riding, you could take the ponies to his house," Vivian said which made Christopher, Nicholas, Joey, Paul, Adrone and Zach all smile and jump around.

"Zach isn't this wonderful?" Zelda asked between her tears.

"This all happened so fast that I wasn't able to contact Gabriel," Hannah said. "So I will write to him today. I hope he doesn't get mad that I did this without him."

"I can promise you he won't get mad," said Luca.

"Zelda, Ike and Wanda won't be completely moved out until Sunday but I am sure they would let us look at the house again if you want to see it today," said Hannah.

"Oh, that would be so wonderful. I just can't believe this. And it will be so nice to be close to all of you," Zelda said. "You are family now."

"Can we all go or do you think that will be too much for Ike and Wanda?" Emeral asked.

"They are lovely people, I am sure they will enjoy the company," said Hannah.

"We are going to have to put up fencing and separate the pastures," Maxwell said. "I was planning to hire the work done but does anyone want to help me figure out the plans?"

"Sure," Sam said.

"I would like to also," Vivian said. "I have to admit that when Elan and I bought those ponies; we were both so excited that we didn't think about how much land we would need. So this makes me happy."

As the family now sat down to eat their midday meal, Miranda's voice was heard in the dining room. "You have a patient in the parlor. She will explain everything." Hannah, Luca and Maxwell were already running to the parlor before Miranda finished speaking.

Jasmine was lying on the sofa in the parlor and tried to sit up as Hannah and the others ran into the room. "Hannah it's not my blood it's Teivel's. I am not bleeding but I have broken bones. The Angels sent me back so I could tell all of you what is happening. You need to bring King Sudfad here."

Jasmine gasped in pain as Luca picked her up. "Take her to my medical room," Hannah said. Elan and Cassandra ran out of the parlor and opened the medical room.

"I'll get Sudfad," Maxwell said and ran out of the house.

"Who is it?" Christopher asked fearfully as Hannah entered the dining room.

"Honey it is Jasmine and she will be alright," Hannah said soothingly.

"I am starting tonics," Vivian yelled from the kitchen.

"Will someone bring water and towels and one of my nightgowns?" Hannah asked and left the parlor.

When Raul, Sorren, Edward, Michael and Simon materialized in the caverns under Teivel's castle they heard the sounds of fighting. But it was not their comrades who were engaged in battle.

"Demons attacked the castle," Archetenus said. "Gabriel wants us to let them battle each other while we get the prisoners out. Most of our people are helping the prisoners. Why are you here?"

"Teivel started transforming," Michael said. "Jasmine stabbed him in the eyes before she jumped out of his carriage. They are on their way here now. We need to get to the room for the transformation."

"That's where all the demons were headed too," Archetenus said. "Let me get some others and we will go with you."

"Quickly, quickly," Clay said as he ushered people through his office and into the wine cellar. "There is an escape route down there. Everyone must be quiet."

"Clay are you coming?" asked one of the waiters.

"No, I will try to divert them, now go."

"I am staying with you," Darla said.

"I don't think that is wise," Clay said as he peered out of the window in his office. "Darla I think they are coming for us."

"Where is the portal?" the Sanuri asked as he ran into the cavern where Michael and the others were waiting for Archetenus.

"In the Mountains of Rihlet, in the highest peak. Emeric and Banaka have a temple there and the portal is in the temple," Sorren said.

"That is near my castle," Erebus said as he ran into the cavern behind the Sanuri. "I will go there."

"You don't have the power to close that portal," said the Sanuri. "It's the warlock you must stop because he is expediting the transformation and the opening of the portal."

"You can't go alone," Raul yelled but the Sanuri had already disappeared.

Stephan and Thaos alone heard Daniel's voice as they followed Teivel's carriage inside of the stone walls that surrounded the castle. "Chaladrone has already sent an army of demons and they are battling Teivel's soldiers. You stay with Teivel. He has started to transform and Jasmine blinded him so he is filled with rage. But you will encounter many more monsters before this is over."

"Well that is a pleasant thought," Stephan said sarcastically as Teivel's carriage stopped in front of the castle.

Two of Teivel's bodyguards were helping Teivel out of the carriage when Thaos ran up to them. "Hurry we must get him inside; the castle is under attack."

"Who?" screamed Teivel savagely.

"I don't know but this place is full of demons," Thaos yelled. "Now get him inside."

"Ratri help me!" Screamed Batina as she pulled her sword out of one of Teivel's soldiers who had just stabbed one of the female prisoners.

"Are you alright?" Ratri yelled as he landed near his wife. The sounds of battle echoed off the stone walls and the din was deafening.

"I am but she is bleeding badly. Can you get her to Lakin?"

Sudfad and Renya ran inside of Hannah's house. "They are still in the medical room," Iris said. "I will take you there." Iris knocked on the closed door. "The King and Queen are here; can they come in?"

Elan opened the door and said, "It will be a few minutes yet; she has a lot of injuries."

They heard Hannah yell, "Iris can you get a robe, Jasmine doesn't want to speak to Sudfad and Renya in a nightgown."

Emeral walked out of the medical room and closed the door behind her. "Why don't you go into the dining room and have some coffee while we wait. Jasmine has a broken leg, several broken ribs and a dislocated shoulder. They are just finishing up with her."

"Did she tell you anything else?" Sudfad asked as they entered the dining room.

"She was covered in blood and she said the blood was Teivel's because she stabbed him in both of his eyes. Jasmine said that Teivel was transforming."

"What on earth was that girl doing with that monster?" Renya asked.

"All I know is that she got some very important information from him and that is what she is going to tell us about," Emeral said.

"How did she get hurt?" asked Sudfad.

"Apparently she was riding in a carriage with Teivel and after she stabbed him she jumped out and landed on some rocks."

"What!" Sudfad said.

"I felt your presence here," Rybkin said condescendingly as Erebus entered the cavern where the transformation was to take place. "Why are you here?"

"To stop you," Erebus said. He knew he had to distract or destroy Rybkin so Michael could enter the chamber.

"Not that you are strong enough," Rybkin sneered. "But I am curious as to why."

Erebus did not answer Rybkin's question but kept walking towards the warlock. "Tell me Rybkin, how much are you getting paid to destroy this world?"

"More than you can imagine," Rybkin said as he eyed up his adversary. "It is not often you see a warlock with a, shall I say a concern for social justice." As Rybkin was speaking the ground beneath Erebus' feet began to shake. Erebus flew into the air as the floor beneath him fell away.

Rybkin screamed from the pain that Erebus inflicted upon him. Rybkin's screams caused rocks to fall from the ceiling. Erebus momentarily disappeared then reappeared behind Rybkin. Lightening shot from Rybkin's hands as he turned and attacked Erebus.

Erebus blocked the lighting strikes and shot huge balls of fire at Rybkin. Neither warlock was injured. They were just starting to access their arsenals of weapons. The two warlocks stared at each other and slowly started to circle each other. Neither man aware that the water of the pond in the center of the room was beginning to bubble.

"Get me down to my chamber," Teivel screamed to his bodyguards who did not understand what was happening to their leader. Teivel's knees were weak and kept giving out on him. He was foaming at the mouth. Blood was running from his nose and ears as well as the injuries to his eyes. Teivel's body was shaking and he was sweating profusely.

Thaos and Stephan led their men inside of the castle as they followed Teivel. They protected him from the numerous demons that were lunging at the dictator. Suddenly Teivel stopped walking and make a loud and horrific sound. The back of his shirt ripped open exposing a grotesque bulge in his back. There appeared to be living things moving inside of Teivel's body. Long dark hair would appear then disappear on his back.

"I think Michael needs to get here now," Thaos said. "Miranda!"

Gabriel had told his army to stay out of the fight between Chaladrone's demons and Teivel's soldiers until the soldiers suddenly started to attack the prisoners. Without provocation the soldiers ran into the caverns where the prisoners were housed and started to kill them. The soldiers were taken by surprise when Gabriel's warriors attacked them.

The bodyguards who were holding Teivel's arms now jumped away from the monster that was growing in front of them.

"I don't think this is supposed to happen like this," Stephan yelled to Thaos as they watched Teivel's body growing and changing shapes. Thaos and Stephan had their men surround Teivel although they were all ordered to keep a distance from the monster. One of the bodyguards screamed with terror as Teivel picked him up and started to devour his face.

"Keep back!" Thaos yelled to his men. "Miranda!"

The castle started to shake violently, causing men and women to fall and to grasp things to help them balance. Teivel too fell forward for he was not causing this disturbance, it was the result of the warring warlocks in the caverns.

"Are you alright?" Matthew yelled as a large stone hit Simon on the head.

"Yes, keep going," Simon said as he tried to regain his balance and wipe the blood from his eyes. Raul, Simon, Matthew and Michael were running up the ancient stone steps from the subterranean caverns to the castle.

Michael was in the lead and suddenly stopped when he reached a landing that had four tunnels leading from it. "Ruth, somebody which way?" screamed Michael.

"Take the one farthest to your left," Daniel's voice called out.

"Misha, Micha help me!" yelled Thor as he tried to lift a large wooden beam that had Joshua pinned to the floor. Dagon and Horace ran to Thor and attacked the soldiers who were running towards Thor and Joshua.

"In here!" Yelled Dagon when he heard Misha's voice.

"Father," Micha yelled as he and Bianca entered the small cavern where Joshua was trapped. "Father," Micha called again as he was filled with fear.

"Thor you will hurt your back. Step away," Calen said as he too entered the chamber.

Dagon and Horace killed the three soldiers they were fighting with and turned to help the others free Joshua. "Thor, Bianca pull him out as soon as we can lift this," Misha said. "But be careful we don't know how bad his injuries are. Joshua was unconscious and there was blood on the floor from his body.

Dagon, Misha, Micha, Calen and Horace had all they could do to lift the wooden beam a foot into the air. Thor quickly grabbed Joshua and moved his body away from the beam. "He's alive," Thor said. "But he is unconscious." Misha picked Joshua up and flew out of the cavern.

"Go with your father," Calen said to Micha, Thor and Bianca and the three Venatores ran to catch up with Misha.

"Back! Get Back!" Stephan yelled as Teivel grabbed another one of his soldiers and started to devour the man. Stephan was not yelling to just the men that he and Thaos led; many of Teivel's soldiers were so horrified at the scene before them that they were frozen in place by their fear.

Both Rybkin and Erebus were exhausted from their battle and both men suffered many wounds. The chamber where the transformation was to take place was all but destroyed. Rybkin shouted and part of the ceiling fell on top of Erebus.

Erebus was struggling to free himself when he heard Ruth's voice. "The altar is giving him power."

Rybkin was walking towards Erebus who was now sitting up. Rybkin sneered as he relished the thought of destroying his adversary. Suddenly he stopped and turned to see what Erebus was staring at. "No!" Rybkin screamed when he realized that Erebus was focused on the altar. Rybkin ran towards Erebus but was thrown across the cavern by the power of the exploding altar.

Screams from hell beasts filled the castle when the altar exploded. Teivel's knees weakened and he stumbled forward but quickly regained his balance.

"Erebus," Rachel screamed and ran into the cavern to help her friend.

"Rachel stay out of here!" Erebus yelled as he tried to stand on his feet. Rachel jumped in front of Erebus and faced Rybkin, who was now standing.

"Erebus you let a child defend you," Rybkin said sarcastically. "I am disappointed."

"Rachel get out of here!" Erebus yelled again as he weakly stood on his feet.

"Why don't you try fighting like a man," Rachel spat. "Fight like a warrior!"

"I am no warrior," Rybkin said and laughed as he was enjoying the banter with Rachel. "Erebus I am going to kill your little friend first."

"You might try," Rachel said and stepped towards Rybkin. "You will have to go through me to get to him." Rachel took another step towards Rybkin.

Dominic and Raphael ran into the cavern. Dominic thrust his sword through Rybkin's back then screamed in pain as lightening flowed through the sword and burned Dominic's arm. Raphael pulled Dominic away from Rybkin and started to chant as he walked towards the warlock.

As Rybkin was trying to pull the sword out of his back, Rachel ran forward and plunged her sword into Rybkin's heart. She too screamed with pain and dropped her weapon. "Rachel," Erebus screamed and ran forward.

While the sword wounds did not kill Rybkin they helped to weaken him. "What are you doing?" Rybkin screamed and swung around to face Raphael who continued to chant and to walk towards the warlock. Smoke started to rise from Rybkin's skin. "Who are you?" he screamed as he backed away from Raphael.

"Erebus get Rachel out of here," Raphael said and continued to walk towards Rybkin, who was backing away from the priest. Rybkin threw lighting at Raphael but Erebus mumbled and a shield materialized in front of Raphael.

Although Dominic's right arm was burned to the elbow he now stood next to Raphael. "Ruth give me the words," Dominic said and instantaneously he started chanting. Rybkin started to cry out in pain and the smoke rising from him became thicker.

"Ruth I can fight too, tell me what to say," Rachel said as Erebus helped her to her feet. "No Erebus I am not leaving." Rachel became light headed and realized she was chanting. Raphael, Dominic and Rachel formed a triangle around Rybkin. They did not lift a weapon for they were calling holiness into the cavern.

Erebus could not get himself to call upon the Angels but neither would he leave his friends. There was no longer power in Rybkin's spells; he could feel himself becoming weaker. Rybkin was facing his attackers as he walked backwards towards the pond. Erebus saw the bubbling in the water of the pond. "Jump away from him," Erebus yelled and with the last of his strength Erebus summoned a wind that blew Rybkin backwards. As Rybkin was losing his balance a giant red tentacle thrust out of the water and wrapped around Rybkin's body; within an instant Rybkin was pulled beneath the hellish waters.

"Well it's about time," Stephan yelled as Michael, Raul, Matthew and Simon ran into the front foyer of the castle. The floor was covered with blood.

"He's been eating his men," Thaos said to explain the grisly sight.

"Teivel," yelled Michael. "Teivel look at me!"

The monster dropped the body of one of his soldiers and looked for the voice that was demanding his attention. "Teivel do you remember centuries ago when you could not overthrow the Clan of Gesmal? Do you remember the old woman who cursed you?" The monster screamed at Michael's words.

As Michael spoke, Matthew, Simon and Raul gathered around him. All four men touched The Scroll of Imari. "I am Michael and I am the fruit of your seed." The monster lunged at Michael and his brothers but they held their ground and concentrated on the scroll destroying Teivel.

An eerie stillness filled the foyer. The men felt as if they were moving within a dream. Teivel's attack towards Michael was slowed. The monster started to howl and thrash around. The men could hear Teivel gasping for air. Teivel's body became less dense and suddenly scenes appeared within the body of the monster. The men in the foyer saw Teivel's life flashing before them. They saw his hatred and his murderous deeds.

As the scenes captivated the on-lookers, Teivel's body was transforming into the shape of a man. "Wait! What was that?" Raul yelled about a scene that had flashed before them. Teivel collapsed onto the floor. The Scroll of Imari disappeared from Michael's hands. Michael ran over to Teivel's body and rolled Teivel onto his back. The dictator, the monster of Ryed was dead. Teivel started to decompose; within moments he was nothing but a skeleton, then the bones turned into ash.

Chapter XIII
On the Wind

As the ashes of Teivel blew across the floor of his castle, Miranda's voice was heard by all, even Teivel's soldiers. "Teivel the monster had been destroyed. But his armies of demons have been unleashed against the citizens of Ryed. Now is the time to make a stand. Who will rule this kingdom the people or the demons?"

"Who do they take orders from?" Gabriel yelled. Gabriel's voice was amplified throughout the castle.

"Chaladrone, a powerful demon. He will show no mercy to the men who were loyal to Teivel. Time is short, decisions must be made."

"Our wounded?" Lakin yelled. "We have to get them out of here."

"They will be transported to the Patronus Headquarters in Nora," Miranda said.

"You healed the prisoners, why not our wounded?" Raphael asked and his voice too was heard by all.

"Your handful of warriors have risked all to save the people of Ryed but you cannot make their decisions for them. This day the people of this kingdom must decide if they will live as free men and women or continue to be the slaves and victims of dark masters. Raphael we are not leaving you on this journey," Miranda's voice was carried on the winds. The soldiers, the citizens of Ryed stopped and looked around in wonderment. Some people cried; many, many others grabbed weapons.

High Priest Othnial walked outside of the monastery at Rubar and looked at the sky as he listened to this conversation between the Angel Miranda, Gabriel and Raphael. Tears fill the eyes of the old priest and he instantly fell to his knees and thanked The Great Ruler for answering his prayers. After a few minutes, Othnial ran inside of the monastery to prepare to care for wounded.

In the Village of Gesmal people ran out of their homes and listened to the words of Miranda. They knew her voice. They had sworn to follow her. Chief Duncan walked up to his tribesmen as they listened to the conversation between Miranda and the two high priests. Duncan pulled his sword from its sheath and thrust it into the earth. "Miranda, Daniel where do you need us?" Duncan's voice was carried on the winds.

Unbeknown to Raul, Simon, Michael or anyone on Gabriel's team; Sudfad had an army waiting to attack Fort Polta. The Angels had suggested that General Craven, the Commanding General of Fort Stanus lead the attack; for Craven too listened to the voices of the Angels.

The prior night, Craven was plagued with dreams in which he kept hearing the voice of the Angel Daniel. Before the sun came up, Craven followed Daniel's orders and moved his army close to Fort Polta. The troops were hidden in the dense forests that surrounded the fort.

Craven and his men were mounted on their horses and had been waiting in the forests for hours. Now before the midday sun was high in the sky, Daniel's voice was heard by all of Craven's troops. "Teivel has been destroyed. The human masks have fallen from Teivel's men inside of the fort. You will recognize them because they have the faces of demons. The gates have been opened for you; it is time."

"Charge!" bellowed Craven and the order was repeated by the leaders of the designated forces that were to attack different areas of the fort. The Horn of Cass was blown by Craven's men so that the few soldiers who battled the demons within the walls of Fort Polta understood they were not alone in this battle.

Nicholas and Joey ran into the bedroom where Jasmine had been taken. The room was filled with the adults in the household as well as Sudfad and Renya, as they listened to Jasmine's story.

"Mama," Nicholas said excitedly. "Natasha and Diana just came home."

Now everyone except Sudfad and Renya ran down the stairs and into the dining room where a group of Ruala warriors were laughing and watching Natasha and Diana hug the children.

"We hit really bad weather and it delayed us," Natasha said tearfully as she hugged members of her family.

"Why are there so many of you?" Maxwell asked Bryce one of the Ruala warriors.

"Because our packs are filled with gifts for families here and in Lentz," Bryce said with a grin.

"Everyone thought they might die so Gabriel let them buy gifts for their families," Diana said as she hugged Iris. Diana's words shot through the family like a lot iron.

Maxwell saw the fear in the faces of the women and turned to Bryce. "You must be exhausted. Elan and Cassandra will show you to rooms then come down here and have a meal."

"We have so much to tell you," said Natasha.

"And we would like to hear it also," Sudfad said as he and Renya walked down the stairs to the dining room.

"The Angels brought Jasmine here," Hannah explained to Natasha and Diana. "She is hurt but she was instructed to tell us about the mission."

"Everyone take a seat and we will bring food and refreshments and listen to what they have to say," Emeral said.

"Can I come down too?" Jasmine yelled from her bedroom.

Luca looked at Hannah and asked, "Should I bring her down?"

"Yes, but we will need to prop her leg up on a chair," Hannah replied.

"What happened to her?" asked Natasha.

"That is a story she should tell you," Luca said. "The short version is she was trying to get information from Teivel about the location of a portal that would open our world to invading demons."

"She was riding in his carriage with him and he started to transform. She slipped him truth potion, got the information, stabbed him in both eyes and jumped out of a moving carriage. She has a lot of broken bones."

"What!" Natasha gasped.

Second in command in the attack on Fort Polta was General Ridon, a seasoned veteran of battle. If he lived through this day, Ridon would be promoted to commanding general of Fort Polta. General Craven carried the promotion papers on him but King Sudfad did not want Ridon to know about the promotion until after the battle. Sudfads' reasoning: Ridon would have demanded to lead the attack but the Angel Daniel told Sudfad he would be wise to have Craven as the leader.

Captain Malard was young but his abilities as a military strategist impressed the Royal Family. Unbeknownst to Malard he too would be assigned to Fort Polta after the battle. Never in the history of any kingdom in Opots had a king been forced to attack his own fort. Sudfad vowed to never again allow the enemy to infiltrate his military. Sudfad spent long months agonizing over job assignments of his officers for Sudfad planned many changes in his military after the battle at For Polta.

Fort Polta was attacked from all four sides by General Craven's troops. The fort had gates at both the front and the back of the huge wall that surrounded it. As soon as Cedrick Teivel was destroyed the human masks fell from the faces of the soldiers within Fort Polta who were demons or members of the Insidiae. With their darkness exposed these beings now attacked the loyal soldiers of Wetpr. Demons blocked the gates to prevent the soldiers from escaping but the Angels opened the gates to allow Craven's troops inside.

The number of the loyal soldiers of Wetpr were significantly smaller than the number of demons and members of the Insidiae within the walls of the fort. These soldiers would have been slaughtered had not Craven's men been waiting outside of the fort.

Fort Polta had one hundred and fifty thousand men assigned to it. General Craven led twice that number. The battle took on tremendous proportions.

By the time that Gabriel and his army reached the City of Teivel it had turned into a war zone. Soldiers and citizens battled legions of demons. People who had been prisoners of their fears for centuries now broke their bonds and fought against the monsters that had enslaved them. Buildings were burning and blood ran through the streets.

The leaders within Gabriel's army led their troops in attacks against the demons. Gabriel, Sorren and a small contingency of warriors went to the Teivel Manor Hotel to find Darla and Clay.

Yells went up from the citizens when they saw the reinforcements and when they realized the freedom fighters fought among them. The freedom fighters had a unique war cry. Dominic and his men screamed the war cry which was taken up by thousands of voices.

"What do you mean they aren't here?" Gabriel asked a cook who was holding a bloody towel against his head.

"What happened here?" demanded Sorren as he pushed his way through the crowd of wounded employees.

"Noel was just about to tell me," said Gabriel.

"When the streets started to fill with soldiers, Clay and that girl ushered all of us, even the customers into the wine cellar to hide us. They stayed in the hotel. We were only down there for minutes before we hear all this noise up here. It sounded like glass breaking and furniture being thrown around. Then we heard Clay yelling." Noel swallowed hard. "He was a good man, he took care of us. The sounds got louder and some of us ran back up the steps and burst into Clay's office. The soldiers were beating both of them. We tried to help but the soldiers attacked us too."

"What did they do with them?" Sorren asked in almost a whisper.

"I didn't see because I was knocked out but some of the others told me that the soldiers dragged Clay and that girl out of here. We looked for them in the hotel but didn't find them. We were afraid to go outside," Noel continued.

"Do you have any idea where the soldiers would have taken them?" asked Gabriel.

"Usually the prisons," Noel said then paused. "When I saw them, I mean Clay and that girl, they looked really hurt. There was lots of blood."

"Why did the soldiers beat them?" asked Gabriel.

"That is what the soldiers do," Noel said.

"Why did they take them and not the rest of you?" Sorren asked.

"I cannot answer that," said Noel.

"Did you find them?" Joao asked as he and Dack joined Gabriel and Sorren in the kitchen of the hotel.

"They were beaten badly and dragged away from here," Gabriel said somberly.

"No, no," Dack said intensely. "I am not losing another friend." Dack quickly turned to leave the hotel.

"Wait son," Sorren said. "I understand how you feel. I promised Darla's parents that I would protect her. We have to get our heads on straight or we won't be any good for Darla and Clay."

"There had to be a reason they only took Darla and Clay," Gabriel said. "And both of them know we would look for them. I am searching his office." Gabriel pushed through the crowded kitchen with Sorren, Dack and Joao behind him. As soon as Gabriel opened the door to Clay's office all four men stopped and stared at the scene before them.

"It looks like there was a massacre in here," Sorren whispered as fear gripped his heart.

153

"Darla would leave us a sign if she could," Gabriel said. "Look through everything."

Panic filled the men as they searched through the blood covered office without finding any clues as to what happened to their friends. Gabriel ran back into the kitchen. "Noel where is the nearest prison. Draw me a map." Gabriel took the map and the four men started to run out of the hotel when they heard a woman screaming hysterically. The screams were coming from inside of the hotel. The men stopped and listened.

"The kitchen," Sorren yelled and they ran through the dining room and burst into the kitchen. Two demons had entered through the back door. Gabriel and Sorren pulled their swords and charged the demons. Joao and Dack flew over the heads of their friends.

"Everyone out of the kitchen," Gabriel yelled as they saw more demons pouring through the door.

Joao cut the throat of the demon that was charging towards Sorren. Dack broke the neck of a monster that had grabbed one of the women in the kitchen. Gabriel held his sword in his right hand and grabbed a cleaver from a table with his left hand. He was a powerful man, but the anxiousness of losing one of his team members surged through him. Gabriel savagely attacked the demons.

Sorren was filled with anger and guilt but he did not let these emotions cripple him. He stabbed and punched his way through the onslaught of demons.

Edward and his men found a group of demons that had trapped five people in an alley. He let out a war cry as he and his men attacked the demons. Edward ran his sword through a demon that was about to stab one of the trapped men; then he jumped off his horse and pulled a demon off from another man. Edward thrust his sword through the demon's chest.

"Are you alright?" Edward asked as he reached down to help the man stand up.

"Yes but the demons are herding people into a building."

"Where?"

"I'll show you," the man said and jumped to his feet.

Edward's soldiers quickly killed the group of demons and now followed this small group of people through several back alleys. Suddenly they saw smoke and heard horrifying screams. The demons had set a building on fire; trapping the people inside.

Edward ordered half of his men to attack the group of demons that was standing in the street watching the building burn. The rest of Edward's soldiers were ordered to get the people from the burning building. The citizens that led Edward's men to the building, also helped to carry people from the fire.

Among Edward's troops were Hangered and Janson; the two mentally challenged soldiers who the terrorists had tried to take advantage of. After the incident when the terrorists planted a weapon on Hangered and Janson, Edward personally watched over these two soldiers. They were among the soldiers who were helping people escape from the burning building.

Hangered ran up to Edward, carrying a badly burned woman. "General some of these people are hurt real bad," Hangered said anxiously. "Where do we take them?"

Edward looked around hoping to see a physician's sign hanging from one of the buildings. The soldiers were laying burn victims on the ground and running back into the building to save others. A loud roar was heard and the building started to collapse. "Get out! Get out!" men were yelling. Edward ran to the building to help the last of his men escape the flames.

The cries and screams of the victims filled the air and added to the din and chaos. Edward looked at these people and felt helpless, a feeling he was unaccustomed to. "Miranda, Daniel, Ruth I have never called to you before," Edward said in almost a whisper. "Please, how do we help these people?"

Ruth's voice was heard only by Edward, "Physicians have gathered in the red brick building down the street to your right but there are many patients there."

"Take these people to that red brick building," Edward yelled to his troops. Then he spoke again to Ruth, "Please help those people."

"We are," Ruth said. "When your troops return you should go four blocks down and turn to the left. Simon and his men are surrounded."

"Miranda help us!" Archetenus yelled as his men were surrounded by armies of demons.

When Erebus regained consciousness he found himself in a makeshift hospital in the Patronus Headquarters in Nora. The scene was chaotic as priests and citizens from Nora were trying to administer to the wounded. Erebus did not know where he was until he asked a woman who was running past him.

Erebus was weak and when he tried to stand up he came dizzy and nauseous. He heard Lakin's voice and tried to focus his sight so he could find Lakin in the crowded room.

"Lakin, Lakin," Erebus called as he slowly walked towards the Ruala healer.

"You should return to bed," Lakin said as he was packing crystals in the wound of a soldier.

"Is the battle over?" asked Erebus.

"Teivel is dead but Chaladrone released armies of demons upon the kingdom. Our warriors are still there fighting and the Sanuri is trying to close the portal."

Erebus became dizzy again as he looked around the massive room which was filled with the wounded. He saw Thor standing over a bed and started to walk in that direction.

As Erebus got closer he realized that Thor was crying and fear filled Erebus' heart. Erebus found Micha and Bianca kneeling near a bed where Joshua was lying. Joshua was unconscious.

"Is he alive?" Erebus asked as he looked upon his friend.

"A huge timber fell on him," Micha said as tears ran down his face. "It took many of us to lift it off. We don't know how bad his injuries are."

Erebus felt overwhelmed as he looked at the faces of his friends and at all of the wounded in the room. He walked out of the hospital and stood outside taking deep breaths of air. "Ruth, Ruth," Erebus whispered. "Help Joshua and, and..." Erebus paused. "Ruth I want to help. How can I?"

"You are in no shape to help anyone," Ruth said as she appeared before him.

"Can you heal me and return me to the battle?"

"Do you believe that I can heal you?"

"I know you can," then Erebus paused again. "But would you heal one as me?"

"Erebus I don't know if you really understand what you are asking. You have devoted your life to darkness and you have been so afraid that The Great Ruler will force you to change the person you are. Do you understand that if I heal you it will be with holiness? Do you want to change your mind?"

Erebus stared at the Angel, "Will I still be able to help the others?"

"Yes."

"Then let me do so, but would you heal Joshua first?"

"Asher!" Screamed Dominic as he saw his brother fall. "Fennel, Asher is hurt." Dominic ducked as a battleaxe swept over his head. Still in a crouching position, Dominic stabbed the demon before him in the thigh then quickly moved to the right and severed the tendons behind the demon's knee.

Finally Dominic jumped on the back of the demon and cut its throat. He pushed the demon to the ground and turned and ran towards Asher. Fennel was squatting and holding Asher's head as blood poured from the knife wounds in Asher's chest.

"Fennel!" Dominic screamed. Fennel ducked as Dominic threw a knife that landed in the chest of the demon standing behind Fennel. Raul heard the screams and turning he thrust his sword into the back of the demon. When the demon collapsed, Raul saw Fennel and Dominic holding their dying brother.

"Michael!" Screamed Raul. Michael turned and saw Raul trying to keep the demons away from Dominic, Fennel and Asher. Michael quickly moved behind Dominic and thrust his sword through a demon's stomach.

"Hang on Asher, you can't die," Dominic said as tears flowed down his face.

Asher grasped Dominic's hand. "Promise me," Asher said then started to choke on his own blood.

"Promise you what?" Dominic could barely utter the words.

"Promise me that you and Fennel will leave Ryed. Start new lives. Do you promise?"

Dominic looked at Fennel, who was sobbing. "We promise." But Asher died before he could hear his brother's words.

"No!" Sorren screamed and fell to his knees. Gabriel, Joao and Dack ran out the back kitchen door of the Teivel Manor Hotel but stopped abruptly. Sorren was holding Darla's lifeless body and rocking back and forth. The bloody bodies of Darla and Clay had been thrown in the back alley with the trash.

Dack and Joao stood in horror as Gabriel felt Clay's body for signs of life. "I have to take her body back to her parents," Sorren said as tears ran down his face.

"Don't leave me," Janson cried as he held Hangered's lifeless body. Janson sat on the ground trembling. His grief prevented him from hearing the demon behind him. "Please don't leave me..." The demon broke Janson's neck. Janson's body fell forward and draped over the body of the only friend he ever had.

"Stephan!" Thaos screamed and ran to his brother who was lying on the ground. Thaos tore his crystal necklace from his throat and shoved it into Stephan's knife wound. "Miranda help us!" Thaos yelled as he covered Stephan's wound with a bandana.

Thaos started to lift Stephan from the ground but both men collapsed as Thaos lost consciousness. The demon behind Thaos swung his club to strike Thaos a second time but he fell on top of his prey as Chaez ran his sword through the demon's back.

Chapter XIV
The Children of Ahriman

Archetenus and Jared were fighting back to back when Erebus suddenly appeared next to them. Jared felt Erebus' presence and turned to stab the intruder. "What the hell!" Jared shouted.

"Quickly cut the heart out of one of those demons," Erebus said.

"Why?" yelled Jared.

"So I can stop them," snapped Erebus.

"Archetenus watch my back," Jared yelled and ran forward to one of the bodies lying on the ground. Erebus started to mumble and the demons surrounding Archetenus and Jared burst into flames.

"Damn!" Yelled Archetenus.

"Here," Jared said as he thrust the heart at Erebus. Black goo was dripping from the organ.

"Give me your crystal necklace," Erebus said. Jared hesitated for a moment then tore the necklace from his neck and handed it to Erebus. The crystal burned Erebus' hand as he wrapped it inside of the heart. As Erebus mumbled his voice became louder and smoke was rising from his hand. Deafening screams were heard as demons burst into flames. Screams were heard in the hell dimensions as holiness surged through Chaladrone's kingdom. The earth shook from Chaladrone's screams.

"His hand is on fire," Archetenus said as he and Jared stared at Erebus.

Erebus continued to chant louder and louder as the demons screamed. People were covering their ears as the vibrations from the screams were causing people to bleed from their noses and ears. Suddenly the screams stopped. Erebus collapsed on the ground and Archetenus and Jared both ran to him. The fire from Erebus' hand had spread to his clothing. Archetenus and Jared were smothering the flames.

Although the demons at Fort Polta were weakened by Teivel's death; Teivel had created various traps within the fort. General Craven's troops battled the demons and the members of the Insidiae. In the midst of battle thousands of red demonic snakes appeared within the walls of the forts. "Angel!" yelled Craven.

"Tell your men to cut the heads off the snakes, we will take care of the rest," Daniel's voice was heard only to Craven.

"Cut the heads off the snakes! Cut the heads off the snakes!" Craven ordered. Other military leaders repeated the command. Craven had no idea what Daniel was talking about when he said 'they would take care of the rest.' Until Craven heard screeching and looking up he saw a battle between Hengers and Talmuth in the sky over the fort.

The demons were destroyed in Ryed but no one felt victorious as they gathered their dead and wounded. Gabriel and Raphael found each other on a back street as they were searching for their warriors. "I hope this was worth the cost," Gabriel said solemnly as he looked at the carnage before them.

"Have you talked to the Angels?" Raphael asked. "What do they want us to do now?"

"No," Gabriel said. "But I found one of our soldiers here. We are taking everyone to the Teivel Manor." Gabriel picked up the body of the soldier and looked at Raphael. "Darla and Clay were beaten to death by Teivel's men. I have never seen Sorren cry before." The two men walked in silence.

When Emeric and Banaka felt the powerful death of Teivel they returned to their temple in the Mountains of Rihlet. These Grand Masters had been in hiding after the Old Ones of Nunc sent death squads after them. But now they returned to protect the portal for they knew that if the invasion was not successful the Old Ones of many worlds would seek to kill them.

Emeric and Banaka had spent centuries conspiring against the Old Ones of Nunc and making grand promises to powerful demons from other worlds. This brother and sister knew that Teivel had many enemies who would try and stop his transformation. What they did not know was who actually destroyed Teivel. The Angels had shielded Gabriel's army from the eyes of these two insidious Grand Masters.

Emeric and Banaka assumed that one of the Old Ones of Nunc killed Teivel and this concerned them because they feared that the Old Ones would be able to sense the energies of the portal. These two traitors to humanity had no idea that time had been reversed for one hour in the World of Nunc. They had no idea that for a short period of time four of The Seven Sons were in possession of The Scroll of Imari. And they had no idea that the Sanuri had just materialized inside of their temple.

Miranda disabled the security alarms that Emeric and Banaka had put into place. They relied on their dark magics to protect them. These children of Ahriman poured wine and toasted each other. With Teivel dead, they could keep more of the riches they would receive for selling out their world.

The Sanuri materialized in a marble hallway. When he realized he was alone, he closed his eyes and tried to sense the energies of the portal.

"You could ask for help," Miranda's voice whispered in the Sanuri's ear. He smiled.

"Would you help me?"

"First you must know that Emeric and Banaka materialized in the temple minutes before you. They know Teivel is dead and they came here to protect the portal. They are in the chamber where the portal was created."

"How do I find it?"

"Wouldn't a better question be to ask how you are going to battle two powerful Grand Masters and stop an invasion which is schedule to start in twenty minutes?"

"Miranda you are right. Would you care to join me?"

"I thought you would never ask." In that instant Miranda appeared next to the Sanuri. "Straight ahead," she said and started to march down the hallway.

"Where are the guards?" he asked as he was amazed at how quiet the temple was.

"Emeral and Banaka trust only each other. When the Old Ones put bounties on them, they feared their men would betray them."

"So it is just the two of them in here?"

"For now," Miranda said and turned a corner.

The temple was made of marble and gold. Huge oil paintings adorned the walls. This temple reminded the Sanuri of the temple were the victims for the blood moon ceremonies had been imprisoned. The presence of evil permeated the building. The Sanuri wondered why Miranda was walking the halls instead of materializing in the room with Banaka and Emeric. Then he realized that Miranda was touching each painting that they passed.

"Miranda what are those paintings?"

"Portals into hell worlds created by both the demons and the humans of this world."

"What are you doing when you touch them?"

"I am collapsing the portals and opening other doors so the victims can escape."

"Won't the demons stop them?"

Miranda turned to the Sanuri and smiled. "I am keeping them busy."

Miranda and the Sanuri walked down four more hallways before they came to a set of beautiful wooden doors. The doors exploded. Emeric and Banaka jumped up from their chairs as they faced Miranda and the Sanuri.

"You children of Ahriman who have brought so much evil into this world. The people who once bowed down to you are now fighting against you. You have no power here," Miranda said loudly as she began to glow. "You sold this world to demons so shall you dwell."

Emeric and Banaka screamed as Miranda hurled them through distant worlds. They looked around fearfully when they suddenly materialized in a putrid swamp. They started to cry when the demon Chaladrone appeared before them.

"The portal is glowing," the Sanuri said and ran towards it.

"Stop!" Miranda yelled. "Let the invaders come a little farther."

The portal appeared as a large oval of energy in the center of the room. The energy surging through it had been causing a buzzing sound which now grew in intensity. Lighting shot out of the portal and into the room. The Sanuri jumped back to keep from being struck by the lighting.

Miranda walked up to the portal and a sword of light appeared in her hand. The Sanuri now walked closer to the portal. They could hear voices and what sounded like thousands of feet marching. Soon an army of demons started to materialize within the portal.

"This world is protected by The Great Ruler," Miranda said and thrust her sword into the portal. The portal exploded as did the temple.

"I thought I would die," Erebus said as he opened his eyes and saw the Sanuri looking at him. "Why am I not dead?"

"Do you want to be?" the Sanuri asked.

"I should be. I acted as a conduit and channeled holiness to the hell regions. I remember starting on fire," Erebus said and tried to sit up but couldn't.

"You have suffered significant burns but Archetenus and Jared stopped the fire from spreading."

"I can hardly move am I crippled?" Erebus asked fearfully.

"You will be for a while, we will take you back to Wetpr to heal. Erebus you know that you marked yourself as a traitor to all of the underworlds. Your life is in great danger now. Did you really understand what you were doing?"

"Of course I did but I didn't think I would live through it. Am I still a sorcerer? I feel very different but that may be pain medicine."

"You cannot have that type of darkness and holiness in your body at the same time. The darkness was eradicated but of course you can always call to it again if you choose. But I would suggest that you try living without it for a while. In a way you have been given a second chance."

Erebus stared at the Sanuri for a few moments then looked around the crowded hospital room. "Are we back in Nora?"

"Yes, the Angels brought all our people back here. Sudfad has built a hospital in Fort Salar which should be completed in a few days. The Angels will transport everyone to the hospital then."

"Why, Sudfad, Renya what a surprise," Emeral said as she moved so the King and Queen could enter Gabriel's house. "Is something wrong?"

"I was going to call a meeting but with all the babies here, we decided to come over," Sudfad said.

"Is that Sudfad's voice that I hear?" Hannah asked as she walked to the foyer.

"He would like to have a meeting with all of us," Emeral said with a look of concern on her face. Hannah stopped walking as fear consumed her?

"Is Gabriel alive?" Hannah asked as tears filled her eyes.

"Yes but there is much that I have to tell you," Sudfad said.

"Thank God," said Hannah. "We can have the meeting in Gabriel's study."

Hannah walked into the playroom. "Boys will you gather everyone the King is here for a meeting?" Paul, Adrone, Nicholas, Christopher, Zach and Joey all jumped up and ran out of the room. "Emeral I will make some refreshments," Hannah said as she saw Emeral leading Renya and Sudfad to the study.

In less than ten minutes all of the adults in the household were in the study with the exception of Melinda who was with the children. Luca was the last to enter since he was carrying Jasmine. Both Hannah and Natasha were nervous as they set up a table of refreshments; they were fearful of the news the King was bringing.

Sudfad stood before the group. "Just after dinner I received a letter. The Enrops who delivered the letter said that the Angels expedited their journey and the birds believed that only minutes had passed since they were in Ryed. The battle is over. Teivel, Emeric and Banaka have all been destroyed. The Angel Miranda destroyed the invading armies of demons. After an arduous battle Fort Polta has now been taken back from the demons and dark lords."

"Michael, Raul, Simon and Matthew combined their powers with that of The Scroll of Imari to destroy Teivel. As it turns out Teivel had many enemies that did not want him to complete the transformation. The demon Chaladrone attacked Teivel's castle. After Teivel was destroyed, Chaladrone attacked the entire kingdom of Ryed with armies of demons. Apparently Miranda's voice carried on the wind and she gave the people of Ryed a choice and most of them chose to fight the demons. But the battle was a nightmare from the sounds of it."

Sudfad continued. "The letter was written by Simon. He said that all our people are wounded and many, many lives were lost. He asked that we not hold a celebration for the returning warriors as they are all injured and grieving. The Angels sent all of our people to Nora. Citizens, the Patronus priests and Padres Bartholomew and Thomas are tending to the wounded. As Hannah knows, The Lion told me several weeks ago to expedite the building of the hospital at Fort Salar. It should be completed in three days then the Angels will send everyone here."

166

"Hannah do you think you will have enough staff?" asked Sudfad.

"I have hired a lot but honestly if all the soldiers are wounded we will need more," Hannah said.

"I will call a meeting of the physicians in Salar tomorrow afternoon; Hannah I would like you to be there."

"Of course Sudfad."

"We can all help too," Cassandra said.

"Sudfad we are all afraid to ask but do you know who has died," Vivian asked fearfully.

"Simon said that most of them would have died had not the Angels helped to heal them. Of your team, Ratri and Batina have serious knife wounds. Joshua was struck by a massive beam. He will live but he will be in bed for a long time. Misha was stabbed in the back multiple times." Diana started to weep. "Thor hurt his back trying to lift the beam off from Joshua. Rachel has severe burns to her arm after stabbing a sorcerer. Calen, Koby, Dagon, Raphael, Gabriel, Joao and Dack are all wounded but not as severely as the others."

"What about Micha and Bianca?" Iris asked fearfully.

"They left the battle to care for Joshua. I believe any injuries they have are minor," Sudfad said. "Jasmine, Darla was beaten to death by some of Teivel's men as was a man named Clay."

"Oh my god," Jasmine gasped and started crying.

"My Lord, do you know of my husband?" asked Zelda.

"To my knowledge he is wounded and will be brought here. Raul, Simon, Michael and Matthew are all injured. Raul worse than the others. Edward lost an eye. Archetenus and Jared are both injured but they all will make it. Stephan was seriously injured and is living only because of the Angel Ruth. Thaos was attacked as he tried to help Stephan and Chaez saved him. The list goes on. Maxwell and Luca I will need you to keep your positions as acting commanding generals for a while."

"Of course," Maxwell said.

"Of that core group of freedom fighters only five survived and they are all injured. They will be brought to Wetpr. Now I am not sure I really understood what Simon said about Erebus. Apparently Teivel had a powerful sorcerer that Erebus battled with. Erebus had many injuries and had been transported to Nora. I am not really sure what Erebus said to the Angel Ruth but she returned him to the battle. He told Jared to cut the heart out of a demon. Erebus took the heart and Jared's crystal necklace and somehow sent holiness to all the hell worlds."

"Because of what Erebus did all of the demons that our people were fighting with burst into flames. It was Erebus who ended the battle. But he too started to burn. Archetenus and Jared put the flames out. Erebus is alive but has significant burns to the right side of his body. He too will come here since the underworlds will probably put bounties on him."

"Thedes and King Neputa are both seriously injured," Sudfad said and took a deep breath. "Simon said they were still searching for bodies but so far over one thousand Wetprian soldiers were killed."

Chapter XV
Moments

Since it was late in the evening, Renya and Sudfad left immediately after Sudfad briefed the people in Gabriel's house. Hannah walked the King and Queen to the door and returned to the study where everyone sat in stunned silence.

"I'm going upstairs and finish Thor's room," Diana said sadly. "Hannah I will take care of both of them."

"Do you want some help?" Vivian asked.

"Sure," Diana said and stood up.

"Vivian before you go," Iris said. "I am going to write to Thomas and Sasha and tell them to come home." Iris was trying desperately not to cry.

"We should write to Ratri's and Batina's parents," Hannah said. "They should be here."

"I'll write to Ratri's family," Emeral said. "They are close friends." Then Emeral looked at Jasmine. "I think someone should stay with Jasmine tonight."

"Thank you but I really need to be alone," Jasmine said as tears ran down her face. "Darla came to the hotel to help me prepare for my meeting with Teivel, that's the only reason she was there." Bekka started to cry and walked over to Jasmine and hugged her.

"I lost my best friend in battle too. I know the guilt you feel," Bekka said. "I will stay with you for a little while."

"Let me know when you want to go upstairs," Luca said to Jasmine.

"I am sorry I am so much work," said Jasmine.

"Jasmine you are a hero," Maxwell said and stood up. "I believe we could all use a little wine."

"You know we haven't handed out the gifts that we brought," Natasha said tearfully.

169

"If everyone is back in three days perhaps we should wait." Then Natasha jumped up. "Vivian with all of this going on I forgot. When Raphael and Edward found the bodies of the Patronus priests, they were in a storage room at our castle looking for Raphael's mother's things. He wants you to have them. I don't know what he sent but let me find them."

"Natasha as sad as we all are maybe we should give everyone the gifts that Calen and Misha had made," said Diana.

When Sudfad received his letter, simultaneously letters were received by the ruling families in Lentz and King Manu in the Ice Caves. Both King Manu and King Mathias decided to wait until the morning to present the news to others. Sorren had also sent a letter to Mathias. Sorren wanted to personally meet with the families of those who died in battle. And Sorren was bringing the bodies of the Nordes warriors home.

Vitomas and Annabelle had not stopped crying since they read Simon's letter. What King Sudfad did not tell the people at Gabriel's house was that Simon had included a partial list of names of soldiers who had died in battle. Vitomas and Annabelle wanted to keep busy so they started writing the many letters for the families of the fallen soldiers.

It was almost twenty minutes before Natasha, Diana and Vivian returned to the study. "Batina and Bianca saw these in a store and Calen and Misha had one made for every women in the house," Natasha explained. "They even had ones made up for Renya, Laurel, Vitomas and Annabelle. Maxwell will you take these to the meeting tomorrow?"

"Of course," Maxwell said. "But there are five packages here."

"Look at the names," Diana said with a smile. "Your sons bought you something too."

"Oh, girls these are just beautiful," Emeral said as she held up her bracelet that was made up of jewels and disks containing the names of her family."

"Calen joked that yours would be so heavy you wouldn't be able to lift your arm," Natasha said and helped Emeral clasp the bracelet.

"Every bracelet is different," Diana said as she watched the faces of the women as they opened their gifts. "I am glad we are giving these out now. Everyone is smiling."

"I got a beautiful pocket watch," Maxwell said as he proudly held up his gift for others to see.

Vivian cried when she opened her bracelet. Then she simply stared at the second package. "I don't know..." Vivian didn't finish her sentence; she took the package and carefully opened it.

"Raphael's family was very poor," Natasha said as she walked over to Vivian. "I am sure that any jewelry his mother had was handed down through the family."

Vivian cried as she looked at a golden locket, two bone hair combs and a golden wedding band. "There is a lock of baby hair in the locket," Vivian said and handed the locket to her mother. "I wonder if it is Raphael's hair."

"I am sorry Zelda, we don't have one for you," said Diana.

"Oh my, I would never expect such a thing," Zelda said and paused. "Unless you need me to help here I think I will start cleaning and preparing our new home tomorrow. Can I leave Zack here to play with the other children?"

"Of course," Emeral said. "And some of us will help you."

Hannah was trying to compose herself after she opened her gift. "Tomorrow morning I am going into the city and stock up on food and supplies. We might be so busy with the wounded that we won't have time to do those things later."

"I'll go with you," Diana said. "I need to buy some more things for Thor's room."

Everyone in the room became silent as they again thought about Sudfad's words. "Well I doubt if any of us are going to get any sleep tonight," Emeral said. "I am going to get paper and pens and perhaps we should start writing letters."

Mathas, Fahron and Claudius were all solemn as they gathered in the King's castle for their morning meeting. None of the men spoke as they poured themselves coffee.

"From the looks on your faces I believe you received letters too," Mathas said. "We should compare the information that we have received..." Mathas did not finish his sentence because there was a knock at the door, then Rosa entered the room.

"I am sorry to interrupt Mathias but a group of Rualas are here. They are carrying packs of gifts for the families of many of the soldiers as well as our families."

"Please show them in dear," Mathas said.

Fifteen Ruala warriors entered the study, Bryce was their leader. "So many people felt they might not survive this mission that Gabriel allowed them to purchase gifts for their families. We have packs full of them. Where would you like us to put them because we must return to Ryed," Bryce said.

"The battle is over son," Claudius said. "Why don't all of you join us for our meeting? We were just going to compare the letters we have received."

Rosa was still standing in the doorway of the study, "I will have breakfast prepared for these men." Rosa said and started to turn.

"Rosa would you send soldiers to bring Fahron's and my families here?" asked Claudius. "I am sure that Bella and Isadore will want to help sort and deliver the gifts."

"Is something wrong? Have you heard more news?" Renya asked as Marie led Renya, Laurel, Vitomas and Annabelle into Sudfad's study.

"No dear," Sudfad said. "I will let Maxwell explain."

172

Maxwell walked towards the women smiling. "Calen and Misha had gifts made up for all the women in our family. And they had similar gifts made for all of you because you have done so much for us." As Maxwell spoke he handed each woman a package.

"This is beautiful," Vitomas said as she was the first to open her gift.

"I just love this," Annabelle gushed. "Sudfad look."

"These are wonderful gifts," Renya said. "Thank you. We needed this right now."

Laurel kissed Maxwell on the cheek, "Thank you so much."

"Of course we will thank the boys when we see them," Renya said. The women were all helping each other clasp their bracelets.

"Ladies you are welcome to join us this morning," said Sudfad.

"Erebus how are you feeling?" Rachel asked as she and Horace walked up to Erebus' bed.

"Better than I should, I guess. How's the arm? You are lucky that jolt didn't kill you."

"It will heal but it does hurt a lot," Rachel said. "Erebus I want to introduce you to my father Horace."

Erebus raised his left hand to shake with Horace. "My daughter has told me a great deal about you. I want to thank you for helping my family."

"You have a lovely family; you should be proud. And they are very loyal to you. They never gave up hope."

"Erebus we heard what you did," Rachel said. "Gabriel said that you can't go back to your castle. He said we will be here for a few days so he wants you to make a list of things you want and he will go with some Rualas and get your things. I will write them down, if you want to tell me."

"I think it would be dangerous for any of you to go there now," Erebus said.

"Actually Ruth has made it possible for everyone to retrieve their belongings. We have all of the books and scrolls you brought to help with research."

"Joshua suggested that I purchase a home in Wetpr so I will need some of my money. I would like many of my books but I don't know where I would store them." Erebus paused for a moment. "Both Gabriel and Simon offered to let me stay in their homes until I can walk again."

"That was something that I wanted to talk to you about also," Horace said. "This morning I received a letter from Zelda. Hannah purchased her neighbors' land to increase their pastures. Hannah said we could have the neighbor's house. Zelda said that it is a wonderful house and very large. You took my family in when they didn't have a home. We would like to do the same for you." Rachel smiled proudly as her father spoke.

"Mother said there are seven bedrooms so you could store your things in one of those rooms. And the house is just down the road from Gabriel's house. Emeral and Maxwell fixed up a home for Dagon and me in Gabriel's house so all of us would be really close to each other."

"I think that is very gracious of you, but I might be in pretty bad shape for a while," Erebus said. "I couldn't impose like that."

"Lakin said that King Sudfad built a hospital and that is where all the wounded will go at first. Apparently it will be ready for patients in two days and that is when we are all leaving. So you might be in the hospital for a while," Rachel said. "Then you could stay with us after that. We would really like you to."

Erebus tried to smile but the right side of his face had burns. "I thank you and I will think about it."

"Well plan to store your things in our house at least," Horace said. "Rachel has paper and can start making a list for you."

Ingr was still crying when Claudius' family arrived at the castle of King Mathas. Isadore, April and Sally arrived a few moments later. Once the families arrived, Mathas asked Rosa, Shara and Angelina to join everyone in the study.

"Fifteen Ruala warriors arrived this morning with packs filled with gifts," Mathas said. "They told us that many people felt they would not return from that mission so Gabriel allowed then to go shopping and sent the gifts here. There are gifts for the families of soldiers as well as our families. The Rualas were exhausted so they are now sleeping but all of those huge packs are piled in a room. First we were wondering if all of you would be interested in sorting and distributing the gifts and secondly it turns out not all of our letters contained the same information plus the Rualas told us more so we wanted to give you as much information as we have now."

"Of course we will take care of the gifts," Bella said. "Do you have the names of all our soldiers who were killed?"

"Not yet," Mathas said. "What are you considering?"

"I would really hate to hand a family a gift and give them a death notification at the same time," Bella said. "We need to deliver those gifts today." Bella turned to Ryan, Ingr and Nikki would you be willing to help?"

"Of course," Nikki said. "But are there gifts for people in Wetpr and our tribe too?"

"The gifts for Wetpr have already been delivered to Sudfad's castle," Claudius said. "And it does sound like there are gifts for your tribe. We can have soldiers deliver those if you aren't up for it."

"No, we will take them," Ingr said. "Do you have the names of the warriors we lost?"

"No, Sorren said that he wanted to personally make the notifications," Mathas said then paused. "I will let you read his letter. He sounds as if his heart is broken."

"All of you can read the letters," Fahron said. "We thought we would brief you first."

175

"We'll help too," Sally said. "This is just all so sad."

"In Chaez's last letter he said that Dominic and the other freedom fighters wanted to come here and personally thank us for paying for their educations. Isadore and I invited them all to stay for a while. So perhaps when everyone is healed we can have a celebration. Chaez says he has gotten close with several of these men and his heart goes out to them because they have led such horrible and lonely lives," Fahron said.

The members of the ruling families of Lentz and Sorren's family tried to be cheerful as they distributed gifts to the families of the soldiers and the Nordes warriors. They waited until after all of these gifts were delivered before they opened their own. They gathered in the parlor of Mathas' castle. Rosa served refreshments and they decided to let the children open their gifts first.

Sally and April were surprised at the beautiful jewelry that Chaez sent them. Sorren's young sons proudly held up the fancy knives and sheaths from their father. Margarit was initially happy with the doll and the necklace that Matthew sent for her but her demeanor soon changed. "I miss Matthew," Margarit said sadly.

The room became quiet when Amy opened her gift. "Why, Amy that doll looks just like you," Bella said. Amy clutched the doll in one arm and flew into Nikki's arms and started to cry.

The next two days were insanely busy for Gabriel's household as well as Sudfad's household as they prepared for the arrival of the returning troops. Hannah brought her baby to the castle every day because she and Sudfad were kept busy trying to hire staff and procure all of the needed supplies for the hospital. Sudfad had hired all of the physicians in Salar to help with the work at the hospital. One of Hannah's duties was to create the schedules for the physicians and other staff.

While Mathas did not have a hospital in his kingdom, he too was making arrangements for the care of the returning wounded soldiers. Mathas and Sudfad had corresponded regularly about the hospital that Sudfad was building at Fort Salar. And the second hospital that Sudfad planned to build within the City of Salar. Mathas was more than intrigued with these projects and planned to visit the completed hospitals. Mathas had talked with Fahron and Claudius about building a hospital in Lentz but all three men knew they would need a strong physician with the skills to oversee such an enormous project.

Chaos reigned at the headquarters of the Patronus priests in Nora. The buildings were filled to capacity with wounded warriors; although many of the wounded Ruala and Shettee warriors were already being transported to the Ice Caves. Hundreds of citizens from Nora arrived at the headquarters every day to help with the wounded and the workload.

There was not a single person who had been on the Ryed mission who was not wounded. High Priest Rueben, who was in charge of the Patronus Headquarters in Nora organized burial details. These men worked around the clock digging graves for the thousands of soldiers from Wetpr and Lentz who would never make it home. Gabriel had asked the Angels to transport the bodies of the men and women who died to Nora for burial. There wasn't a leader among Gabriel's army who wanted to leave their dead in the dark kingdom of Ryed.

Simon, Matthew and Michael were gathering the names and possessions of the dead. The possessions were carefully packed so they could be returned to the families. Raul was not able to leave his bed to help because of the multiple knife wounds he had received.

With Ruth's assistance, Gabriel and Raphael were gathering the belongings of the wounded and having them packed for transport to Wetpr and Lentz.

The warriors who had suffered only minor injuries worked day and night to help care for their comrades and to help Simon, Matthew, Michael, Gabriel and Raphael with their projects.

While all of the warriors looked forward to returning to their homes they could not overcome their sadness and grief. The losses were great; hearts and spirits were broken.

Chapter XVI
Aftermath

On the fourth morning after the battle in Ryed, the Angels transported the men and women of Gabriel's armies to their homes. The numbers of wounded Wetprian soldiers filled the new hospital and a good portion of Sudfad's castle. All of the wounded members of Gabriel's team were moved from the hospital to Gabriel's house.

In Lentz, King Mathas had set up two large makeshift hospitals and both of these buildings were filled to capacity. King Manu also had set up a makeshift hospital in the Ice Caves but the majority of wounded Ruala and Shettee warriors had been flown home in small groups so the impact was not as severe as in Wetpr and Lentz. Chaos reigned as family members wanted to see their loved ones while the medical staff were trying to organize and care for the wounded.

"Gabriel I can't leave here with all these wounded," Hannah said as Gabriel kissed her again and again. "Go home and meet your son. Vivian is taking care of both babies. And get some rest you look awful. I will be home as soon as I can."

"I don't ever want to let you go," Gabriel said as he hugged Hannah tightly. "This is the last mission the team will be working on for a while. We all need to stay home and heal and I don't mean just physically."

"Gabriel do you really mean that?"

"Yes, this was a horrible mission."

"I am so glad to hear you say that," Hannah said and kissed him again but their embrace was interrupted.

"Hannah we need Hannah over here," a voice cried out.

"They're here," Christopher yelled. "Nicholas, Cerey, Gabriel is coming. Zack I think your daddy is with them."

"Is Raphael here?" Vivian asked but all of the children had already run out of the house.

Gabriel, Raphael and Horace dismounted from their horses and hugged the children and cried. Zelda ran out of the house and jumped into Horace's arms. The tears were flowing down her face. "I thought I would never see either of you again," Horace said as he hugged his wife and son.

Vivian and Iris walked up to the men. Both women were crying and carrying babies. Vivian was so emotional she couldn't talk as she put Robert in Raphael's arms. Gabriel put Nicholas and Cerey down and stared with awe as Iris walked up to him and put Daniel in his arms. Within moments the members of the team who were not taking care of wounded came to the front lawn to greet Gabriel, Raphael and Horace.

Thedes and King Neputa were two of the first Shettee warriors to be flown to the Ice Caves. Both men had serious wounds and were originally put into the makeshift hospital. Since Ibula was a healer she was caring for many of the warriors in the hospital besides her husband.

"Ibula you look exhausted; you need to rest," Thedes said with concern. "You are pregnant you can't overdo it."

"Thedes I am fine," Ibula said as she was cleaning his wounds. "I think you will be able to go home in a day or two. But you will have to be careful; which means you can't carry the boys."

"I understand," Thedes said with a grin.

"I believe you understand," Ibula said as she smiled. "But it is whether you will follow my orders that concerns me."

The adult members of the ruling families of Lentz were at the makeshift hospitals taking care of the wounded. King Mathas walked among his soldiers with a heavy heart when he saw their broken bodies.

"Shara will you please look at Stephan?" Ingr called as tears ran down her cheeks. "Can we take him home?" Both Matthew and Thaos were wounded but their wounds were minor and both men were able to walk, whereas Stephan was bedridden.

Shara walked up to Stephan's bed which was nothing more than one of the hundreds of cots in the building. She carefully cut off his bandages and looked at his wounds. When Stephan saw the look on Shara's face he said, "The Angel Ruth did something to me to help me heal."

"I think she did quite a lot for you," Shara said. "Stephan you could easily have died from this." Shara turned to Bella and Ingr. "I am telling you because I know Stephan won't do as I say. This is a serious injury. He must stay in bed for several days and he can't lift anything not even the babies."

"Stephan do you hear that?" Ingr asked anxiously. "Now you do what Shara says."

"Oh he will," Bella said. "We brought a boca to take you home in.

"Mother I am not hurt that badly," Chaez said as Isadore, Sally and April hovered around him. "I can go home. You should probably help with the others."

"Chaez don't you tell me what to do," Isadore said. "You are my first child to come back from battle. Wait until you have children and you will understand."

"I am sorry Mother; I didn't mean to hurt your feelings," Chaez said guiltily.

"I know dear," she said and hugged Chaez again. "Your father is helping with the wounded. When he is done, we will take you home then I am coming back here to work."

"We can stay here and help," Sally said. "Why don't you stay with Chaez?"

"Do you girls know what to do?" asked Isadore.

"Angelina and Shara can tell us," said Sally.

"April now be honest with me; do you think you can do this?" Isadore asked.

"Yes," April said sincerely. "I want to help; this is all so sad."

"What are you doing?" Misha asked when he saw Maxwell and Diana helping Thor into the bedroom.

"I am putting you both in the same room for the day," Diana said. "You can keep each other company and it will be easier for me to take care of you."

"Ok but he's not spending the night with me," Misha said and tried to grin.

"I should hope not," Thor said and chuckled as Maxwell helped him into bed.

"Maxwell don't they look cute together?" Diana asked teasingly.

"Like two peas in a pod," Maxwell said and laughed.

"Maxwell did you notice how upset Melinda got when she saw that Thor was hurt?" Diana asked and giggled. "She's coming back later to help me take care of them."

"Diana do you ever stop with the matchmaking?" Misha asked with a grin.

"I'm telling the truth," Diana said. "Thor you are awfully quiet." Thor shook his head and smiled.

"Iris you need to come upstairs," Bianca said as she ran into the kitchen. "Joshua is practically fighting with Micha because he wants to get out of bed."

"I'll help," Luca said as he, Iris and Bianca ran up the stairs.

"Joshua what are you thinking?" Iris yelled as she ran into the room and saw Micha trying to hold his father in the bed.

"I can't stay in bed," Joshua said angrily.

"Joshua just stop and look at me," demanded Iris. "Hannah said there is a lot of damage to your back and if everything doesn't heal right you might never be able to walk again. Now do you want that?"

"I didn't know that," Joshua said as he stopped struggling.

"If you force me to I will keep you drugged until you heal," Iris said sternly. "Now are you going to do as we tell you?"

"I didn't realize it was that serious," Joshua said. "I will stay in bed but I will go crazy without something to do."

"Vivian knows you so well that she already made arrangements for Padre Markle to tutor you. He will be here tomorrow," said Iris.

"Alright," Joshua said reluctantly.

"Mother I have never heard you like that before," Micha said with a grin and kissed Iris on the cheek.

"They're both sleeping," Emeral said as Natasha walked into Ratri's and Batina's bedroom. "I gave them the pain tonic."

"Take a break," Natasha said. "I will watch them for a while. Their families are coming so that will help. It may be a while before either of them are on their feet."

"Are you still mad at me?" Raul asked as Vitomas brought a tray of food to his bed.

"Raul you act like this is a joke," Vitomas said emotionally. "You have come close to being killed several times just since I have known you and you have children now. You need to start thinking about them once in a while. We are all so sad when you are gone," Vitomas paused. "And I don't want to have to explain to them that their papa isn't coming back. Just think about that." Vitomas sat on the edge of the bed and tears ran down her cheeks.

"Jasmine," a letter came for you," Bekka said as she walked into Jasmine's bedroom.

"I feel so useless," Jasmine said sadly. "Raphael and Gabriel came to see me. They said that the Angel sent everyone to their homes. I was hoping that Sorren would take me home."

"Jasmine, you are in no shape to travel," Bekka said and sat down in a chair next to the bed.

"I wanted to go to the funerals," Jasmine said and started to cry as she opened her letter. "Bekka, Hannah wrote to my parents and asked them to come and stay with me. They are coming with Batina's parents."

"Why do you sound so surprised?" asked Bekka.

"I am surprised that Hannah wrote to them."

"Why? Jasmine I don't know if you want to be on the team after all this but everyone thinks of you as a member. Your parents should be here so you don't have to go through this alone."

"Darla and I asked to be on the team and Gabriel told us to get our parent's approval. We never got a chance to write to them," Jasmine said with tears in her eyes.

"Do you still want to be on the team?"

"I don't know," Jasmine said softly.

Ryan drove the boca to the front door of the castle of Claudius. Then Ryan got down and walked to the passenger side of the boca and helped Bella down. Thaos dismounted his horse and called to some soldiers to help carry Stephan into the castle. Ingr and Nikki rode in the back of the boca with Stephan.

The front door of the castle opened as Nikki's mother tried to stop Amy from running out the door. "Papa, Papa," Amy screamed loudly as she ran to Thaos and jumped into his arms. Amy was sobbing as she and Thaos hugged and kissed.

Then Amy pulled back so she could look in Thaos' face. She slapped his shoulder and scolded, "Don't leave us again."

Thaos laughed and kissed Amy again, "I don't want to Honey."

Amy suddenly looked scared and asked, "Where is Uncle Stephan?"

Thaos was holding Amy and now turned so she could see the soldiers carrying Stephan into the house. "Amy, Uncle Stephan is hurt so you can't jump on him," Thaos explained as he walked up to Nikki and put his arm around her. The family walked into the castle, following the soldiers who were carrying Stephan.

Thaos set Amy down as Nikki's mother handed him baby Titus. A few minutes later Ingr opened the bedroom door and told the family they could come in and visit Stephan, who was sitting up in bed. Stephan was not wearing a shirt so his massive bandages were visible. Amy walked up to the bed and gently touched Stephan's arm. "I missed you Uncle Stephan," Amy whispered.

"You don't have to whisper," Ingr said and smiled.

"I missed you too Amy," Stephan said and smiled as she held his hand and cried.

Hannah, Cassandra, Elan, Koby, Calen, Dagon and Rachel came home from the hospital for the midday meal. "Every one of you looks exhausted," Emeral said as the group entered the dining room.

"Cassandra, Elan and I will be returning after we eat," Hannah said. "But I want the rest of you to stay here and get some rest." Hannah looked at Calen and the others as she spoke.

"Don't worry about anything here," Ella said as she was setting the table.

"They haven't set their sons down since they came home," Vivian said to Hannah as Raphael, Vivian and Gabriel entered the dining room. Both men were proudly holding their babies.

185

Gabriel kissed Hannah then said, "I can't believe how much these boys look alike."

"Now that Daniel's hair is starting to curl it is easier to tell them apart," Hannah said and smiled. "At first Vivian and I were afraid we would get them mixed up."

Diana came out of the kitchen carrying a tray of food, "Just so you know we didn't give the gifts out after we heard everyone was coming home."

"Where are they?" asked Koby.

"I can show you when I come back down; I have to get another tray," Diana said.

"I'll show them," Luca said. "Then I'll get Jasmine."

"Where are my parents?" asked Rachel.

"Zelda and Zack are showing Horace your new house," Ella said. "It will be nice having them live so close. Zelda and Zack fit right in." Rachel smiled at Ella's comment.

"Oh my," Emeral said. "With everything going on we forgot. Dagon, Rachel you haven't seen the home we prepared for you. Maxwell how could we have forgotten that?"

Maxwell put his arm around Emeral's shoulders and kissed her cheek. "Dear we can show them now. Does everyone want to come up and see it?" Maxwell asked. Emeral and Maxwell led the family up the stairs.

An hour later Dack and Joao walked into the dining room. Both young men had been greatly affected by Darla's death and neither of them wanted to tell Jasmine the details. This moment was the first time they entered Gabriel's house since they were transported back to Wetpr.

The dining room was filled as everyone was eating the midday meal. Both Dack and Joao stopped and stared when they saw Jasmine, who was sitting next to Luca.

Neither Dack nor Joao were aware of the significant injuries Jasmine had incurred during the mission. They were now shocked to see her bandages and braces.

Jasmine was facing the door and saw her two friends immediately. The three young warriors all stared at each other then Jasmine started to cry. Both Joao and Dack ran to Jasmine and hugged her.

"What happened to you?" asked Joao.

Jasmine was crying too hard to speak so Luca said proudly "She will have to tell you the details but she jumped from a moving carriage after she drugged and stabbed Teivel."

"What!" Joao said. "How did we not hear about this?"

"I thought I told you," Gabriel said. "I am sorry. I think we were all so overwhelmed in the aftermath of that mission."

"Where have you been?" asked Natasha.

"We were helping at hospital," Dack said and kissed Jasmine on the forehead.

"I am sorry I am crying," Jasmine said as she wiped the tears from her cheeks. "I have been like this since I heard about Darla."

"I know," Joao said. "Honestly Dack and I didn't want to see you right away because we didn't want to have to tell you the details."

"You were there?" asked Jasmine.

"Yes when we found the body," Dack said angrily.

"Perhaps the three of you should have a long talk after lunch," Emeral suggested and glanced at the children who were all watching Jasmine, Joao and Dack.

Dack turned and looked at the children's table. "You're right," he said and took his seat at the table.

Hugo and Greta were originally planning to go to Wetpr with Thomas and Sasha after the family received Iris' letter; but just before they were to leave the village, Hugo received a letter from his brother Sorren. Hugo and Greta prepared the village's Great Hall for the bodies of the warriors who Sorren was bringing home.

Sorren had asked his brother not to speak of the deaths because he wanted to give the death notifications in person. Other members of the village saw Hugo and Greta preparing the room and they too helped; fearfully no one asked questions.

This morning the Angels transported the members of the Nordes Tribe to the Kingdom of Lentz. While many were sent to the hospitals, Sorren and fifteen bodies of his warriors appeared in the Great Hall. Several women were in the hall arranging bouquets of flowers. They gasped when everyone appeared.

"Please get Hugo and Greta," Sorren said.

One of the women hugged Sorren then left the building. The other two women also hugged their chief. "We will start preparing the bodies," one of the women said with tears running down her cheeks.

"I wanted to tell the families in person," Sorren said sadly. "Many of our warriors are injured and they are either at the King's hospitals or at Gabriel's home in Wetpr. After I meet with the families, I want to have a meeting of the tribe."

Chapter XVII
To Honor

Archetenus re-fractured his leg in the battle in the City of Teivel. Other than the broken leg he suffered only minor cuts and bruises. Jared was not so lucky. A demon had tried to cut Jared's throat. Jared killed the demon but not before the demon stabbed Jared twice in his chest. Because of the injuries that Archetenus and Jared sustained, Renya moved them and their families into chambers on the first floor of the castle.

Edward lost his left eye in a battle with two demons. Had Dominic not come to his aide Edward would have lost his life. Edward had thick bandages around his head and his wound affected his sense of balance so Renya moved Edward to chambers on the first floor also.

Of the original group of freedom fighters only Dominic, Fennel, Seth, Noah and Lawrence survived the battle in the City of Teivel. All five of these men were wounded. Simon and Michael transported them from the hospital at Fort Salar to Sudfad's castle where they were given individual chambers.

Dominic was in his late twenties with dark curly hair and brown eyes. His body bore many scars from battle. His brother Fennel was three years younger with light curly brown hair and brown eyes. Seth was a cousin to Dominic and Fennel. Seth was a soft spoken man in his early twenties with brown hair and green eyes. Noah was the oldest of the group. He was in his mid-thirties with black hair and brown eyes. And Lawrence was in his mid-twenties with red hair and blues eyes.

This handful of warriors were all men of integrity and courage. They had sacrificed all they had to stand up to a totalitarian regime. These men felt both in awe and out of place in their luxurious chambers in Sudfad's castle because they had spent years living in caves to evade the armies of Teivel.

Dominic and his followers had been idealistic men in their youth. On this day as Sudfad and Renya met the freedom fighters of Ryed; the King and Queen saw the sadness and loneness in the eyes of these warriors.

"They seem so lost," Renya said as she and Sudfad returned to the King's study. "Sudfad isn't there more that we can do for them?"

The following morning a small group of people from the Nordes Tribe arrived at the house of Gabriel. Thomas and Sasha, Edgar and Cora, Batina's parents, and Leta and Conrad who were the parents of Jasmine. The reunion was emotional for all of the family members; especially for Edgar and Cora because they were not prepared for what they found. Both Ratri and Batina had suffered multiple stab wounds; had the Angels not given them healing energy both of these brave warriors would have died.

Because of the extent of Ratri's and Batina's injuries, Hannah kept them heavily medicated. Members of Gabriel's household were taking turns sitting with Ratri and Batina so they would not reopen any wounds.

It was Hannah, not Jasmine who wrote to Leta and Conrad telling them of Jasmine's injuries and the death of her best friend. Jasmine experienced a wide range of emotions when she saw her parents.

"Child why didn't you tell us?" Conrad asked as he hugged his only daughter.

"I was going to write but I was on a lot of pain medication at first and then after I heard about Darla I couldn't stop crying. I wasn't trying to hide anything from you," Jasmine said between sobs.

Leta was sitting on the side of the bed and stroking Jasmine's hair. "Hannah didn't tell us everything about your mission but she said that everyone on the team is so proud of you. She said you are a hero. Jasmine know that your father and I are always proud of you. Do you feel up to telling us what happened?"

"Well you certainly look better than I thought you would," Thomas said as he and Sasha walked into Joshua's bedroom.

"Micha said Mother had to threaten you to keep you in bed. I wish I could have heard that," Thomas said as he hugged his father. Sasha kissed Joshua on the cheek.

"I am glad to see you two," Joshua said. "Yes, Iris told me that if I don't heal right I could be crippled. Thank god Vivian made arrangements for one of the Patronus priests to tutor me or I would lose my mind. You know I can't stand to sit around."

Sasha started to laugh, "Thomas predicted you would say those exact same words."

"Well, we are moving in here for a while," Thomas said as he moved a chair closer to Joshua's bed. "Got time to tell us what happened?"

When Ratri's parents, Joseph and Clair, arrived later that afternoon they found both Edgar and Cora sitting next to the bed of Ratri and Batina. Both patients were sleeping. Clair started to cry when she saw her children.

"Edgar why don't you take Joseph and Clair down to the dining room and tell them what happened," Cora said. "I will stay here."

"There are four other bedrooms in these chambers," Edgar said. "Why don't you choose your room and put those packs down first."

Sorren spent his first day back in his village giving death notifications to the families of the fallen warriors. Normally Shara would have been at his side for such solemn proceedings but she had not left the hospital where she and Angelina were taking care of the wounded soldiers and warriors.

Sorren had been a warrior since an early age. He had seen a great deal of death in his lifetime and it never got easier for him. The deaths of these warriors were particularly difficult for him; one, because of the young ages of many of the warriors.

And two because he had personally asked some of the warriors to join the mission in Ryed. While Sorren always felt responsible for his people, that emotion was now weighing heavily on his heart.

It was late at night on that first day; that Sorren held a meeting with all the members of the village after the death notifications were given to the families. Now on this second day after Sorren's return; the entire village was preparing for the funerals. Women were preparing the bodies and gathering flowers as men were digging the graves. The entire village was in mourning.

Just before noon, King Mathas, Claudius, Fahron and their families led a small caravan into the village of the Nordes Tribe. Soren was as surprised as the rest of the villagers to see the leaders of the kingdom riding down the main street of the village.

"Sorren we would like you to gather the members of your tribe for a meeting," Mathas said as he dismounted his horse.

Sorren turned to a couple of villagers and told them to gather everyone then he turned back to the King. "Mathas is something wrong?" Sorren asked with concern.

"Only with this world," Mathas said with a heavy heart. "The deaths of so many of our people are weighing heavily upon me."

Since the bodies of the dead filled the Great Hall the meeting was held at the training field of the village. King Mathas, Claudius and Fahron stood in front of the large group of people.

"Sorren please come up here with us," Mathas said then he turned to the group. "I hope that everyone will be able to hear us. We have come this day to honor your tribe and your families for service to our kingdom. Over the last two years members of your tribe have fought valiantly in numerous battles to protect this kingdom. In addition your warriors have fought to protect other peoples from the darkness that would overtake us all."

"The actions we take today will not bring back our dead or heal our wounded but we hope to honor those among you," Mathas said to the villagers then he turned to Sorren. "Sorren will you please stand before me?" Sorren was surprised by the King's request.

192

Mathas pulled his sword from its sheath and as he spoke he touched both of Sorren's shoulders with the blade. "Sorren from this day forward you are one of the ruling members of the Kingdom of Lentz. You will sit with Claudius and Fahron and share the responsibilities and benefits of such a position."

Fabron stepped forward and handed Sorren a sheathed sword. The handle of the sword as well as the sheath contained the crest of the Royal Family and the colors of the kingdom. Sorren was speechless as he was presented with this gift.

Fahron returned to the side of the King and Claudius stepped forward and handed Sorren a scroll. "This is a deed to greatly increase your land holdings. You now own a percentage of the diamond mines." As Claudius spoke, Matthew walked forward and handed Sorren three large leather pouches of gold coins. "Sorren this is but a small payment for your service to this kingdom. We have brought payment also, for the men and women who have also served this kingdom but we will need you to call them forward. But before that, will you turn and face your people."

Everyone in the village applauded and yelled war cries when Sorren turned around. Matthew motioned to the soldiers behind him and several now carried large chests of gold coins off the bocas and brought them to the King. Rosa, Bella and Isadore now walked to the front of the group and stood with their husbands. Each woman was holding a large basket.

King Mathas again spoke, "We have recently designed two different medals for our soldiers and warriors. One medal is to be awarded to those who have fought in battles to protect our kingdom and the second medal will be awarded to those who have volunteered for the many dangerous missions we have performed. Sorren will you turn around so we can award you both of these medals then will you assist us in presenting these honors upon your people?"

It took over three hours for the members of the Nordes Tribe to receive their medals and pouches of gold coins.

Sorren, as most of the villagers was both proud and overwhelmed by the presentations. When the last presentation was made the entire village applauded again.

"It is our understanding," King Mathas said. "That your tribe holds a feast after funerals. Since all of these brave warriors died in service to this kingdom we have brought provisions for your feast. If you could just tell the soldiers where you would like these things put."

Again there was applause from the villagers. Sorren turned and shook hands with Mathas, Claudius, Fahron and Matthew. "Thank you for these honors," Sorren said emotionally. "We have all been so overwhelmed by the deaths that this brings light back into our hearts." Then Sorren kissed Rosa, Bella and Isadore on their cheeks.

Shara, Angelina, Nikki and Ingr did not attend the ceremonies at their village because they were busy taking care of the wounded and the dying. Ryan, Sally and April assisted the women in their duties. But there were many others who also worked at the hospital for the need was great.

Mid-afternoon these seven people took a break to hastily eat a late lunch. Exhaustion consumed them and there was little talking among their group. Sally and April kept looking at each other.

"Is something the matter?" Angelina asked. "You two look like there is something on your minds. If this is too much for you; you don't have to help."

"Oh no, that is not it at all," Sally said. "In fact it is just the opposite. We want to ask you something but we haven't said anything to Isadore and Fahron yet."

As Sally was still talking, April blurted out, "If our parents approve will you train us to be healers?" Everyone at the table smiled as April continued. "They ask us all of the time what we would like to study. Sally and I decided we would like to study medicine and help people like you do."

194

"Angelina and I would be proud to have you as students," Shara said. "And I believe that Isadore and Fahron will be very pleased with your choices. Would you like us to come with you when you ask them; that way we can explain the training?"

Both Sally and April got big smiles on their faces. "That would be wonderful," Sally said.

"Angelina, Claudius told us that Mathas wants to build a real hospital but he needs to find someone to oversee the project; like Hannah is doing in Wetpr. Maybe you and Shara should talk to him," Ingr said.

"I know Mathas has been writing back and forth with Sudfad about the hospital in Wetpr," Angelina said. "But I didn't realize he had made a decision."

"Claudius said anyone can build a building," Ryan said. "But they need someone with medical experience to set everything up and to help hire people. This is the first time I have really watched you two work, I think you both have the experience. But it would probably take up a lot of your time."

Angelina looked at Shara and asked with a grin, "Mother would you like to have an audience with the King?"

"Yes but we should probably talk with your father first."

Chapter XVIII
Healing

"What?" Shara asked loudly when Sorren arrived at the hospital that evening to tell her that they were now one of the ruling families of the Kingdom of Lentz. "Sorren, really I am not sure I understand what you are saying, tell me again." In that moment Shara saw April walking through the large room. "April, I need you to get the girls and bring them here."

"Is something wrong?" asked April.

"No," Sorren said with hearty laugh. Sorren showed Shara the medals he had received while they waited for Angelina, Ingr and Nikki.

"What is the matter?" Angelina asked as the three young women quickly walked to Shara and Sorren. Ryan saw the group gathering and also joined them as did Sally and April.

The first thing all of these people noticed was that Sorren was smiling because he had seemed so broken after his return from Ryed. "Now that the family is here," Sorren said with a big smile. "I have much to tell you. Early this morning Mathas led a caravan into the village and asked me to gather everyone. We met on the training field. Mathas, Claudius and Fahron presented me with these medals and made me one of the ruling men of the kingdom. I will be sharing duties with Claudius and Fahron. Then Matthew hands me a fortune in gold coins..."

"Mathew! He didn't tell me about any of this," Angelina said loudly.

"Oh, there is more. Shara we were given a deed to land that includes part of the diamond mines. Then after I received these honors, Rosa, Bella and Isadore stood next to their husbands with baskets of medals. They asked me to call the villagers forward and Matthew would hand them a bag of gold coins and the others were awarding medals to our people."

"Did any of you know about this?" Angelina asked those around her. Everyone responded 'no'. "I can't believe they kept this a secret."

"I am still not sure I understand all of this," Shara said in amazement.

"We are one of the ruling families of the kingdom now," Sorren said. "All of you have been working around the clock since the warriors returned. Mathas would like to have us all at the castle for dinner to celebrate. Do you think you could leave for a while? And I am talking to all of you," Sorren said as he looked at the faces of the young people gathered around him."

"Of course we can," Angelina said as she could see her mother was stunned by the news. "There are many others here now to help and the real emergencies have been taken care of."

"Sorren will Fahron and Isadore be there?" asked Sally.

"Yes."

"Shara could we ask them or would you prefer we wait?" Sally asked.

"I am sorry I think I am in shock by all of this," Shara said. "Of course we can talk to them." Shara said to Sally then turned to Sorren. "Since the girls have been helping us here they decided they want to study medicine and become healers. They have to ask Fahron and Isadore."

"I think your parents will be proud of your decisions," Sorren said to Sally and April. "We have much to celebrate."

That evening during the celebration at King Mathas' castle Sorren was told that he received the position as a ruling member of the kingdom not only for his dedication, service and leadership skills but also because of the threats against the people of Lentz.

It was not surprising to the leaders of both the kingdoms of Lentz and Wetpr that rumors of retaliation from both the Insidiae and demons against those involved in the mission in Ryed were surfacing.

But the Kingdom of Lentz had additional threats to be concerned with. There were rumblings that the warlord Usman of the Valdore Tribe was not going to allow the Nordes Tribe and King Mathas to form an alliance. In addition, the day before the armies were returned from the Kingdom of Ryed a trade ship docked in the port city of Langer.

The few remaining crew members on this ship were seriously wounded and said they had been attacked by a ship of creatures from the Continent of Tansof. The sailors said they had been trading with villagers along the western coastline of Tansof and recognized the creatures as being from the Dura Tribe. The sailors said that although they had no problems in Tansof this ship of creatures followed them for days but did not attack until the sailors were close to the Kingdom of Lentz.

While the sailors said they did not understand why the creatures waited so long to attack them, the ruling families of Lentz understood that the creatures of the Dura Tribe were sending them a message. Two decades earlier the Dura Tribe had launched a violent and savage offensive against the people of Lentz. The war lasted for almost two years and took a great toll on both the Kingdom of Lentz and the vicious Dura Tribe.

Usman took advantage of the attack and also declared war on King Mathas' regime. Now as it appeared that history might repeat itself, Mathas, Claudius, Fahron and Sorren wondered if there was an alliance between the Valdore Tribe and the Dura Tribe.

"We need to discuss the timing and manner in which we make the announcement about Sorren," Claudius said. "Because we should be prepared for an attack from Usman."

"I agree," Mathas said. "And it is Sorren's people who will likely be attacked first. Sorren I know that some of your people were opposed to soldiers patrolling the lands between your tribes, but I feel we should increase the presence of the military."

"Usman has spies everywhere," Thaos said. "If you increase the military presence he will know something has changed. Perhaps it is time for a few of us to frequent the bars where Usman's men hang out."

"Stephan is too weak," Ingr said. "He barely made it here for dinner. And besides doesn't everyone know who you are now? Do you really think Usman's men will talk in front of you?"

"Actually I have been thinking about that," Thaos said. "Dominic and his men want to come here to meet all of you. I know Fahron and Isadore are planning on having a big celebration for them but what do you say we ask them to spy for us first? Hell after the lives they lived in Ryed, Usman's men are nothing."

"I like that idea," Matthew said. "But all of those guys are wounded. And after losing Asher and the others they may not be up to it."

"Let's write them a letter tonight," Stephan said. "I bet they will do it but we will need to know how long it will be before they are healed enough."

"I already have chambers prepared for them," Isadore said. "Do you think spies are watching our homes?"

"I think we live in a time when there are probably spies everywhere," Fahron said. "Those boys will stay with us like we planned but we should postpone the big celebration if they will work with us."

"Well, I am looking forward to meeting those boys," Bella said. "I was hoping we could host something too."

"I believe we all want to meet them and we should be able to do smaller gatherings like this," Mathas said. "It is my understanding that Chaez will be returning with them; perhaps we can say they are Chaez's friends from school."

Stephan, Thaos and Matthew all started to grin. "Dominic and his men look like hired fighters," Stephan said. "That story may not work."

"Speaking of school," Sorren said with a grin and winked at April and Sally. "Fahron and Isadore your daughters have been waiting all night to tell you something."

199

Sally and April started to grin as everyone at the table now looked at them. "Girls do you want to talk in private?" Fahron asked.

"No," Sally said and looked at April with excitement. "Both of you have been asking us what we want to study in school and we finally decided."

"We love working with Shara and Angelina and we want to be healers too," April said enthusiastically.

"They have been doing very well," Shara said. "And you might say they jumped right into the fire helping us with all of the wounded."

"Some of the injuries were horrible," Nikki said. "But Sally and April didn't hesitate and kept asking us for more to do."

Isadore got out of her chair and hugged both of her daughters, "Why, I am just so proud of both of you."

"We both are," Fahron said with a big smile. "Shara, Angelina I will pay you for their training."

"You will do no such thing," Shara said. "They are family too and I think it pleases all of us that they want to become healers."

"Calen will you stay in bed!" Natasha said loudly. "You need to rest to heal."

"I am healing just fine and you know I can't stand to lay around," Calen said. "Besides there is work to do."

"Calen you are in no shape to work."

"What I want to do will not be strenuous," Calen said with a grin. "Since we have another baby coming I want to draw up plans to make a few changes to our chambers and I was thinking of doing the same for Misha and Diana."

"What sort of changes?"

"It will be a surprise."

"You have company," Emeral called out as she knocked on the door to the chambers of Calen and Natasha.

"Come in," Calen yelled. "Mother when do you have to knock?"

"I thought it was appropriate since I have part of the Royal Family with me," Emeral said with a coy smile.

Emeral, Renya, Laurel, Vitomas and Annabelle walked into the small parlor where Calen and Natasha were standing.

"Emeral tell your son to stay in bed," Natasha said then laughed. All the women smiled at this comment.

"We won't keep you," Renya said. "We just wanted to thank you for the beautiful gifts. And we received them at the perfect time."

"I am glad that you like them," Calen said. "You have done so much for our family that the bracelets are really nothing."

"We love them," Vitomas said. "They are beautiful and sentimental."

"We want to thank Misha too," Renya said to Emeral.

Calen and Natasha both laughed loudly, "You might want to wait on that," Calen said. "It might not be safe to go in there."

"What do you mean?" asked Annabelle.

"During the day Diana puts Thor and Misha in the same room so they can keep each other company and play cards," Emeral explained and started to grin. "Those two men are so bored that they have been acting like little kids and Diana is fit to be tied."

"Yesterday they were taking the apples out of their fruit basket and throwing them at the vases of flowers in the room, then they made bets on where the glass would splatter," Natasha said with a big grin. "Thank god Calen isn't that bad."

"Stay in bed!" Diana yelled as she marched into the bedroom. "Misha you aren't supposed to be walking yet."

"I'm helping him," Thor said with a mischievous grin.

"Oh, like that is any better. I hope you two are healed before the babies come because I can't take care of four children! What are you laughing at?" Diana turned around and saw Emeral, Renya, Natasha, Vitomas, Laurel and Annabelle standing in the doorway. "I am sorry you had to hear that," Diana said to the women then she laughed. "Emeral I am ready to tie your sons up."

"I think we could help you with that," Emeral said with a grin and walked up to Misha and Thor. "Diana is right, if you break open your wounds you will just be in bed longer. Do I have to spank you boys?" Everyone laughed at this comment.

"Alright," Thor said and laughed loudly again.

"Actually I would like to see that," Misha said and grinned as Emeral helped him back to bed.

"Diana, you can certainly come for a visit if you need to get away from these two," Annabelle said and giggled.

"Actually I just thought of something," Renya said with a voice of authority. "Diana would you get some paper and pens?" As Diana was leaving the bedroom Renya continued, "We came over to thank you for the wonderful gifts; we all love them."

"You're welcome," Misha said and laughed. "We had that poor jeweler so confused because there were so many orders and every bracelet was different. We gave him a good tip."

"Well, we really appreciate them," Laurel said.

Diana returned to the bedroom and handed the paper and pens to Renya who took the items and walked up to the bed where Misha and Thor were sitting. "The Learning Center will be opening soon and both of you will be instructors so start working on your lessons and the lists of supplies you will need," Renya said and handed the men the paper and pens.

"What are we supposed to teach?" asked Misha.

"Well, you wanted courses for the new members of our team," Emeral said. "And Raul said all you boys were going to teach about our culture and fighting styles."

202

"And anything else that you can think of," Renya said.

"I already have an idea about what I will be teaching," Thor said. "My question is will I be teaching adults or children?"

"Now that we have everyone home we need to have some meetings about all of this," Renya said. "I would suggest that you draw up lessons for both."

"Actually that brings up something else that we wanted to talk to all of you about," Vitomas said. "We know that you have some of the Patronus priests holding school for the children in the house. But the building is completed for the children's classes. We have the furniture and supplies. We thought it might be fun to have the children paint the walls in a couple of rooms like you did with your playroom here. And we were wondering if you would like to help decorate."

"Right now we are only starting out with two classrooms for the children. One for the young ones and the other for the older children. And you still have to pick out the rooms you want for training your team," Annabelle said.

"Well, let's go downstairs and meet with everyone," said Emeral. "I believe we could all use a nice diversion like this."

"Diana go with them," Thor said. Diana gave Thor such a disapproving look that both Misha and Thor roared with laughter which caused them to both wince with pain. "I am serious. You know the types of things I will be teaching so you should help set up the training rooms. We will be good, I promise," Thor said with a grin.

"Why don't I believe you?" Diana asked and laughed. "But you are right. Now if you two can behave I will bring you some treats."

"Feel up to company?" Gabriel asked as he and Raphael walked into Dominic's chambers. Fennel, Seth, Noah and Lawrence were all sitting with Dominic.

"Yes, please come in," Dominic said and started to get out of bed.

"No, please don't get up," Raphael said. "But we are glad to see all of you up and walking around."

"Some of us still need a little help," Seth said with a shy grin.

"Do you think you would feel well enough to come over for dinner tomorrow night?" Gabriel asked. "Sudfad said you could ride in one of the carriages. And if you start feeling badly, my wife is a physician," Gabriel added with a grin.

"Our family has heard so much about all of you that they want to meet you," Raphael said. 'But be honest if you aren't ready to travel yet."

Dominic and his men all looked at each other then Dominic said. "We would have to take the carriage, most of us aren't ready to ride yet but I believe we could make it. Thank you."

"No, it is our pleasure," Gabriel said. "So have you had a chance to walk around the castle yet?"

"No," Fennel said. "This is pretty much the first time we have been out of bed for more than a couple of minutes. But people keep coming to visit us and everyone is so nice."

"Chaez showed us a letter from his parents," Dominic said. "We are planning to visit them so we can thank them for paying for our educations. Chaez's mother already has rooms prepared for us and they want to have a big celebration when we get there."

"You will like them," Raphael said. "In fact, I think you will get along well with all of the members of the ruling families. Do you have any idea how long you will be there?"

"No, why?" asked Dominic.

"Because the Patronus training facility is almost finished. High Priest Nicholas has sent a list of applicants and we are trying to figure out a time frame to start the training. Now, of course if you want to wait until the following session you certainly can; especially since you are all injured," Raphael explained.

"We originally planned to start training in two weeks but so many of our men are injured that it may be more like two months now," Gabriel said. "Many of the men who were with us are also the instructors."

"We should all be in good shape in two months," Fennel said. "How long of a ride is it from here to Lentz?"

"Three days each way," Raphael said. "But I would plan to be there for a couple of weeks because knowing King Mathas and the others they will have a lot planned for you."

Chapter XIX
The Dinner Party

"Hannah so what do you think?" Ratri asked with a hopeful smile. "Batina and I are going crazy being stuck in bed."

"I think you two can start getting out of bed and walking, but only with your parents helping you and for short periods of time," Hannah said. "You both lost a great deal of blood and I doubt if you realize how weak you are."

"We will make them mind," Edgar said and winked at Joseph and Clair.

"Now on another note," Hannah said. "Since everyone is doing better we are having a dinner party here tomorrow night. We want all of you there which means Ratri and Batina you can't over do it."

"Do you need help?" Clair asked.

"Actually yes if you wouldn't mind," Hannah said to Cora and Clair then she turned to the men. "Joseph and Edgar since most of the men in the house are injured would you mind helping with something? Alexander will be delivering some tables for the party and will need help bringing them in."

"Of course," Joseph said. "We can help with other things also."

"Joseph I didn't bring anything to wear to a party," Clair said. "We will need to go shopping."

Batina's face lit up and she asked, "Hannah did Natasha find my packages?"

"Yes, they are on the table in the parlor. Now I have to check on Jasmine," Hannah said and turned to leave the room.

"Hannah how is Jasmine doing?" Cora asked. "We haven't spent much time with her."

"She has a lot of injuries and they are healing fine but she is very depressed about Darla. She feels guilty even though she has no reason to."

"Can we visit her?" Ratri asked.

"Her room is too far away for you to walk but perhaps someone could carry her here," Hannah said and left the room.

"Mother, Father would you bring the packages from the parlor?" Batina asked excitedly. "Then we need all of you to stay in here."

"What on earth is all of this?" Cora asked as she and Edgar piled armloads of packages on the bed.

"Natasha gave us spending money and ordered us to shop so Ratri and I have gifts for all of you because you have done so much for us. We have toys and clothes for my brothers and sisters too so we will have to sort this out. Actually could all of you turn your backs for a moment?" Batina asked and giggled as she and Ratri emptied the packages."

"You can turn around now," Ratri said after a few moments. "I want all of you to know that Batina picked these gifts out."

"Mother and Clair you might not need to buy anything for the party," Batina said as she handed her mother a dress then handed Clair a blouse and jeweled hair combs.

"Batina this is so beautiful," Cora said as she held the dress up. "Edgar look."

"Batina I absolutely love this but how did you know my size?" asked Clair.

"I saw a woman who looked your size in the store and asked her to help me. Do you really like them?"

"We love them," Cora said and both women kissed Batina on her cheeks.

"Father, Batina bought you these pipes and different kinds of tobacco," Ratri said as he handed his father a box and several pouches.

"These are beautiful," Joseph said as he showed the ornately carved pipes to the others. "Edgar do you enjoy a pipe?"

"It has been a while."

"We will have to try these out," said Joseph.

"And Edgar, Batina said that you have always wanted one of these," Ratri said with a big smile and handed a pouch to his father-in-law."

"Children," Edgar said emotionally as he showed the golden pocket watch to the others. "I am very touched."

"These are all wonderful gifts, thank you." Joseph said.

"Oh, there are a couple more," Ratri said as he and Batina each handed their mothers a pouch.

"Oh, I saw Hannah's," Cora said as she took her family bracelet out of the pouch. "I just love this. Thank you so much." Cora kissed both Batina and Ratri on their cheeks as Clair thanked them for the gifts.

Batina looked at Ratri, "I guess we should have gotten more gifts for our fathers."

"Nonsense," Joseph said. "These gifts are wonderful and I think all of us agree you spent too much on us."

"All of you have done so much for Batina and me; we want you to know how much we appreciate you. Since you came here so quickly," Ratri said. "We know you didn't prepare for a party. So if any of you need anything; we can't go shopping with you but we will pay for it. Cora you probably need shoes and a shawl for that dress and Mother you will need a skirt and shoes. And Father and Edgar whatever you want."

"Son, you don't have to pay for these things," said Joseph.

"Besides everything they provide for us, Gabriel and Raphael are paying us for our work. So please let us do this for you," Ratri said.

Joao and Dack were sitting in Jasmine's bedroom with her and her parents. "You know Jasmine is a lot nicer to us with you here," Dack said jokingly to Leta and Conrad.

"Yeah, she hits us a lot," Joao said and laughed.

"I would if I could," Jasmine said with a grin. "Mother, Father don't let them fool you; these two can be awful. They always thought they had to protect..." Jasmine stopped talking. "I'm sorry," she said and started to cry.

Before anyone could say anything there was a knock on the door. "Come in," Conrad called.

Edgar walked into the bedroom and saw that Jasmine was crying. "Ratri and Batina want to visit with Jasmine but Hannah won't let them walk this far. Jasmine if you are up for a visit I could carry you to their room."

"Yes, I would like to see them. I just feel so stupid having to be carried around," Jasmine said as she wiped the tears from her cheeks.

"I'm not saying a word," Dack said with a grin which made Jasmine laugh.

"Why don't all of you come down for a visit," Edgar said. "Did Hannah tell you about the party? Because Cora and Clair are going shopping if you want to go with them Leta."

"That does sound like fun; I think I will," Leta said. "Unless you want me here?" Leta asked Jasmine.

"No go Mother. In fact neither of you have been into the city. Salar is incredible you both should go. You will have fun."

"Where do you want these?" Dagon asked as he carried an armload of packages into the house of Horace and Zelda.

"Just put them on the kitchen table," Zelda said.

"I still can't believe those people left so much behind," Dagon said. "Did they take anything with them?"

"They were moving in with their daughter and her family so they didn't need the furniture; which was a gift for us," Zelda said. "And they left tools and a boca and all sorts of things. We are very blessed."

209

Horace walked into the house with an armload of packages. "Dagon did Gabriel tell you that he is giving us some of this land? I told him that I wanted to pay for it but he said they didn't need the money but might be asking me to help on missions. I will help but it doesn't feel right not to pay for these things."

"Both Gabriel and Hannah were each very wealthy before they married. They really don't need the money but honestly we always need help with the missions. So that would mean more to Gabriel. And speaking of money; Horace I know you keep saying you are going to return that pouch of coins to Erebus but I would think twice about that," Dagon said.

"What do you mean?" asked Horace.

"I think if you do that you will be greatly insulting him. Erebus is a very wealthy man but he has no one to share anything with. It made him feel good to give that money to your family. I think that if you want to pay him back you have him over for dinner once in a while."

"Actually I was going to ask Hannah if we could get Erebus out of the hospital and bring him to the party," Horace said. "It might make him feel better."

"I think that is a good idea," said Dagon. "And when the dust settles a little we all need to sit down and talk. Rachel and I want to have another wedding with all of our family and we would like you to help us with the planning."

"That makes me very happy," Zelda said.

Excited energy filled Gabriel's household as everyone prepared for the dinner party. The event gave the people a much needed distraction from the horrors of the mission in Ryed. Now on the eve of the party the energy turned into a fervor.

"Something really smells good in here," Raphael said as he entered the kitchen and saw almost every woman in the house working in the large room.

"Where's Robert?" Vivian asked as Raphael kissed her on the cheek.

"With your father."

Vivian laughed, "Between the two of you always holding him I bet I will have trouble teaching him to walk."

"We will cross that bridge when we get there," Raphael said with a grin. "Do you need help?"

"Yes, if you want to go to the wine cellar and start bringing things up," Hannah said. "Wine, whiskey and probably some ale."

As Raphael was walking out of the kitchen Emeral asked, "Raphael I haven't seen the Sanuri since he returned. Is he still in Wetpr?"

"Yes, he has been spending all of his time at the hospital," Hannah said. "I did invite him."

"Also, Erebus gave him a mountain of scrolls and books," Raphael said. "I would assume that when he is at the castle he is in his chambers reading. In fact, Renya is having new chambers designed for the Sanuri with an office and a library."

The few men in the house who were not wounded were assigned to help all of the wounded warriors to the dining room. This was the first time most of the injured had been out of their bedrooms.

"I am so looking forward to this," Batina said as Edgar carried her down to the dining room.

"Well you look very pretty," Maxwell said to Batina as he was helping Thor down the steps.

"But I feel like child again," Batina said. "Our parents had to help Ratri and me get dressed."

"We are all in the same boat," Thor said with a grin. "But it is good to get out of the bedroom."

211

"Petra is here with the pups," Christopher yelled excitedly and now all of the children and Jasper the dog ran towards the front door.

Gabriel and Raphael quickly walked to the front door. There were soldiers and carriages stopping in the front yard. Sudfad, Renya, the Sanuri, Petra, Kyra, Laurel, Alexander, Gala, Raul, Michael, Simon, Vitomas, Annabelle and all the children were climbing out of the first four carriages.

Archetenus, Delilah, Jared, Zoya and the babies were riding in the next carriage. Edward, Chaez, Dominic, Fennel, Seth, Noah and Lawrence rode in the last two carriages.

"You're going to have a house full," said the Sanuri with a big smile as they walked through the front door.

"We are so glad you could all come," said Gabriel.

"Let me show everyone our new nursery and playroom," Emeral said as she greeted the guests. "In case you want to put the babies to bed."

Jasmine was sitting at the table with her broken leg propped up on a chair when Fennel, Seth and Lawrence walked up to her. Lawrence and Fennel were helping Seth to walk. "Jasmine will you watch Seth for us, he is supposed to stay off that leg?" Fennel asked with a grin. Seth looked embarrassed by his cousin's comments.

"Of course it will be nice to have company," Jasmine said with a sweet smile as she could see that Seth was embarrassed. "What is wrong with your leg?"

"Just a knife wound," Seth said shyly.

"A really bad knife wound," Lawrence said. "He could have lost his leg."

"How are you doing?" Fennel asked. "We are so sorry to hear about Darla."

"And I am sorry to hear about Asher, Martin and Oliver," Jasmine said sadly.

212

"I miss my friend and as for the injuries, the worst part is that I have to have help doing everything. I feel so useless."

"Well, you are alive and rather a hero from what we heard," Fennel said. "You just have to be patient with the rest."

"And you look very pretty," Lawrence said and kissed Jasmine on the cheek. "Doesn't she Seth?"

Seth again turned bright red and said, "Yes." Fennel winked at Jasmine then kissed her on the cheek. Fennel and Lawrence walked away.

"Seth, I know they were teasing you but you don't have to sit with me if you don't want to," Jasmine said.

"No, I want to. You see everything is so different here. You know we were living in caves and we certainly didn't go to fancy parties or get a chance to talk to a pretty girl. I am just still getting used to everything. I heard what you did Jasmine. You were really brave you should be proud. You saved a lot of lives."

"But so many were lost. I think that is all I can focus on," Jasmine said softly. "I wanted so badly to be a part of Gabriel's team, now after all this I don't know if I am cut out for it."

"Your actions show that you are cut out for the work but understand you are grieving. You shouldn't be making any big decisions now."

Natasha walked up to Jasmine and Seth with a tray full of glasses of wine. "If you two promise you won't try to dance I will give you some wine," Natasha said jokingly.

"Sure," Seth said and took two glasses from the tray.

"Excuse us," Micha repeated as he and Thomas carried a large overstuffed chair into the dining room.

"Put it over there," Iris said. "Then after you bring your father down we will need another chair for Erebus; they should be arriving shortly."

213

"Hannah, Horace and I are trying to figure out how we can pay you and Gabriel back for everything," Zelda said as the women were working in the kitchen.

"Really it was nothing Zelda. We got the land we needed and it is nice to have you living so close. I think it is amazing how everything worked out."

"This has all been like a dream," Zelda said. "Life here is so different. And a few weeks ago we were all total strangers and now it feels like we are all family."

"We are," Ella said. "Personally I was surprised at how quickly you and Zack just fit in here; and now Horace and Rachel. Doesn't it seem like we have all known each other for a very long time?"

"That is part of what I mean," Zelda said. "You have to understand that in Ryed people can't trust their own neighbors. Why, we never did things like this."

"That sounds like such a sad way to live," Cora said. "Our tribe is like one huge family. I would trust all of them with my life."

"That is why Rachel and I were so shocked that Erebus took us into his home. You have to understand how feared the sorcerers are in Ryed. We thought they all worked for Teivel. So it seemed like our enemy gave us shelter when our friends would not. That is why we would like Erebus to stay with us until he is well."

"When you listen to all of our stories, isn't it strange how we all came together," said Vivian.

Rachel walked into the kitchen, "Everyone is here now and the King is going to speak."

"Before Sudfad speaks," Gabriel said. "Raphael and I would like to make a toast. So everyone grab a glass of wine. For many of us the mission in Ryed was the most difficult and frustrating mission we have ever worked. And the number of lives lost has overwhelmed us all. But there have been many bright moments and we have much to be grateful for."

"We are alive and healing and we have made new friends and added to our family members. Let's not lose sight of these good things in all of the darkness. To blessings," Raphael said and held up his glass of wine. Everyone followed the toast.

"Our team has been working back to back missions for almost two years and we will be taking a break. Raphael and I feel that everyone needs to heal both physically and emotionally. As many of you know I had asked Dominic and his men to work with us on occasion. He was just showing me a letter he received from Stephan and Thaos. They were asking Dominic and his men to come to Lentz to help them gather information about two new threats against the ruling families. It sounds like Dominic and the others will go to Lentz so if any of my team wants to accompany them; you can." said Gabriel.

"What is the mission?" Thor asked.

"You can't even walk," scolded Diana.

"We won't be leaving for a while," Dominic said. "Here's the letter, any of you can read it."

"I would like to see that too," Chaez said.

Sudfad and Renya now stood in front of the room. "I will try to keep this short. Since most of you are wounded we are improvising tonight. Simon and Michael are going to be pinning medals on you as I speak. The medals are for valor in battle and for working on the missions. Normally we would do this before the entire military but most of you won't be ready for that for a while. But if you would like such a ceremony please tell me."

"We get medals too?" Natasha asked in amazement.

"You sure do," Sudfad said. "As the boys are awarding the medals I don't know if all of you have heard that Sorren was made one of the ruling members of Lentz. He will share duties with Fahron and Claudius." Edgar yelled a war cry and everyone applauded.

"Mathas also expanded the lands of the Nordes Tribe which now includes parts of the diamond mines and he gave pouches of gold to all of the members of your tribe who served in battle or lost a family member in battle. So I assume many of you will be receiving gifts when you return home."

Raul slowly stood up and addressed the group. "For those of you in our military you will be required to wear these medals on your uniforms. I don't know what Gabriel and Raphael want to do with the team and the Patronus priests."

"We will have to think about that," said Gabriel.

"Sanuri would you please step forward?" Sudfad asked. "Renya and I have been trying to think of what we could do for you besides build you knew chambers. Then Petra told us something that was so obvious we could not believe we had overlooked it. We are truly sorry we did not give you one of these before." As Sudfad spoke Renya handed the Sanuri a small box.

"A family ring," the Sanuri said with a big smile. "I will wear this proudly."

After Sudfad and Renya sat down, Erebus said loudly, "I want to thank you for including me tonight. It is certainly a treat to get out of the hospital and enjoy good company. Horace and Dagon I apologize that I was so difficult to move."

"You weren't difficult; we were just afraid that we would hurt you," Dagon said.

"The tonics that Hannah is giving me really help the pain, I have been pleasantly surprised," said Erebus.

"Hannah, Zelda has prepared a room and we would like to bring Erebus into our home while he heals. Do you have any idea when we can move him?" Horace asked.

"Well in a way that is up to you and Erebus," Hannah said with a sweet smile. "He will be on pain medicine for a long time and we can't let his wounds get infected. But I can come over every day and check on him."

"I can't impose on you like that," Erebus said.

"You don't want to stay in the hospital do you?" asked Dagon. Erebus didn't say anything.

"Well then; our house is much closer than the hospital," Horace said. "If we bring him home tonight will he need medicine before the morning?"

"I can give you some," Hannah said with a big smile. "Erebus I think you will heal better with Zelda's cooking."

"Then that is it," Horace said and looked at Erebus. "You move in tonight and tomorrow Dagon and I will get your things from the hospital."

Rachel smiled at her father's words. Not only was she happy that Erebus was going to move in with her family but Rachel was pleased at how bonded her father and her husband had become.

Edward was sitting in a chair and Vivian and Diana quickly walked up to him and sat down on opposite sides of Edward and stared at him. "You two are making me nervous," he said and laughed.

"They should," Thor yelled and chuckled. "They are trying to match you up."

"We noticed you didn't bring a date tonight," Diana said with a coy smile. "So none of your girlfriends are taking care of you?"

"I'm not sure I want to answer that," Edward said with a big grin. "Is this about Kate?"

"How did you know?" Vivian asked with surprise.

"Raphael told me you had a friend you wanted to introduce me to."

"He did, well what did he say?" Vivian asked.

"That she is beautiful and a warrior and you two think we would get along. Although you two don't really know me that well."

217

"We know you well enough," Diana said and giggled. "So will you meet her? She wants to visit us so we were thinking of having some of the Rualas bring her here."

Micha and Bianca had been listening to the conversation. "Edward, Kate is beautiful but she is just like Vivian and Diana were," Micha said. "She is more interested in hunting demons than dating."

"Yes, we aren't telling her that we really want the two of you to meet," Diana said. "So you will agree to come over for dinner when she is here?"

"Edward say yes; what can you lose?" Vivian said persuasively.

"Ok," Edward said with the grin that had not left his face. "But you might want to tell her I lost an eye. It might make a difference."

"Edward, Kate is a Venator," Diana said in a scolding voice. "Besides you look even more handsome with that eye patch."

Chapter XX
Plans

Over the next few weeks as Dominic and his men healed they were invited to join Sudfad's morning meetings. A common topic of discussion was the situation in the Kingdom of Lentz. Almost once a week a ship would pull into dock in the City of Langer that had been attacked by the creatures of the Dura Tribe from the Continent of Tansof. From the stories of the sailors the attacks were similar in that a ship from Tansof would follow the sailors; then attack when the ships were close to the Kingdom of Lentz. Some sailors were always kept alive to tell the story.

"While Mathas believes the Dura Tribe is responsible for these attacks he has not ruled out that someone or something could be trying to draw Lentz into a war with the Dura Tribe," Sudfad said. "When the Dura Tribe attacked Lentz twenty years ago it was a major offensive; they weren't attacking merchant ships to send a message."

"The Valdore Tribe has not attacked anyone yet," Sudfad continued. "But Usman's men have been seen more frequently in Langer and they are purchasing large quantities of supplies which is apparently unusual."

"We all know that when Juleta was alive she was trying to start wars to distract her father so she could take the throne," Simon said. "And although Mathas has not ruled this out; do they have any other leads?"

"Isn't Juleta dead?" asked Dominic.

"Yes, but she cut deals with demons and paid bounties before she died," Raul said. "She has made a lot of people's lives nightmares."

"Would demons want to take over the throne?" asked Fennel.

"It is hard to say," Simon said. "But we did find out that she had a husband in Zorta and he is the father of their daughter."

"Does he know about the child?" Michael asked.

"We don't think so," Sudfad said. "Juleta put the baby in a monastery and the Sanuri returned the child to Mathas and Rosa who adopted her."

"You mean that little girl with the dark hair is Juleta's daughter?" asked Michael. "She looked just like a normal little girl."

"She is as far as we know," Sudfad said.

"If you would have met Juleta it is really hard to believe she would leave her baby at a monastery, I mean she tried to sacrifice her baby sister to a demon," Raul said with disgust.

"You are going to have to tell me that story," said Michael.

"Tell us all," Edward said.

"Are you sure about this?" Dagon asked Misha as the family was gathered in the dining room for the midday meal.

"Dagon, I thought Misha was going to pass out when he was coming down the stairs just to eat," Diana said. "And look at how big I am getting already. And besides that Thor is injured he might go on that mission to Lentz. So you and Rachel should have your big wedding ceremony before us. We will have ours later."

"If you are inviting the people from Lentz, you might want to have the wedding sooner than later," Gabriel said. "They might be going to war at some point."

"I know everyone has been talking about having all of the babies christened at the same time," Dagon said. "Have you picked a date yet?"

"We were going to discuss that today," Raphael said. "The Sanuri is leaving for Lentz in two weeks so we were thinking about having the christenings next Sunday. How does that work for everyone?"

"Ella and I have Ian's and Emma's outfits and blankets done," Iris said.

"We just have to finish the ones for Robert and Daniel. But that will give us almost a week."

"I will start making the arrangements today," Emeral said. "Does everyone still agree on the new chapel?" Several people nodded to answer Emeral's question.

"Hannah will father be able to stand for that long?" Vivian asked.

"This is my first grandson," Joshua asked. "I will stand."

"Well I guess you have your answer," Hannah said with a smile.

"We have got some work to do," Dagon said to Rachel with a grin. Then Dagon looked at Emeral and said, "We have discussed some of this. We want our parents there and we want everyone here in the wedding but Rachel isn't for a lot of frills. So if I give you the money will you and Zelda plan everything?"

"Why did I know that was coming?" Maxwell asked with a laugh.

"I would love to," Emeral said. "Have you talked about it to Zelda yet?

"No," Rachel said. "They have been so busy with the new house and everything that we haven't really talked to them about it."

"After lunch why don't the four of us visit Zelda and Horace," Emeral said then she turned to Maxwell. "Do you have to get back to the fort right away?"

"I'll make time for this," Maxwell said happily.

"So if we are all in the wedding; you are going to need more girls," Diana said with a coy smile.

"Oh no, I can see the wheels turning," Thor said and laughed.

"Well, Vivian and I are going to ask Kate to visit; we could ask a few more friends unless Batina, Sasha, Bianca and Jasmine have some girls from their tribe," Diana said with a big smile. "But we are inviting Kate to meet Edward so don't bring any girls for him."

"Oh this will be fun," Bianca said. "Let's talk about this after lunch."

"Since two of the girls will be for us, Dack and I want to be part of that conversation," Joao said with a big grin.

"Now I have a suggestion," Iris said. "Everyone understands that the girls are looking for dates for all of you for the wedding so don't think more than that." Iris turned to Luca, "There is a beautiful woman in our tribe who lost her husband almost a year ago and she is raising their infant son by herself. I don't think that either you or Natalie are ready to meet anyone romantically but you have so much in common you might become friends. Would you consider being in the wedding with her?"

Before Luca could answer Vivian said, "Luca, Natalie is really nice and she isn't looking for a husband. But Mother is right; I could see the two of you becoming good friends."

"I am not ready for a romantic relationship as long as she understands that but I would be fine with meeting her," Luca said.

"Actually you may have already met," Joshua said. "She was helping with the wounded from Ogg. Her husband had only been dead a couple of weeks and Natalie was trying to keep busy so she was working around the clock with the wounded. She is a good mother and a brave warrior but she has seemed so lost since Troy died that it might do her good to come for a visit."

"What does she look like?" Luca asked. "I mean so I might remember if I met her."

"She's about my height," Vivian said. "She has blonde hair but it is really curly and brown eyes."

"Does she have a scar on her right shoulder?" asked Dack.

"Yes, she was stabbed by a demon," Vivian said.

"I talked to her several times; I was wondering why she seemed so sad. If Luca doesn't feel ready to be in the wedding I will walk with her," Dack said.

"I am glad you said that," Luca said. "I will meet her but I may not be ready to be in the wedding."

"Elan and I remember her too," Cassandra said. "She was a really hard worker."

"How old is her son?" Emeral asked.

"He must be almost a year now. He was only a few weeks old when Troy was killed," Iris said. "Natalie doesn't really have any family. I mean our entire tribe is like a family but both of her parents and grandparents were Venators and died in battle."

"Troy went hunting, not for demons but for food one day and never returned. We had search parties looking for him," Joshua explained. "After a week we found his remains. We think a bear killed him and other animals ate him. He was a fine young man."

Everyone was quiet for a few moments then Diana said, "Ok, we are inviting Kate and Natalie, who else?"

King Mathas called his second meeting of the day. Claudius, Stephan and Thaos entered the study just minutes after Fahron and Sorren.

"It's the same damn story," Claudius said before he even sat down. "Another ship came into port. Only a few sailors left alive with the same story about the creatures from the Dura Tribe. Something is really wrong here, I can feel it in my bones."

"You mean besides the attacks?" asked Matthew.

"All of you boys were babies when we were at war with the Dura Tribe," Fahron said. "They are merciless butchers. They often attack at night, they give no warnings or messages and they slaughter everything and everyone in their paths; like the Hutas. I agree with Claudius; I am beginning to think more and more that someone is trying to get us to attack the Dura Tribe and start a war."

"Who besides Juleta and Usman have wanted to take the throne?" asked Thaos.

"I am sure there are others but those two were the only ones who verbalized it," Mathas said. "Are you thinking Juleta's husband is still doing her biding?"

Thaos looked at Stephan before he spoke. "Now you know I am the only one in this room who is not originally from here. When I was working for Juleta I spent a lot of time here spying for her. I heard a lot of things but unless they effected my mission I didn't pay much attention. I talked to Stephan about some of these things so he and I have been spending time in some of the taverns again."

Stephan looked around the room then said, "Thaos is trying not to insult anyone but you know how Sudfad and his family got so focused on the missions and the threats to their families that Shanksaw and his men took over Salar and a whole lot of people were hurt and killed. Well, Thaos and I aren't so sure the same things aren't happening here."

"I kept hearing stories about a man named Deckor," Thaos explained. "From what I heard he has a gang of men who have been trying to extort some of the businesses and ship captains. This kind of stuff is pretty normal in large cities. I told Stephan and he tells me that Deckor is the mayor of Langer. Now I have no proof about anything; just listening to drunks talk in taverns but this Deckor sounds like he has his hands in a lot of things in the city. And if things don't go his way; people get hurt."

"So Thaos and I have been trying to look at all of these threats and attacks with new eyes," Stephan said. "Who would profit by us going to war; and I don't even mean taking the throne. I think we all need to really think about this; we might have enemies we haven't even considered."

"I have never liked Deckor," Claudius said. "He is one of those politicians that speaks out of both sides of his mouth as far as I am concerned. But the boys are right we don't have any proof of wrong doing but we need to look into him."

"I don't think any of us in this room have ever liked Deckor," Mathas said. "But he has always been a man to get results. We may have just found out why. But Stephan and Thaos are right; our focus has been too narrow."

"Ok so tell me some of the ways that Deckor or someone like him could profit from war," Sorren said.

"We will need more supplies and weapons," Claudius said. "To say nothing about ships if we fight the Dura Tribe. So that is a big boom for the economy and if Deckor is extorting money from the business he will raise his rates."

"There are other ways too," Thaos said. "For a large port city, Langer is pretty clean. Most of them have lots of whore houses and gambling joints and they bring in big money. And I don't mean the kind of ma and pa gambling taverns you have here; where you are served a Sunday meal while you play cards. I mean like that tavern that Shanksaw took over. If the economy booms here we will probably see more of those kinds of places opening up."

"Did Archetenus ever tell you about some of the places he would frequent in Port Friada?" Stephan asked. "Every night they would just stack the bodies on the curb. We a few of those here but that is nothing for a city the size of Langer."

"But back to Shanksaw; he was able to thrive because the eyes of the military and the Royal Family were focused on other issues. The citizens of Salar love Sudfad's family yet no one came forward and let the cat out of the bag about the murders and kidnappings. Thaos is right someone could make a lot of money here," Stephan said. "I was thinking about writing to Dominic again to get an idea of when they will be coming."

"Thor and Michael are both healing from wounds but they are thinking about coming too," Mathas said. "Sudfad said that Gabriel is giving his team a break to heal since they have had back to back missions for almost two years. Gabriel said that his team members were free to help us but some of them are still in pretty bad shape."

"You know it might be nice to have some of the Rualas here," Fahron said.

"Now Fahron don't get mad at what I am going to say," Thaos said. "Both Chaez and Thor want to help. Chaez has changed a lot and you should be proud. But neither of those boys look like criminals. Dominic and his men are good men but they have been on the run for a long time and look like it. And well you have seen Michael. We can't send Chaez and Thor into some of the taverns because they will be made right away. But that doesn't mean they can't work in other areas."

"I am not offended and I think everyone in this room agrees with you," Fahron said. "All of us are men who are used to battle not these types of what should I call them, investigations? But after some of the stories that all of you have told about Ryed and some of the other missions, I would like us to ask Gabriel to help set some things up. I understand he won't want to participate but he could help us with plans and strategies. Of course we would pay him."

"Thaos and I keep saying it but watching Gabriel's team in action is really something and the women are just as impressive as the men," Stephan said.

Chapter XXI
Children

There was a huge celebration at the house of Gabriel for the christening of four babies. The christenings were held in the new chapel in the early morning hours. There was a luncheon afterwards, then games and contests followed by a feast in the evening and a dance.

The Sanuri, Dominic and his men, Batina's parents, Jasmine and her parents, Thor, Chaez, Gabriel, Raphael, Joao and Dack were all leaving for the Kingdom of Lentz early the following morning. Gabriel and Raphael had no intention of becoming involved with the mission other than helping to devise strategies.

Fahron and Isadore had originally invited Dominic and his men to be their quests and now opened their home to the others from Wetpr also.

While Hannah and Vivian were not particularly happy that their husbands were leaving again; the women did take comfort in knowing that Gabriel and Raphael would not go to battle. At this point the men planned to be in Lentz two to three weeks.

After the feast that evening, Raphael, Gabriel, Luca and Calen walked up to Jasmine who was sitting with Seth and her parents. "Is anything wrong?" Jasmine asked when she saw the looks on the faces of the men."

"No," Gabriel said. "Jasmine we know you still have a lot of healing to do and that you want to go home. But we would like to offer you a position on the team. You don't have to give us an answer now. In fact you should probably talk it over with your family first."

"Do you mean a permanent position?" Jasmine asked with amazement. "I know we had talked about Darla and me helping out now and then."

"Yes a permanent position," Raphael said.

"Since our team has had so many back to back missions everyone lives here in Wetpr but you certainly can stay at home in between missions," Gabriel said. "Or live here with us."

"I think Seth would like you to stay," Luca said and winked which made both Seth and Jasmine blush.

"A few weeks ago I would have said no," Jasmine said. "I was so depressed after Darla died that I didn't think I could do something like this again. But I am feeling much better. Let me talk with my parents. When do you want an answer?"

"That is up to you," Gabriel said.

"Hannah said I should be able to walk just fine for Dagon and Rachel's wedding. That gives me almost seven weeks to heal. If I move back it will probably be then," Jasmine said as she started to get excited about the idea.

"Honey, the decision is yours," Conrad said. "Your mother and I are very proud of you and the work that Gabriel's team does. And as Edgar says, it is only three days travel from our village. If you want to work on the team you have our blessings."

"I will move to Wetpr when I return for the wedding," Jasmine said with a big smile. "Gabriel I know I can't do a lot now but I am willing to help you in Lentz; if you can find something for me to do."

"For our parts we will be gathering information," Gabriel said. "Perhaps you can help. But right now your healing is the most important thing."

"She may hit me," Seth said to Leta and Conrad. "But I will watch out for her." Jasmine's parents smiled.

Joseph and Clair decided to stay with Ratri and Batina a few more days. Ratri didn't want his parents traveling to the Ice Caves by themselves. He talked them into waiting until a small group of Ruala warriors who were patients in the hospital at Fort Salar flew home.

Sam and Ella were sitting near one of the bonfires watching Bekka and Koby dance. Ella held baby Emma while Sam held his grandson Ian. Joseph and Clair sat down with Sam and Ella.

"Can I hold her?" Clair asked and Ella handed baby Emma to her friend. "Joseph and I were just talking and we can certainly understand why you and Sam are staying here."

"Yes we came for a funeral and never left," Sam said with a grin. "We have never said anything to our children but I think Ella and I were in the same situation as Maxwell and Emeral. We had good lives but once the children were gone, well, it was just too quiet. Here, well..."

"What he is trying to say is that we feel needed again," Ella said. "And we both like that. Everyone in the household is so appreciative of what we do. And it is crazy here but it is a good crazy. And we just love all of the children."

"What's wrong Nicholas?" Christopher asked loudly and ran up to Gabriel who was walking into the dining room carrying Nicholas, who was crying.

"He is sad because I am leaving after breakfast," Gabriel said emotionally. "Christopher would you watch out for him?"

Gabriel sat down at the table and put Nicholas on his lap and kissed his son on the forehead. Christopher now climbed onto Gabriel's lap also. Christopher too was sadden that some of the family members were leaving that morning.

Hannah and Natasha walked out of the kitchen carrying platters of pancakes and eggs. "Where is Cerey?" Gabriel asked.

"She and Daniel are sleeping in the big nursery," Hannah replied. Then she bent down and kissed both Nicholas and Christopher on their heads.

"I'll get her," Adrone said and got up from the children's table and ran out of the dining room.

Misha was the last person to enter the dining room. "We aren't waiting on Thor and Melinda," Misha announced as he sat down. "I just locked them in his bedroom."

"What on earth!" Emeral gasped.

"They are fighting about Thor leaving with his injuries," Misha said with a grin. "They both care about each other but neither of them will make a move so everything is in limbo. This way they are going to have to work something out to get out of that room." Calen and Koby roared with laughter at Misha's words.

"I'll check on them," Diana said to Emeral.

"No you won't," Misha said. "Just let them work this out."

There was silence and many of the adults were aware of the sad faces of the children. After so many of the family members were gone for months in Ryed, no one wanted them leaving again.

Dagon looked at Rachel who was sitting next to him. "Maybe you should tell the children about what we are doing?"

"But they aren't done," said Rachel.

"Maybe they would like to see your father working on them," Dagon said.

"What are you talking about?" asked Paul.

"It was Dagon's idea," Rachel said with a proud smile. "But we are planning a party for all of the children. My father is making puppets and is going to put on a show at the party."

"Oh, that is wonderful," Hannah gasped.

"What are puppets?" asked Christopher.

"They are like dolls with strings attached to them and they talk and move around," Maxwell said. "You will really like them."

"Father is still making them," Rachel said. "But after breakfast why don't I take all of you to their house and you can watch him."

"Vivian, can we ride the ponies?" Paul asked excitedly.

"Yes, and I will go with you if Mother and Father will watch Robert."

"Like you have to ask," Raphael said teasingly as he was holding his infant son.

"I was planning on checking on Erebus this morning," Hannah said. "Cassandra would you watch Daniel, then I can drive the boca and take Cerey and Cicely too?"

"Of course and I think this is a wonderful idea," Cassandra said.

"Does Horace need any help?" Sam asked.

"He still has to build the stage," Rachel said. "And Mother is making the outfits."

"Perhaps Ella and I should go with you," said Sam.

"Sam you just can't stand to sit still a moment," Koby said with a grin.

Natasha squealed as an Enrop flew into the dining room and landed next to her. Soon several more Enrops flew into the room. The children ran from their seats to pet the giant birds.

"These letters are all from Ryed," one of the Enrops said.

Gabriel quickly read his letter then addressed the group, "High Priest Othnial says that Ryed has turned into a war zone as different factions fight for control of that kingdom. He says that with Teivel destroyed the people are trying to take their homeland back from the demons and dark lords. Othnial is giving shelter to many in the monastery." Gabriel put the letter down and shook his head. "So many lives were lost; I wonder if we will ever find out if it was worth it."

While Gabriel was talking, Vivian motioned for Diana to come to her. Both women were reading a letter that Vivian was holding. "We have something to discuss with all of you," Vivian said and handed the letter to her mother. "The Sanuri told Duncan not to allow the Venatores to hunt. The Sanuri fears for the safety of the village and believes all of the warriors should stay together. Everyone in our village knows you and the work we do."

231

"We told you that we had asked Kate and Natalie to come here for the wedding. They are bored and wonder if we need any help?"

"Of course Natalie would be bringing her baby," Diana said.

"Do they mean help around the house or on a mission?" Raphael asked.

"Both," Vivian said. "You can read the letter. Kate feels like she is trapped in the village and wants to be working. Natalie has more work to do with Hunter; that is her son. But she is still grieving and would like to keep busy."

Gabriel and Raphael looked at each other then at Vivian. "I would say yes, have them come unless any of you have objections," said Gabriel.

"They are Venatores," Joshua said. "They will perform well wherever you want them."

"Natasha teach them some of the things they will need to know to work on a mission and get them some outfits," Gabriel said. "If we need them in Lentz I will send for them."

"Do you want us to go get them?" asked Koby.

"All of you are still healing," Maxwell said. "I will send a message to the Ice Caves."

"Visterle will you stop laughing," Nada snapped irritably. "I don't know what you think is so damn funny."

"You my pet. I have never seen anyone eat so much. Are you sure we are having just one baby?" he asked with a grin.

"I am not sure about anything. And look how big I am already. You do know I have had twins before don't you?"

"I would be alright with that," Visterle said. "I will just hire another midwife. But what I want to know is do you always get so grouchy when you are pregnant?" Nada scowled at Visterle which made him roar with laughter.

"Matthew just settle down," Rosa said sweetly. "Shara is with her, everything will be alright.

"But she is late; that might be a bad sign," Matthew said as he paced outside of the bedroom door.

"Honey not everyone gives birth at exactly the ninth month mark and you might have calculated the time wrong," Rosa said. "Angelina is healthy and strong, don't worry so."

"Are they in the bedroom?" Nikki asked as she and Ingr ran into the parlor of Matthew's and Angelina's home.

Before Matthew could finish saying, "Yes." Ingr and Nikki ran into the bedroom and shut the door.

"I sent soldiers to bring Sorren and the boys here," Mathas said as he walked into the parlor. We were lucky that Shara was visiting."

"Honey, Matthew is so nervous, why don't you play cards or something?" Rosa asked and stood up from her chair. "When are the others coming?"

"I would expect soon," Mathas said. "I sent soldiers to tell Claudius and Fahron as soon as Angelina started to go into labor."

"Then I am going to tell the cooks to prepare some food," Rosa said and left the parlor.

"You horse's ass," Thor said loudly to Misha as Thor and Melinda entered the dining room. Almost everyone sitting around the table laughed at this comment.

"Thor, the children," Hannah scolded although she was smiling.

"Sorry," Thor said and laughed.

"Well, you two look like you are getting along better," Misha said as he saw that Thor and Melinda were holding hands. "How did you get out of the room?"

"Melinda flew us down from the balcony," Thor replied as he held a chair out for her.

"I was going to check on you," said Diana.

"No, she wasn't," Misha said. "You two care about each other but it's like neither of you will admit it."

"I think we've realized that," Thor said as he took a seat and gave Melinda a sheepish look.

"We've got a lot more talking to do," Melinda said with a voice of authority that no one had heard before. Joao and Dack roared with laughter.

"I have never felt this guilty in my life," Gabriel said to Raphael as their group was riding towards the Kingdom of Lentz.

"You mean because of the children?" Dominic asked. Dominic was riding close to Gabriel and Raphael.

"Yes, Nicholas cried all morning then Cerey and Christopher cried after breakfast. And then leaving Hannah and the baby too, I never realized it would tear me up like this."

"I feel it too," Raphael said solemnly.

"For a man who never wanted his team members to be distracted on a mission," the Sanuri said. "You both have many distractions." The Sanuri was driving his boca and Jasmine was riding in the front seat with him.

"So what are you saying?" asked Gabriel.

"After you leave Lentz, go home and take some time off. Both of you have always wanted children and now that you have them you are never home. Do you want to come home someday and find your children are grown and you don't know them anymore?" the Sanuri asked.

"I agree with what you are saying," Gabriel said. "That is why I told the team we would take a break but with all the threats..." Gabriel paused.

"Annabelle and Vitomas are really upset with Simon and Raul for leaving so much too," Michael said. "In fact I heard Vitomas saying something very similar to what the Sanuri just said."

"Sanuri, I know you. What are you really saying?" Raphael asked.

"These old bones are telling me the threats are going to increase; this dark time is long from over for our world. But as good and faithful as all of you are, you can't be every place at once. I think when you get back home you should start thinking about who you can train to fill your shoes then let them take some of the missions. As bad as all of this has been I believe it will get much worse before it is over."

"You mean from within the team?" asked Gabriel.

"While all of the members are very talented and competent for something like this I would ask for guidance," the Sanuri said.

"It is none of my business," Chaez said. "But all of you have been seriously injured many times. What will happen to your team if you are killed? That is why Mathas has my father, Claudius and Sorren as ruling members. They are all trained in the King's duties so if Mathas is killed the kingdom will not go into chaos."

"As dedicated as your team is, they have seen so much battle and horror and they too are now taking families," the Sanuri said. "All of you could use some help and a break whether you want to admit it or not."

"So you are actually saying we should develop several teams?" Gabriel asked. "Actually I think that is a very smart idea, but..."

"But what?" Jasmine asked.

"I was just thinking about the sacrifices," Gabriel said.

"Everyone who is riding with us here knows about sacrifices," the Sanuri said. "Just be honest with the people upfront."

Jasmine's father Conrad and Edgar were riding next to the boca. "This is my first time meeting most of you," Conrad said. "But everyone in our village has heard so much about you and your work. Just like with the Rualas it is a great honor for us to work with you. I don't think it will be difficult for you to get volunteers."

"Dominic could lead one of the teams," Seth said.

Dominic turned and looked at his cousin, "I would have much to learn before I could run something like Gabriel does."

"Would you be willing to learn?" Gabriel asked. "Because Raphael and I have already talked about you joining us on a regular basis." Dominic did not answer.

"It is a lot of hard work," Raphael said. "And you and your men have sacrificed so much already. But you can still have lives and families, especially if we split up the missions."

"Let me think about this and talk with my men," said Dominic.

"Dominic you already know we will all follow you," Noah said with a grin. "But I'll bet that young Seth here wants Jasmine to work on our team." Jasmine and Seth both turned dark red with embarrassment. Conrad and Edgar laughed loudly.

"Is that a baby's cry already?" Bella asked with astonishment as all of the guests sitting in the parlor of Matthew's and Angelina's home jumped to their feet.

"You don't think anything is wrong do you?" Matthew asked loudly but he directed the question to no one in particular.

Shara opened the door and peaked her head out. "Give us a few minutes and you can come in and meet baby Mathas Sorren," Shara said with a proud smile.

"Shara the baby came so fast is everything alright?" Matthew asked fearfully.

"Honey the baby was almost four weeks late; I think when he finally made up his mind nothing was stopping him. Don't worry they are both just fine," Shara said and closed the door.

Sorren let out a war cry and everyone in the parlor laughed. "I believe we are going to need to make a toast," King Mathas said and walked out of the parlor.

Both Stephan and Thaos slapped Sorren on the back as Sorren was beaming with pride. "You're a grandfather again Sorren; let's just hope this baby doesn't take after your wild ways," Stephan said teasingly.

The bedroom door opened and Ingr and Nikki both walked out carrying armloads of soiled linens. "You can go in now," Ingr said with a grin.

"Matthew the baby looks just like you," Nikki said. "And he is so big."

Before Nikki finished her sentence, Matthew ran into the bedroom and knelt next to the bed where Angelina was lying and holding their son. Matthew kissed Angelina once, twice, three times before he spoke. "How are you feeling?"

"Pretty good but I hope all of our children don't wait so long to be born," Angelina said as she handed the baby to Matthew. "Matthew take your son."

Matthew cradled the baby in his arms and kissed his infant son on the head; then Matthew turned around and introduced baby Mathas Sorren to the rest of the family.

Chapter XXII
Treachery

"You are sure no one saw you?" Deckor snapped.

"Boss, I told ya three times; I had Jake and Giles be look outs. The streets were dark. We grabbed those damn sailors before they knew what happened to them. No one knows them so no one will be looking for them," Ackley said.

"I can't afford any mistakes," Deckor said as he poured two glasses of whiskey. "I have been planning this far too long and last week Jessie's team almost got caught. If I lose this election there will be hell to pay for all of you."

"Boss, I'm telling ya; no one will ever find out."

"I'm sorry to call all of you here this time of night," King Mathas said to the small group of men who were gathering in his study. "But..."

There was a knock on the door. Queen Rosa opened the door and she and Shara both entered the room carrying large trays. "We have a few treats for you since everyone had to come out on such a cold and damp night."

"Thank you," Mathas said and waited until the women left the study before he continued talking. "As you know; several years ago we assigned our troops to patrol the border between the lands of the Nordes Tribe and the Valdore Tribe. Thaos is the one who told us that Usman dismembers the bodies of those he believes to be traitors and dumps the body parts on the border as a warning to others. During the last couple of years our soldiers have discovered no more than a handful of bodies dumped on the border. Earlier this evening they found the bodies of seventeen men lined up on the border."

"The patrol had passed that area several hours earlier so Lieutenant Harrison believes the bodies were dumped late in the afternoon. Harrison said that two of the bodies appeared to be wearing suits; which he found very unusual."

"Harrison's men did not find anything to identify the bodies. Sorren before you ask, none of the bodies were wearing the warrior uniforms of your tribe. Here is Harrison's map; you can all see where the bodies were dumped." Mathas spread a large map out on the table in his study.

"These bodies were dumped on the shores of the Sea of Grevdt," Thaos said as he studied the map. "Every body I have found was dumped on the western boundary of the Valdore Lands. Usually around Arora."

"Usman lives in the Village of Bask which is North of Arora so that would make sense," Sorren said. "But I have found bodies north of Snakes Crossing also, but that is still just east of Bask. And in all my years I have never heard of a mass slaughter like this. Mathas did Harrison say if all the bodies looked fresh?"

"He said that the blood was dried on all of the bodies," Mathas said. "But the bodies were so destroyed it was difficult for Harrison's men to determine anything else."

"So, where the bodies were found is a straight shot north from your castle Mathas and Langer," Claudius said with a frown. "This could be some kind of message."

"Normally Usman kills his own people or hired fighters," Sorren explained. "If there were men wearing suits, they must have been from Langer."

"Who in their right mind goes into the Valdore Lands?" Stephan asked. "Everyone knows what Usman does to strangers."

"They could have been abducted," Fahron said.

"That's a long way to transport bodies," said Stephan.

"It might be worth it if you want to start a war," Claudius said solemnly.

The following morning King Sudfad addressed his group of leaders in his usual morning meeting.

"Before I begin I must say to Joshua that it is good to see you again," Sudfad said.

"I don't make a good patient," Joshua said sarcastically. "I will be coming on a regular basis now."

"He means that Iris is sick of having him grumbling around the house," Misha said with a grin.

"That too," Joshua said and smiled.

"Speaking of being grumpy, I have to go back to work soon," Edward said.

"Has Hannah cleared you?" Sudfad asked.

"She will today," said Edward and laughed loudly.

"Well, Edward you are one of the topics of conversation this morning," Sudfad said.

"That's never good," said Jared sarcastically.

"Last night I received a very long letter from the Sanuri, Gabriel and Raphael," Sudfad said. "And we all need to discuss its contents. They will be arriving in Lentz today and their trip has been uneventful. But the Sanuri told the men that this plague of darkness that has descended upon Opots is going to get much worse. The Sanuri said that our experience in Ryed should have taught us that a handful of men cannot be the sole protectors of our kingdoms. He said that all of you have seen too much battle and need to heal and need time with your families."

"The Sanuri is suggesting that we establish several highly trained teams like Gabriel's and have these teams rotate missions. Gabriel wants all of you to think about this and he and Raphael will have meetings when they return. Because of the amount of training that will need to be done, especially for the leaders of the teams; they are wondering if Edward would be interested in leading one of the teams since he has already undergone some of the training and has experience working on covert operations."

"Absolutely," Edward said with a proud look. "But would I still be in the military? And I need more training."

"At this point, I believe there are many questions and everything is on the table for discussion," said Sudfad. "You can all read the letter. Gabriel and Raphael have also asked Dominic to lead a team. Dominic has not given them an answer yet."

"Would we be able to work between the different teams?" Archetenus asked.

"I would imagine the answer to that is yes," Calen said. "The missions will dictate the number of members needed and the skill sets."

"But each team should have a core group," Luca said. "And that group should include Rualas."

"I believe that Venatores should be included also," Joshua said.

"Father what does that mean for us?" Raul asked. "I mean The Seven Sons."

"Probably that you go wherever you are needed, like now," Sudfad replied. "But as I said everything is on the table for discussion. Now I am throwing something else on the table. Gabriel's team lives together and that works well for them. If the other teams want that also I will provide suitable housing."

"Sons," Maxwell said addressing Luca, Calen and Misha. "I think when we get home tonight, all of you who are the core group of Gabriel's team should meet and make lists of both questions and suggestions. And I think we should send a letter to King Manu and King Neputa so they can ask for volunteers."

"I think it is smart that Mathas is holding the morning meeting at Fahron's castle," Stephan said as he, Thaos and Claudius rode to the meeting.

"I agree," Thaos said. "But if Mathas is afraid there are spies watching his castle, well, there are probably spies watching all of our homes."

"I agree with both of you," Claudius said. "But it is known that Chaez is going to school in Wetpr and we are going with the story that Dominic and his men are friends of Chaez."

"While I personally don't think some people will buy that story," Stephan said. "Chaez has grown up a lot since he left home."

"Thaos you have been awfully quiet since the meeting last night," Claudius said. "Is something bothering you son?"

"Yes, but I can't put my finger on it. While much of this is so similar to what Juleta was manipulating when she was trying to steal the throne; I don't know there is something else," Thaos said.

"You mean like you feel we are being watched?" Stephan asked.

"No, it's more like I saw something out of the corner of my eye but I can't remember what it was."

"Isadore, please settle down," Fahron said with a grin. "Everything is perfect; you can't do any more."

"It is just such an honor to have these guests in our home," Isadore said as she moved a vase of flowers for the third time. Then she turned and looked at Fahron. "I know that Dominic and his men are just that they are grown men. But after reading Chaez's letters, I don't know how to explain it. I feel like they are lost boys who need a home and I want them to be comfortable here."

"They were living in caves I am sure they will be very comfortable here," Fahron said jokingly and put his arm around his wife.

"You know what I mean Fahron. Reading Chaez's letters about the people in Ryed made me realize even more how blessed we are."

"They're here," Sally said excitedly as she and April ran into the parlor where Fahron and Isadore were talking.

"Let's meet our guests," Fahron said and took Isadore's hand. Sally and April ran ahead of Isadore and Fahron and out the front door.

"My, how you have grown," the Sanuri said with a broad smile as he hugged Sally then April.

"Sanuri where is Chaez?" Sally asked as she looked at the faces of the men dismounting their horses. "Is he alright?"

"He will be here in just a moment, don't worry," the Sanuri said then walked forward to shake hands with Fahron.

"Please everyone come in," Isadore said. "I know it is early but I have a feast prepared for you."

"I'll have some of the men take your horses to the stable and feed them," Fahron said. "We have chambers prepared if you. Do you want to put your things away first?"

"That might be a good idea," Gabriel said. "It won't take long."

"Of course," Isadore said. "Actually we gave you the entire eastern wing. Fahron said you might have others join you and that you would be holding meetings. So if you would like to follow us we will take you to that wing and you may choose your rooms."

As the group walked towards the eastern wing of the castle Fahron said, "Mathas will be holding the morning meeting here, with all of you so we expect them soon."

"I could use some help here," Chaez's voice rang out as he walked a few feet behind the small crowd.

"Chaez what on earth .." Isadore did not finish her sentence.

"Oh my god, puppies!" Screamed April. April and Sally ran to Chaez who was having difficulty holding two wild puppies.

"One's a boy and the other is a girl," Chaez said as April and Sally grabbed the puppies from his hands. Everyone smiled as they watched the two girls hugging and kissing their gifts.

"Honey," Isadore said and hugged Chaez tightly. Isadore stepped back and stared at her son. "Chaez are you alright? You have so many cuts and bruises."

"You should have seen him before," Michael said with a laugh.

"I am fine Mother," Chaez said and hugged Fahron. "Has everyone been introduced yet?"

"Actually we were going to do that when we got to the dining room. Your mother has a feast prepared for our guests," Fahron said. "We gave them the entire east wing, I don't know if you will want to stay with them or in your room."

"I should probably stay with them," Chaez said and turned as Helen, one of the housekeepers quickly approached the group.

"My Lord I am sorry to interrupt but the King and others have just arrived."

"Thank you Helen, would you take them to the dining room and we will be right down," said Fahron.

"Perhaps we should just leave our gear here and choose our rooms later," Gabriel said.

King Mathas, Matthew and Sorren had barely entered the dining room when April and Sally ran up to them. "Look at what Chaez brought us," April said excitedly and thrust her puppy at Sorren. The men laughed.

"Those are some handsome pups," Sorren said as he pet both of the puppies.

"I see you met the newest members of the family," Fahron said and laughed as he led his guests into the dining room. "Now would be a good time for introductions; Chaez do you want to do the honors?"

Chaez stepped forward. "This is King Mathas you know his son Matthew and Chief Sorren of the Nordes Tribe. Chief Sorren is also one of the ruling members of the kingdom. My father Fahron and my mother Isadore, also ruling members of the kingdom. My little sisters Sally and April." Chaez turned towards the group standing in the doorway.

"You all know the Sanuri, Prince Michael, High Priest Gabriel, High Priest Raphael, Thor is a Venator and a member of Gabriel's team. Joao and Dack are also members of the team.

"Dominic was the leader of the freedom fighters in Ryed. His brother Fennel, his cousin Seth, Noah and Lawrence." The two groups stepped forward and all of the men shook hands.

"We have heard much about you and your men," Mathas said. "It is an honor to have you here and we are grateful that you have agreed to help us."

"The honor is ours," said Dominic.

"Well look at this," Stephan said kiddingly as he, Thaos and Claudius walked into the dining room. "Father let me introduce you."

"Good morning My Lord," Jenny the secretary said as Mayor Deckor walked into his front office. "Would you like some coffee?"

"Yes and the paper," Deckor said as he walked through the lobby and into his private office. "What are you doing here?" Deckor demanded and quickly closed the door.

"You aren't glad to see me?" Hector asked with a grin.

"Did Jenny let you in?"

"No, I was here when she arrived."

Deckor quickly opened the door, "Jenny, I changed my mind about the coffee and paper. I don't want to be disturbed for a while."

"Just checking on my interests," Hector said smugly. "My wife gave you a great deal of money; I want to make sure she invested wisely."

Deckor walked over to a table in his office and poured two glasses of whiskey, then turned and walked towards Hector. "You will not be disappointed but these things take time and I have had other distractions."

"You mean the election?" Hector asked as he took his glass of whiskey.

"Yes, if I lose it will be harder for me to, shall I say, work for your interests."

"How many men are running against you?"

"At this point just Tetly. I've scared or bribed the others."

"And what; you can't scare Tetly?"

"I guess we will find out today," Deckor said with a smirk. "I had two of his hired men killed. I expect the patrols will find the bodies soon."

"Where did you dump them?"

"On the border of Usman's land. Of course I added a few others just to throw everyone off."

"Did you kill them like Usman does?"

"Yes and what a damn mess."

Since the food was prepared, Mathas held his meeting in the dining room of Fahron's castle. "So what exactly are you saying?" Gabriel asked Claudius.

"While both Usman and the Dura Tribe are credible enemies, we all feel something is very wrong here. Of course we could just be paranoid because of all the plots Juleta has sent against us. Basically we really don't know how many enemies we have or who they really are; we would like you to help us determine that," Claudius said.

"Compare the Dura Tribe to the Hutas," said Mathas. "And Usman is a barbarian. He butchers his own people if they talk about the tribe to strangers. Fortunately for us, Thaos knows what bars Usman's men frequent."

Thaos looked across the table at Dominic and his men. "What Mathas hasn't told you is that I was hired by Juleta to spy on her father and to help incite wars in this kingdom. As I got to know more about Juleta and what she was doing I came here and warned Claudius and Stephan."

"I can't prove a damn thing but all of this has the earmark of something that Juleta would do. And before we go any farther all of you have to know that if Usman's men get their hands on you they tie all of your limbs to horses and let the horses pull your body apart. So you might want to reconsider helping us."

Stephan looked at Gabriel and Raphael, "The taverns where Usman's men hang out are like that place that Shanksaw had. We don't want to piss anyone off but we feel that both Chaez and Thor don't look enough like criminals and will stick out like sore thumbs."

"This is the second time," Thor said with frustration. "What do I have to do to look like a criminal?"

Raphael laughed then said, "Natasha sent along a lot of disguises and makeup and stuff. Perhaps we can dirty Chaez and Thor up a little and they can come with us just to watch."

"I don't think that is going to work for Chaez," Fahron said. "Everyone knows who he is."

"Well can't we gather information at other places besides those specific taverns?" Chaez asked.

"We were getting to that," Claudius said. "Ryan recently opened a shop in the main business district of Langer. Besides that Ryan's fine work brings people in, every morning Bella sets up a table with coffee and treats in the front window of the shop. People come in now just to have a cup of coffee and socialize. Ryan is a little on the shy side so he doesn't engage in a lot of conversation but he has been hearing some interesting things which Stephan and Thaos say reminds them of the problems you had with Shanksaw."

"People are saying that someone is abducting people from Langer and everyone is getting paranoid that men are being stolen to work on the ships," continued Claudius.

Stephan was looking at all of the faces around the table and added, "We will take you into Langer, it is a huge port city with ships coming and going every day."

"We've been looking into these stories," said Matthew.

"But so far we haven't found any proof they are true. But people might be afraid to tell us so that is another reason we want your help."

"What kind of shop does Ryan have?" asked Gabriel.

"He works with wood and sells furniture and toys," Claudius said proudly.

"Lawrence is a fine woodcarver," Fennel said. "Maybe he should help in the shop."

"Chaez you and Ryan have become close friends," Claudius said. "I would appreciate it if you checked in on him too; it wouldn't look suspicious if you were hanging out at the shop. Ryan is a fine woodworker but he couldn't defend himself in a fight."

"Are you saying that there are men here like the one that stole me and April and Amy?" Sally asked.

"Honey, we don't know if they are stealing little girls but we think there are some pretty bad men here who might be stealing other people," Isadore said.

"Stephan you told us that you were trying to get information about those other men when you heard about us, didn't you?" asked Sally.

"Yes," Stephan said. "And as soon as we did we came looking for you."

Sally looked at the men sitting around the table, "Stephan, Thaos and the Sanuri saved us from a horrible monster. You know we can help too."

"Sally it is too dangerous," Fahron said.

"When you are a kid everyone talks in front of you like you aren't there. We could work in the shop and just listen to people," said Sally.

"And what would happen if someone caught you listening to them?" the Sanuri asked.

Sally set her puppy on the floor and put her hands on her hips, "Before you saved us April and me saw a lot of really bad things. We aren't stupid and besides Sorren is training me to be a warrior. April and me can make up stories or pretend to cry or I don't' know, hit someone if we have to. Don't laugh!"

"We aren't laughing at you," Gabriel said. "You sound like a young warrior."

"In my tribe warriors are hunting demons by themselves when they are your age," Thor said to Sally. "I think we give the girls a chance. I agree, who is going to suspect them of anything. I will go to the shop too."

"I don't like this idea at all," said Isadore. "It is too dangerous."

"We haven't agreed on anything," Fahron said.

"You know we have been to Ryan's shop before," said April. "We helped to clean it before he opened. And we've gone there to visit with Bella and Nikki and Ingr. There's always lots of people but I never saw anyone scary."

"You two remind me of my little sister," Gabriel said with a smile. "We have not agreed to let you help but if we did there would be rules."

"What sort of rules?" Sally asked.

"You would always have to stay where one of our men could see you. You would have to do what we say and not take any chances."

"We can do that," said Sally with a grin.

"You know I am not brave like Sally," April said. "But if someone would have heard about us before, maybe Margo would still be alive."

Hector held out his glass for Deckor to pour more whiskey in it. "I really don't like you showing your face in my office," Deckor said. "You look too damn much like Thaos. People will get suspicious."

"That was the idea," Hector said with a sneer and took a gulp of his whiskey.

"What are you saying?" Deckor asked.

"This wasn't always my face. My dear wife changed it."

"What are you saying man?" Deckor gasped.

"You heard me; Juleta changed my appearance."

"How on earth did she do that?"

"Her black magics and I am not the only one."

"What! Who?"

"Wait and see, the fun hasn't started yet."

Chapter XXIII
Terrorists among You

As Mayor Deckor and Hector talked there was a knock on the outside door to Deckor's office. This door opened to an alley. "Make sure no one comes in the front door," Deckor said to Hector and quickly walked across the room and opened the back door.

Two men who Hector recognized as hired fighters pushed another man into the room. "Deckor what is the meaning of this?" demanded the portly man. "Who do you think you are sending your thugs after innocent people?"

"So you think you are innocent Wickfield?" asked Deckor.

"What are you trying to say?" Wickfield asked. "I have committed no crimes, which is more than I can say for you."

"See there you go again Wickfield; shooting off your mouth," Deckor said angrily. "And if that isn't bad enough you write it in your damn paper."

"We have freedom of speech here; you haven't taken that away from us yet," Wickfield said as he walked closer to Deckor and stared into the Mayor's eyes.

"Mr. Wickfield doesn't seem to fear you Deckor," Hector said. "Does he have a family?" Deckor sneered at Wickfield.

"You keep my family out of this," Wickfield said.

"Then you stop writing your lies about me," said Deckor.

"You are scared because I print the truth and you don't want people to know what you are really like," Wickfield said.

"Well if you know how bad I am then you know that you and your family are in great danger if you piss me off," Deckor said. "Do you understand me?" Deckor and Wickfield stared at each other with hatred in their eyes. "Well do you!"

"Yes," Wickfield said and turned to leave the room.

"Wickfield you know better than to tell anyone about this conversation don't you?" Deckor asked in a stern tone. Wickfield didn't say anything but stomped out of the office and slammed the door behind him.

Deckor turned to the two hired fighters, "Ackley keep an eye on him and let me know if he meets with any members of the ruling families."

"Sure boss."

"And Ackley keep a low profile," Deckor said. "Wickfield is the owner of the most powerful newspaper in Lentz. People watch him and will notice you following him."

"I am finding this conversation upsetting," Isadore said. "These girls have been through enough. So can we please change the subject for a moment?" No one spoke so Isadore continued. "I know we want to keep this work a secret but honestly we are so proud to have all of you under our roof that I invited a few people here for dinner. Now Gabriel and Raphael you have met most of them. It will be the families of all of us here and a few friends."

"When she says friends, she means our wives invited women from the Nordes Tribe to meet you," Matthew said. Joao let out a war cry and everyone laughed.

"All the women are warriors and will not talk about your presence here," Sorren said with a grin. "But don't be surprised if a few of them volunteer to help you."

"We might take them up on it," Gabriel said. "Sorren we know how well you train your warriors but you will have to decide who you think can work covertly."

"Jasmine wants to help," Dack said. "She could teach them the ropes."

"Let's see what the night brings and we will talk about this later," Gabriel said. "After we unpack I would like to have another meeting."

"Would some of you be able to stay and help us to get a better understanding of the politics and histories of this area?"

"We already planned to have Sorren, Stephan and Thaos stay," Mathas said. "The rest of us have a ceremony at the fort that we must attend. Stephan, Sorren and Thaos can give you three uniquely different prospectives. And I brought these along," Mathas said and picked up a satchel from the floor. "These are records from our war with the Dura Tribe. You may make copies of any of this information but I do need these records back."

"Isadore since the baby is only three days old, Angelina and I won't be coming tonight," Matthew said.

"My dear, I didn't expect you to but I do have some gifts for you to take home."

The Sanuri looked at Gabriel and Raphael and said, "Why don't you take a few minutes and tell them what we have been discussing."

"The Sanuri believes that the darkness that is plaguing our world will get considerably worse," Raphael explained. "He said that after Ryed we should realize that a handful of warriors cannot fight all of the battles of this world. The Sanuri suggested that we form other teams like Gabriel's and those teams can rotate missions."

"I like that idea," Sorren said with a nod.

"All of this is just in the preliminary stages," Gabriel said. "So we have much to decide. But we will train the teams so they aren't going into anything blind. Since many of you have worked with us you could recommend people."

"I think we should have a team in this kingdom," Stephan said. "But we would need some new faces."

"And these are the things we need to work out," Gabriel said. "When we return home, Raphael and I will hold meetings and of course all of you are invited. We will keep you informed. We feel that our team is strong because we embrace the differences of our members and try to learn from their cultures. I would strongly suggest you consider this when forming a team."

"I think that any of us that have worked with your team agrees," Sorren said. And I agree with Stephan, with all that is going on we should have a team here." Sorren paused. "Michael are you alright?"

"I dreamt about all of this last night," Michael said. "I mean everything, the food on the table, what you are saying, even the puppies in the room. But in my dream I kept feeling like all of you were in great danger."

"After Ruth showed us your dreams, we should probably take this as a warning," said Sorren.

"It is like I am seeing everything from my dream again," Michael said with a confused look on his face. "Isadore the dinner tonight you said it was only the families and women from the Nordes Tribe?"

"Yes, why?" Isadore asked.

"I didn't remember all of this in my dream but I see a huge celebration at a castle. Everyone here is there and I am sensing danger," said Michael.

"We have a huge celebration planned for all of you at our castle," Mathas said. "We just haven't set the date because of the mission."

"I think the Angels were sending Michael a message," the Sanuri said.

"Why me and not you or Gabriel or Raphael?" Michael asked with a hint of annoyance.

"Because they are trying to get you used to communicating with them," the Sanuri replied.

"I don't think it comes as easy for me as it does the rest of you," said Michael.

"It didn't come easy for any of us," Matthew said. "But with what we are doing it is necessary. And they always help us."

"I don't know," Michael grumbled.

"Son is something else going on?" Sorren asked. Michael did not answer.

After the meal, Gabriel's group, Thaos, Stephan and Sorren went to the east wing of Fahron's castle. The first thing the group did was to set up a large meeting room. Then Michael and Fennel walked around the wing to determine security issues, while the other men moved into chambers. Isadore sent trays of coffee and sweets to the east wing just as the men were reconvening in the meeting room.

"Ok I know I am not cultured," Thor said with a laugh as he poured himself a cup of coffee. "But not only is my room fancy but there are bottles of wine and whiskey besides fruit and a big plate of chocolates."

"All the rooms are like that," Raphael said. "We are being treated well."

"Chaez you grew up like this?" asked Dack. "Because you seem so normal."

Chaez laughed loudly. "My parents are going all out for you. They are very proud to have you here. Believe me I never had chocolates and whiskey in my bedroom."

"Michael and Fennel why don't you start and tell us what you found," Gabriel said.

"Since we are on the first floor every set of chambers has a small courtyard and garden attached. While these are very nice the gardens have lots of large bushes and trees where people can hide. There are locks on the balcony doors but it wouldn't take much to break them open," said Fennel.

"Chaez we know there are soldiers stationed here," Michael said. "And we are not showing disrespect but since Sudfad has had so many issues with spies in his military and castle you really can't rule out the same thing. And that goes for all of you," Michael said as he looked at Stephan and Thaos.

"I am sure you all noticed that there are heavy drapes that can be pulled across the windows in the balcony doors. Of course that can prevent us from seeing out as well as someone from seeing in," Fennel said.

"It is our understanding," said Dominic. "That the way you have organized the power here is that someone would have to kill Mathas, Claudius, Fahron, Sorren and Matthew to take the throne. Is there anyone else on that list?"

"No," Stephan said. "But if someone was killing them off they would go after Rosa, Angelina and the children also."

"I want to set some ground rules for these meetings," Gabriel said. "We need to explore ideas and examine information. So no one should take offense at what is being said. And if someone does we should discuss that so there are no hard feelings. Now that I have said that; I have only met Queen Rosa a handful of times. I believe she is a loving and charming woman but she is no threat for the throne. Angelina on the other hand is a different matter. Sorren you raised her to lead your tribe. She is more than capable of leading a kingdom or a revolt against terrorists."

Sorren smiled proudly at Gabriel's words. "In my opinion if I were trying to ruin the families I would put Angelina on that list. One because of her power and two because it would cripple Matthew. I believe that was Juleta's plan when she had Angelina kidnapped. Now, Stephan and Thaos you are forces to be reckoned with in your own rights. And any terrorist who is doing their homework would know you would never stand around while the ruling families were being murdered."

"To my understanding all of the attacks against the ruling families over the last few years have been sponsored by Juleta. And you don't really know if she has more bounties on you. And even if she doesn't I am sure Usman and any other enemies you might have, have been watching how you react to these attacks."

"Gabriel can I interrupt for a moment?" Chaez said as he stood up. "Timothy wasn't a dark lord but it is our understanding that he made many promises to powerful demons, who may not have been the same ones that Juleta dealt with."

"Thank you; that is a good point." Gabriel said. "And the Angels told us that there are bounties on all of us who entered into Baal's regime. The point that I am trying to make is that if I were your enemy I would change my strategies."

Raphael stood up. "Like our team, when all of you are together you can't be defeated. Your enemies have tried to separate a few of you and that too did not work. Gabriel and I fear that plans will be put into motion to get each and every one of you alone and these attacks will be launched simultaneously. Now we know you aren't going to live in fear but we believe you really need to be aware of this."

"Now that we are here," Raphael continued. "We would really like all of you to take a back seat and let us work on this mission," Raphael was looking at Thaos, Stephan and Sorren as he spoke.

"I was with you right up until that last sentence," Thaos said. "While it has merit, we aren't going to sit around and wait to be picked off."

"You aren't going to be sitting around," Raphael continued. "You will be preparing for war. Now of course these are our opinions with the information we have to this point. Chaez you have changed greatly since you left home and anyone who sees you now will realize that; you too will be considered an obstacle."

"Thank you," Chaez said which made the others grin.

"Sanuri you have been quiet; what are your thoughts?" Sorren asked.

"Unfortunately I don't have any easy answers for you. I believe that you have more threats than you realize and from the message that the Angels sent to Michael I believe some of your threats are basically in front of your faces," the Sanuri explained. "It has been my experience that when the Angels or The Great Ruler sends me messages…well, let's just say there is more to it than what appears on face value. They want us to think and to stretch past our boundaries."

"While Michael's dream or vision took place at a celebration at Mathas' castle do not limit your thinking about this matter."

"I feel the message was that you know your enemies but you don't think of them as enemies. I believe you have a similar situation as Sudfad had. I think your families should look with new eyes at some of the people you deal with every day. Sorren, I know you are new to this position but previously when I have stayed here, Mathas, Fahron and Claudius routinely had meetings in their homes with many different types of people. While I have no facts I believe this is an area of concern."

"As I did when Juleta was alive," the Sanuri continued. "I have called for flocks of Enrops to watch over your families." The Sanuri paused and appeared to be listening to something the other men could not hear. "Dack and Joao fly to the fort and tell Mathas and the others what we are talking about and tell Matthew that he and his family should travel here tonight with the others. Tell him that Angelina and the baby will be alright. I don't see any direct threats but I don't believe it is a good idea to leave them behind."

   After Dack and Joao left the room the Sanuri continued. "Sorren your tribe is a very tight knit group but don't rule out the fact that you too could have spies and terrorists among you."

   "Why, Luca I have never seen you act nervous before," Diana teased. "We aren't trying to set you up with Natalie."

   "And you are sure that she knows that?" Luca asked.

   "Luca, Natalie and Kate are some of the friends who Vivian and I write to. We didn't even think to ask Natalie here until Iris suggested it. Natalie knows about you and Lila only because we have written about everyone in the family. We have never said that we wanted the two of you to meet," said Diana. "Although now that I think about it I could see the two of you liking each other."

   "There she goes," Misha said. "It's like she can't turn it off. Luca they really haven't tried to set you up and I will make sure that doesn't change once Natalie gets here."

   "Thanks," Luca said. "I am not looking for a girlfriend and I have no idea why I am so nervous."

Diana kissed Luca on the cheek, "Because your heart is still healing. Luca don't feel pressured into anything and please don't tell Kate that we are trying to set her up with Edward. Misha go to the fort and tell Edward that he can't tell Kate we are trying to match them up. Don't laugh I am serious."

"Why?" Misha asked with a grin.

"Because Kate will get mad and then she won't even give Edward a chance. Kate is, I am trying to think of the right word. She is really nice and smart but she is…"

"She is what?" asked Luca.

"She is rather headstrong," Diana said.

"Oh, like you and Vivian aren't?" Misha teased.

"Oh, she is a lot worse than we are," Diana said and started to laugh. "If Edward makes her mad she is liable to punch him."

"Luca I think dinner tonight will be a lot more fun than I thought," Misha said and laughed.

"Misha don't you stir things up," Diana scolded.

"Please excuse us," Isadore said as she, Sally and April walked into the meeting in the east wing. "I just wanted to tell you that our guests will be arriving within the hour."

"It is that late already?" Raphael asked with astonishment.

Isadore smiled, "You've been at it for six hours, I wasn't sure if I should interrupt you. "If this is how you plan to work I can have your meals served in here."

"No, we will eat with the family," Gabriel said. "But thank you for your graciousness. We very much appreciate it."

As Gabriel was talking both Sally and April walked up to Chaez and hugged him. "We didn't thank you for the puppies," Sally said. "We love them."

"Isadore is this a formal affair?" Gabriel asked.

"No, all of you are dressed just fine. But the celebration at Mathas' will be formal. If you don't have suits I can have Fahron's tailor come to the castle."

"That might not be a good idea," Raphael said. "One of Renya's seamstresses was a spy."

"Well, wouldn't the Sanuri be able to tell?" asked Isadore.

"Why don't you have him come to the castle tomorrow and I will see what I can find out," the Sanuri said.

"They're here!" Christopher yelled as he and Nicholas ran into the house.

"What on earth are you boys doing?" Emeral asked. "You are soaking wet. You weren't at the river were you?"

"What!" Hannah gasped as she and Vivian walked out of the kitchen.

"No, we are trying to give Jasper a bath cuz he got into something stinky but he doesn't like baths. Joey, Paul and Adrone are trying to hold him in the tub so we've got to get back," Christopher said without taking a breath.

"Mother can you hold Ian?" Bekka said as she laughed. "I'll go out with the boys."

"We are by the sandbox," Nicholas said and he and Christopher ran out of the house.

"Wait for us," Diana said as she and Iris walked out of the kitchen.

Six Ruala warriors landed in the front yard of Gabriel's house. They carried Natalie and her baby and Kate. Both women stared with amazement at the mansion in front of them.

"We are so glad you are here," Vivian said as she and Diana ran up to their friends and hugged them.

Emeral walked up to the Ruala warriors, "We have rooms prepared for all of you and we are having a dinner party tonight. The boys are looking forward to seeing you but none of them are here right now."

"A dinner party," Natalie said shyly.

"We are glad to have you here," Hannah said. "Actually most of our team is gone right now but we can tell you all about that over dinner."

Everyone remained in the front yard as introductions were made; as the group was turning to walk into the house they heard yelling.

"No Jasper, come back here."

"Jasper don't."

"Oh no he rolled in it again."

The group laughed as they watched a muddy and wet dog running around the yard with five little boys behind him. All of the boys were as wet and muddy as the dog. Bekka walked up to the group of adults with an armload of towels. "I'm not even going to try and catch them," she said with a grin.

The meeting ended in the east wing and the men all walked directly to the Great Hall of the castle, which was filled with guests.

"We should have ended the meeting earlier," Gabriel said with embarrassment to Raphael. "I forgot something; I will be right back."

"Jasmine you are walking," Seth said with surprise as Jasmine walked towards him on crutches.

"I'm not very good on these things but at least people don't have to carry me anymore," Jasmine said. Then was taken by surprise when Seth kissed her on the cheek.

"I am glad you are here," Seth said shyly. "I've been thinking about you."

Jasmine smiled and blushed, "I've been thinking about you too. What have you been doing all day?"

"Meetings about the mission. Are you going back to your tribe or are you staying here to help us?"

"I'd like to help if they will have me."

"Let's talk to Raphael," Seth said. "You might be able to help gather information in the city. There are rumors that people are disappearing." As Seth and Jasmine walked up to Raphael, Gabriel reentered the Great Hall and walked up to Claudius and his family who were standing together in a group.

"Christopher would kill me if I forgot to give this to Amy," Gabriel said as he handed a small box to Thaos. Nikki and Thaos were standing next to each other and each holding one of their small sons.

"It's not a wedding ring is it?" Thaos asked with a grin.

"Thaos," Nikki scolded then she looked behind her and called to Amy.

"Amy this is a gift from Christopher," Thaos said and handed her the box.

Amy's eyes grew wide with excitement. "What is it?"

"We don't know," Thaos said and laughed as Amy tore the ribbon off the box.

"Oh Papa, Mama look," Amy said and took a golden bracelet out of the box.

"Amy that is beautiful," Nikki said. "Thank Gabriel for bringing it then show the rest of the family."

Gabriel squatted down and hugged Amy, "Thank you Gabriel. I just love it." Then Amy turned and yelled, "Grandma, Grandpa look!"

"Just wait until Cere gets older," Thaos said to Gabriel with a grin.

"Gabriel, Thaos acts like he thinks Christopher and Amy are going to run away and get married," Nikki said. "I think it is cute." Thaos looked at Gabriel and winked.

Diana, Vivian and Cassandra showed their guests to their chambers. Kate and Natalie wanted to share chambers as did the two female Ruala warriors Nana and Risa. Adin, Enzo, Ralf and Sol decided to all stay in one of the larger chambers.

"We have quite a bundle of letters for you," Adin said as he handed a large pouch to Vivian.

"Thank you, Mother and Father will be so happy. They love it here but they miss their tribe too," Vivian said.

"I can't believe how fancy this home is and look at the two of you," said Natalie.

"You mean because of the way we are dressed or how big I am already?" Diana asked with a grin.

Kate and Natalie laughed. "Both I guess," said Natalie.

"It is a different life but it's a really good life," Vivian said. "You'll like it here. I hear voices; maybe we should go down stairs."

Chapter XXIV
Celebrations

"Your friends are lovely girls," Emeral whispered to Vivian. "Why don't you introduce them to everyone and we'll get the refreshments.

"Natasha I want to introduce you to some friends," Calen yelled in the dining room.

"Honey I had to get Lily," Natasha said as she approached the small group. Calen, Luca, Koby, Dagon and Misha were standing with the newly arrived Rualas. "This is my wife Natasha and our daughter Lily," Calen said proudly. "And these are old friends of ours: Adin, Enzo, Ralf, Nana, Sol and Risa. We all grew up together."

"When we heard the Venatores needed to be brought here; we jumped at the chance," Enzo said. "We thought it was time for a reunion."

"Well, we are glad you are here and we would like to talk a little business too," Luca said.

"What do you mean?" Adin asked.

"We are forming more teams, but we can go into all that over dinner," said Luca as he saw Vivian and Diana walking towards the group with Natalie, Hunter and Kate.

"Is Ratri here?" Nana asked. "We heard he got married."

"Actually they just flew into Salar with Father," Misha said. "They had to pick up some things for Emeral."

"We are going to interrupt for a minute," Diana said and giggled. "Kate, Natalie this is my husband Misha." Misha put his arm around Diana as she spoke. "And these are my brothers-in-law: Luca, Calen and his wife Natasha, Koby is married to Bekka you met her earlier and Dagon. Dagon where is Rachel?"

"Helping her mother with a few things. They will be here soon," Dagon said. "I remember seeing both of you when we were in the village," Dagon said to Natalie and Kate.

"All of you look familiar but I don't think we ever got a chance to talk," Kate said. "But we have heard a great deal about you."

"Wait a minute; that may be good or bad depending on who you heard it from," Misha said teasingly.

"It was all good," said Kate.

"We have to make some more introductions," Diana said as she saw Edward, Jared, Zoya, Archetenus and Delilia walking into the dining room with their babies.

"We'll be back," Vivian said.

As soon as the women left the group Misha said, "Luca did you notice how Diana introduced everyone. She made it clear you are single. You better watch out."

"What is going on?" asked Risa.

"Vivian and Diana thought Natalie and I might become friends because we are both widowed and have children," Luca said. "But I am not ready for anything more than friendship."

"They are both really nice," Risa said referring to Kate and Natalie. "I certainly don't get the impression that either of them are looking for a husband. But I think Natalie could use a friend; she seems kind of broken."

"Luca!" Christopher yelled and jumped into Luca's arms.

"Elan helped me to clean up the boys and Jasper," Bekka said as she laughed. She walked up to Koby and kissed him.

"What did you do?" Luca asked Christopher.

Christopher took a big breath and said, "Jasper rolled in something really stinky and we were afraid Hannah wouldn't let him in the house. So we tried to give him a bath but he kept jumping out of the tub and getting dirty again."

"You should have seen them," Elan said as he held Joey's hand. "All the boys were as muddy and stinky as Jasper."

"What, did you roll in it too?" Luca teased.

Christopher's mouth fell open, "Luca! No, Jasper rolled on us."

"The King and Queen are here," Emeral announced as the entire Royal Family entered the dining room. Which included Petra's three dogs.

"Luca put me down," Christopher said excitedly. All of the children in the house now ran towards each other.

"Boys take your guests into the playroom," Emeral said loudly. With these words Raul's and Simons four sons and Petra ran wildly towards the playroom with Joey, Nicholas, Christopher, Adrone, Paul and four dogs.

"It's a good thing you have a big house," Raul said and laughed.

"Dominic I want you to meet my family," Stephan said. "Where are the others?"

"Fennel bring everyone here," Dominic yelled to his brother. Within moments the freedom fighters of Ryed were gathered around Stephan and Ingr.

"This is my beautiful wife Ingr, our children Marcus Stephan and Sicily Bella and this is Dominic, Fennel, Lawrence, Noah and Seth," Stephan said. "And as you can see we will have another baby soon," Stephan said proudly.

"Stephan talked about you and the babies all of the time," Dominic said as Stephan handed him Marcus. "It's been a long time since I held a baby," Dominic said with a sadness to his voice that touched Ingr.

"Does anyone want to hold Sicily?" Ingr asked.

"I will," Fennel said quickly and took the baby. "Stephan may have told you that we haven't had normal lives for a very long time."

"Well, we are all very proud of you," Ingr said. "We have so many freedoms here that is was difficult to read the letters from everyone in Ryed. It sounds like an awful place to live."

"After seeing what life is like here and in Wetpr," Lawrence said. "I think the people in Ryed merely exist."

"We know that this mission is kind of secret but Bella really wants to have all of you over to our home for a celebration. It would mean a lot to her," Ingr said.

"I am sure we can work that out," said Dominic.

"Well, I should tell Mother it should be soon because you are going to have that baby in a few weeks," Stephan said.

"As long as the celebration isn't the night I give birth we will be alright," Ingr said and winked at Dominic. "Stephan was at war and missed the births of the twins so he is really nervous about this one."

"I am and I can't even begin to tell you why," Stephan said with a grin.

"Now I hope you don't get mad," Ingr said with a big smile. "But you see that group of girls standing with Joao and Dack; well we asked them here to meet all of you. Are you ready for introductions?"

Sally walked up to Fahron, Isadore, Chaez, Sorren and Shara. Sally looked at Shara and grinned then at Chaez, "Chaez can I talk to you?"

"Have you even put that pup down today?" Chaez teased.

"Yes, I fed him and he had to go to outside but that's not what I want to talk to you about," Sally said and looked at Shara again.

"Chaez those two are up to something," Sorren said and winked.

"Chaez I want you to meet someone," Sally said. "She's a warrior and she's really pretty and really nice."

"Are you fixing me up with girls?" Chaez asked and laughed loudly.

"No, just one," Sally said with a grin. "Shara tell him, Lana is really nice."

"Lana is a lovely girl," Shara said. "She's been helping with the training; that is how Sally met her."

"Did you know about this?" Chaez asked his parents who were both grinning.

"No, neither of us did," Fahron said. "But I would be interested in seeing who Sally picked out for you."

"I'll go get her," Sally said enthusiastically and ran from the group. A few moments later Sally was walking towards the group and holding hands with a beautiful young woman who had long black curly hair and large blue eyes. "Lana this is my brother Chaez; I told you about him. And Chaez this is Lana." Both Chaez and Lana blushed at the introduction.

"It is nice to meet you," Chaez said nervously. "This is our father Fahron and our Mother Isadore." Both Fahron and Isadore were grinning.

Fahron shook hands with Lana, "Shara says you are one of Sally's trainers."

"Yes," Lana said shyly. "She is very enthusiastic and learns quickly."

"Chaez why don't you get Lana a glass of wine and show her around the castle," Isadore said.

"Do you want to see it?" Chaez was clearly embarrassed.

"Sure," Lana said as she too felt uncomfortable.

Chaez took Lana's hand and they walked towards one of the refreshment tables. "I told you she was pretty," said Sally.

"And I think Chaez thinks so too," Fahron said with a grin. "Sally I would say you did a good job." All the adults laughed

"Sally talks about you all of the time but I didn't know she was..." Lana paused.

"She was trying to fix us up?" Chaez said and chuckled. "She told me moments before we met. I am sorry that was so awkward. Do you really want to see the castle or did you just say that to get away from everyone?"

"No, I would like to see it. You live so differently from us."

"Ryan come here," Claudius yelled and motioned for Ryan to join him, Bella and Gabriel.

"Thank you," Ryan said. "Elexas is here."

"Who is Elexas?" Gabriel asked with a grin.

Claudius glanced at Bella then said, "A female predator might be a good description."

"She's an awful girl," Bella said disapprovingly. "She is always chasing men and she wanted to have sex with Nikki and Thaos, can you believe that?"

Gabriel could see that Bella was mad so he was trying very hard not to laugh. Gabriel turned to Ryan. "Claudius and Bella have been telling me about the toys you are making for the orphanage in Wetpr. I think that is a wonderful thing you are doing and you know my wife works there. You should send Hannah a letter and she will help set up a time for you to distribute them."

"Hannah works there?" Ryan asked.

"Yes, she is one of the physicians for the children."

"Oh, I will. It would help for me to know how many boys and girls there are and some of the ages."

"Erebus you look so good," Diana said and hugged her friend as he walked slowly into the dining room with a cane.

"Hannah says I am doing better every day although I would argue that," Erebus said and smiled.

269

"Erebus these are two friends from our tribe, this is Natalie and her baby Hunter and Kate. They are visiting us," Diana said. "Erebus is from Ryed; we wrote to you about him."

"Yes, I am the sorcerer who can't seem to die," Erebus said and laughed.

"Vivian and Diana have told us a great deal about you," Kate said. "I have to admit you are not what I would expect a sorcerer to be."

"Is that good or bad?" Erebus asked with a wink.

"Good," Kate said. "Do you need help?"

"No, I probably look worse than I am," Erebus said. "But I could use a glass of whiskey."

"I'll get it for you," Diana said.

"Wait," Erebus said. "Horace, Rachel, Zelda and Zack will be here in a few minutes. Horace is going to put on a puppet show for the children. I don't know how much room he is going to need."

"Kate and Natalie can you help Erebus get a seat and a glass of whiskey so Diana and I can set up a space for the puppet show?" Vivian asked.

"Luca go over there and talk to that poor girl; she looks so out of place," Emeral said.

"What should I say?"

"Did one of my sons actually ask me how to talk to a girl?"

"Well this is a little different."

"Luca you are probably the only person here that she can relate to right now. You have Emma, take her over and introduce her to Natalie and Kate."

Luca looked uncomfortable as he walked up to the two women. "Thought I would introduce you to my daughter Emma."

"She's a beautiful baby," Natalie said.

"She looks exactly like Lila," Luca said with a mixture of pride and sadness. "Natalie I have got to be honest. Everyone wants you and me to talk because we are both in the same situation. But I have to tell you I am not looking for anything more than a friend."

"I am so glad to hear you say that," Natalie said. "The way everyone is acting I thought they were trying to fix us up."

"No, the family knows neither of us are ready for something like that. I think they hope we can both heal if we have someone to talk to."

"Luca I don't know you," Kate said sweetly. "But for my part I think that is a good idea. I am going to leave the two of you alone."

Luca looked at Natalie. "I would like that," she said as tears ran down her cheeks.

Vivian and Diana helped Horace and Rachel set up the stage for the puppets in the main parlor of the house. Zack's job was to tell the adults about the surprise as Zelda carried in dishes of food. Ten minutes later Annabelle, Vitomas, Cassandra, Melinda, Iris and Ella brought all of the children into the parlor. Some of the children squealed with excitement while others stared at the stage in awe. All of the adults gathered around and the show began.

Edward walked up to the crowd and stood next to Kate, who smiled at him. "How long are you and Natalie going to be in Wetpr?" Edward asked.

"I don't know, why?"

"Because your names came up at the meeting we had today," Edward said. "Expect Joshua to talk to you later but basically we are forming several more teams like Gabriel's and we are looking for the right mix of people. I will be heading one of the teams."

"You and Natalie are welcome to train with us to see if you would be interested in being on a team."

"Really? You don't even know us."

"That is true but we have nine members of your tribe here who do know you. We are planning on talking to you, Natalie and the six Rualas who brought you here after dinner. So something for you to think about."

"I will be at your meeting but I doubt if Natalie will. She and Luca are talking about, well, you know they both lost their spouses recently. I hope it helps them. I don't mean to say Natalie won't be interested in joining a team."

"I know what you are saying. Luca is a great guy but he has been like a walking dead man since Lila died. We could talk to him but I think it is different to talk to someone who has suffered the same experiences. We should just let the two of them be."

Thaos pulled Noah aside. "My wife wants me to warn you about Elexas," Thaos said with a grin.

Noah laughed, "Thaos we weren't living in caves that long. I know what she wants. She's not exactly subtle. And she is a beauty."

"Well don't get attached because you're probably not the only man in her bed tonight."

"I expect you are right," Noah said and laughed as he walked back towards Elexas.

Natalie and Luca walked out to one of the gardens and sat on a bench; each of them holding their babies. "Luca when Lila died did you feel so, I don't even know how to explain it. I don't even feel like I am alive anymore."

"The Angel Miranda, she was in your village. She said that I lost my spirit. I don't really know what that means but I felt like you do. I don't really remember much for weeks after Lila died, it is all a blur."

"How did you get your spirit back?"

"When Miranda said that to me she kissed me on the forehead and after that I started to get better."

"I wonder if she would help me," Natalie said. "I have Hunter to take care of and sometimes it is scary because it's like I can't think."

"Then it's good that you are here because the family can help. I wouldn't even go near Emma for days afterwards because I blamed her for Lila's death. Then Emeral told me that from watching Lila die, Emeral thought that Lila knew something really bad was wrong with her but she hung on until she could give me Emma as a gift. Then when I saw Emma I don't know how, but I realized that Emeral was right."

Natalie was crying as she listened to Luca speak, she reached over and squeezed Luca's hand. "Troy was huge and he was such a fierce warrior. We hunted packs of demons all of the time. Who would think that Troy would be killed by an animal? We aren't really sure what killed him because by time we found his body..." Natalie paused. "Other animals had gotten to his remains."

Both Natalie and Luca were quiet before she spoke again. "I am so thankful for my tribe. I don't have any family and I am so unfocused; others were hunting and bringing food for us. A Venator that can't even hunt," Natalie said and started to cry harder.

"I don't care how well you are trained as a warrior, you are grieving. I adopted Lila's little brother as my son, Christopher. I'll be honest, I don't remember taking care of him right after Lila's death; thank god we were here with the family." Luca paused. "Natalie I am going to tell you something but don't get mad. We are forming more teams like Gabriel's and Joshua suggested you and Kate be on the teams. But after talking to you, I don't think you are ready. Because I know what you are going through."

"I do want to get back to work."

"Well stay here with us for a while. Give yourself some time before you make those kinds of decisions. That was Natasha calling us in for dinner. Are you ready?"

Natalie nodded and wiped the tears from her cheeks. Luca took her hand and the two stood up and walked into the house.

"Luca you missed the puppet show," Christopher yelled when Luca and Natalie walked into the dining room.

"That's my son," Luca said with a grin.

"You said he was adopted but he looks like he could really be your son," Natalie said.

"I know," Christopher said loudly and nodded. Christopher could hear what Natalie and Luca were saying because everyone in the huge room had stopped talking and were watching Luca and Natalie walk in.

Both Luca and Natalie noticed that the only empty chair was next to Luca's. Luca helped Natalie into her chair then said loudly, "You can all start talking again."

"Sorry, I guess that was kind of rude," Natasha said then giggled. "Luca do you want me to hold Emma so you can cut your meat?" Natasha stood up and walked to Luca and took the baby. "You did miss a good puppet show," Natasha said and returned to her seat.

"Horace that was absolutely delightful," Renya said. "Could we hire you to come to the castle and put on shows?"

"I won't take any money. I get pleasure from the children's reactions. I would be glad to do it," Horace said.

"Father has one entire room in the house filled with puppets he is making. They are in various stages of, I guess I don't know how to describe it," Rachel said.

"Coming alive," Horace said with a grin.

"Can Kyra and I come over and see how you make them?" Petra asked.

"Certainly," Horace said. "Anyone can come over, we would enjoy the company. But since I do a lot of carving I don't want the smaller children touching the tools."

"I am coming over," Sam said.

"Why did I know you were going to say that?" Koby said with a grin. "Being a grandfather suits you."

"We should probably get back to the celebration," said Chaez. "The meal will be served soon."

"I can't believe how big this castle is," Lana said. "Our entire tribe could live in here."

"We certainly don't use all these rooms but all of the castles are large so people can take shelter here if they need to. And that includes your tribe too," Chaez paused. "Lana I know Sally put us both on the spot but I have really enjoyed talking to you. Would you do me the honor of sitting at the head table with me at the feast?"

"I have never sat at a head table; what do I do?"

"Nothing special, just eat and drink. Sorren and Shara will be there as well as the heads of all the ruling families."

"Alright," Lana said shyly.

As Chaez and Lana entered the Great Hall they saw Joao, Dack and Thor surrounded by a group of women. Dack saw Chaez and waved. "We really like it here," Dack yelled with a grin.

"You know you don't have to stay with us old married guys," Gabriel said kiddingly to Dominic and Fennel. "There are a lot of beautiful women here, you should mingle."

Dominic grinned. "Maybe later."

"Noah and Lawrence look like they are having fun," Raphael said with a mischievous smile.

"They deserve it," Dominic said. "We couldn't afford to have relationships; it was just too dangerous for everyone."

"Seth is the youngest and has been with us since he was a small boy," Fennel said. "Jasmine is his first crush. We tease him but it is nice to see him acting like a normal young man again. I guess we were so used to our lives that we didn't see how awful they were until we left Ryed. It was normal for us and now we see our pasts as all of you did."

"I think I speak for everyone in this room when I say we are all glad you came back with us," Raphael said. "Dominic we know you are still considering our offer to make you the leader of a team. Gabriel and I were talking and we feel it is a little unfair to ask you to make that decision without knowing everything it entails. And that includes not only your training for the position but also the training for becoming a Patronus priest. Would you and Fennel like to stop by our chambers after the celebration for a short meeting?"

Chapter XXV
Meetings

"Ackley what is the meaning of this?" snapped Deckor. "It's the middle of the night. This better be important." Deckor was tying his silk robe as he walked into the study of his home, where Ackley was waiting.

"Boss, you know I wouldn't come to your home unless it was important. Me and the boys found a bunch of these posted all over the city. We've been tearing them down." Ackley handed Deckor a poster.

The veins started to protrude from Deckor's neck as he read the poster. "Do you know who is behind this!" Deckor demanded.

"No but I got the boys asking around. I figure it is either Tetly or Wickfield."

"It could be supporters of Tetly so I don't want your men ruffing anyone up; at least not yet." As Deckor talked he moved closer to the fire in the hearth and examined the poster. "This isn't printed it is hand written. I don't think Wickfield is behind this, especially after we threatened his family."

Deckor walked over to his desk and opened a small drawer. He took out a pouch of gold coins and threw it to Ackley. "You did well. We are too close to the elections for any mistakes. I want your men to keep their ears open but no one takes any action until I say so; got it."

"Luca I agree that I am not ready for a mission but I would like to go to the meeting but I have to put Hunter down first," Natalie said as everyone was leaving the dining room table.

"I'll take him," Cassandra said. "Elan and I just adopted two children so we won't be going on missions away from home for a while."

"Are you sure?" asked Natalie.

"I love babies," Cassandra said. "Just come to our chambers when the meeting is over."

"The girls are taking the children home," Raul said as he, Simon and Sudfad walked into Gabriel's study. "Hope you don't mind if we sit in."

"Of course not," Calen said. "We will be set up in a few minutes. Please help yourselves. Hannah bought cigars and brandy for us. I have to get some more chairs."

"Our wives went back to the castle," Jared said as he and Archetenus walked into the study and poured themselves some brandy.

"Emeral, Ella, Iris and Zelda are watching all the babies," Natasha said. "Sorry we are late." Natasha, Hannah and Vivian entered the study together.

"You aren't late," Misha said. "We know it is late so we don't plan on having a long meeting. For some of you who are new here I am going to explain a little of our history. Gabriel and Raphael are both Patronus priests. For years Gabriel has led a small team which specializes in clandestine missions. In this room Natasha, Calen, Luca, Dagon, Koby and me primarily made up the team. While Raphael worked with Gabriel, Raphael was a leader of troops."

"Without going into lots of detail there has been more need for Gabriel's team and the missions have gotten bigger and bloodier. Because we have won most of our battles the demons and dark lords are hunting us now. Most of us in this room have been on constant missions for the last two years. While we are all warriors this has taken a toll on all of us and our families. Calen will explain the next part," Misha said and sat down.

"As you can see our team has gotten bigger," Calen said. "And that is out of necessity. But we are all married now and having babies so while there are a lot of members often times we are still greatly shorthanded. Some members of our team are in Lentz on a mission. With them are five of the original freedom fighters from Ryed and the Sanuri."

"The Sanuri told Gabriel and Raphael that there are going to be many missions and battles in our future and we will need more teams like the one that Gabriel established. Today some of us had a very long meeting and we want to tell you some of the things that we came up with. Of course this is all for discussion."

"Gabriel carefully picks the members of the team and as we have become more involved with other groups such as the Nordes Tribe and the Clan of Gesmal we realize these new members greatly add to our team. So today this is what we came up with. We would like to create six new teams. Edward stand up. Edward has experience in clandestine operations and has already received some of the training. He will be leading one of the teams."

"Dominic, the leader of the freedom fighters of Ryed has been asked to also lead a team but he has not given us an answer yet. While all of us are experienced in battle, anyone who has seen Gabriel's team in action realizes this is an entirely different set of skills. We would like to establish core members for each team then allow many of the rest of you to work on missions as needed."

"Raul, Simon, Jared and Archetenus will you please stand up?" Calen asked. "These men are not specifically members of the team yet they have worked with us almost constantly for the last two years. The missions themselves will determine the members that we need. Now I will let Dagon talk."

"Traditionally Gabriel, Natasha and maybe one or two other humans would be playing roles and would make direct contact with whoever. The role of the Rualas has been to provide protection for the humans. We can't be seen because the demons and dark lords know we work on behalf of The Great Ruler. Although the actions of Morgan, Bruno and Nada may have changed that. Normally we aren't seen until there is a battle. So there has to be a least one Ruala warrior for every human on the team."

"Because of the nature these missions are taking we would like one team member with some level of medical training."

"And Natasha possess many skills that have been game changers on the missions. We want her to train a least one member of every team with her skills."

"We also recommend having at least one woman on each team and we would like Natasha to train the women in covert skills. We have come to realize that Venatores are our experts on demons besides being fierce warriors. We would like at least one Venator on each team as well as at least one member of the Nordes Tribe."

"Now what we are suggesting is just the most basic core group. Our missions have become more elaborate and many people in this room have different skills that have been absolutely necessary for different missions. We don't want to set a minimum or maximum number of team members because as we said the missions will dictate who we need. Is anyone against what we have proposed?"

"No," Raul said. "But after working on several missions I think you need someone on each team who can vanquish demons because powerful demons are attacking us all of the time."

"We thought about that," Luca said. "But we were going to talk that over with Gabriel and Raphael because we don't know if every Patronus priest can do that. If no one has any objections to what has been said. We are going to have Joshua be in charge of the Venatores for each team. And of course Chief Sorren will be the person we go to with the Nordes Tribe. Recently the only Nordes warriors on our missions have been women and that was dictated by the missions. But we welcome both men and women warriors on the teams."

"If we volunteer for a team does that mean we have to move here?" asked Kate.

"There was a time when we would go months between missions and now it seems like we have multiple missions going on at any time. So the answer is probably yes. But you can always just volunteer for a mission instead of the team. Ratri worked dozens of missions with us before he became a permanent member," explained Luca.

280

"Kate and Natalie you have to understand that being on a team isn't like going to battle," Diana said. "We play roles, which means that sometimes we flirt with people or act scared if we need to. Once Vivian and I pretended to be homeless and starving so we could get jobs as cooks and cleaners in a tavern."

"Let me say that was an important and dangerous mission," Jared said. "And those two girls got more information than the rest of us. And I am talking information that saved lives."

"Most of us have been trained to fight demons and criminals," Joshua said. "But Gabriel's team goes after the leaders who send the demons and thugs. So far on every mission I have been a part of we have saved captives; which is why the team plays roles."

"Well you talked me into it," Adin said then he looked at Enzo, Ralf, Sol, Risa and Nana. "Is there any one of you who doesn't want to work on a team?"

"I think we all do," said Sol. "But part of the reason Calen and his brothers and Ratri are effective is because they have trained and fought together as a group their entire lives. The six of us on this side of the table have done the same thing. I would suggest we basically stay together."

"I'm taking all of you for my team. Welcome aboard," Edward said.

"Edward, I have medical training," Nana said. "I am not on the level of Lakin or Ibula but I have lots of experience."

"Even better," Edward said. "Tomorrow I am going to start looking for a house for my team to live in. I want an area where we can train and is outside of the city."

"Kate and Natalie what do you think?" Joshua asked.

"I will give it a try," Kate said.

"Then you will be on my team also," said Edward.

"Aren't you having your girlfriend from the Nordes Tribe on your team?" Jared asked kiddingly. "Cuz she doesn't take kindly to other women."

"I don't want to cause problems," said Kate.

"No, you are on the team," Edward said. "Toni is a nice girl but she isn't my girlfriend and she causes problems. Gabriel has made rules that I too will impose. All of you who are on my team now are experienced warriors. You know you can't be distracted when you go into battle. On these missions many more lives than ours are usually at risk. I am not saying we can't have lovers and families but I don't want anyone on the team that I know from the beginning is going to cause problems."

"That sounds fair," Ralf said. "How does Toni cause problems?"

"She really likes Edward," Batina said. "And Toni is so jealous of any woman who even looks at him and I mean any woman. She's even said things to Bianca and me and we are married."

"I didn't know that," Ratri said. Batina rolled her eyes and nodded.

Batina continued, "Toni would pay more attention to the other women than she would the mission so Edward is smart making that call."

"You know Jasmine and Seth kind of like each other," Bianca said. "If Dominic has a team, Jasmine may want to work with them."

"We thought about that," Luca said then he turned to Natalie. "What are you thinking?"

"I find all of this really interesting and I would like to work on a team but I am still too unfocused after Troy's death. I think I need a few weeks."

"Joshua I told Natalie she should stay with us for a while, then when she feels better she should make her decisions," said Luca.

"I think that is a fine idea," said Joshua.

"I have to tell you I like everything that I am hearing," Sudfad said. "Now I have a few things to say. You are all risking your lives for this kingdom, so starting today you are all employed by me and will be receiving weekly pay."

"And for some of you that means a considerable amount of back pay. I will pay for the buildings, equipment and anything else you need. So Edward meet with me tomorrow morning and Calen I believe you are in charge when Gabriel and Raphael are gone. You should be in that meeting too."

"Most of the Learning Center is completed so you could do your training there. Simon and Raul will take you on tours tomorrow if you want to look at the facilities and choose your rooms."

"Sanuri; Raphael, Dominic, Fennel and I are having a short meeting in our chambers if you would like to join us," Gabriel said. "We want Dominic to have a clear understanding of the work involved to become a Patronus priest and to lead a team. It's not fair to ask him to make such a decision with limited information."

"I agree and I would like to join you," the Sanuri said. "When are you planning on getting together?"

"Things are winding down so we thought we would say goodnight and go to our chambers. But you don't have to leave this early."

"No, I think we can leave the young ones to enjoy the rest of the celebration. Perhaps Michael would like to join us," the Sanuri said.

"Where is he? I haven't seen him all night," asked Raphael.

"In his chambers studying. All of this is still new to him and he doesn't always feel comfortable at these galas," explained the Sanuri.

Gabriel, Raphael, Fennel, Dominic and the Sanuri thanked their hosts for the celebration and walked to the east wing of the castle. "I'll get Michael," Raphael said and walked towards the closed door to Michael's chambers. Just as Raphael was about to knock on the door he heard a loud noise and glass breaking inside of Michael's room.

"Gabriel!" Raphael shouted as he threw himself against Michael's door. Three times Raphael threw his weight against the door before it opened.

Raphael, Gabriel, Dominic, Fennel and the Sanuri all charged into the room which was illuminated by candles and a fire in the hearth. Furniture was overturned and the door to the patio was open but there was no sign of Michael. The men ran out onto the patio and followed the sounds of fighting.

"Over here!" Dominic yelled and jumped on the back of one of the men who Michael was fighting with.

"Keep them alive," the Sanuri yelled as he grabbed one of the assailants by the back of his shirt. The Sanuri spun the man around and punched him in the face with enough force that the man lost consciousness.

Gabriel, Fennel and Raphael each attacked one of the group of men who had surrounded Michael. Of the two remaining assailants, one tried to run away but Michael grabbed him and got him in a choke hold with his right arm. Michael kicked his remaining attacker in the knee; a second kick struck the man's crotch.

"What is going on?" Joao yelled as he and a female Nordes warrior ran towards the fight.

"Joao quickly tell Fahron there has been an attack against the castle," the Sanuri yelled.

The meeting ended in the house of Gabriel. "Natalie I am going to talk to Edward for a little while; don't wait up for me," Kate called across the room.

Natalie nodded to her friend then turned to Luca. "Luca, Cassandra and Elan have Hunter. Will you tell me how to get to their chambers?"

"I'll take you," Luca said. "They live on the other side of the house."

"I've never seen one building this big before," Natalie said several times as she and Luca walked through the hallways. Luca noticed that Natalie was looking for identifying marks on the walls and he laughed.

"I'll walk you to your room. All of you that came today are staying in the same wing where I live."

"I'm really embarrassed. I never get lost in the forest."

"We're here," Luca said and knocked on a door.

Cassandra opened the door with Hunter in her arms. "He's been sleeping since you left," Cassandra said and handed the child to Natalie.

"Thank you so much," Natalie said. "That was very kind of you."

"Luca, Zack stayed here so all of the boys are camping in the playroom. Cere and Lily are having a sleep-over here with Cicely. So you can tell the others they can work later if they want."

"Thanks I will go back downstairs after I get Natalie to her room."

"Everyone here is so nice, I feel like I am back with my tribe," Natalie said as they left Cassandra. Natalie was silent for a few moments then asked, "Luca where is Emma?"

"Bekka and Koby take her at night so Bekka can feed her. The entire family is helping with her. I am very fortunate."

As Luca and Natalie walked down the hallways they heard Jasper barking. "That means the boys are horsing around," Luca said with a grin. "Here is your chambers. Let me go in first and light some candles so you don't trip with Hunter."

Natalie stood in the doorway as Luca lit a dozen candles. "I will get a fire going for you," Luca said and bent down by the hearth. Once the fire was roaring Luca stood up and looked around the room. "Do you have a cradle for the baby?"

"Not here, I was going to have him sleep with me."

"Come on, my chambers are just down the hall. Lila and I got so many baby gifts that we have an entire room filled. I haven't even looked at them since Lila died. But I do know there is more than one cradle."

"Oh my," Natalie said as Luca led her into his chambers. "This is really beautiful."

"When each of us get married our parents give us a home." The chambers where illuminated with candles and a fire in the hearth in the parlor. "Let me show you something," Luca said and grabbed a candle from one of the tables. "Christopher was the first child to come to the house. Look at this room have you ever seen so many toys?"

"Oh my gosh; look at all of this little furniture. This is so cute."

"He sleeps with me a lot because he has nightmares."

"About Lila dying?"

"Sometimes but when I found Lila and Christopher their home was being attacked by Hutas. That is a long story that I will tell you some other time. Here this is the room with all of the baby gifts. Take anything you want."

"I can't take your things."

"Well borrow them while you are here. See there are two cradles over there. Look for some blankets."

Ten minutes later Luca and Natalie returned to her chambers. Luca set up the cradle then turned to leave.

"Luca thank you for everything."

"You're welcome. I am glad that you came."

"So am I," Natalie said and closed the door.

Chapter XXVI
Revelations

Within minutes people from the celebration and soldiers ran into the east wing of Fahron's castle. The six men who had attacked Michael were taken to one of the chambers in that wing tied up and gagged. Thaos and Stephan were in the lead and the first two to enter these chambers.

"What happened?" asked Stephan.

"Michael hasn't had time to tell us the whole story," Gabriel said but he was attacked by these men. Where are the soldiers here?"

"Fahron is checking into that," Thaos said. "And Mathas is making sure the guests are guarded."

"Is anyone hurt?" Shara asked as she and Sorren pushed through the crowd. "Michael let me look at you."

"It's not the cuts on my face," Michael said. "I might have a broken rib; but we can deal with that later. I was lying in bed reading when I heard something on the patio. As soon as I got out of bed three of these guys busted through the patio doors and tried to grab me. I think they thought I would be an easy mark. I was winning the fight so they tried to run away but I followed them and ran into the rest of their buddies; that's when the rest of you arrived."

"Here's the truth potion," Thor said to Gabriel. "I've got pen and paper too."

Mathas, Fahron and Chaez pushed their way into the room. Mathas looked at Thacs and Stephan and said, "Matthew is staying with your families. What happened here?"

"Like I just said; I was reading when I heard a noise on the patio, three of these guys busted through the patio doors and jumped me. When they couldn't take me out they ran out the doors and I followed them and then the other three were on top of me. That's when help came," Michael explained again.

"We found three of our soldiers with their throats cut," Fahron said angrily. "Captain Powell is doing a head count. I want to be part of the interrogations."

"Got another one!" Noah yelled through the crowd as he pushed a large man who was covered with bruises. "Elexas and I found him lurking around the castle. I told your Captain and he told me about the others." The crowd separated so Noah and his prisoner could enter the chambers. "Where do you want him?"

"We'll take him," Dack said and grabbed the man.

"Fahron, Sudfad had a lot of problems with terrorists infiltrating his army," Sorren said. "You can't discount the same. I think my people who are here should be guarding our families and the guests."

"I think they already figured that out," Noah said. "When we came in the Nordes warriors were taking over."

Early the next morning Kate and Natalie heard a knock on the door to their chambers. Kate opened the door and saw Luca standing in the hallway wearing the uniform of the Wetprian Military. "You're in the military?" Kate asked but before Luca could answer she said. "You look really handsome in that uniform." Kate moved so Luca could enter the parlor.

"Thanks," Luca said as he blushed at the compliment. "Most of us here are in the military. Sudfad had problems with terrorists. That's a long story for another time. I wondered if the two of you needed help finding the dining room."

Kate laughed and turned to Natalie who had just entered the parlor. "Last night I got lost and Luca had to show me to our rooms."

"I was checking on the boys and saw Kate wandering around the house," Luca said with a grin.

"We are ready," Natalie said. "I just finished feeding Hunter. Luca, Kate and I were talking and if we are staying here we want to help with the chores."

"I am sure the women will be happy to hear that. Just tell them when we get downstairs," Luca said. "So Kate what did you and Edward talk about last night?"

"The team and some of the missions they have been on. Wait, why did you ask it like that?"

"Like what?"

"With that smirk Luca. You are still smirking. What is going on?"

"What makes you think something is going on?" Luca asked with a big grin on his face.

Kate slammed the door shut and stood with her back against it. "Listen, you aren't getting out of here until you tell me." Luca laughed loudly at Kate's statement.

"What do you think is going on?" asked Luca.

"Natalie listen to him. Luca don't play with me. If I knew I wouldn't ask." Kate's eyes widened. "Did Edward say something about me?"

"No, Edward is a good guy. I know that Jared and Archetenus were kidding him a lot last night and I don't want you to get the wrong impression. Because Edward is so nice, Renya and Diana have been trying to fix him up with girls. Basically he has at least four women who are interested in him. But Edward is a warrior who is dedicated to his work. He isn't dating any of them."

"Why would it matter if I got the wrong impression?" Kate asked then her eyes widened again and Luca and Natalie laughed. "Diana is trying to fix me up with him."

"Vivian is part of that too. They didn't want to tell you because they thought you wouldn't come. All they wanted was for the two of you to meet, the rest is up to you."

"Let me think about this," Kate said with a grin. "I could have some fun with this."

"Well don't aim your revenge at Edward because he had nothing to do with it," Luca said.

"If he asked you on the team it was because he thinks you are a capable warrior. In fact, having you on his team may have killed any chances of a romantic relationship between the two of you."

"I don't understand," said Natalie.

"Edward is a professional and serious about his work. He will make the team a priority."

"Luca, really, is that why they asked me here too? To match me up with you or someone?" Natalie asked.

"I told you last night that from what I know, they think we can help each other heal. It was Iris who first suggested that you come here. And I will be honest, it helped talking to you."

"I feel the same way," Natalie said. "And I wouldn't be mad; I just am not ready yet."

Every guest who attended the celebration at Fahron's castle spent the night because of the attack on Michael. Bella and Rosa helped their longtime friend Isadore as she arranged lodging and meals for the guests. Mathas, Claudius, Sorren and Fahron took part in the interrogations which lasted until well after dawn.

"Captain Powell lock these men in the dungeons here," Fahron ordered. "And make sure they are separated. I don't want them to be able to talk to each other." Fahron turned to King Mathas. "I believe we should have our morning meeting here after breakfast. We need to make some plans."

"I agree," said Mathas.

"All of you are welcome to stay here and get some sleep too," said Fahron.

"Let's deal with that later," Claudius said. "Can we hold the meeting in the Great Hall? I think all of Gabriel's team at the very least should attend the meeting."

"It worked," Luca whispered to Vivian after he led Kate and Natalie into the dining room. Then in a louder voice Luca said, "Natalie and Kate want to help with the work. I told them to talk to all of you."

"We can always use the help," Emeral said with a smile then she turned to Rachel who was pouring coffee into cups. "Rachel after breakfast you should tell your parents that Zack will be staying here for a while. The boys are finally asleep."

"Those boys were up all night giggling," Elan said with a grin. "Luca and I kept running into each other as we checked on them."

"You are both good fathers," Emeral said with pride.

"Gee Emeral, did you say that for anyone's benefit?" Misha asked and chuckled. "Kate and Natalie I have to warn you that my mother and wife are notorious matchmakers."

"Funny, I heard it was Vivian and Diana," Kate said with a grin.

"And who did you hear that from?" asked Vivian.

"I really don't remember," Kate said. "But I can tell you he looks very handsome in his uniform."

"Well that would be all the men," Natasha said. "They are all in uniform today."

As the rest of the team entered the dining room Melinda asked, "Why are all of you in uniform? Ratri are you in the military now?"

"Because of all of the spies and terrorists, Raul and Simon want all of the men here to be acquainted with the fort and to have some idea of procedures in case they need to help or to go in disguise," Maxwell explained. "So today is a training day."

"And that includes us," Joshua said as he, Micha and Thomas entered the dining room wearing military uniforms.

"I can't stop staring at Thomas," Sasha gushed. "He looks so handsome."

"Vivian I will help with breakfast but where should I put Hunter? Where are the other babies?" asked Natalie.

"I'll take him," Luca said and took the boy from Natalie, which made Emeral smile.

"I am the nanny," Melinda said. "But since the boys are sleeping Cassandra, Iris and Ella are with the smaller children. They will be here soon. One of us is always with the children."

"It works out well," Hannah said. "That way we can get more done."

"We know that many of you are still eating," Claudius said as he, Mathas, Sorren and Fahron stood up in the Great Hall of Fahron's castle. "But we feel you deserve an explanation of what happened here last night. And after the meal Mathas will be holding the morning meeting here and all of you are invited to attend."

"Gabriel's group is staying on the ground floor of the east wing," Claudius continued. "Last night Michael was in his room studying when three men broke in and attacked him. As any of you who know Michael will attest he is not an easy victim. The three men ran back into the garden and Michael followed. There were three more men in the garden and all six attacked Michael. But it as it happened, the Sanuri, Gabriel, Raphael, Dominic and Fennel were going to have a meeting and stopped at Michael's room to ask him to join them."

"As this was going on Noah and Elexas found another intruder lurking in the gardens. Three of Fahron's soldiers were murdered by the intruders. King Sudfad has a very powerful healer who makes a potion that forces people to tell the truth. Gabriel and Raphael brought bottles of this potion and administered it. We have been up all night interrogating those men." Claudius now turned to Mathas.

"I don't know if all of you are aware that we have been concerned about two powerful foes," Mathas explained. "One is the Valdore Tribe. We had heard rumblings about Usman preparing for war before Sorren became one of the members of the ruling body of Lentz. Although we have not had the big celebration yet, we believe that Usman is aware of this information and is in a rage. Our soldiers have found many dismembered bodies dumped on the border between the Nordes and Valdore lands."

"Then we have another foe who many of you in this room are probably too young to remember. Across the Sea of Grevdt lies the Continent of Tansof. Twenty years ago savages from the Dura Tribe of Tansof launched a major attack against us. The Dura Tribe have the skill and the mentality of the Hutas. The battles were savage and the war lasted two years. While we were defending our shores from those monsters Usman took advantage of the situation and launched an attack against us from the north."

"Over a number of weeks we have had ships docking in Langer that claim they were attacked by members of the Dura Tribe. So far there have been eight ships in all and the stories are identical. A ship follows them from Tansof but doesn't attack until they are near our shores. Some sailors are always left alive so they can tell us who attacked them. Besides that all these identical stories are suspicious this is not how the Dura Tribe operated in the past." Mathas turned to Gabriel and Raphael. "Do you two want to explain about the potion?"

Both Gabriel and Raphael stood up. "To our knowledge no one can lie to us once the potion has taken affect. The person acts drunk and obliging. We've only had one instant where the person was giving us confusing answers and that was moments before a demon caused him to burst into flames. We separate the people being questioned so they can't hear the answers of the others." Gabriel said then looked at Mathas, "Do you want us to share what was said?"

"I will," Fahron said angrily. "I can't tell you how damn angry I am that my men were killed and our home attacked."

"The one thing that has not been said yet is that Gabriel and his men are here to help us gather information to find out who our enemies are and during the interrogations we were all taken by surprise. We expected the intruders to say that Usman sent them. But the men work for Mayor Deckor of Langer; he sent them to spy on us. The men said they don't know why Deckor wants us watched but they have been watching all of the ruling families; including Sorren's."

"They didn't know who Michael was when they attacked him. They saw the Great Hall filled with warriors and men who looked like hired fighters. Michael was the only person they found alone and they planned to take him to Deckor for questioning. The intruders will be killed but right now we need to figure out some plans..."

"Stephan," Ingr yelled. "My water broke."

"What! Why didn't you say something?" asked Stephan.

"I just did," Ingr snapped. "Dominic take her," Ingr said and turned to Dominic who was sitting to her left and handed Sicily Bella to him."

"I'll take him," Lana said who was sitting next to Chaez. Stephan handed Marcus Stephan to Lana and helped Ingr out of her chair. Isadore, Shara, Bella, Rosa, Sally and April all jumped out of their chairs.

"Father take the baby," Angelina said and followed her mother and friends out of the Great Hall. Nikki handed Titus to Ryan and followed the small group. Matthew was holding Jacob and Alexas Rose and he too decided to follow the group.

"In light of these events," Fahron said with a smile. "And the fact that most of you have not slept, I am offering you our home. If Isadore has not already assigned you to chambers, please let me know."

"Now that all of you know the same information that we have," Mathas said. "I would like to gather for a meeting later this afternoon and we welcome any information and ideas you may have."

Mayor Deckor was enjoying an exquisite lunch with several wealthy bankers at the Cool Springs Restaurant when he looked through the front window and saw Ackley standing on the street. Deckor nodded to Ackley and excused himself from his dining companions. Twenty minutes later Deckor opened the back door to his office and Ackley walked in.

"Boss I didn't want to disturb you but we might have some problems," Ackley said.

"Did you find out who made those posters?" asked Deckor.

"No, it's something else. You know how I have a couple of men outside of every castle watching the ruling families." Ackley did not wait for Deckor to answer. "Well since you want them watched around the clock I schedule my men in shifts. When the morning shift showed up at all three castles they couldn't find the night shift. They let me know and I've sent more men out searching for them. That was a little after dawn and still no sign?"

"They are missing at all three castles?" Deckor asked nervously. "How many men?"

"Seven and we haven't found their horses or anything."

"Did the morning shift see anything suspicious around the castles?"

"Well, you know they can't get that close during the day but they said it looked like normal business."

"Ackley this could be very bad. Let me know even the littlest piece of information."

"Sure boss."

"Got two more," Sorren said proudly as he and six Nordes warriors pushed two men who had their wrists tied into Fahron's study.

295

"Where did you get these?" asked Mathas.

"Your place," Sorren said with a grin. "They were right were the others said they would be."

"Our men wouldn't tell you anything," snapped one of the captured men.

"Before this day is over you both are going to be singing like birds," Sorren said with a laugh.

"Ryan go get Claudius," Bella said happily when the family heard the cry of a baby. Ryan ran out of the room.

"I only hear one so you didn't get twins this time," Matthew said kiddingly to Stephan who was standing at the door.

"I can't believe how nerve racking this is," Stephan said. "I would rather be in battle." Matthew, Sorren and Thaos laughed loudly at Stephan's remark. "Can I come in?" Stephan yelled through the door. Laughter was heard from inside of the bedroom. A few moments later Shara opened the door.

"Meet your son," Shara said with a smile.

Stephan walked quickly to the bed. "Another baby that looks just like you," Angelina said to Stephan with a grin.

Stephan smiled at Angelina's words but his focus was on Ingr and the baby. "Stephan look at all the black hair he has," Ingr said proudly.

"Honey how are you feeling?" asked Stephan.

"Fine. After having the twins this birth seemed a lot easier." Stephan kissed Ingr then took the baby from her arms. "I haven't told anyone the name yet," Ingr said with a coy smile.

"Shara I hear Father's voice. Would you ask everyone to come in here?" Stephan asked. As the room filled, Stephan showed his son to family and friends. "I want you to meet Matthew, Thaos, Sorren, Ryan. A little baby with a big name."

"He's a big baby," Ingr said with a grin. "Now tell them the rest."

"Since he has such a long name we are going to call him Matty T."

"No!" Matthew said and started to laugh.

"Matty was Matthew's nickname when he was little," Rosa said happily.

"Thaos do you really not have a middle name or did you just tell us that?" Ingr asked.

"I really don't," Thaos said and grinned. "But I guess this little one makes up for it."

Chapter XXVII
Agendas

"Gabriel would you pass the word that the meeting will be postponed until after dinner tonight," Mathas asked. "I don't think anyone has had a chance to sleep yet between searching for Deckor's hired killers and Ingr. Besides I would like the interrogations done before the meeting."

Fahron entered his study where Mathas, Gabriel and Claudius were talking. "That's twenty hired killers that we have captured. The dungeons here aren't as big as at Fort Langer. We won't be able to keep them all separate. So should we execute the ones who killed our men last night or move them to the fort?"

"I say we execute them," Claudius said. Mathas nodded in agreement.

"Gladly," Fahron said angrily and walked out of the study.

After numerous introductions Matty T began to cry so people walked out of the bedroom to leave Ingr with her baby. "Father I don't want to travel with Ingr and the baby for a couple of days," Stephan said. "I need to go back to the castle and get things for the children and Ingr."

"I was thinking the same thing but with all of Deckor's spies I am sending soldiers with you," said Claudius.

"I think we are all staying here for a few days," Thaos said. "Bella if you will watch the children, Nikki and I will go home and get things. Why don't you make a list of what you want?"

"I want to check on our castle too," Stephan said as he turned to go back into the bedroom. "Give me a few minutes so I can see what Ingr wants us to bring."

"Stephan when you go in there tell Angelina that we will bring extra things for her and her babies too?" Nikki said. "That's the nice thing; so many of our children wear close to the same sizes."

"What about Jacob?" asked Thaos.

"Bella has gotten us outfits for when our boys are older, they are big enough to fit him," Nikki replied.

"Well, let's get going," Thaos said. "We should leave before it gets dark."

"We've got one more for dinner," Calen yelled as he entered the dining room with all of the team members who had been at the fort and with Edward and his team.

"So, did you find a place?" Natasha asked Edward as she put an additional setting on the table.

"Yeah, it's a couple miles north of here," Edward explained. "It's a big old house with about twenty acres of land. It needs a little work and a lot of cleaning but it's a sound house. I figure we can move in it in about a week."

"Edward, we can all move in now and work on the place," Sol said as he took a seat at the table.

"Well, actually I have already hired some of Sudfad's people to start cleaning and painting. We need to set up a weapon's room, a medical room, the kitchen and bedrooms. I would like all of you to start on that tomorrow. We need to get the money from Sudfad in the morning. Do you want me to make assignments or can you work it out?"

'We can work that out," Ralf said with a grin.

"After that, we need to set up a training area, library and meeting room," Edward said. "Natasha I want you to set up the area and things for the disguises and outfits."

Now, everyone was seated at the dining room table. "I've been thinking about that," Natasha said. "Normally Laurel helps with the outfits but with all these new teams we will need more help. Iris and Ella you both sew well, would you help?"

"Of course," Iris said.

"Mother is a great seamstress," Rachel said. "I will ask her to help tomorrow."

"Along those lines," Luca said solemnly. "Last night Natalie came to our chambers to borrow some things for Hunter and that made me realize that none of you have been in there since Lila died. I haven't touched any of her things. And she had so much clothes that she never even had a chance to wear. Natasha why don't you take those things for the teams."

"Are you sure?" asked Natasha.

"Yes but I don't want to sort through them," said Luca.

"Honey, there are some things you should save for Emma and Christopher too," Emeral said to Luca.

"That brings up something else," Luca said. "I have been in such a fog that I have never asked anyone if they wanted something to remember Lila by. Emeral would you take care of all that? Whatever you decide is fine by me."

"Of course dear."

"And last night was the first time I have gone into that room that is filled with baby gifts. If any of you want some of those things help yourselves," Luca continued.

"After that huge baby shower that Renya had for us we all have a lot," Vivian said. "But maybe Natalie could use some things."

"Of course," Luca said and looked across the table at Natalie. "Just let me know."

There was a lull in the conversation so Edward turned to Kate and asked, "Are you going to live here or at our place?"

"I was planning on living with the rest of the team, why?" Kate asked.

"I didn't know if you wanted to stay here with Natalie. It's up to you; whatever you want," said Edward.

"Kate doesn't need to stay with me," Natalie said with a smile. "Edward we are trained to be lone hunters and here I am with a houseful of people."

"Well, that's not really what I meant," Edward said. "I didn't know if she wanted to stay with you for support."

"I'll be fine," Natalie said. "I just have to work through this."

"Luca I once saw the most beautiful thing," Hannah said. "I'm not really sure what it is called; but it was a large wooden frame with a sheet of glass in front of it. And behind the glass were mementos of this woman's father. Everything was arranged beautifully with material and dried flowers and it hung on the wall."

"Hannah draw me a picture and I will make one," Sam said. "I was thinking about making small chests for each of the children. They would be big enough to hold things, but not huge. Why don't I start with ones for Emma and Christopher and Emeral can pack some of Lila's things in them?"

"Why Sam, that is an absolutely wonderful idea," Emeral said. "And I very much like what Hannah suggested too. I will look for the right things for such a project." Emeral paused as she looked at the faces around the table. "Since many of you were so close to Lila, why don't you help me?"

"I know what needs to be in that frame," Bekka said. "Luca got stabbed saving Lila and Christopher from Hutas. Lila taught herself that special stitch and fixed Luca's robe but she kept a little piece of the material to remember him by. This was before they fell in love. She keeps it in that jewelry box that Luca bought her."

"I didn't know that," Luca said in almost a whisper.

"We should put one of your wedding invitations in there too," Cassandra said. "Luca if you didn't save any, I still have ours."

"I won't build the frame until you have picked out all of the things you want in there," Sam said.

"Luca, I think these projects will help us all heal," Emeral said. "Would it be alright if we started after dinner?"

301

"That is fine," Luca said to Emeral as Christopher got up from the table and ran from the room. "Christopher are you alright?" Luca yelled and started to get out of his seat.

"I'll be right back," Christopher yelled as he continued to run. A few minutes later Christopher ran back into the dining room. "Luca put this in there," Christopher said and handed Luca a small chain with a golden disk. "Lila bought that for me when I started having nightmares."

"Are you sure you want this in the frame?" asked Luca.

"Yeah, that way we can all remember her," Christopher said.

Luca looked as if he was going to cry so Maxwell said, "Christopher why don't you bring that here and I will read it to everyone." Christopher took the chain from Luca and ran to his grandfather.

"I never saw that before," Luca said.

Maxwell hugged Christopher then said. "The disk is engraved. It says *You are loved.*

"There's four men watching you from that ridge to your right," an Enrop said to Stephan and Thaos as they led a small contingent of men from Fahron's castle to the castle of Claudius.

"Does Deckor have an army?" Stephan asked out loud but did not expect an answer.

"If he does you know there is more going on here than his men know about," Thaos said to Stephan. Then Thaos turned to the Enrop. "Do you think those men have clear sight of all our troops?"

"No, they probably can't see the ones at the end because they are still concealed in the trees," Remi the Enrop replied.

"Remi will you go to the rear of the formation and lead those soldiers to our spies?" Thaos asked.

"Certainly," Remi said and flew over the formation.

"Do you think this is another of Juleta's plots?" Nikki asked with frustration. "I wish she was alive so I could kill her myself."

"Gabriel and Raphael have been asking Deckor's men about her," Stephan said. "They claim they don't know Juleta; for what that is worth."

"Since we've got a little time now," Thaos said to Stephan. "Tell us what you do know about Deckor."

"He has been mayor for about ten years. He always wins the elections by a landslide. He's been in all of our homes...," Stephan was interrupted by Nikki.

"Remember Michael's dream?" Nikki asked.

"Oh trust me I thought about that," Stephan said. "Deckor seems to be effective in that he gets things done but now I think we are all wondering by what means."

Suddenly they heard yells and the small flock of Enrops that were escorting the troops now flew quickly towards the ridge. Stephan stopped the troops and waited for their soldiers who were returning to the formation with the captives. "One is dead," Sergeant Kerns said. "But we brought his body."

"Sergeant take half of the men and return to Fahron's castle with these spies," Stephan said with disdain. "The rest of us will proceed forward."

"Ackley what have you heard?" Deckor asked nervously as he met the hired killer in the study of his home.

"Boss, I sent a lot of the boys out and I don't have any good answers for you yet. But there is something else. Is your wife awake?"

"No Karin went to bed early; why would you ask about her?" Deckor demanded.

"Because I stopped your girlfriend on the street; outside of your place. She looked really pissed and said you better see her tonight or she was going to tell her husband about the two of you."

"What! Are you sure that's what Linda said?"

"Boss, I wouldn't make something like that up. And as mad as she was I wouldn't put anything past her. Do you know why she is so pissed?"

"She found out about Sharon," Deckor said. "It's the damndest thing. Linda doesn't seem to mind that I have a wife but another girlfriend has made her insane. And this is the last thing I need before the election."

"Well boss, I ain't no expert on women but I got a bad feeling about this. Is there something you need me to do?"

"No, I'll take care of it."

"Kerns just led a group of men back here with three more of Deckor's men," Matthew said as he walked into Fahron's study where Mathas, Claudius, Sorren, Fahron and the Sanuri were meeting. "There was a fourth man but he was killed by our soldiers. The Enrops spotted the men spying on the troops that Stephan and Thaos are leading."

"Were any of our men hurt?" asked Claudius.

"No and from the sounds of it these four men may have only intended to spy on us," Matthew replied.

"Son, take them to Gabriel and Raphael for interrogation," Mathas said.

"Already done," said Matthew.

"Is anyone else concerned about the number of men Deckor has employed?" the Sanuri asked. "Why would the mayor of a city with relatively little crime need an army of hired killers?"

"Chaez wait up," Sally called as she ran towards her new brother.

"Are you still holding that pup?" Chaez asked with a grin. "He'll forget how to walk."

"No he won't," Sally said with a big smile. "I've named him Lucky because April and Amy and me are all so lucky that we were rescued and have good families."

"Did you tell Mother and Father his name?"

"Not yet; they are all so busy."

"You should tell them tonight; I think it will make them smile," Chaez said.

"Where are you going?"

"Some of the soldiers just brought three more spies here. I am going to sit in on the interrogations. Why?"

"I just wanted to know what you thought about Lana," Sally said with a coy grin.

Chaez stopped walking and turned and faced Sally with a big smile on his face. "Well, I think you were right about everything. She is very beautiful and really nice. But Sally you know I am going back to Wetpr."

"Forever?"

"I don't really know Sally. If I can get accepted as a Patronus priest I believe I have to go wherever they send me."

"Don't we have any Patronus priests here?"

"No."

"Why not?"

"That's a good question. I don't know."

"Well do you like Lana?"

"Yes."

Sally stared at Chaez for a few moments. "I've got to go."

"Sally I am sorry I didn't mean to upset you." Sally didn't respond to Chaez as she ran down the hallway.

"Can I come in?" Sally asked as she peaked her head into Fahron's study. "I have to ask you something and it's important."

All the men smiled. "Certainly come in," Mathas said.

Sally walked up to the desk where Mathas, Sorren, Claudius, Fahron and the Sanuri were gathered. "Why don't we have any Patronus priests in Lentz?"

"That is a very good question," the Sanuri said with a big grin.

"I don't have a good answer for you," Mathas said.

"Well, can we get some here like they have in Wetpr?" asked Sally.

"Honey what is all this about?" asked Fahron.

"If Chaez gets accepted as a priest he may never come home. He said he will need to go wherever the Patronus priests are sent." Sally took a big breath. "And he and Lana really like each other but Chaez says nothing can happen because he is going away."

"I see," Sorren said with a grin. "So Sally what do you think we should do about that?"

"Well, how did they get the Patronus priests in Wetpr?" Sally asked.

"They gave them a place for a headquarters," the Sanuri said with a smile that had not left his face.

"Really that is all it takes?' Fahron asked the Sanuri who nodded. "I am not saying this because of Chaez but perhaps we should consider setting up a headquarters here. It certainly would be advantageous for us."

"Sally we will talk with Gabriel and Raphael after they are done with the interrogations," Mathas said. Sally smiled brightly.

"Sally that was a very good idea you had," Claudius said.

Sally turned and walked a few steps towards the door then returned to the desk. "Chaez told me I should tell you this now."

"I named my puppy Lucky, because April and Amy and me are all so lucky that you found us and gave us such good homes."

After dinner Emeral, Natasha, Hannah, Bekka, Vivian and Cassandra went with Luca to his chambers. "I really don't want to help you sort through things," Luca said as he opened a closet door that was filled with women's clothing. "That dresser with the mirror has her things too."

"If there are things that we aren't certain about, we will ask you," Emeral said and kissed her son on his cheek.

"Luca be honest," Vivian said. "Kate and Natalie really don't have anything. Would it bother you if you saw them wearing some of Lila's things?"

"I don't know," Luca said with a hoarse voice.

"I think perhaps we should take those girls shopping," Emeral said. "I think it is still too soon for Luca."

"Can we help?" Adrone asked as he, Christopher, Nicholas, Joey and Paul walked into the room.

"Here Grandma," Nicholas said and handed her a bracelet made from twisted flower stems. "Lila made this for me. Put it in the frame."

"Are you sure Nicholas?" asked Emeral.

"Sure," Nicholas said and ran to the bed and sat down with Christopher.

"Luca do you mind if they are in here? It might help them," Emeral asked.

"No, of course not," Luca said.

"Luca would it be too painful for you to find something to put into the frame too?" asked Hannah.

"Actually I was thinking about that," Luca said. "I really do like that idea."

Once again King Mathas postponed the meeting with all of the people at Fahron's castle. There were two reasons for the postponement. Stephan, Thaos and their men did not return to Fahron's castle until late that night and Gabriel and Raphael were still conducting interrogations.

It was well after midnight when Gabriel and Raphael completed the interrogations. They immediately went to Fahron's study to see if any members of the ruling families were still up. To Gabriel's and Raphael's surprise the study was filled with people.

"We're glad you are here," Claudius said. "You have been the subject of conversation."

"Is that good or bad?" Raphael asked as Chaez handed both high priests glasses of whiskey.

"Earlier today Sally, she is one of Fahron's adopted daughters came in here and asked us why we didn't have a headquarters for the Patronus priests in Lentz. She was greatly disturbed by this because she idolizes her new brother and was afraid she would never see Chaez again. And the more we thought about the idea we didn't know why it never occurred to us to offer you a headquarters. What would we need to do to bring some of your group to Lentz?" asked Claudius.

Both Gabriel and Raphael got huge smiles on their faces. "Let us write to our superiors and it will be approved," Raphael said. "Now you need to decide how much of a presence you want in your kingdom so our superiors can determine how many men to send."

"With all of the problems you have suffered here," Gabriel said. "I would suggest you establish an outpost and not just a small office. You have seen the headquarters in Nora; that would be considered a huge outpost. The headquarters in Salar is slightly smaller than the one in Nora. When the priests in Wetpr aren't on assignment they are studying, tutoring, helping with building the Learning Center and administering to people in Salar."

"But we aren't keeping their presence a secret in Salar; that is another decision you will have to make."

"What would you need from us for a headquarters?" Mathas asked.

"A large building with plenty of space for training and our horses," Raphael said. "And the way things have been going; the location will have to be defensible by the priests. Our men come from all walks of life and have many talents. So they can fix up whatever building you give them."

"But they will need a library," Gabriel said.

"Our sons, who have worked many missions with the Patronus are all for this idea," Claudius said. "In fact they have already been looking at maps for the right location for the headquarters. We can always have the buildings built for your men too; just tell us what you want."

"We know you don't want to be away from your families for long," Mathas said. "But while you are here would you help find a location?"

"Certainly," Gabriel said. "We would be honored and we feel this is a very wise decision on your part."

"All the time we have spent with you and your men and it takes a child's question to make this happen," Matthew said with a smile and a shake of his head.

"Do you want to talk about the interrogations now?" Raphael asked.

"Did you find out any new information?" asked Sorren.

"We told you before that Deckor has a foreman who hires the men. That is the man named Ackley. We found out tonight that Ackley hires different groups of men and keeps them separated so one group doesn't know what the other groups are doing. The men that were watching Stephan and Thaos were sent to find the missing men who were assigned to watch all of you. Those three men didn't know about your spies because their normal assignment is to spy on a man named Wickfield. Apparently he is the editor of a big newspaper and an enemy of Deckor's," Raphael explained.

"I used to do the same type of work as Ackley," Thaos said. "And if he is keeping his men in segregated groups it is because Deckor is afraid of information leaking out. It's Deckor who is calling the shots. The more we hear the more you've got to wonder what Deckor is hiding."

"The men we just interviewed have worked for Deckor longer than the first ones you captured," Gabriel explained. "These men say they don't know for sure how many hired fighters Deckor has in Langer but they all guessed the numbers to be at least one hundred men. So you have a mayor with a lot of secrets and a small army of hired killers. This is reminding Raphael and me of the Shanksaw mission we had in Wetpr. Deckor strikes me as intelligent and ruthless. We will need to proceed with caution because there may be innocent lives at risk."

"If Deckor has over one hundred killers in Langer you know people know about them," Thaos said. "And if no one has come forward it's because they are being threatened in some manner. I think we are going to need more new faces here. Can we get some of the Patronus priests to help like they did on the Shanksaw mission?"

"We were going to suggest that to you," Raphael said. "We will send a message to the Cicero Headquarters before we go to bed. I believe this is much bigger than any of us realized. Surely you know people who will be honest with you about what is going on?"

"Unless their families are being threatened and they probably know that we are being watched, so they are afraid to come here," said Thaos.

"Perhaps it is time for a huge celebration," the Sanuri suggested. "You know you will have spies here but also people will have an excuse to come into the castles. Maybe you can separate a few and talk to them."

"While I think that is a good idea," Stephan said. "I hate to have them around the children. You know what happened at Sudfad's castle."

"Everyone in our tribe knows each other," Sorren said. "If we have this celebration we will have my warriors guarding the babies."

"Well, perhaps it is time to announce Sorren's new role in the kingdom," Mathas said.

"I'll want to let all my villages know first so they can be prepared for attacks from Usman," Sorren said.

"Gabriel, Raphael did you get any other new information from the interrogations?" Fahron asked.

"Deckor pays his men well, they are told to follow orders and not to ask questions. But a couple said they think Deckor is worried about this upcoming election. They suspect he has some plans in the works and he needs to be elected again to complete everything. But these men don't know what Deckor is planning. It sounds like the one man who knows what is going on is Ackley," Raphael said.

"Ackley doesn't frequent one particular tavern, but he makes the rounds at all of them almost every day and night so he can keep up on the gossip. Ackley drinks whiskey although none of the men have ever seen him so drunk that he talks about business and he likes to play cards. They described Ackley as tall and thin with a scrubby beard that is brown. He has brown hair and eyes. One of the men said Ackley isn't the kind of man that attracts women; that could work to our advantage," Gabriel said. "I think we need to get some of our female team members here."

311

"One of my men did say something interesting," Raphael said. "Apparently Deckor is quite the lady's man but his wife doesn't know about it. Deckor has several girlfriends and they are all married women."

"Then he likes to live dangerously," Sorren said. "Gabriel, I don't think it is a good idea to have any of the women from my tribe go in disguise in Langer because they will be recognized. And that includes Batina and Bianca."

"Raphael and I haven't met them yet, but we have two Venators visiting at our house. Hannah said they are both very beautiful women. And Edward already talked one of them into being on his team. The other woman is mourning the death of her husband and has a baby; her name is Natalie and she said she feels too unfocused to work on a mission right now. And we also have Rachel, no one will know her."

"I think we should give Fahron's daughters a chance too," Thor said. "April is really quiet but that little Sally is smart as a whip and she thinks like a warrior. All they will do is work in Ryan's shop and keep their ears open."

"Were does Michael keep disappearing too?" Thaos asked.

"We don't know what the Angel Ruth said to him in Ryed," Gabriel said. "But he is reading all kinds of prophesies besides translating some manuscripts for us."

"Tomorrow morning after breakfast we are going to have a meeting with everyone here," Mathas said. "Besides giving them information we want to hear some of their ideas. Then unless something else comes up I think you should start sending your people into Langer."

Chapter XXVIII
Murder

Two days passed before all of Fahron's guests returned to their homes. In that time, the soldiers of the ruling families discovered five more of Deckor's men spying on them. "At some point Deckor has to realize that we are on to him because the men he sends to spy on us disappear," Matthew said at the morning meeting.

"We need to make Deckor think he has other enemies," Thaos said. "Got any ideas?"

"That we need to think about," said Claudius.

This morning the meeting included the ruling families and some of the members of Gabriel's team. "Lawrence, Thor, Sally and April are already in Langer in Ryan's store," Gabriel said. "Fahron you should know that I told the girls if they did not follow my rules they would not be allowed to help."

"Ryan is going to have them paint the toys he is making for the orphans," Claudius said. "So I don't know how much the girls will actually be in the front of the store."

"So you know," Fahron said. "I am not as worried about the girls as Isadore is. The more I get to know those girls the more I am impressed with them. They managed to survive a horrible situation with their wits. Sally is really showing her true self with the warrior training. And April is changing since she is studying to become a healer."

"This is changing the subject," Raphael said. "But still speaking of girls. We got a message this morning. Edward's new team is already on route and Dagon and Rachel are with them. Edward's team hasn't had much time to work together, it consists of Edward, six Ruala warriors, two of which are women and Kate the Venator. According to Edward's letter, Natasha was working with Kate around the clock to teach her some of the skills. And since everything happened so fast, Luca gave Kate a great deal of Lila's things to wear for disguises."

"Raphael and I haven't met any of Edward's team members but we know they are all highly trained warriors. But we need to find them a place to stay before they get here. With all of the spies, I don't know if you want them seen in your castles. And actually that may go for the rest of us too," Gabriel said. "You aren't planning on releasing any of Deckor's men are you? Because they will recognize us."

"No, we are working on Thaos' plan, we will execute them for treason but we want to make it look like someone else is responsible for the deaths to throw Deckor off," Fahron said.

"I just got a great idea," Matthew said proudly. "Just south of Fahron's castle is an old lodge. It was kind of a hotel before all the nice hotels were built in Langer. It is about two hundred yards from the ocean and it has some cottages. It is probably in pretty rough shape but it should be big enough for all of you. No one goes there anymore. I would be surprised if the road leading there is ever traveled. We can look at it after the meeting."

"Now you girls promise me you will do exactly as Thor and Lawrence tell you," Bella said to April and Sally as they were setting up the table in the front window of Ryan's shop. Every morning Bella put pots of coffee and trays of deserts on the table. Some mornings people would line up in front of the store for the treats.

"Bella we will be fine," Sally said. "But I have a favor to ask of you." Sally looked around the shop to see if anyone was listening before she continued speaking. "I know Chaez and Lana really like each other. I can tell by the way they act around each other. But they both are shy and I am afraid that Chaez thinks he is leaving forever so he won't ask Lana to be his girl."

Bella laughed loudly and asked, "Why are you trying so hard to match those two up?"

"Bella, don't forget that April and I didn't know any of you before Timothy killed Tabeth. April and I love Isadore, Fahron and Chaez but they always seem sad. I know they try to act like they aren't. Did you see Lana and Chaez together?"

"They both looked really happy. So that is the biggest reason. But also I don't want Chaez to go away and never come back. I think that if he has a girlfriend here he will come home more often."

"Well, I think Chaez is lucky to have a sister like you," Bella said and hugged Sally. "Let me think about this. Since you are so good at matchmaking maybe you can find a girl for Ryan. He is really shy." Bella laughed loudly again when she saw Sally's eyes light up.

Diana and Natalie were clearing the breakfast dishes from the table when Christopher and Nicholas walked up to them. "Natalie, Paul and Adrone said that your parents were killed when you were little," Christopher said. "Did you have nightmares?"

"Yes for a long time. I was a little older than you and I was hunting with them when we ran into an ambush of demons. I saw my parents murdered. And honestly I still don't know how I survived. It was like the demons didn't see me. Luca told me you have been having nightmares. Do you want to talk about them?"

"Well mostly I want to know if they will stop," said Christopher.

"Sometimes talking about them helps them to go away," Natalie said. "I know you saw awful things but in your dreams are you also afraid that the Hutas will get you?" Christopher didn't speak but nodded. Natalie sat down and set Christopher on her lap. "Nicholas here sit next to us," Natalie said.

"Do you remember when almost everyone in this house went to my village to help free the captives of Ogg?" Natalie asked and both boys nodded. As Natalie talked to the children her back was to the kitchen door. She did not see Diana open the door and motion for the women in the kitchen to come into the dining room. "Did your parents tell you that Angels came to our village too?"

"Daniel and Miranda," Nicholas said. "My brother is named after Daniel the Angel."

"That's right," Natalie said with a smile. "I can't even begin to tell you what an experience it was to be in the presence of Angels. They were in our village for several days before I got up the nerve to talk to them. I wasn't afraid of them but I would cry whenever I was in their presence. I wanted to ask them if my husband was in heaven. But we started to talk about all different things. You know I am trained to be a Venator and we are trained not to fear anything. But I was afraid. I didn't know how I would go on without Troy and I didn't know if I could give Hunter a good home."

"Miranda told me something that I will never forget," Natalie continued. "She said that whenever I was really afraid I should pray to The Great Ruler and ask that He surround me with His Light. She said the Light would heal me and protect me. And you know what; I believe it works. I don't own anything fancy but I asked Miranda to bless my necklace." As Natalie spoke she removed a necklace made of wooden beads from her neck. "I think it is very special to have something that has been blessed by an Angel. Christopher why don't you wear this necklace and see if it helps you with your nightmares."

Natalie fastened the necklace around Christopher's neck. "It's too long for you. Let me shorten it," Natalie said and took the necklace off from Christopher.

"Natalie can you make two necklaces from that?" Nicholas asked. "So I can wear one too."

"I have more leather and beads," Vivian said and quickly walked out of the dining room. Natalie turned around and realized most of the women in the house were standing in the doorway listening to her talk with the children."

"Thank you," Hannah said. "I think that is a wonderful thing you are doing. The children are trying desperately to understand their feelings about losing their families." Natalie smiled but did not speak.

A few minutes later Vivian returned with a basket filled with small pouches. "Natalie I have lots of beads here. Would you mind us mixing them with the beads on your necklace then we can make a necklace for each of the boys."

"Of course," Natalie said. "If we are taking the necklace apart, let's make one for Hunter too, for when he is older."

"Can we help?" asked Cassandra.

"You can all help," Vivian said. "But we need to clear more dishes off the table so we have room."

"Natalie, Joey lost his parents too," Cassandra said. "If we bring all of the boys in here would you mind repeating what you just said to Christopher and Nicholas?"

"Linda keep your voice down," Deckor said angrily and walked past his girlfriend and opened the door leading to the waiting room of his office. The waiting room was empty. Deckor closed the door and turned to Linda. "Did anyone see you come in here?"

"Why does that matter?" Linda asked angrily. "Are you ashamed of me now?"

"No Honey, you know better than that. I believe I am being watched is all."

"No, you are trying to change the subject," Linda's voice was getting higher and louder as she spoke. "For months you have been telling me you were going to leave Karin and now I find out you have another girlfriend. How could you do that to me? You said you loved me!"

"Linda I do."

"Then why are you sleeping with Sharon?"

"Linda, keep your voice down I don't want to have to tell you again."

Linda picked up a small statue from Deckor's desk and threw it at him but missed hitting him by a considerable distance. "If you love me get rid of Sharon!"

"Linda," Deckor said through clenched teeth. "You are not my wife and you cannot tell me what to do. Now keep your damn voice down."

Linda's eyes filled with tears. "You are such an ass. All you really care about is that election. Well, I won't be a burden for you anymore." As Linda spoke she grabbed her shawl from a chair and stomped towards the door to the waiting room.

"And just what do you mean by that?" Deckor asked as he roughly grabbed Linda's arm and pulled her back to him.

"Let go of me. You are hurting me." Linda struggled to free herself from Deckor's grasp.

"Tell me what you mean by that."

"That we are through!"

"I will tell you when we are through. Now calm down. Linda I am a powerful man and I can make a lot of trouble for your husband so I would think twice about threatening me."

"People told me that you were a monster but I wouldn't believe them. I think it is time everyone found out what you are like." As soon as Linda said the last word, Deckor slapped her with the back of his right hand with great force. She fell on top of one of the small tables in the office.

Deckor grabbed Linda by the front of her dress and pulled her to a standing position with his left hand then he punched her in the stomach with his right fist; she collapsed on the floor. Deckor jumped on top of her and punched Linda repeatedly in the face with both his left and right fists. Linda's blood spattered onto the furniture and carpet. Her blood splattered onto Deckor's face and suit. Deckor had worked himself into a frenzy and he kept hitting Linda over and over; then he tore her clothes off.

"This is perfect," Gabriel said. As all of the men from the King's morning meeting, walked through the old lodge.

"I'll send some Enrops to intercept Edward's group and lead them here," Raphael said and walked out the door.

"Gabriel this place is filthy," Fahron said. "I will have some of my people clean it."

"I would prefer you didn't," Gabriel said. "The fewer people who know about this the better. We can clean it."

"I've lived in worse places," Michael said as he picked up an overturned chair.

"Well, then let me provide you with supplies and linens from the castle so you don't have to purchase those things in the city," Fahron said.

"We would appreciate that," said Gabriel. "We'll move in here today."

"Can we take one to Zack?" Paul asked as Vivian tied a bead necklace around his neck.

"Sure," Diana said. "We have enough beads."

Christopher walked up to Emeral who was sitting at the dining room table and whispered in her ear. "Why, Christopher I think that is a wonderful idea," Emeral said with a warm smile. "We can go after we give Zach his necklace." Emeral looked at the other women who were around the table. "The boys would like to go into Salar."

"I can drive the boca," Hannah said. "I also need to take some supplies to my office."

As Deckor was pulling up his pants he heard movement in the waiting room of his office. Deckor walked to the door but did not open it. "Jenny," Deckor called to his secretary. "I am not seeing anyone this morning. Something urgent has come up. Did you hear me?"

"Yes sir. Do you need anything?" Jenny asked through the closed door.

"Only not to be disturbed." Deckor listened at the door for a few moments then walked across his office, stepping over Linda's naked body. Deckor opened the back door and silently called to a messenger. A lone raven landed on his arm.

"Find Ackley and bring him here at once," Deckor said and walked back inside of his office.

Thor was sitting in the front of Ryan's shop painting toys. The store was filled with people but most of them weren't looking at the wares, they were eating the sweets and drinking the coffee that Bella had put on the large table that stood in front of the big front picture window. Sally was dusting the shelves and trying to listen to every word that was spoken by the customers. She went into one of the back rooms and brought out another tray of cookies. She gave one to Thor, then put the tray on the table.

"Why, thank you," an old man said. "This is the friendliest place in town."

Sally got a big smile on her face. "Do you want to see my new puppy?"

"The two old men grinned. "Sure thing," one of them said.

Sally ran into the back room and carried Lucky to the front of the store. "You can pet him he is really friendly," she said proudly. "I am keeping him in the back room because I don't want him running out the door," Sally said as the two men pet her dog. "I've heard it isn't very safe around here. I don't want anything to happen to him."

"You're a smart girl," one of the old men said. "It's not a safe place for any of us."

Sally turned around and smiled at Thor as she saw that he was listening to the conversation.

Ackley knocked on the alley door to Deckor's office. Deckor opened the door just enough to allow Ackley to walk through. "I need you to help me clean up a mess," Deckor said and nodded towards Linda's body which was now rolled inside of a large carpet.

"What do you want me to do with it?" Ackley asked.

"Just dump it some place far from the city; I don't care."

"I'll have to get a boca," Ackley said. "Do you want me to stop by your house and get you some clean clothes?"

"Yes, Karin should be up by now."

Gabriel and his group spent the remainder of the day cleaning and setting up the lodge. Fahron had sent two bocas filled with supplies for the men. "It's really beautiful here," Raphael said as he looked at the ocean. "I am surprised people don't come around here."

"There are so many beautiful places on this coast that this place may be forgotten," Gabriel said. "Are you thinking about this site for the headquarters?"

"Yes, but I want to wait until Dominic and his men come back from searching the area."

That evening as everyone gathered around the dining room table in Gabriel's house Emeral made an announcement. "While many of you were gone, Natalie did a very nice thing for the boys today and they wanted to do something for her. Boys."

Christopher, Joey, Adrone, Paul and Nicholas got up from their chairs at the children's table and ran up to Natalie. "Since you gave us your only necklace we got you this," Paul said as Joey handed Natalie a small pouch.

"You didn't have to get me anything," Natalie said.

"Open it," said Nicholas excitedly.

"Oh boys, this is so beautiful," Natalie got tears in her eyes as she held up a golden chain with a golden locket hanging from it.

"Grandma says you can put some of Hunter's hair in the locket so you can remember when he was a baby," Christopher said with a huge smile. "Put it on."

"I will put Hunter's hair in it," Natalie said as she clasped the necklace around her neck. "Thank you so much." Natalie bent down and hugged each of the boys.

"What is all of this about?" asked Maxwell.

"Natalie had a wonderful talk with the boys about being afraid and words that Miranda told her," Hannah explained. "She had Miranda bless her necklace which was made of beads. Natalie gave the necklace to Christopher to help him with his nightmares but it was too big so we took it apart and made necklaces for all of the boys."

"We added extra beads," Vivian said. "But all of the necklaces have beads that were blessed by Miranda."

"Well, let's see," Maxwell said. "Boys why don't you show all of us your necklaces."

"How was your day dear?" Karin asked as Deckor entered the dining room and kissed her on the cheek.

"Busy, like every other day. How was yours?"

"I went to a luncheon today and met a friend of yours. A very handsome man. He said his name was Hector and he would be visiting you tomorrow."

Chapter XXIX
Riley

"Natalie, Natalie," Christopher yelled as he ran into the dining room the next morning for breakfast. "Batina where is Natalie?"

"She's in the kitchen; Christopher is everything alright?" Batina asked.

"Yeah," Christopher said and ran into the kitchen. "Natalie, I didn't have any nightmares last night." Christopher yelled as he ran past the other women and ran up to Natalie who squatted down and hugged him. "Thank you so much."

"I think it is Miranda who you should thank," Natalie said.

Christopher looked up at the ceiling and yelled, "Miranda thank you." Everyone in the kitchen smiled.

Luca had followed Christopher into the kitchen. "He told me what you said to him," Luca said with a warm smile. "Thank you."

"I am just glad that he is doing better," said Natalie.

"Luca, I've got to tell the others," Christopher said and ran into the dining room.

By the time that Edward's team arrived at the lodge, Gabriel and his men had the building prepared for the mission. The Sanuri was the only member of the group who remained at Fahron's castle.

"Fennel is a great cook," Raphael said as he was leading Edward's team into the lodge. "He's prepared lunch for you."

"I can't believe how beautiful it is here," Risa said.

"After this mission the ruling families are tearing these buildings down and building a headquarters for the Patronus priests," Raphael said proudly. "I hope you don't mind but everyone has to share rooms. But Fahron sent beds and clean linens here."

"I don't think any of us care about that," Ralf said. "But I want to take a walk by the ocean. I have never seen one before."

"And who are you?" asked Raphael.

"I've written you so many letters about them that I forgot you haven't met. Sorry about that," Edward said. "Ralf, Risa, Nana, Sol, Adin and Enzo this is High Priest Raphael. Where did Kate disappear to?"

"She was walking down to the water," Nana said. "I will need to set up a medical room."

"Already done," Raphael said. "Let me take you to your rooms and Fennel said lunch will be ready soon."

"Where is everybody?" asked Edward.

"The Sanuri and Gabriel are still at King Mathas' morning meeting. Everyone else is in Langer working except for Dack and Joao who are pulling guard duty here. We take turns with that. I'll brief you on everything over lunch," Raphael explained.

Rosa knocked on the door to Mathas' study but opened it before Mathas said anything. She quickly slid inside of the door and closed it behind you. "I am sorry to interrupt but there is a man here and I think all of you need to listen to him." As Rosa spoke she walked closer the men who had gathered for the morning meeting.

"It's Geof Thurstand; he is beside himself because his wife Linda has been missing since yesterday morning. Yesterday Geof asked some of our soldiers to help him look for her and one of the soldiers was told she was seen entering Mayor Deckor's office very early in the morning and that she was often seen at his office. The soldiers didn't tell Geof anything but they brought him here to see you."

"Of course, bring him in," Mathas said as he stood up from his chair.

"Can I have some paper and pen?" Gabriel asked. "I will take notes."

As Matthew found paper and a pen for Gabriel, Rosa escorted Geof Thurstand into the study. It was obvious to everyone that Thurstand had been crying. Sorren stood up and poured Thurstand a small glass of whiskey. "Here," Sorren said as he handed Thurstand the glass. "You look like you could use it."

"Please have a seat Geof," Mathas said. "Geof this is the Sanuri and High Priest Gabriel, I believe you know everyone else." Mathas turned to the group. "Geof owns a small shipping company here in Langer." Mathas turned back to Geof. "Rosa told us why you are here. We will look into this matter so Gabriel is going to take notes to help us in the investigation."

"Thank you all so much," Geof said. "My wife's name is Linda. We have been married for three years. I work a great deal so Linda involves herself with many civic duties. The night before last," Geof stopped speaking so he could compose himself. "Linda was sleeping when I got home from work. When I awoke she was gone. That has happened before but she usually leaves me a note telling me where she is or asking me to meet her for lunch. We always have lunch together."

"When I didn't hear from her I went to every restaurant that we normally go to and no one had seen her. Then I went to her friends and the other ladies who she serves with in the organizations. No one saw her. Then I saw some of your soldiers patrolling on the streets and I went up to them and asked them to help me. They were very kind. Your Sergeant Halsal called for extra troops and they went to every home and business in the city. They didn't get done until this morning. Halsal told me that several people had seen Linda walk into Mayor Deckor's office just after sunrise."

"I have no idea why she would go to his office." Geof stopped talking and started to cry for a few moments before he could compose himself. "The soldiers said many people told them that they would see Linda at the Mayor's office. I was going to go to Deckor's office but Sergeant Halsal brought me here. He is sending troops to patrol the countryside to see if they can find Linda."

"Geof I need you to think," Gabriel said softly. "Was there any signs in your home that you might have had an intruder?"

"Actually I thought about that last night so I went home and spoke to the staff and searched the house myself. Nothing was out of place or even missing except for Linda's purse but she would have that with her."

"Geof I am going to ask you some personal questions but the answers are necessary for us helping you. Has Linda been acting different the last few days?" asked Gabriel.

Geof paused for several moments before he answered. "No, but like I said I work a great deal."

"Geof why do you think Linda was going to Deckor's office?" Geof started to sob and Sorren got up and poured more whiskey into his glass.

"I don't really know," Geof said. "I thought we were happily married but everyone knows what an animal Deckor is."

"What do you mean?" Gabriel asked.

"He has the sweetest wife but he is always seen with other women and I don't mean in a professional manner. He has a private dining room in The Peacock Hotel where he takes his dates."

"Geof, I am new to this area. What else can you tell me about Deckor?" Gabriel asked.

"He is a power hungry and ruthless man," Geof said passionately. Then he stopped talking and stared at all of the men in the room.

"Geof you and I have known each other a long time," Claudius said. "So you know I am a man of my word. Lately the soldiers have heard some disturbing things about Deckor but we have no direct witnesses or proof. If he is a criminal we can't stop him if we don't know what he is doing?"

"Geof, we will protect you and your family if that is what concerns you," said Mathas.

"For all I know my Linda is already dead," Geof said as tears ran down his face. "Can I have some more whiskey?" Sorren poured more whiskey into Geof's glass and he gulped it down for courage. "What I am about to tell you is putting a target on my back."

Geof paused again, "The streets of Langer are filled with Deckor's hired men. Some of us have wondered how the soldiers don't realize what is going on. Every business and sea captain has to pay protection money to Deckor. Wickfield is one of the only men who has stood up to Deckor and the other morning some of Deckor's men destroyed Wickfield's office and dragged him to Deckor's office. Wickfield hasn't printed a paper since."

"How the hell can this be going on and no one tells us," Stephan said angrily as he hit the arm of his chair with his fist. We have soldiers patrolling the streets night and day."

"Geof is Deckor paying off some of the soldiers?" Gabriel asked.

"I can't prove anything but I have heard stories about soldiers turning their backs as Deckor's men ruffed people up."

"What!" yelled Fahron.

"Geof can you tell us anything else about Deckor?" Gabriel asked.

"Before you disinherited Princess Juleta she was often seen with Deckor. I don't know if it was business or personal," the room became silent at this statement. "Deckor is always scheming and he seems to have come into a great deal of money over the last couple of years. Did you know that he bought a small fleet of ships?"

"No," Mathas said. "Are they for trade?"

"Understand that I have no proof," Geof said. "But since Deckor bought those ships there have been lots of attacks on ships up and down the coastline."

"Do you mean besides the attacks that the Dura Tribe may be behind?" Claudius asked.

327

"Oh yes; the sailors think pirates are attacking the ships. They rarely kill anyone they usually steal the cargos. I have had that happen to a couple of my ships too. And as for the Dura Tribe; well some of us think something else is going on there. It is all just too suspicious."

"Geof you said that people wonder why the soldiers don't recognize Deckor's men. How do you recognize them?" Gabriel asked.

"They all wear those black bandanas around their necks. Have you ever seen a black bandana before?"

"Geof other than The Peacock Hotel do you know any other places where Deckor or his men frequent?" Gabriel asked.

"I know you can't tell that now, but I normally am not a drinking man. I work and go home. But everyone says that Deckor's men are in all of the taverns daily. As for Deckor he is often seen at the Cool Springs Restaurant for lunch. He only goes to the best places."

"Geof, I have been told that Deckor always wins the elections by a land side," Gabriel said. "How does he do that?"

"His men intimidate all the people into voting for him and Deckor gets rid of his competition. We are all expecting Tetly to disappear soon. Two of his body guards have disappeared."

"Geof why don't you stay with us; for your own protection," Matthew said.

"No, I have to go home, in case Linda returns."

"Geof can you tell me what Linda looks like?" Gabriel asked.

"She's beautiful," Geof said and started crying again. "She is short with long curly blonde hair and blue eyes."

Luca and Christopher knocked on the door to Natalie's room after lunch. "Are you busy?" Luca asked when she answered the door.

"No, I just finished feeding Hunter. Why?"

"Grab the baby; Christopher has a surprise for you," Luca said with a big smile.

"What sort of surprise?" Natalie asked as she picked up Hunter who was crawling on the floor.

"You'll see when we get there," Luca said.

Emeral smiled at Luca, Natalie and Christopher as they walked through the dining room. Christopher was walking between Luca and Natalie and holding both of their hands. "Emeral you know what Christopher's surprise is don't you?" Natalie asked.

"I might," Emeral said with a coy smile. "You have fun."

Luca helped Christopher and Natalie into the small boca that was hitched in front of the house. As he sat down and grabbed the reigns Luca laughed. "I have to tell you that I don't often drive a team of horses but I can't carry all of you. So this may not be pretty."

"If you are too bad, I can drive," Natalie said and laughed.

"Natalie why doesn't Hunter ever cry?" Christopher asked as he sat in the front seat between Luca and Natalie.

"Oh, he will cry if I don't feed him on time of when he gets his teeth. But he is pretty easy going. Troy was like that too. I am very lucky."

Christopher barely waited for Natalie to stop talking before he spoke again. "Natalie did you know I have a girl friend?"

"No," Natalie said with a big smile.

"Her name is Amy and she is really pretty and really nice; like you. But she lives in Lentz so I don't get to see her often. But I already asked her daddy if I could marry her when we get old like you and Luca. Both Luca and Natalie laughed loudly.

"What did her daddy say?" asked Natalie.

"He said that people change when they get older but if we still want to get married then he will give us his blessing."

"Christopher I am very impressed," Natalie said.

329

"I bought her a ring but her daddy said it can only be a friendship ring," As Christopher spoke Natalie looked at Luca who grinned and nodded.

"You must really like Amy," said Natalie.

"Yes, I will marry her someday," Christopher said wistfully which made both Luca and Natalie laugh again. Christopher paused then got a mischievous look on his face. "Maybe when you and Luca stop being sad you could be boyfriend and girlfriend. I would like that."

"Christopher you are sounding more like Emeral every day," Luca said and Christopher giggled loudly.

"Here we are," Luca said and stopped the boca on a busy street in Salar. Luca dismounted from the boca and hitched the horses to a rail then he grabbed Christopher and set him on the sidewalk. "Christopher you stay right here until I help Natalie and Hunter. Do you understand?"

"Yes," Christopher said as he simultaneously nodded his head.

As soon as Natalie and Luca were on the sidewalk Luca said, "Give me Hunter," and took the baby from her arms.

Christopher grabbed Natalie's hand and pulled her forward. "Where are we going?" Natalie asked as she laughed.

"In here," Christopher said and pulled Natalie into a shop.

An older women walked up to them, "Hello my name is Eloise, can I help you?"

"I am buying some things for my friend," Christopher said proudly. Eloise grinned and looked at Luca who nodded.

"Luca I can't let you buy me things," Natalie said.

"Please let him do this for you," said Luca.

Natalie looked at Luca for a moment then turned to Christopher. "Christopher why don't you pick out the things you want to buy."

"Alright," Christopher said excitedly. "But I don't know what size you wear."

"I can help with that," Eloise said as Christopher ran to a rack of dresses.

"You may be really sorry you are letting him pick out your clothes," Luca said with a broad smile.

"Clothes. Just how much are you buying?"

"That depends on Christopher," Luca said and sat down on one of the chairs.

Both Natalie and Luca laughed loudly when Christopher walked up to them with an arm load of clothes. "That lady said you should try these on," Christopher said and handed the clothes to Natalie.

"The changing room is right over there," Eloise said and pointed to a door to the right. As soon as Natalie closed the door to the changing room, Christopher ran back to Eloise and grabbed more clothing.

"Natalie come out so we can see you," Christopher yelled.

"Christopher I am not coming out in these nightgowns. I think they are nightgowns. I've never seen anything so fancy."

"Do they fit?" Luca called through the door.

"Yes but they are very thin. I am beginning to think Christopher has ulterior motives here," Natalie joked.

"Try on the yellow dress," Christopher said excitedly. A few minutes later Natalie walked out of the changing room wearing a yellow dress. Both Christopher and Luca looked at her and shook their heads and said, "No." Natalie laughed and walked back into the changing room. She came out several moments later wearing a blue dress. "Oh, you look really pretty in that one," Christopher said. "We're buying that one." Christopher ran back to Eloise.

Two hours later they left the store and climbed into the front seat of the boca. The back of the boca was filled with packages. "I can't believe you bought all of those things," Natalie said.

"And I can't believe I am exhausted from trying on clothes. Thank you Christopher and Luca."

"Do you want to go to the Dragon's Inn for some chocolate cake?" Luca asked.

"Sure!" Christopher said. But stopped talking then screamed as Luca stopped the boca and literally flew out of the seat. Two drunken men were kicking a large dog and laughing. The dog looked badly injured. Luca kicked one of the men in the head then landed in front of the other man. The man could see how angry Luca was.

"I ain't gonna fight you over no damn dog," the man said and turned and staggered down the sidewalk. Luca picked the dog up and placed it in the back of the boca. Then got into the front seat and they sped back to Gabriel's house.

"Hannah, Hannah help us!" screamed Christopher as he ran into the house. Hannah dropped a plate when she heard Christopher scream. Within moments everyone in the house was running out the front door.

"Ratri hold the door," Luca said as he picked up the whimpering dog.

"What happened?" asked Natasha.

"Two drunks were trying to kill this poor dog," Luca said.

"Elan, Cassandra come you are going to have your first animal patient," Hannah said. "Natasha would you get some hot water and towels?"

"Mother why would someone hurt a dog?" Adrone asked as tears ran down his face.

Iris hugged her son and said, "Honey who knows why people can be so cruel."

An hour later when Hannah opened the door to her medical room she saw Christopher, Joey, Nicholas, Zach, Adrone and Paul all sitting on the floor staring at the door. Jasper the dog sat with them. "Is he going to live?" Paul asked fearfully.

"Yes but he has several broken bones," Hannah said. "He is going to need a lot of rest and I don't want any of you trying to make him walk or play until I tell you it is safe for him."

"We won't Mama," Nicholas said. "Can we go in and see him?"

"Yes but be very careful he has a lot of injuries," Hannah said. Hannah walked back to the examination table with the boys.

"He's trying to wag his tail," Christopher said happily.

"That means he likes us," Joey said. "Mama, Papa can we keep him?"

Cassandra, Elan and Hannah all looked at each other and smiled. "Yes," Elan said. "But remember he won't be able to play like Jasper does for a while."

"We made him a bed in the playroom and Natasha is making him food," Adrone said as he walked closer to the dog.

"We picked out a name," Paul said. "We are going to call him Riley."

Chapter XXX
Preparations

"Look who followed me home," Gabriel announced as he entered the lodge in the late afternoon.

"Jasmine!" Dack yelled and walked up to his friend and hugged here. "Wait until Joao finds out you are here. You aren't even on crutches anymore."

"No, but I can't ride a horse yet. Lana drove me in a boca," Jasmine said.

"Where is she?" asked Dack.

"Taking care of the horses," Jasmine said. "Could you help us bring our things in?"

"Are you staying?" Dack asked.

"Yes, I am going crazy knowing all of you are here working and I am just sitting around. I may not be able to fight yet but Gabriel said I can help."

"Did Edward and his team arrive?" Gabriel asked.

"Yeah, Raphael and Fennel are showing them around. Sol and Ralf just replaced Joao and me on guard duty. Everyone else is still in Langer."

"Look who I found," Joao said with a grin as he and Lana walked into the lodge. They were both carrying large pouches."

"Is there more?" Dack asked.

"Our weapons," said Jasmine.

"I'll get them," Dack said then turned to Lana. "So are you going to help us too?"

"Yes, I am looking forward to this."

"Does Chaez know about this?" Joao asked.

"No, do you think that will be a problem?" asked Lana.

"No, I think he will be pleased," Joao said. "He likes you he just is shy."

"I went into Langer and told all our people to be back here for dinner," Gabriel said. "I have a lot to tell you."

"Can we camp in the playroom with Riley and Jasper," Paul asked as soon as everyone was seated at the dinner table.

"Yes but be gentle with Riley," Hannah said.

"Can I stay too?" Zach asked.

"Dear it is alright with us," Emeral said. "But one of us will take you home so you can ask your parents."

"So Luca, the boys said you beat those guys up that were hurting that dog," Joshua said.

"I wanted to. I just kicked one in the head and the other ran away," said Luca.

"We are glad you did," Nicholas said from the children's table.

"We were so busy with the dog we didn't ask about your shopping trip," Diana said with a coy smile.

"Oh, you should see the beautiful things they bought me. I will show all of you after dinner," Natalie said.

"She let Christopher pick out her clothes," Luca said with a large grin.

"You didn't," gasped Natasha.

"You should see some of the things he picked out," Natalie said and blushed.

"Are they bad?" Diana asked in a lowered voice.

"No, they are..." Natalie didn't finish her sentence and looked at Luca.

"They are sexy," Luca said and laughed. "Yes, my son is seven going on twenty."

"They are pretty," said Christopher.

"Yes they are," said Natalie with a loving smile.

"Did you coach Christopher?" Calen asked with a grin.

"Nope, he did it all on his own. I will say he has good taste," Luca said.

"Christopher do you have a crush on Natalie?" asked Calen teasingly.

"No Calen I have a girlfriend," Christopher said with such indignation that everyone at the table laughed. "But Luca doesn't," Christopher added with a mischievous grin.

"He's turning into you," Misha said sarcastically to Diana. "Another matchmaker in the family."

"He told us that when we aren't sad anymore he would like Natalie and me to be girlfriend and boyfriend," Luca said as Christopher grinned and nodded his head.

"I have been trying to think of how I can pay you back," Natalie said. Then she looked at Emeral. "They bought Hunter clothes too." Natalie turned back to Luca. "I could help take care of Emma sometimes. I am not working on any missions now."

"You mean feed her?" Luca asked.

"Well yes but everything. I am still nursing Hunter."

"That would be nice," Luca said. "And it would give Bekka and Koby a break."

"You can feed her?" Christopher asked loudly then got out of his chair and walked up to Luca and Natalie who were sitting next to each other at the adult table. "We can bring Emma home then."

"Honey, Emma is home," Emeral said.

"No, I mean with me and Luca," Christopher said. "Luca said Emma can't stay with us because we can't feed her. But if Natalie feeds her then she can sleep with us."

"Honey, Emma wakes up a lot in the night to eat," Bekka said. "Natalie would have Emma in her room so she could feed her."

"Well then move in with us," Christopher said to Natalie which made Calen and Koby roar with laughter. "We have plenty of room for you and Hunter. Don't we Luca?"

"Here Luca take Hunter," Natalie said and handed Luca her baby. "Christopher come up on my lap. I really understand why you are asking this but I don't think you understand what you are asking."

"Yes I do."

"Christopher you are asking Luca and me and you and the babies to live as a family. Honey, we just aren't ready for something like that."

"I don't understand," Christopher said and started to cry which surprised everyone at the table.

"Honey, you know how much you care about Amy, well that is how Luca feels about Lila and how I feel about Troy," Natalie said. "Christopher I know you want a family but..." Christopher started to cry harder so Natalie stopped talking and hugged him. Luca stared at Christopher then looked at Emeral and Maxwell. "Christopher I tell you what," Natalie said. "If it is alright with Luca sometimes, Hunter and Emma and I will come over for a sleep over. But it will be as friends."

Christopher looked at Luca who smiled and nodded. "Give me a hug," Luca said. Christopher jumped off Natalie's lap and hugged Luca then ran back to the children's table. Luca looked at Maxwell and Emeral and asked, "Could I talk to the two of you after dinner?"

"Why don't both you and Natalie come to our chambers right after dinner?" Maxwell asked.

Thor, Lawrence and Chaez were the last three team members to arrive at the lodge that evening because they took Ryan to Claudius' castle and Sally and April to Fahron's castle.

"Jasmine," Thor said happily. "Are you joining us?"

"Lana and I both are," Jasmine said with a big smile as she watched Chaez's face.

"Lana," Chaez repeated and turned around to see her walking out of the kitchen carrying two platters of meat. "Lana why are you here?"

"To help. Aren't you glad to see me?"

"Yes, I just didn't expect this," Chaez said as everyone in the dining room watched him and Lana.

"Lana tell him what Sally said," Jasmine said and laughed.

"Your little sister the matchmaker told me that we are both shy and one of us has to make the first move. So here I am," Lana said as everyone roared with laughter.

"I am glad you are here," Chaez said and kissed Lana on the cheek.

"Does someone want to make the introductions again?" Gabriel asked. "Then we are going to have a long meeting after the meal."

"Are we too late?" Luca asked as he and Natalie walked into the chambers of Maxwell and Emeral. "Natalie fed Emma and Hunter first."

"Nonsense it's not late at all," Emeral said happily. "Maxwell will you pour us some wine?"

"I'll take whiskey," Luca said as he and Natalie sat next to each other on one of the sofas in the parlor.

"Natalie you don't really know us yet but Maxwell and I are basically the parents of everyone here; so know you can always come to us with anything," said Emeral warmly.

"Thank you," said Natalie. "Actually that is nice because my parents were killed when I was little."

"There are a couple of reasons that we thought we should talk," Maxwell said as he handed out the drinks and sat down next to Emeral on the second sofa. "Luca you looked so shocked when Christopher started to cry at the table."

"I was. I didn't understand why he was so upset. I feel awful," Luca said.

"Luca you know that Christopher worships the ground that you walk on. He seems so much older than his age that we forget he is a seven year old boy who saw all of his blood family and a close friend die horrible deaths. Other than his nightmares, Christopher seems to be handling things well but we all have been waiting for something to surface."

"Luca every child in this home, except for Hunter and Emma have two parents," Emeral said. "Now, everyone loves the children here so much that they don't go without but...Now Natalie I hope you don't take this the wrong way. But you are a natural mother and Christopher is really responding to you. Then when you told him about your parents dying that was one more connection the two of you have. And then when you helped him with his nightmares, well we think Christopher just decided you are who he wants for a mother."

"While he hears what you say about grieving and not being ready for a relationship; he probably doesn't really understand," Emeral continued. "And it seems that he is looking at the two of you and the babies as a family and we think that makes Christopher feel safe and secure."

"Both of you are wonderful with him," Maxwell said. "And I think he needs both of you right now. But don't let your guilt or your feelings for Christopher push you into a relationship before you are ready."

"I think we know that," said Luca.

"Son, you two agreed to have sleep overs. Do you really think you can pull that off without something happening?" Maxwell asked.

"Before you answer that question," Emeral said. "Maxwell and I want you to know that we are very happy you two have become friends. Luca whether you realize it or not you have changed. It's like you are coming back to life. And Natalie that is what Iris and Joshua said about you too. And know that we would be thrilled if your relationship became romantic. It's just that both of you are so fragile now; we want to make sure you think things through."

"I think we can handle it," Luca said and looked at Natalie who just stared at him.

"Natalie what do you think?" asked Maxwell.

"Well now that I hear you two talking; I don't really know. Luca today was so much fun and I just realized it was like we were a family. Maybe Christopher read that all wrong," Natalie said.

"Don't stop spending time with Christopher because he needs both of you right now," Maxwell said again. "We just don't want to see the two of you get hurt either."

"So you don't think Natalie and Hunter should spend the night?" Luca asked his parents.

Before Maxwell and Emeral could answer Natalie said, "Luca I promised him. We have to do it at least once. We are adults we should be able to deal with this."

Luca squeezed Natalie's hand and said, "I agree."

"Just so all of you know, I think Christopher is the most precious child and I would like to help him if I could," Natalie said. "I'm just not sure how."

"My dear just be yourself," Emeral said warmly. "You are so loving to him; that is what he needs."

After Gabriel told the team members at the lodge about the meeting with Geof Thurstand, Raphael said.

"This sounds like Shanksaw all over again."

"I was thinking the same thing." said Thor.

"For those of you who aren't familiar with the mission we are talking about. King Sudfad and his sons were involved with different enemies which caused them to take their eyes off from the City of Salar. Like in Langer the soldiers patrol the streets of Salar to protect the citizens. Well, a man who I shall say sounds similar to Deckor took advantage of the situation. Once we started finding out about Shanksaw's crimes no one could understand why the citizens weren't coming forward about them," explained Raphael.

"Then we find out that Shanksaw was kidnapping people and forcing their families to pay monthly ransoms to keep those family members alive. All of the captives were held in an old farm house and the guards were told to kill the people if anyone approached the house that was not one of Shanksaw's men. We were able to save those people but we planned several attacks to be launched simultaneously," Raphael continued.

"You should have seen the conditions those poor people were in," Thor said. "That was when I realized how important these missions are."

"Chaez don't be offended but Fahron was so enraged that he wanted to send troops into Langer and arrest all of Deckor's men. But the Sanuri and I told him about the kidnappings in Salar. You know that Deckor is doing something to paralyze that city and if we act too hastily innocent people might die," Gabriel said. "So for now we will keep the same plans but now you can recognize Deckor's men. The Sanuri sent out flocks of Enrops to search the country side for anything suspicious."

"But bear in mind," Raphael said. "That now we know there is an association between Juleta and Deckor, which means he could be a dark lord, a demon or a member of the Insidiae. So be careful but keep your eyes and ears open for such things."

"Kate it is our understanding that Luca gave you a great deal of clothing is that correct?" Gabriel asked.

341

"Yes." Kate replied.

"I am not saying this to offend you but Diana had a horrible time learning to wear the shoes that women wear here," Gabriel said. "Do you think you can function in that clothing well enough so you don't draw attention?"

"I think so, the girls were helping me," Kate said.

"I can help her too," Rachel said. "I also brought a lot of things."

"Good," Gabriel said. "Edward how about you?"

"Natasha sent along all kinds of clothing for me."

"The three of you are going to be disguised as people of means. I already sent a message to Natasha and she will be forging paper work for you. Edward you are going to be a ship owner who is interested in expanding your fleet. Kate you are his wife and Rachel you are his sister. Rachel and Jasmine since you have worked on a mission before I want you to pass your knowledge to Kate and Lana."

"Lana and Jasmine, Sorren said we shouldn't use you two in Langer because people would recognize you as members of his tribe. So I was thinking you could just be yourselves. I will give you money and have you shop at the markets, especially the ones close to the docks. I want you to talk to people and listen. I know you are both well trained but don't take any unnecessary risks because we don't really know what we are dealing with."

"Edward, it's going to take a couple of days for you to get your paperwork. Dack, Joao and I will take your team out and train them in our roles," said Dagon.

"Excellent," Edward said then he turned to Kate. "If we are pretending to be married we are going to have to get a little affectionate at times and maybe fight at times. Tell me now do you think you can handle that?"

"What do you think I am going to hit you if you kiss me?" Kate asked and laughed.

"Honestly yes," Edward said with a grin.

"I'll play my part but Rachel told me I will need to learn how to dance in fancy shoes," Kate said.

"We can all help teach you," Dack said.

"I don't know if I need all of you to teach me," said Kate with a grin.

"Kate if you are as bad as Diana you will," Thor said and laughed heartedly. "Misha has scars on his feet and ankles and I'm not kidding. To dance like they do here, the woman has to follow and Venators are trained to lead."

"Oh, this might be a problem," Kate said. "Maybe someone should start teaching me tonight."

"Dack and I will start working with you tonight," Joao said with a grin. "Just don't hurt us too bad."

"Kate they are really good dancers, they taught me and Darla," Jasmine said.

"Chaez I know you probably want to go with Lana but everyone knows you are a member of one of the ruling families. "It's better that you stay with Ryan," Gabriel said.

"I can go with Jasmine and Lana," Thor said. "I don't really know what I am doing in that shop. But Lawrence is really talented. He could be a professional wood carver."

"I could go with them too," Seth said.

"I don't think that is a good idea Seth," Dominic said. "When you are around Jasmine you can't see anything else. I am not saying this to be mean, it's the truth." Both Seth and Jasmine looked embarrassed.

"Michael, you have been so quiet this entire mission," Gabriel said. "Is anything wrong?"

"Ever since we left Wetpr I have been feeling like I had a dream about all of this and I am trying to remember it. And it is driving me nuts. And I don't know if Sudfad told you but after I left my prison the first time I tried to stay in the area in case my mother needed me."

"I got all kinds of jobs. At one point I was working in the diamond mines here. You might want to tell the Sanuri to send Enrops to the mines. They are huge. You could hide just about anything in those mines."

"That is really good information," Gabriel said.

"And just so you all don't think I am mad at you. The Angel Ruth gave me homework you might say. I've been doing a lot of reading but I haven't found anything that seems important for this mission, although she didn't tell me that I would," Michael continued.

"Michael since we are going to be spending a lot of time together maybe you can teach me that language those scrolls are written in," Dominic said. "Cerfic."

"I'll take a stab at that too," Fennel said.

"Before we end this meeting there are some rules we need to tell you about," Raphael said. "For those of you who are new at this I think you are realizing nothing is black and white and a wrong decision or act on our part can get innocent people hurt. The first rule is to communicate with all of us. No matter how insignificant you might think something is, tell us. Watch each other's backs; we've lost too many of our friends in battle."

"And a lesson that Gabriel and I had to learn; you are all good people, warriors with integrity. But you will have to understand how our enemies think to defeat them. And that means you have to get into their minds and think like criminals. And trust me that is easier said than done."

The next morning Edward, Kate, Rachel and Michael remained at the lodge while everyone except Gabriel and Raphael rode into Langer.

Dominic and Seth pretended they were gathering information for their boss who was a wealthy businessman. In every business they entered, Dominic gave the same story. He said his boss was looking for businesses to invest in.

The clerks and secretaries were more than willing to give Dominic information about land owners, businesses and ship owners in and around the City of Langer.

Gabriel and Raphael attended the morning meeting of the leaders of Lentz. Thaos and Stephan had spent the previous day gathering all sorts of information about ships, sailing and the sea trade. They brought several large pouches of books, scrolls, and maps to the meeting which they gave to Raphael and Gabriel.

"We'll keep looking for information for you," Stephan said. "Thaos and I are really frustrated because we want to take a more active role in this mission."

"How often do you go into the taverns?" asked Gabriel.

"Since we got married, not that often," Thaos said. "But it wouldn't be suspicious for us to make an appearance now and then."

"Fennel and Noah are in Langer now checking out the taverns. Do you want to join them?" Raphael asked.

"Do you want us to be seen with them or just go in the same places to point things out?" Stephan asked.

"We'll leave that up to you," Gabriel said. "It would help if you would point out Usman's men to them."

"Mathas do you need us here?" asked Stephan.

"No, go and have fun," Mathas said with a grin. "Matthew do you want to go with them?"

"Actually I was going to take a carriage out to the lodge for Edward to use then I am looking for a place the Patronus priests can stay unless; you want them put up in hotels because there isn't any more room in the lodge."

"How many are coming?" Mathas asked Raphael.

"One hundred and fifty but they are coming in groups of twenty or thirty. Putting them in hotels isn't a bad idea. We should have them come to the lodge first so we can give them money," Raphael said.

"I think my boys can take care of setting up the rooms," Claudius said. "When are you expecting them?"

"They should start arriving in two days," Raphael said.

"Stephan, Thaos I am sure you can set up rooms without making it look suspicious," Claudius said.

"Most of our people are in Langer," Gabriel said. "They could help with that."

"Any thoughts about when we should have the big celebration here?" Mathas asked.

"Wait at least two weeks," Gabriel said. "I want to get everyone in place and to see if we can find out any information about a possible attack by the Valdore Tribe."

"We almost forgot," Raphael said and turned to the Sanuri. "Michael said that since he started this mission he keeps having the feeling like he dreamed all of this before and can't remember everything. He said that before he came to live with Sudfad, he traveled around getting jobs where he could. He said he worked in the diamond mines here and that they are large enough to hide anything. He suggests you send Enrops searching in those areas."

"That is an excellent idea," Fahron said. "We so rarely go to the mines that we don't think about them."

"Gabriel if your people need proper clothing for the celebration, let Matthew know, he will set everything up," Mathas said.

"Lana will need a dress; Natasha provided dresses for Kate, Rachel and Jasmine. Dominic's men have the clothing. We should have some of the Patronus inside and do you want to have the Rualas here? I don't think it would be suspicious for them to be at the celebration."

"I think the Rualas should be here," Matthew said. "I will make arrangements. We'll have our tailors make the clothing. You will have to set me up with the Patronus."

"Did you say Lana?" Fahron asked.

"Yes, she and Jasmine volunteered to help," Raphael said. "Apparently Sally told Lana that she and Chaez were both too shy and one of them needed to make the first move. So she volunteered for the mission." Fahron roared with laughter as Raphael spoke. "Jasmine and Lana are spending time in the markets and shops trying to gather information. Thor is with them today."

"We'll check on them," Stephan said and he and Thaos left the meeting.

"Ackley I don't care how you do it; just make it look like a damn suicide," Deckor said. "I can't have Thurstand shooting his mouth off all over the city."

Ackley turned to walk out of the back door of Deckor's office then stopped and turned around. "Boss, I don't know if it is just my imagination but is sure seems like there are a lot more troops patrolling the city."

"It's probably because of Thurstand," Deckor said with disgust. "I heard he asked the military to help him find Linda."

"Well they won't find her body," Ackley said smugly. "I threw it in the diamond mines."

"Michael will you give it a try," Edward asked. "If Kate kicks me one more time I won't be able to perform the mission."

"Am I really that bad?" asked Kate.

"Yes," Edward said. "You refuse to relax and let me lead. And you act like you are going into battle. Doesn't your clan do any kind of dancing?"

"Yes, it's just different than this," Kate said. "I will try harder."

"I think it's a trust issue," Rachel said. "Believe me I didn't trust any of Gabriel's team when I first met them and now they are all family. Dagon could help you learn how to dance too."

"Kate I just learned how to dance too so I am not as good as Edward," said Michael. "But I will tell you it was a necessary skill for the people who were playing parts in Ryed. You know you can do it; you just have to change your mindset."

"Kate I am going to ask you something that is probably going to piss you off but I need to know the answer if you are going to work on the team. We all admire the Venators and understand that they are trained to be lone warriors. Vivian, Diana and Thor had to decide if they could work with a team. You need to make that same decision because the lives of others depend on you."

"I've made that decision." Kate said. "I will work as a team member."

"Then perhaps you and I should have a talk in private," Edward said and pointed to the kitchen. After Kate entered the kitchen Edward closed the door behind them. "Kate, you are smart, you're beautiful and you are a highly trained warrior but you have been acting, I'm not sure how to explain it; like you have a chip on your shoulder ever since you joined us. Some of the others, actually myself included are afraid to even joke with you because you get so tense and angry. Thor said that is not how you normally act so I have to ask did I or someone else here do something to offend you?"

"No," Kate said almost angrily.

"I am sure none of us intimidate you. Is it because Diana and Vivian wanted to set us up because I didn't have anything to do with that. You don't have to like me but you have to work with me."

"Honestly Edward I didn't realize I was acting like that and I can't really tell you why. Maybe I just feel out of my element. But I will tell you I want to be on this team and on this mission, so tell me what I need to do."

"You can start by trusting us. How can the other members trust you when you make it so obvious you don't trust us? Part of my job is to make sure this team can work together Kate. I'm not trying to come down on you but you need to change."

"Start conversations with the others, tell a joke, ask someone about their life; find a way to break the ice."

"You are right, I will do that tonight when the others return. I am sorry I have been so difficult. My mother says I am headstrong."

"Oh, I think you are way past headstrong," Edward said and laughed.

"Edward I will tell you it has been a long time since someone scolded me. Let's make a deal; I will work on these things and you will point them out to me when I am doing them."

"Deal."

"And Edward, I wasn't mad that Diana and Vivian were trying to match us up; I can understand why. But Luca told me you wouldn't allow anything to happen after I agreed to be on the team. So it isn't an issue."

"What do you mean you can understand why they were trying to match us up?" Edward asked.

"I think you already know the answer to that question," Kate said with a coy smile. "You are handsome, you are nice and you are a great warrior. You are also funny and I am sorry that I make you feel you can't be funny around me. I started thinking you were mad at me."

"I wasn't mad at you but I was surprised and confused by the way you have been acting. And Kate we certainly could date as team mates but I can't allow anything to disrupt or endanger the team and you are already doing that. If you weren't on the team I would have asked you out. Are you mad because I haven't?"

"No, you asked me why I was acting like this and I wanted you to know it wasn't because of anything with us. And everything you have said makes sense. I will work on it."

An hour later Raphael, Gabriel and Matthew arrived at the lodge without any soldiers. Matthew was driving a fancy carriage and Gabriel was driving a boca filled with supplies.

As soon as the three men walked into the lodge they saw Michael and Kate dancing. Kate stopped and walked up to Gabriel. "I want to apologize for being difficult and not working as part of the team. I promise I will do better."

"Glad to hear that," Gabriel said. "Do you want to help us bring things in?" Gabriel dropped two large pouches on the table. "Edward this is information you will need to study. And Matthew has your carriage outside."

"Gabriel we just got a message from Natasha," Michael said and handed the note to Gabriel. "Calen and Luca left last night. They are bringing forged papers, money, disguises and more clothes."

"Good then we can get started," Edward said. As he spoke both Rachel and Kate entered the lodge carrying supplies. "Girls I will help you in just a minute. When we get done with that we have a lot of reading to do."

Chapter XXXI
Taking a Stand

Thaos and Stephan found Fennel and Noah in a dirty smoke filled tavern near the docks. The Ocean's End Tavern was open twenty-four hours a day, seven days a week. It was never really cleaned; the bartenders would simply throw buckets of water on the floor to wash away the vomit and blood. The side alley was half filled with decaying bodies. Bodies of men no one ever claimed or even thought about.

Although it was late morning the tavern was filled with customers. When Thaos and Stephan walked through the front door sunlight flooded some of the tables, blinding some of the men. "Shut the damn door," an angry voice yelled and a hunting knife flew through the air and imbedded itself in the wall near Stephan's head.

"Got him," Noah yelled as he picked a drunken sailor up from his chair and rammed the sailor's head into the wall. Two, three more times Noah rammed the man's head into the wall. The man lost consciousness and slumped on the filthy floor.

"Thanks," Stephan said. "It's so damn dark in here; our eyes hadn't adjusted. You two sure picked a great place." As Stephan spoke he and Thaos were searching the bar with their eyes for more adversaries but no one wanted to fight. They saw Fennel sitting at a table and walked up to him.

"Everyone take a seat," Fennel said in almost a whisper. "There's three guys sitting at a table near the bar that seem really interested in you," Fennel said to Thaos and Stephan. "They aren't wearing black bandanas."

"I'll get a bottle and some more glasses," Thaos said and walked slowly to the bar. Thaos was studying the room and the faces as he walked. He ordered a bottle of whiskey and two glasses. While Thaos was waiting for his order, he turned so he could face the three men at the table. After a moment he smiled. As Thaos stared at the men he yelled loudly, "Stephan here's three of the men who kidnapped the King's daughter."

The tavern became quiet. Even this room of killers didn't want to get involved with the situation that was unfolding before them. Men started to get up from their chairs and move out of the line of fire.

"Hector with you?" Thaos asked the men as he walked towards them. Stephan, Fennel and Noah were already out of their chairs and approaching the three men from different directions.

"Thought you were him for a minute there," one of the men at the table said as he slowly stood up. Instantly Thaos grabbed a wooden chair and used it to block the knife the man threw at him. Fennel, Stephan and Noah charged the three men as did Thaos.

"One of the men at the table screamed a war cry and charged towards Stephan with a huge butcher knife. Fennel grabbed a chair and threw it at the man who was charging at Stephan. The chair hit the man in the head, momentarily stopping his momentum and giving Stephan a small advantage. Stephan threw a knife which lodged in the man's stomach but did not take the man off his feet, he continued his attack towards Stephan.

Thaos charged the man who had thrown a knife at him. Thaos had already figured this man was the leader and had no intention of killing him. Noah had smashed the table that once stood between Thaos and his attacker. Thaos threw a knife that landed in the man's upper thigh and blood spurted out. The man knew he would quickly bleed out so he threw himself to his left as he pulled off his belt to use as a tourniquet on his leg. Thaos grabbed a whiskey bottle and smashed it into the right side of the man's head. The man collapsed on the floor. Thaos grabbed the man's belt and applied the tourniquet to his leg.

Fennel and Noah had overpowered the third of Hector's hired killers. They beat the man into unconsciousness and tied his wrists. When Fennel looked up he saw that Stephan was still fighting with his attacker. "Stephan duck!" Fennel yelled and threw a knife that struck a man wearing a black bandana who was creeping up behind Stephan.

When Fennel yelled, Stephan did not duck but went into a forward roll.

Stephan stood up behind his attacker and thrust his knife into the man's kidney. The man screamed in pain and fell forward. Stephan grabbed the man's hair and pulled his head back exposing the man's neck. Stephan cut the man's throat and quickly turned to see Thaos fighting with a man wearing a black bandana.

"We don't allow no damn women in here; get the hell out!" the bartender yelled as Jasmine, Thor and Lana ran into the tavern.

"You do now," Jasmine yelled as she threw her knife into the back of one of the men who were fighting with Fennel. Thor let out a war cry and grabbed one of Deckor's men off from Noah. Thor broke the man's neck and threw him to the ground. Lana jumped on the back of another one of the men who were attacking Fennel and cut the man's throat.

Jasmine knew she couldn't kick because of her injuries so she carried extra knives on her. "Lana right!" Jasmine screamed. As Lana threw herself to the right, Jasmine's knife penetrated the throat of the man who was behind Lana.

Thor did a side kick to the knee of one of the men who were surrounding Stephan. As the man dropped. Thor broke the man's neck. Thor stood back to back with Stephan as they fought four more of Deckor's men.

Thaos had a knife in each hand and grinned at the two men who were coming at him. Thaos threw one of his knives which landed between the eyes of one of his attackers. Thaos threw himself to the left as a knife sped past him; then he was just about to release his second knife but stopped as the attacker fell forward with blood running from his mouth. Lana had stabbed the man in the back.

"Anyone else want to join in?" Noah yelled challengingly as the last of their attackers were defeated. None of the bar patrons moved.

"Watch the crowd while we search the bodies," Thaos yelled. Noah, Jasmine, Lana and Thor formed a semi-circle facing the crowd as Stephan, Thaos and Fennel searched the bodies of their attackers.

"We've got five alive," Thaos yelled to his comrades. "We're taking them with us."

Jasmine and Lana backed towards the door and faced the crowd as Thor, Noah, Stephan, Fennel and Thaos dragged their prisoners out of the tavern. "Any of you try to follow us and you're dead," Jasmine said as she and Lana backed out of the door.

Thor had parked the boca immediately outside of the tavern's door. Three of the five prisoners were unconscious. Thor punched the other two prisoners so hard that they lost consciousness. All five prisoners were not only tied up but also tied to the sides of the boca.

"I'm wondering why we haven't seen any of our soldiers around here," Stephan said as he mounted his horse.

"I was thinking the same damn thing," Thaos said and looked up. A small flock of Enrops was circling over them. Thaos motioned to the birds and one of them landed on his arm. "We are going to take these men to the lodge. Send word to Gabriel that we are coming and expect to be attacked."

"Some of the flock flew to Gabriel when we realized you were fighting," the Enrop said. "We will watch over you as you travel."

"We're taking a back way," Stephan said and started to lead the group away from the docks.

"Wait!" Jasmine yelled. "Noah there is blood coming through your shirt. "Let me look at it."

"It's nothing," Noah barked.

"Let them look at it," Fennel said. Noah dismounted his horse and his knees started to buckle. Lana jumped off from the boca and Fennel jumped off from his horse. They both grabbed Noah and held him up as Jasmine opened Noah's shirt.

"Here," Stephan said and handed Jasmine his and Thaos' crystal necklaces. Jasmine took her necklace off too and packed all three of the crystals into the knife wound.

Jasmine was not wearing her warrior's outfit but a dress. She tore pieces from her skirt and bandaged Noah's wound. Noah was helped into the front seat of the boca where he sat between Lana and Jasmine. Thor mounted Noah's horse.

"I've got a bad feeling," Thaos said. "Let's get the hell out of here."

"How did you know we were in a fight?" Stephan asked Thor.

"We were at the market down the street and the Enrops told us."

"Well we were damn glad to see you kid," Stephan said with a grin.

Matthew was still at the lodge when a small flock of Enrops flew through the windows squawking. "There's a fight, they need help," the birds were saying. None of the people in the lodge took the time to ask the birds any details; everyone ran out of the lodge, saddled their horses and left the lodge at a full run. The Enrops guided the group towards Langer.

"Fahron's castle is the closest," Matthew yelled to the Enrops. "Some of you go there and get more help." Three Enrops left the flock and headed towards the castle.

Stephan was leading the group south along the shoreline of the Sea of Grevdt instead of taking the main roads through the City of Langer. This route was not only closer to Fahron's castle but was not highly populated. The group did not want to advertise that they had captured some of Deckor's men.

"Fahron they need help! Fahron they need help!" The Enrops screamed as they flew over the troops who were stationed at the castle and flew into the castle. The birds continued to yell their message as they flew around the castle looking for General Fahron. Fahron ran down a hallway towards the sounds of the birds.

"We will follow you," was all that Fahron said. Since the soldiers heard the screams of the Enrops first, Captain Powell had a company of men mounted on their horses and waiting for Fahron whose horse was saddled. General Fahron led his troops north towards the City of Langer at a full run.

"There's a group of men riding behind you," one of the Enrops screamed to Stephan and Thaos.

"It's too open here to take a stand," Thaos yelled to the others. "Keep moving!"

Dagon, Joao and Dack had been in Langer training Adin, Enzo, Ralf, Sol, Nana and Risa. These warriors were working on the far northern end of the large city and didn't know that Stephan and Thaos had entered the city or been in a fight.

"Your friends need help," screamed a single Enrop and the Ruala warriors quickly followed the bird. While Rualas cannot fly as fast as an Enrop they can travel faster than a horse can run. "That dust is the men chasing your friends," the Enrop screeched and the Rualas propelled themselves forward.

"We can't outrun them with the boca," Stephan yelled to Thaos. "We'll have to take a stand."

"Not yet," Thaos yelled and they continued southward.

"I can see the dust clouds," Michael yelled and sped ahead of Gabriel and the others.

"Tell them we are coming," Gabriel yelled to the Enrops.

The nine Ruala warriors flew over the army of Deckor's men who were chasing Thaos, Stephan and the others.

The Rualas shot arrow after arrow into the mass of men. The hired killers leading the army didn't realize the men at the rear of the formation were being attacked.

This army of killers was so focused on the prize in front of them that they also did not notice two separate dust clouds moving towards them.

"Gabriel and others are just ahead of you and Fahron is bringing soldiers," an Enrop screamed to Stephan and Thaos who did not know that the Rualas were attacking their enemies.

"Now we take a stand," Thaos yelled. Thaos, Stephan, Thor and Fennel stopped their horses and turned to face the army of killers behind them. Lana was driving the boca and stopped it. Noah had passed out in the front seat. Lana and Jasmine grabbed their knives as they prepared to protect Noah and the prisoners.

"There's Rualas flying over them," Thor yelled as the army of mercenaries got closer. Michael, Edward, Gabriel, Matthew, Raphael, Rachel and Kate stopped their horses and formed a line with Thaos and the others. They faced Deckor's army.

"They are just ahead," the Enrops screeched to Fahron.

"Captain Powell, have them blow the horn so our men know they are not alone," Fahron ordered.

Captain Powell repeated the order and a private took the Horn of Shana from the horn of his saddle and blew the notes that announced the presence of the army.

The army of mercenaries heard the horn as did Thaos and his group. But the mercenaries continued forward.

"Ready yourselves," Stephan yelled. "Charge!" And the small group of warriors rode into the arms of death.

The Ruala warriors had taken a heavy toll on the army. Rualas were expert archers; every arrow hit its mark. The Rualas now flew forward to fight alongside their comrades.

"Left Powell!" Fahron ordered and Powell led half of the soldiers to the left while Fahron led an attack against the mercenaries from the right.

Two soldiers jumped onto the boca and helped Jasmine and Lana fight the men who were trying to free the prisoners.

Edward screamed a war cry as he rode through the approaching army with a sword in his right hand and a battle axe in his left.

Kate quickly rode to her right and jumped from her horse when she saw that Thor was on the ground fighting with three men. Kate stabbed one of the assailants with her sword then stood back to back with Thor.

Raphael too had been pulled from his horse but he maintained his balance on the ground. Raphael was fighting with one of the mercenaries when another grabbed him from behind. As the man was pulling Raphael's head back to cut his throat, Dagon shot the man in the back with an arrow.

Stephan, Thaos, Gabriel, Matthew, Fennel and Michael were able to stay on their horses and rode through the mercenaries stabbing and hacking. Now that the Enrops had brought all of the groups together they too joined the battle, attacking the eyes and faces of the mercenaries.

"No one escapes!" Fahron yelled as he led a small group of soldiers after a dozen mercenaries who had turned and were riding back to Langer.

The bloody battle ended. Nana immediately started to attend to the wounds of her team members. Captain Powell ordered his men to search the bodies of the mercenaries and to tie up any who were still alive.

After Fahron and his men killed the group of mercenaries who were trying to escape he rode up to Stephan, Thaos and Matthew who were standing together. "What happened?" Fahron asked.

"Fahron it's a long story but two of our prisoners are Hector's men who kidnapped Margarit," explained Thaos. "While we were fighting with them Deckor's men attacked us. We think they are working together."

"Grab the wounded and everyone back to the castle now!" Fahron ordered.

The Sanuri was at Mathas' castle talking with Mathas, Rosa, Claudius and Bella about the arrangements for the christenings of their grandchildren when Enrops entered the castle.

"There has been a battle," one of the Enrops explained. Everyone is at Fahron's castle now but they have two of the men who kidnapped Margarit and some of Deckor's men as prisoners. The Rualas have gone back to Langer to get Dominic, Seth and everyone from Ryan's shop. Because they are afraid they might be targeted because it was Thaos and Stephan who first got into the fight."

"Ryan and the girls," Bella gasped.

"I'm sending a company of men to escort everyone home," Claudius said and left the room.

"Bella why don't you stay here with Rosa while Claudius and I go to Fahron's," Mathas said and turned to the Sanuri. "Do you think our families will be safe if we are all at Fahron's?"

"At this point I will say yes and I am coming with you," the Sanuri replied.

Gabriel and Raphael rode back to the lodge to get vials of the truth potion while the rest of Gabriel's group tied the prisoners up in separate rooms in the east wing of Fahron's castle.

Mathas had sent Enrops to Fahron's castle to tell him they were coming and were bringing the Sanuri. Lana waited by the front door and as soon as she saw the Sanuri she ran up to him.

"You must come quickly," Lana said. "It's Noah. The Sanuri dismounted and ran into the castle behind her. "He's here," Lana said as she burst through the door of the bedroom that Noah was in. Fennel, Jasmine and Kate were with Noah.

"I put crystals in his wound but he is still bleeding," Jasmine said excitedly. "Please help him."

The Sanuri quickly walked over to Noah and held his hands over Noah's body. The Sanuri closed his eyes and moved his hands the length of Noah's body without touching him. After a few moments the Sanuri placed the palms of his hands over Noah's wound and started to hum. Jasmine, Fennel, Lana and Kate stared at the Sanuri in awed silence.

After three minutes the Sanuri opened his eyes and said, "He will be alright but he should not be moved. He will have to stay here for several days."

"I will stay with him," Fennel said.

"Fennel you are hurt too," Kate scolded. "We will take turns taking care of Noah." Then Kate asked the Sanuri. "Would you look at Fennel's wounds too?"

Dominic and Seth were walking along a sidewalk in the main business district of Langer when Dominic heard Joao call his name. Dominic looked up and saw Dack and Joao standing on the roof of a building. Dack pointed to the alley on the left side of the building. As soon as Dominic and Seth walked into the alley, Dack and Joao swooped down and picked the men up.

"There's been some problems," Joao said. "We'll explain on the way."

"Where are we going?" asked Dominic.

"To Fahron's castle," Dack replied.

"What about our horses?" Seth asked.

"We'll come back for them," Joao said.

Dagon, Enzo, Adin, Ralf, Sol, Nana and Risa burst through the back door of Ryan's shop. Both Lawrence and Ryan jumped at the intrusion. "We have to get all of you out of here now," Dagon said. "Ryan get rid of any customers and lock the doors. Where are the girls?"

"In front with Chaez," Ryan said. "I'll get them."

"There has been a family emergency," Ryan said loudly as he ran into the front of the store. We all need to go home."

"What happened?" Sally asked.

"Just grab your pups and go into the back," Ryan said as he walked up to two old men who were sitting at a table in the front of the store.

"We heard," one of the men said as he was standing up to leave. "Hope everyone is alright."

"Why don't you take that plate of cookies with you," Ryan said and handed one of the men the plate. Ryan locked the door behind the two men and ran into the back room."

"Ryan you did good," Dagon said. "Girls hang on to those pups; we are flying all of you to Fahron's castle."

"What is going on?" Lawrence asked.

"Deckor's men attacked our people," Dagon said. "Ryan lock this back door and I will carry you."

"Did anyone die?" Lawrence asked.

"All I know is that Noah is hurt pretty bad," Sol said as he soared higher into the air.

As the Rualas were flying south they saw the troops that Claudius had sent into Langer. Dagon and the others landed near the troops. "Claudius sent us to bring everyone home," the young lieutenant said who was leading the troops.

"We got everyone out of the city but their horses are left behind. If we tell you where they are will you get them?" asked Dagon.

"Of course," the lieutenant replied.

Lawrence and Chaez told the soldiers where all of the horses could be found, then the Rualas resumed their flight.

Chapter XXXII
Answers

Before Gabriel gave truth potion to the first of Hector's men, the Sanuri wanted to look into the man's mind. The man was tied to a chair in a room that was filled with members of the ruling families and members of Gabriel's team.

"What the hell are you doing?" the man yelled and struggled to free himself from the Sanuri's grasp. The Sanuri stared intently into the man's mind for several minutes before he looked at Gabriel and said, "Go ahead."

As Raphael pulled the man's head back and Gabriel poured the potion down his throat Mathas asked the Sanuri, "What did you see?"

"Fragments but I hope to have a better understanding listening to the interrogation."

"He is ours as soon as this is done," Matthew said angrily.

When the potion started to take hold, not only did the man act drunk but he started to laugh hysterically. Gabriel looked at the Sanuri who said, "He's not a demon."

"Why are you laughing?" Gabriel asked.

"I don't know," the man said and continued to laugh hysterically.

"What is your name?"

"Max."

"Max do you still work for Hector?"

"Yeah." Max started to calm down once the questioning started.

"How long have you worked for him?"

"Don't know for sure; maybe five, six years."

"Do you know Juleta?"

Max sneered. "The witch Hector married. That bitch messed him all up."

"What do you mean?"

"She changed him."

"How?"

"I don't know but he never looked like that before."

"Are saying she changed his appearance?"

"Yep and he said that he wasn't the only one." Now people in the room stared at Max with horror.

"Who else did she change?"

"I don't know. Hector said he wasn't going to let her practice on him first."

"Do you know how many people she changed?"

"Not sure but it sounded like seven or eight."

"Were they all men?"

"Can't tell you."

"Why can't you tell me?"

"Cuz I don't know."

"Why did she change Hector's appearance?"

"All I know is that she told Hector it was for an important job then he finds out she made him look like some guy she had the hots for. He was so pissed. He started to beat the shit out of her but she did something to him with her magic."

"Can you explain what she did with her magic?"

"I don't know, hurt him somehow so that he would stop hitting her."

"Why did he marry her?"

"I don't think it was a real marriage, I mean like normal folk."

"How was it not normal?"

"She took him to her witch's altar and they cut each other and swapped blood. Sounds damned strange to me."

Gabriel looked at the Samuri who did not speak. "Ask him about Sarah," Mathas said.

"Max did Hector and Juleta have any children?"

"Max started to laugh, "Hell no. Hector wouldn't even touch her when he found out what she did to him."

"How long were they together before Hector found out?"

"Do you mean married? Maybe a week or two but we worked for her for three months before that. She changed his looks after the first month and we spent that time doing jobs for her."

"What sort of jobs?"

"Robbing banks and mines and such."

"So are you saying that Hector and Juleta didn't have sex?"

"If they did it wasn't much because she was always sending us away on jobs."

"How did Hector find out what Juleta did to him?"

"Some of her other hired men kept telling him how much he looked like their foreman. Boy was he pissed. Then when those troops came to the castle to get that little girl back, Hector saw the guy. He was so pissed he told us to just ride away and let the witch fight her own battles."

"Were you one of the men who kidnapped Juleta's sister?"

"Yeah, she paid us big for that job."

"Why did she want you to take her sister?"

"To lure her father to her castle so she could kill him."

"Did you know she was going to sacrifice her sister to a demon?"

"Hell no!" Max yelled. "That just gives me the damn willies."

"Where is Hector now?"

"He's rented three different rooms in different hotels but who really knows where he stays. That guy is like a ghost. He was never paranoid like that before he got involved with that damn witch."

"Where are those hotels?"

"In Langer."

"What are the names of the hotels?"

"The Blue Sky, The Pirate's Cove and The Excelsor."

"Why is he here?"

"Don't rightly know for sure but it has something to do with that mayor. Hector don't talk to us like he used to."

"Is Hector a dark lord?"

"I don't know what that is."

"Is he a warlock?"

"Do you mean a man witch? I don't know but I can tell you his personality is as different now as his looks."

"What do you mean?"

"He used to be a regular guy. Now he's all secretive and mysterious. We never know what he is doing or thinking no more. Before we met the witch he was our boss but we was all friends."

"What can you tell us about Mayor Deckor?"

"Now that guy's a man witch or something. He has those damn voodoo statues and crap in his office like Juleta had in her castle."

"Why is Hector dealing with Deckor?"

"I already told ya I don't know. But some of the guys said that the witch paid Deckor a lot of money cuz they delivered the chests. So maybe that is why Hector is here. He don't seem to like that mayor much. But then Hector don't seem to like nobody no more."

"If Hector wasn't the father of Juleta's baby who was?"

"The witch had a baby, that's a damn scary thought. She must have got someone drunk cuz no one ever wanted to go near her she was such a crazy bitch."

"Didn't she have a boyfriend who worked for the King of Zorta?"

Max laughed loudly. "You mean that old man. We would make bets on when she would give him a heart attack. But he ain't alive no more and it wasn't in the bedroom."

"Did she kill him?"

"The witch had that poor old goat wrapped around her finger. But when he heard she had her little sister kidnapped he actually got pissed. We was on a job, but the other guys said the old guy came to the castle and started yelling at the witch. The next thing they know is she is telling them to carry the guy's body out."

"Where does Hector live when he's not in Lentz?"

"In Port Friada."

"Not in Zorta?"

"No, he never lived in Zorta."

"We were told the witch's husband lived in Zorta and was finishing some of her plans."

Max laughed loudly again. "Oh damn, Hector is really gonna be pissed when he hears she had another husband."

"Have Hector's men been spying on the ruling families?"

"Naw, that's all Deckor. He's damn paranoid too. I think he is afraid they are gonna find out what he is up to."

"What's he up to?"

"You don't think he is gonna tell me. That prick treats us all like we are scum on the bottom of his shoe. He treats his own men the same except maybe for Ackley. But he still gives Ackley a lot of shit."

"Do you think Deckor has anything to do with those attacks on the ships?"

"Don't rightly know."

"Ask him if he has other men working for him besides the ones wearing the black bandanas," the Sanuri said.

Max heard what the Sanuri said. "Don't know about that either," Max said. "But he's got all those damn people so scared; the whole damn city probably works for him."

"What is Deckor doing to scare all those people?"

"Besides having people beaten up and killed, don't know."

"Do you know anything about rumors that people are missing from Langer?"

"Nope."

Gabriel immediately interrogated the second prisoner who worked for Hector. He gave similar information as Max. The Sanuri also stared into this man's mind without telling anyone what he saw. The interrogation lasted until early evening. When Gabriel was done asking questions, Matthew, Stephan and Thaos took Hector's men outside and killed them.

The people who had been involved with the interrogations in Fahron's castle took a break to eat dinner but planned to interrogate Deckor's men after the meal. As King Mathas walked towards the interrogation room he said to Claudius and Fahron, "I am so glad Rosa didn't hear any of that. As bad as I know Juleta was it is still difficult to hear those things about our child."

On the second night of their journey, Calen and Luca sat near their campfire eating dinner.

"Luca you have been so quiet this entire trip; are you ever going to talk about it?" Calen asked.

"Talk about what?"

"Well let's start with why is Natalie staying in your chambers and taking care of your children while we are gone. Are you a couple now?"

"No, it's because of Christopher."

"Well, don't stop there, tell me what is going on. Does this have anything to do with you two talking to Emeral and Maxwell the other night?"

"Yes and I feel really guilty because I have been so depressed about Lila that I haven't realized what is going on with Christopher. Apparently Christopher realizes that he and Emma are the only children of the team who don't have two parents and he has talked about this many times. Maxwell said that except for his nightmares that Christopher seems to be handling all of the tragedy in his life well. Maxwell and Emeral have been waiting for something else to surface with Christopher and they think that is happening now with Natalie."

"Emeral said that Natalie is such a natural mother that Christopher is drawn to her. Then when Christopher found out her parents were killed when she was little that increased their bond. And when Natalie helped him with his nightmares; Maxwell and Emeral said they saw a change in Christopher. They think he has decided that he wants Natalie for his mother and he is both confused and frustrated with us because we aren't becoming a family."

"I can understand all that but I still don't understand why she is staying with him and Emma."

"Our parents think that Christopher really needs Natalie right now. I mean he needs both of us but he always has me. Natalie cares about Christopher and wants to help him."

"But Luca don't you think he is going to be even more attached to her after this?"

"Honestly I don't know. Do you think it is a bad idea?"

"I'll tell you what I think after you tell me how you feel about Natalie. Are you attracted to her?"

"She's beautiful and so sweet who wouldn't be attracted to her. And I think that both of us are coming out of our fogs since we have been talking. But Calen I still think about Lila all of the time. I don't think I can consider having a relationship with someone else until I am over Lila."

"Ok now I am going to tell you what I think. First of all everyone in the house is pleased that both you and Natalie seem to be coming out of your depressions. But Luca I know you. You like to take care of others and Natalie needs someone to take care of her right now. So don't get that confused with emotions. But the more I see the two of you together the more I think you two are a really good fit. Now before you say anything let me finish."

"Luca I can't even imagine what you have been going through. I know I would fall apart if Natasha died. But when you love someone that much I don't think you ever really get over them. I think you will always have feelings for Lila and I think that Natalie will always have feelings for Troy. And you know there isn't anything wrong with that. You two need to accept that and decide when you are ready to move forward, whether it is with each other or not."

"That makes a lot of sense," said Luca.

"Luca I don't know if you and Natalie are ready to move forward now but I don't think you two should just dismiss each other either. Because I am pretty sure that when you are ready for a relationship the two of you could have something good."

"You really think so?"

"Actually everyone in the household thinks so but everyone worries about the two of you too. You are both in such difficult positions right now."

"Maxwell is afraid that we will let Christopher push us into something we aren't ready for."

"I can certainly see that too. Luca unless something unforeseen happens I bet that when we return Christopher is going to be even more adamant that he wants the two of you together. You need to start thinking about what you are going to do or at least what you are going to say to Christopher."

Chapter XXXIII
Exposed

"What!" screamed Deckor. "They attacked Stephan and Thaos? You know this will expose me! Damn it Ackley they may have ruined everything. Who the hell gave them the damn order to attack?"

"Boss no one did, I think the men just took it upon themselves because they had captured some of our boys," Ackley said. "I'm pissed too. But I can't do much about it cuz they is all dead."

"What! Ok, Ok, I have to calm down," Deckor could hardly choke out the words. He quickly ran over to the table in his office that held bottles of whiskey. Deckor poured two glasses and thrust one at Ackley. "Ackley tell me everything. First how did they capture some of our men?"

"From what I've been told Claudius' boys walked into The Ocean's End Tavern and before they are through the door some drunk throws a knife at them. Well the bartender said there was these two other fellers sitting at a table minding their own business but one of them jumped up and walloped the guy who threw the knife. So Claudius' boys go over to that table to thank those fellers and to buy them a drink."

"The bartender told me that Thaos walks up to the bar to get a bottle and see's three of Hectors guys staring at him. Well Thaos knew who they were and he yells real loud to Stephan that the guys who kidnapped the King's little girl are at that table. Well the whole damn place knows there's gonna be a blood bath now so everyone grabs their drinks and moves out of the way. Stephan gets up and so do the two men at the table and the fight is on. Well Claudius' boys kill one and take the other two prisoner and as they are tying them up a bunch of our boys jump them."

"Why?" Deckor demanded.

"Hell if I know; they should have just let them be."

"Well I heard that our boys were winning until two Nordes women and a guy bust into the place. Those women fight like men and I heard the guy was a giant and just went around breaking necks. They killed most of our guys and took a few as prisoners," Ackley paused. "Boss one of them said something like we've got Deckor's men. I think that's why our boys went after them." Deckor slumped down into a chair and gulped his drink.

"Well's as soon as I hear about this I grab me a bunch of the boys and we go after our men. About five miles south of here I find them; forty-three bodies and they is all ours."

"We lost forty-three men!" anger overwhelmed Deckor again.

"And a whole bunch had these strange arrows in them."

"Were they Nordes arrows?"

"No, I've seen Nordes arrows before. Boss I don't know how many of our boys went after them so's I don't know if they've got more prisoners." Deckor turned white as he listened to Ackley because he understood that such a direct attack on the members of the ruling families was treason.

"Boss, I'm thinking that they got our boys who was spying on them and found out yous was paying them. I'm a thinking they haven't come for you cuz they is trying to figure out what ya are doing."

Deckor sat in silence for a few seconds then he asked, "Does Hector know about this?"

"Hell if I know. Boss you is the one paying me. I came straight to you. So is we going to war or running?"

"Let me think about this. I might be able to pin this whole damn thing on Hector; that would kill two birds with one stone."

Because of the urgency of the situation the interrogations of Deckor's men lasted through the night. Unlike Hector, Deckor never spoke directly to any of his men other than Ackley. Deckor didn't know the vast majority of his men; he would only recognize them by the black bandanas that they wore.

Deckor did not want to be directly involved with his men or their assignments for two reasons. First he thought it would protect his identity and secondly his sense of superiority. Deckor felt that he paid Ackley to get his hands dirty so Deckor wouldn't have to.

Ackley was shrewd and understood Deckor's desire for secrecy. While Ackley worked and talked with the men he revealed little about Deckor or any of the assignments. Because of this Deckor's men revealed little about their bosses during the interrogations. The men told of crimes they had been ordered to commit and specific assignments but they gave no insight into Deckor or his involvement with Juleta and Hector. The men didn't even know Hector but they knew the men who were working for him.

While none of Deckor's men knew the exact number of men who worked for Deckor, the interrogations revealed that Deckor's army was larger than originally thought. The estimated number of men that Hector had in Lentz was approximately fifty.

When Deckor's men were asked who ordered them to attack Stephan and Thaos in The Ocean's End Tavern, they all gave the same answer. The mercenaries were not under orders they simply thought they would take advantage of the situation. All the men knew that Deckor was having the ruling families watched. The men involved in the bar fight planned to kill Thaos and Stephan and to blame it on Hector's men.

When word came that Thaos, Stephan and their comrades had taken prisoners; Deckor's men took it upon themselves to rescue their partners and to protect their bosses.

Every man who was interviewed said that although Deckor and Hector were involved in some type of business the word was that these two men did not like each other. These sentiments of hostility were passed down to their men and conflicts were occurring between the two camps.

The one thing of real interest to the ruling families was that most of the mercenaries believed that although Deckor had always been a criminal he didn't really gain power until the past two or three years. This is the time frame that the ruling families believed Deckor became involved with Juleta.

All of the prisoners were executed the following morning. Ryan did not open up his shop this day because Claudius was concerned about retaliation.

Since Mathas, Claudius, Matthew, Stephan, Thaos and the Sanuri had spent the night at Fahron's castle to listen to the interrogations the morning meeting was held in Fahron's study. Before everyone was seated Matthew said, "I am wondering if Deckor is one of the men who Juleta changed in appearance or either she made him a dark lord."

"I think we are all thinking that," Stephan said then Stephan turned to Thaos and said kiddingly, "She must have liked you a hell of a lot more than me because she didn't make me a twin."

"That we know about yet," Thaos said with a grin.

"The thing that really concerns me," the Sanuri said. "Is that we have not discovered how Deckor maintains his chokehold on the city. Langer is a city of sailors, dock workers and other tough men. While I believe threatening and killing some people would intimidate them I don't think that would go for everyone. I fear more and more that we might have a situation like we did with Shanksaw. We need to tread carefully."

"Thanks," Noah said after Kate removed his breakfast tray and helped him to lie back down.

"You are just lucky the Sanuri was here," Kate said as she pulled the covers over Noah. "We were all afraid you were going to die."

"I don't even remember any of that. How is Fennel?"

"Better than you. Everyone stayed up all night to interrogate the prisoners and now they are in a meeting. I expect your friends will be in shortly to visit you."

"I'm afraid I will be sleeping by then," Noah said as his eyelids were getting heavy.

"Do you want me to wake you?"

"You don't have to stay."

"We decided to take turns watching you," Kate said then she grinned. "Fahron's girls are learning to be healers and they want to help watch you too. We told them not to put their dogs on your bed." Noah started to laugh then grabbed his side in pain. "I'm sorry," Kate said. "I shouldn't have joked."

"No, that's alright. It was funny. Yeah wake me if someone comes."

Calen and Luca arrived at Fahron's castle late that afternoon. "Please come in," Isadore said. "Are you hungry?"

"Starving," Calen said with a grin.

"I'll have the cooks prepare you something while I show you to your rooms. Gabriel and his people were staying at the lodge but everyone was up all night interrogating those awful men who attacked Stephan and Thaos."

"What! Are they alright?" asked Luca.

"Yes, but it is getting like a war around here. Honestly I don't know all of the details and everyone is sleeping except for me and the girls."

"So is everyone here?" Calen asked.

"Yes, they are in the east wing. I will take you there. That wing is for your team to use any time you want."

"Isadore you know how our family is," Calen said. "Luca and I have all kinds of gifts in our bags. Some for babies, some for Sorren and honestly I don't know about the rest but they have names on them. If we can't get with everyone would you be kind enough to make sure they get in the right hands?"

"Of course," said Isadore.

"Actually I think we have something for you too," Luca said. "The girls packed our bags."

Isadore stopped in the kitchen to speak with the staff then she led Calen and Luca to the east wing of the castle. As they walked Isadore was telling the men about the battle the previous day. "Understand I didn't hear everything but it sounds like if Thor, Jasmine and Lana hadn't run into that awful tavern that Stephan, Thaos, Noah and Fennel would have been killed. As it is Noah is badly wounded. Thank The Great Ruler that the Sanuri is here. Fennel is hurt too but not as bad."

"Here we are," Isadore said in a lower voice as she led Calen and Luca into the east wing. A lot of the rooms are empty so just take what you want. But I should tell you one night some of Decker's men broke into Michael's room and attacked him."

"We didn't realize it was so bad here," Calen said to Isadore then turned to Luca, "Maybe we should stay and help out."

"I was thinking the same thing," Luca said. "Let's send a note to the girls right away."

"Luca I have to tell you that Amy is so proud of that bracelet that Christopher sent along for her. Nikki said that Amy won't take it off."

"Actually I wish that Amy lived closer. He does better when he is with her."

"What do you mean?"

"I'll tell you over dinner. But you know all that he has been through; I think it is catching up with him."

"Well I am sorry to hear that. Christopher is such a precious child. Do you know how to get back to the dining room or would you like me to wait for you?"

"We can find our way back," Calen said. "It won't take us long."

Isadore left the wing and Luca and Calen assumed that all the chambers with closed doors were taken. They didn't knock on the doors because they didn't want to wake anyone. They walked into the first open door they found. The chambers were huge and had three bedrooms.

"Let's just check to see if we have gifts for Isadore and Fahron before we go out there," Luca said as he dumped the contents of his backpack on one of the beds.

"While you do that I am going to check these doors and the courtyard," Calen said.

Calen walked back into the chambers about ten minutes later. "There are a lot of thick bushes and trees around the courtyards. Anyone could hide out there. But there are locks on the doors. Are you ready?"

"Yeah, I'm glad I looked; there are some things," Luca said. "We've got gifts too. Do you want to open them now or tonight?"

"Tonight. I know who my gift is from," Calen said with a grin. "Do you think Natalie got you a gift?"

"What do you think?" Luca asked and laughed as he held up a box that was wrapped in paper that was covered with childish drawings."

Calen and Luca returned to the dining room where they found a small feast set on the table. "You let me know if I can bring you anything else," Isadore said as she set a bottle of wine and a bottle of whiskey on the table.

"Isadore we have gifts here for your family and some of them look like they might be from Renya. Calen and I have no idea what anything is. Should we just put them on this end of the table?"

"Yes, your family is always so generous. Would you like me to tell you as much as I know about what has been happening while you eat?"

Vivian, Iris and Joshua knocked on the door to Luca's chambers. Natalie answered the door with baby Emma in her arms. A big smile came on Natalie's face when she saw her friends.

"We brought a gift," Iris said. "Joshua just made it for you."

"A backpack," Natalie said excitedly. "Thank you so much. I can really use it."

"We know," Joshua said. "We have been watching you struggling with carrying two babies, this way you can carry one on your back."

"Natalie put it on and we will adjust the straps," Iris said.

"So what is it like staying in Luca's chambers?" asked Vivian.

"It's a little strange. This is so fancy I am afraid I will break something," Natalie said.

"Dear if Christopher hasn't broken it I doubt if you will," Iris said as she adjusted the straps of the backpack."

"The children have been wonderful," Natalie said. "I let Christopher sleep with me the first night but he got annoyed because the babies kept waking up so he moved back to his room."

"He seems really happy having you here," Vivian said. "Have you and Luca talked about what you are going to do? Because you know Christopher isn't going to want you to leave."

"Luca and I are just playing this by ear. We need to talk more. Emeral and Maxwell really feel that Christopher needs a mother right now and I agree but this is all so complicated."

"Do you think you could ever get interested in Luca?" Vivian asked.

"Honestly since all this came up with Christopher I have been asking myself that same question. I really like him. And I think he is a good man and a good father; it's just that I still have Troy in my heart."

"Honey it was my idea for you to come here," Iris said. "I thought it would help both you and Luca to heal. It was never anyone's intention to try and fix you up with Luca. But I have to say you two have something together. He is a good man and I don't think Troy would want you to go through life alone and depressed. Neither of you might be ready for a relationship now but..."

"But what Iris?" asked Natalie.

"We think you should consider staying here longer. We know you planned to leave right after the wedding. Is there any reason you really need to get back now?" Iris asked.

"Iris I do like everyone here but are you saying I should stay and hope that Luca and I can work something out?"

"I find that an interesting choice of words," Joshua said with a grin.

Edward did not want to waste any time starting his part of the mission. After he received the paperwork, money and disguises from Calen and Luca, Edward met with his team which now included Rachel, Dagon, Calen and Luca. They planned to return to the lodge early the following morning to get their things and the carriage then they were going to ride into Langer. Michael and Dominic were going to join them and act as body guards.

Gabriel, Raphael and the Sanuri walked into the meeting as it was ending. "Many of you are new on these missions," the Sanuri said. "I want to remind you that while you are powerful warriors you cannot kill a dark lord or a powerful demon. I do not want to make my presence known in the city until I am needed but leave the demons and dark lords to me. At this point we should expect that both Hector and Deckor are not normal humans."

"Also," Gabriel said. "Deckor has to know that we killed his men. He does not appear to be a fool so he will know that the ruling families are on to him. He is probably wondering why they have not taken him out of office. Deckor will suspect that the ruling families are trying to figure out exactly what he is doing. Which means he is either going to run or make some changes to his operations."

"If he is smart he will change the identifiers of his men. So don't believe only men wearing black bandanas work for him," Raphael said. "And we believe he will try to create some kind of smoke screen like blaming the attacks on Thaos and Stephan on someone else."

"Since there is no love lost between Hector and Deckor we expect Deckor to try and blame Hector for the spies and the attacks. Be careful not to get caught in the crossfire."

"Deckor might also create a massive distraction which could be more attacks on ships," Gabriel said. "So be prepared for anything. Raphael and I are known here. So we are going to disguise ourselves and meet you for lunch at The Peacock Hotel at noon. We will play the parts of investors. Once again this is primarily a fact finding mission don't expose yourselves unless it is necessary. Rachel did you talk to Kate about a distress sign?"

"Not yet; I was going to," Rachel said with some embarrassment.

"Kate this first mission is going to be a real test for you; it is for everyone," Gabriel explained. "Sometimes you have to fight your instincts to maintain your disguise. Natasha was very cleaver at creating subtle signals for us to come and help her. For example she might be in a crowded room talking to someone and she believes he has caught her in lie. If Natasha runs out of the room or punches the man she has exposed herself and the team. So she would drop a scarf or raise a glass of wine and one of us would come to the table with an excuse to get her away or a back-up plan. Whatever signal you choose, your entire team must be aware of it."

"In Ryed Natasha and I were going to drop an earring," Rachel said. "It has to be something natural yet obvious enough that the other team members can see it. We may be changing the signal depending on what we wear."

"I can fill you in on more about the signals," Calen said. "Natasha is very clever."

"If Deckor believes your stories he may try to put the moves on either of you girls. No matter how disgusting you may find him we would like you to be flirtatious," Raphael said.

"What!" said Kate.

"Kate that is what I thought at first in Ryed too," Rachel said.

"But you could not believe the information Natasha could get from people just from batting her eyes and smiling. Once I saw how much information she was gathering it was easier for me to do it."

"Kate do you think you can pull that off?" asked Edward.

"Edward I know how to flirt," Kate said with a laugh. "Do you want me to practice on one of you?"

"You can practice on me," Joao said with a grin.

Early the following morning all of Gabriel's and Edward's team members left Fahron's castle except for Noah, Fennel, Jasmine and Lana. Jasmine and Lana were taking care of Noah and Fennel until they were well enough to move to the lodge. The teams arrived at the lodge shortly after sunrise and were immediately met by a small flock of Enrops. The birds carried only one note which was from Matthew. *Thirty Patronus priests in The Day's End Hotel. Twenty-five in The Peacock Hotel. Thirty-five in The Blue Sky Hotel. Twenty-seven in The Excelsor Hotel. Thirty-five in The Pirates Cove Hotel.*

Michael was driving the carriage and Dominic sat next to him in the front seat. Edward, Rachel and Kate were riding inside of the carriage. "There's a hell of a lot of smoke ahead," Michael yelled out as they entered the City of Langer. People were running wildly in the streets and yelling. Bells were clanging.

"What is going on?" Dominic yelled down to a man who was running past the carriage.

"A ship is on fire," the man yelled without stopping.

"Guess that is the diversion," Edward yelled out of the window.

Michael stopped the carriage in front of The Peacock Hotel which was only a few blocks south of the fire. Smoke filled the air. People on the streets were coughing and choking. Edward signed for three suites on the third floor of the hotel.

All of the suites had balconies facing the back of the building so Rualas and Enrops could enter the rooms unnoticed.

"Most people like to face the ocean," the hotel clerk said as he handed Edward the keys.

"Not with all that smoke," Edward said. "That fire's not going out any time soon."

When Edward's group got to the third floor they found that each suite had three bedrooms. "I would prefer that all of us stay in the same suite, unless any of you have a problem with that," Edward said.

Everyone looked at each other and Michael said, "I think we are all fine with that. But we should still check out all of our rooms."

"I was planning on it," Edward said. We can set this suite up for the main meeting area. Michael would you open up the balcony doors in the other two suites so the rest of the team can come in."

"That's the nice thing about the fire," Dominic said. "I doubt if anyone will notice the Rualas."

"Edward I just thought, Dagon is probably going to want to stay with me. Would that be alright?" Rachel asked.

"You two can have the room," said Kate. "I will sleep on the sofa."

"There's two beds in each room," Dominic said. "You know you don't have to worry about any of us."

"I'm fine with that," Kate said. "Should we draw straws?"

"Why don't you stay with Edward," Michael said. "I am teaching Dominic the Cerfic language so we are studying every night."

"Fine," Kate said and grabbed her bags.

Chapter XXXIV
Streets of Blood

The following morning Vivian walked out of the kitchen with a big smile on her face and a hand filled with letters. The other members of the household were just sitting down to their breakfast meal. "Enrops just delivered mail from Lentz. I told them to stay and eat while we write letters." Vivian walked around the room handing out envelopes.

"Children, Emeral and I will help you read your letters," Maxwell said as the children left their table and ran to their grandparents.

"I got one," Natalie said with surprise.

"That's Luca's handwriting," Vivian said with a big smile.

"Oh no," Hannah said as she read her letter from Gabriel. "I am sure your letters say the same," Hannah said to everyone at the table. "Gabriel says the situation is very bad and they will probably be staying longer than planned."

"I had a feeling that would happen," Vivian said sadly as she sat down and opened one of her letters.

"Well, I am not sure if I should be mad about this or what," Natalie said out loud. "Luca and Calen are staying to help and it sounds like he is afraid that I am going to leave the children after two days. Does he really think I would do that?"

"Dear I am sure he just feels guilty leaving you with everything," Emeral said.

"Emeral he said he wrote to you to ask you to help with the children if I didn't want to take care of them," Natalie said with annoyance. "I promised to watch Christopher and Emma and I will no matter how long he is gone. What kind of person does he think I am?"

"Natalie read my letter," Emeral said. "He is just worried about you because of everything you are going through and he feels guilty leaving you with so much work."

"Emeral read my letter. Am I just overreacting?" Natalie asked and handed the letter down the table to Emeral.

"Can I read it?" Maxwell asked as the letter was passed to him.

"All of you can read it," Natalie said then she turned to Christopher. "Christopher, Luca said that Amy loves that bracelet you gave her and she never takes it off." Christopher's face broke into a huge grin.

"Natalie are you mad at Luca?" Christopher asked.

"I'm not sure," Natalie said. "He asked me to watch you for four days and now that he is going to be gone longer he is concerned that I won't watch you anymore."

"You aren't going to leave us are you?" asked Christopher.

"Of course not Honey," Natalie said.

"I know what Luca means but I will admit he could have worded it better," Maxwell said as he handed the letter to Emeral.

"Natalie I can help you with the babies," Diana said. "Misha is doing so much better that he doesn't need me watching over him every second anymore."

"Thank you Natalie," Misha said sarcastically with a big grin. Diana punched Misha's arm.

"Emeral that last sentence," Natalie said. "Is Luca afraid I am going to just leave the children and go home?"

"I don't think he believes you will abandon the children," Emeral said as she reread the letter. "I think he was taken by surprise when Calen told him you really didn't plan on staying here that long. But it is difficult to understand the way that he wrote it."

"We already asked Natalie to stay here longer," Joshua said. "There is no reason she needs to go to Ryed any time soon."

"Natalie is staying here with us," Christopher said with such a voice of authority that many people laughed.

Ratri and Batina were whispering to each other as they read a letter from Joao and Dack. "Batina and I are doing much better," Ratri said. "We are going to Lentz and help. If anyone wants to send things with us we will wait."

"Ackley burn them," Deckor said. "All the bandanas. Find another way to identify our men." Deckor paused. "Better yet; give the bandanas to Hector's men."

"They don't run we us," Ackley said. "Why would they wear them?"

"Tell them that Hector is ordering it."

"But ain't he here?"

"No, he went back to Port Friada," Deckor said. "Since he got that territory he's been keeping busy."

"I don't understand."

"He's a, he just got promoted in the organization he works for so I don't expect him to be coming around as much."

"Well, I don't like it at all," Bella said vehemently.

"It's up to you Ryan," said Claudius

"None of the rest of you would hide," Ryan said. "I want to open my shop. But I don't want Sally and April there."

"I think we all agree on that," Claudius said.

Both Ingr and Nikki smiled at Ryan's words. Ingr got out of her seat and kissed Ryan on the cheek. "I will prepare the coffee and treats," Ingr said and left the room.

"Bella will you watch the children? I will set up the table in the shop today," said Nikki.

"I'll go with you," Thaos said. "And I think we should have some men in the shop."

"Already thinking about that," Stephan said. "I'll have the soldiers wear their civilian clothes and I'm coming with you. I don't want to miss out on any fun."

When Gabriel and Raphael entered the main dining room of The Peacock Hotel, Edward, Kate, Rachel, Michael and Dominic were seated at a table waiting for them.

"You look so different," Kate whispered with amazement as Raphael and Gabriel sat down. Both men smiled.

"Sorry we are a little late," Gabriel said. "We attended the morning meeting. Because of the attacks, Sorren is having his warriors patrolling the streets also. He wanted you to know that Toni volunteered to patrol. Since Sorren does not trust her temper he told her you were on a mission and not to jeopardize your disguise."

"Another one of your girlfriends?" Kate asked sarcastically.

"For my part she is just a friend," said Edward.

"And for her part?" Kate asked with a grin. Edward did not answer the question.

"Kate you are the one she will go after and the Nordes warriors are trained as well as you," Rachel said. "I would expect anything."

"In that case maybe you should tell me what she looks like," Kate said.

"She's really tall with long straight white blonde hair. She is very tan and beautiful," Edward said. "And I can handle her." Everyone at the table grinned.

"Edward if I am going to have to fight for you; you better make it worth my while," Kate said with a mischievous grin.

Edward laughed loudly. "What do you want?"

"I'll think of something," Kate said and laughed.

A few moments later a waiter approached the table. "We just got to town," Gabriel said to the waiter. "And we would like to talk to Geof Thurstand about buying one of his ships. Could you please direct us to his office?"

"That's one of his ships that's burning," the waiter said. "That poor man has had a string of bad luck. First his misses disappears, then his office is ransacked and today one of his ships is set on fire."

"Why, that is awful," Rachel said with feigned concern. "That poor man. Who would do such a thing?"

The waiter did not answer the question. "I can give you directions to his office and nothing more," the waiter said.

As Stephan, Nikki and Thaos were leaving Ryan's shop Stephan said, "Gabriel and Raphael said they were going to meet Edwards' team at The Peacock for lunch. Let's just walk past the window and make sure they are alright." Smoke still filled the streets.

"Why aren't you two coughing?" Nikki asked as she was choking on the smoke.

"Don't know," Thaos said with a grin. "Maybe we are too mean."

"You mean crazy," Nikki said with a grin.

"Here we are," Stephan said. "Just look don't motion to them."

"Do you think I am stupid?" Nikki asked with annoyance.

Edward, Gabriel and Raphael saw Thaos, Stephan and Nikki glance into the dining room as they walked past the large picture window of the restaurant. "I don't think anything is wrong," Gabriel whispered. "I think they are just checking on us."

As the three men continued to look out of the picture window they saw people running towards the docks. "Something else is going on," Raphael said.

"Dominic and I will check it out," Michael said and the two men quickly left the dining room. As they were about to enter the front lobby of the hotel they walked past Mayor Deckor and an attractive woman with black hair who was wearing expensive clothing. Michael and Dominic did not recognize Deckor until they heard the host say Deckor's name. Dominic looked back at the table and nodded to Edward then nodded towards Deckor.

"Game on," Edward whispered to the people at his table. The people at Edward's table watched as the host of the restaurant escorted Deckor and the woman through the main dining room to Deckor's private dining room. Deckor was a large man with straight black hair that he greased back from his forehead. He had a very thin black mustache and small dark eyes.

"I can't believe he is a womanizer," Kate whispered. "He looks like a giant rat to me."

"You may be flirting with that giant rat," Edward whispered with a grin.

"This may be harder than I thought," Kate said kiddingly.

"He's no worse than those two old generals in Ryed," Rachel said and Raphael and Gabriel laughed.

Within minutes Michael and Dominic returned to Edward's table. "Geof Thurstand was just found hanging in his office," Michael said. "The soldiers wouldn't let us in but Stephan, Thaos and Nikki are inside and looking around."

While Edward and the others ate lunch the Ruala warriors who were working on the mission entered the two suites that Edward had purchased for them.

"We rarely do something like we just did now," Calen was explaining to the members of Edward's team. "Normally we wouldn't expose ourselves in daylight like this unless there was an emergency but with the distraction of the fire and all of the smoke we used it to our advantage."

"So we almost never reveal our presence?" Sol asked.

389

"It really depends on the mission," said Luca. "We usually don't have to worry around most normal people but dark lords and those who work for them know there is going to be trouble when they see us. For all we know Deckor and Hector are dark lords and it sounds like Deckor owns this city."

"There will be times when you also play parts in the missions," Dagon said. "We did in Ryed. But we usually have to lay the ground work for that first."

All of the Rualas were meeting in one suite when there was a knock on the door. None of the Rualas moved. "It's Rachel," a woman's voice said through the door and Dagon walked across the parlor and opened the door. Rachel quickly came inside.

"We didn't know if you were here yet," Rachel said. "Edward has ordered baskets of food that he told the waiter he wants to give as gifts but they will be brought to this room soon so I will answer the door. Obviously the food is for you. Also there is a slight change in plans. Gabriel and Raphael are getting rooms here now. That ship that is burning belongs to Geof Thurstand and his body was just found hanging in his office. Gabriel thinks Geof was killed because he talked to the ruling families."

"Quiet," Adin whispered. "I hear people."

"Quickly everyone get into the bedrooms," Rachel said. Within moments there was a knock on the door. "Oh my," Rachel said when ten men walked into the room carrying large baskets of fruits, breads, sausages and sea foods. "I had no idea my brother had ordered so much," she said and laughed. "Just set the baskets anywhere." As the men were about to leave Rachel said, "Here." And handed each man a gold coin for a tip. "I have to warn you my brother is quite extravagant this may not be the only time you come up here."

"We thank you My Lady," one of the men said. "You just let us know whenever you need anything." Rachel watched the men walk down the hallway then down the staircase before she returned to the room.

"Lunch time," she called out. "But we don't have any plates. I will buy some."

"We come prepared," Dack said with a grin when he saw all of the food in front of them. "We always carry food and utensils."

"I guess I should have realized that," Rachel said. "Dagon, Edward wanted all of us to stay together so you and I have a room next door."

"Good, I was wondering about that," Dagon said as he filled his dish with seafood."

"Dagon, this is such a beautiful city. Do you think we will have a chance to buy some gifts?"

"I am sure that Edward will let you and Kate go shopping. I probably can't go with you but I brought plenty of money."

"Natasha would get some of her best information when she would go on shopping trips," Luca said. "I would bring that up to Edward."

"Well, why don't all of you make lists and we will get your things for you," Rachel said. "And if you don't know what you want Kate and I can look around and come back and tell you."

"We might need more wine," Joao said as he looked at the three bottles on the table.

"Edward ordered wine and whiskey too so we will have another delivery," said Rachel.

"When you go shopping listen to everyone talk," Dagon said to Rachel. "Markets and shops are a place where people gather and gossip. And Gabriel always says that you have to really buy things or you will look suspicious."

Calen laughed, "When we were on a mission in Taperia the local butcher shop was a place to hear gossip. Natasha would bring home bocas full of meat. I don't think we've ever eaten that well on a mission."

Joao was standing near the front door and now held up his hand for the others to be quiet. "It's Gabriel," a male voice said and Joao opened the door. Gabriel entered the room and quickly closed the door. "Raphael and I have the room immediately across the hall. It faces the front street."

"Deckor is in his private dining room so Edward and Kate are waiting for him to come out. Edward is going to try and make a first contact. Raphael and I are going down to the docks and see what we can find out about Thurstand's death. Michael is going to stay with Edward and Kate and Dominic is coming with us. Do any of you have questions?"

"Rachel wants to buy gifts and we were telling her how Natasha would gather so much information on shopping trips," Dagon said.

"Great idea," Gabriel said and took a large pouch of gold coins out of his pocket and handed it to her. "Let me know when you need more because you really need to buy things or you will expose your disguise."

"Thanks," Rachel said with a big smile. "I already told the others to make lists, why don't you and Raphael too. I am sure you want to bring back gifts."

"Are you supposed to be here?" Ryan asked as Chaez and Lawrence walked into his shop.

"We just heard you were open for business," Lawrence said with a grin. "Those toys aren't going to make themselves."

"There's soldiers in the back room and at the table," Ryan said and nodded at the man who was sitting in front of the window.

"We heard," Lawrence said. "But we still thought we would keep you company."

"Ryan do you have any beads here?" Chaez asked. "Lana and Jasmine want to teach Sally and April how to make jewelry. All the girls are staying at the castle taking care of Noah and Fennel."

"Yeah, jars of them. Just take what you want."

"We might be getting some company," said the soldier loudly who was sitting at the front window. "And they don't look like the shopping kind."

392

"We heard you," yelled one of the soldiers in the back room.

"Ryan go in back," Chaez said.

"No, it's my shop; I have to be here."

Three men entered the shop. One of them pushed the door open with such force that it slammed into the wall. Lawrence and the soldiers recognized the men as hired fighters. "Can I help you?" Ryan asked nervously.

"Are you Claudius' boy?" one of the men asked with a sneer.

"Yes," Ryan said proudly. "What do you want?"

"We've got a message for your daddy," the same man said.

"Why don't you tell me yourself," Claudius said as he had followed the men into the store and was standing behind them. All three men quickly turned around and Claudius punched the man closest to him in the face. Lawrence, Chaez and the soldier at the window attacked the other two men before any of the soldiers in the back room made it to the front of the store.

"Don't kill them yet," Claudius ordered and picked one of the men up and slammed his head into the wall so hard he lost consciousness. "We're taking them with us but first I am paying Deckor a visit." The soldiers tied up the intruders while Lawrence and Chaez followed Claudius out the door.

Claudius was filled with rage and marched the two blocks down the street to Deckor's office. Claudius burst through the door and entered the lobby. "Where is Deckor?" he bellowed.

"He's at lunch," Jenny the secretary said. "Wait you can't go in there!"

Claudius kicked the door to Deckor's office open. "Boys grab those things." Claudius said as he pointed out objects of black magic to Chaez and Lawrence. Claudius stormed back into the lobby. "Where is he?"

"At The Peacock Hotel. In his private dining room," Jenny stammered. Claudius marched out of the office.

Claudius looked so enraged as he walked down the street that one of the soldiers went to Thurstand's office to get Stephan, Thaos and Nikki while other soldiers fell in behind their general.

"Where is Deckor's private room?" Claudius bellowed as he entered the main dining room of The Peacock Hotel. Claudius saw Edward, Raphael, Dominic, Michael and Kate sitting at a table staring at him. Claudius shook his head from side to side to indicate to them that they should not expose their identities.

The host fearfully pointed out the door and Claudius sped past him with Lawrence, Chaez and a dozen soldiers close behind. Claudius kicked the door with such force that it shattered. Deckor and his female companion were kissing and now Deckor jumped up from the table. Claudius yelled his words so that everyone in the restaurant could hear.

"You viper!" Claudius yelled as he punched Deckor so hard in the jaw that Deckor flipped backwards over the table. "You send your hired killers after two of my boys and just now after Ryan." Claudius knocked the table over and ran up to Deckor and kicked him in the side. Deckor flew a short distance. "I just found all of your damn demon crap in your office. You are under arrest for treason." Claudius picked Deckor up and punched him in the stomach.

Stephan, Thaos and Nikki now ran into the room. "They went after Ryan," Claudius yelled when he saw his family. "Boys clean this place out. Get Ackley and the rest of Deckor's men." Claudius picked Deckor up from the floor and punched him in the jaw again.

"Where do you think you are going?" Nikki asked as she grabbed Deckor's girlfriend who was trying to run out of the dining room.

"Let go of me!" the woman demanded. Nikki punched Deckor's girlfriend in the mouth then grabbed her by the hair and slammed her head against the wall.

"I like her," Kate said with a grin.

Stephan and Thaos had run out of the hotel when Claudius told them to arrest Deckor's men. Suddenly a woman in the restaurant screamed as a man was thrown through the front picture window of the restaurant. An army of mercenaries stormed The Peacock Hotel's restaurant to save their boss.

"Now!" Edward yelled and everyone at his table jumped up and attacked the mercenaries.

Gabriel and Rachel were just returning to the dining room. "Rachel get the others," Gabriel said and grabbed his sword from its sheath and ran into the dining room.

Rachel burst through the door of the suite where the Rualas were still eating. "There's a battle in the restaurant. Gabriel wants you down there."

"Where are you going?" Dagon asked as Rachel ran out the room.

"Kate and I need more weapons," Rachel ran into the suite she was staying in and opened one of the large pouches. She grabbed two swords which she removed from their sheaths and several knifes then she ran down the stairs and into the dining room.

Customers were screaming and trying to either hide or run out of the hotel as more mercenaries and soldiers ran in. Kate had just stabbed one of Deckor's men when Rachel ran up to her and handed her a sword and another knife. "Move!" Kate screamed and pushed Rachel to the left as a mercenary was about to stab Rachel in the back. Kate ran her sword through the man's stomach then pulled it out and cut off his head as he fell forward.

Chaez and Nikki protected Claudius' back as he continued to beat Deckor. Two of Deckor's men threw themselves through the window of Deckor's private dining room. "Gabriel!" Chaez yelled and turned and thrust his sword through one of the intruders. Gabriel and Luca ran into the small dining room as more of Deckor's men were entering through the broken window.

Deckor was now lying unconscious on the floor so Claudius joined the battle which was no longer limited to The Peacock Hotel.

395

Deckor's hired killers were fighting with the soldiers of Lentz. Citizens of Langer were screaming and running for cover. The Horn of Shana was heard as General Fahron led troops into the City of Langer.

Dagon and Rachel fought back to back as the sea of hired killers seemed unending.

Stephan and Thaos were leading the troops who were doing battle in the streets of Langer. Not since the war with the Dura Tribe had the streets of Langer been filled with blood.

Michael was a monster of a man and was crushing skulls with his fists. Dominic and Lawrence watched over each other as they fought the mercenaries. Both men were stabbing and hacking their way through the crowd.

A hired killer punched Raphael in the face causing his false beard to fall off. This surprised the man momentarily giving Raphael the advantage. Raphael cut the man's throat then turned and stabbed one of Deckor's men who was behind him.

Flocks of Enrops were gathering all of the Patronus priests from the various hotels. It was Enrops who told Fahron of the battle. Thor was at Fahron's castle helping with the wounded when he heard about the battle. Thor rode into Langer with Fahron's army but separated from them and ran into The Peacock Hotel to fight with his team.

Edward fought his way to Kate. "It's me!" Edward yelled and jumped back as she turn on him with her sword.

"This damn dress is hard to fight in," Kate said as she positioned herself at Edward's back. Edward laughed and thrust his sword into the stomach of a man who was running at him.

The Patronus priests put their green armbands on over their civilian shirts as they joined in the battle. This was a prearranged signal so that the priests could be identified.

Once again the sounds of the Horn of Shana were heard in the streets of Langer but this time it was the soldiers who Matthew was leading into battle who were giving the signal.

Thor ran through the battling crowd in the dining room of The Peacock Hotel. He saw Joao fighting with two men. Thor kicked one of the men in the back of the knee then broke the man's neck as he fell forward.

"I was wondering where the hell you were," Joao said to Thor with a grin and stabbed the man in front of him as Thor stabbed the man from behind.

Chapter XXXV
Karin

The Sanuri led an army of soldiers west towards the Langa Woods. This old forest covered acreage in western Lentz and eastern Wetpr. Simultaneously Raul and Simon were leading troops from Fort Salar in Wetpr to the Langa Woods.

An hour earlier the Sanuri was in the castle of King Mathas preparing for the christening of the King's grandson when Deckor's wife Karin entered the castle to speak to the King. "Please I have to see him, lives are at stake," shrieked Karin. "Tell him I am Mayor Deckor's wife and I have information."

Mathas, Matthew and the Sanuri could hear Karin's voice and ran out of the parlor. "Come to my study," Mathas said and quickly ushered the woman down the hallway.

"I don't know where to begin," Karin said as she was trying to control her crying. She sat down and Matthew handed her a small glass of wine. "Here take this," Karin said and thrust a large traveling case at Matthew. "This morning when I heard that Geof Thurstand was dead and Linda was missing I knew my husband was somehow involved. He has all these late night meetings with strange people and he thinks I don't hear. I know Linda was one of his lovers." Karin started to cry again.

"I could close my eyes to his adultery but not to murder. I went into the safe he has hidden in his study. He gave me the combination once and told me to open it if anything happened to him. Look at those papers. They were in the safe." As Karin talked Matthew pulled large stacks of papers from the suitcase. "Look at that map first." Matthew spread a map of the Kingdom of Lentz out on his father's desk. "Look there," shrieked Karin and pointed to a large circle in the Langa Woods.

"I don't understand those words," Matthew said. "Sanuri can you read this language?"

"My husband is Lithanize. Those words are of his ancestors. They mean prison and children," Karin said frantically.

398

"That is his hold on the city," Mathas gasped.

Two Enrops flew into the window of King Mathas study. "There is a huge battle in Langer with Deckor's men; Claudius needs help," screamed one of the birds as Matthew ran out of the castle.

"Great Ruler help me," the Sanuri prayed. "I need your help," the Sanuri said to the Enrops. He stared into the eyes of each bird and spoke to them with his mind. The birds disappeared.

"What just happened?" Mathas asked in amazement.

"The Great Ruler is sending them to Sudfad. This could be a trap; you must remain here. I will get the children," the Sanuri said.

Mathas quickly walked into the hallway and called to one of the soldiers, "Take the Sanuri to Fort Langer and have one thousand men follow him. They will need medical supplies."

"Yes My Lord," replied the young soldier and he and the Sanuri ran out of the castle.

Almost instantly the two Enrops disappeared from Mathas' study and reappeared in King Sudfad's study. "The Sanuri sent us. Deckor is holding children in a prison in the Langa Woods. The Sanuri is leading troops from Lentz but he wants your men to come too. They don't know how many children or Deckor's men are at the prison. We can show you the way."

"King Mathas I didn't take the time to read everything but you need to look at all those papers," Karin said. "There are awful things in them."

Rosa and Angelina walked into the study. "Karin would you like some coffee?" Rosa asked.

"Honey, prepare a room for Karin. I don't believe it is safe for her to return to her home," Mathas said. "Angelina would you like to help me sort through these papers?"

Even after the arrival of Matthew and his two companies of men the battle in Langer did not end for some time. After the last of Deckor's hired killers were killed or captured Fahron and Matthew had their soldiers search every building and house. The fear was that some of Deckor's men may have taken refuge and hostages in some of the businesses and homes.

Stephan was having the bodies of the dead mercenaries searched and removed from the streets. Thaos was overseeing the incarceration of the captives.

Gabriel's and Edward's teams escorted Claudius and Deckor to King Mathas' castle. Nikki and Thor ran to Ryan's shop and got him so he could travel with this group. While everyone had sustained injuries, none of them were serious. Nana was tending to the wounded.

Suddenly panic filled Dominic as he looked at the companions he was riding with, "Wait! Where is Seth?"

"At Fahron's castle," Thor said. "Jasmine and Lana asked us to help them get Noah and Fennel out of bed to walk. Just as we were getting Noah up I heard about the battle and left. Seth was holding on to Noah so he stayed."

"Did you boys manage to hang on to all of Deckor's black magic crap?" Claudius asked Chaez and Lawrence.

"In our saddle bags," Lawrence said with a grin. "Hope to hell demons don't start jumping out."

Deckor was still unconscious. His wrists and ankles were tied and he was thrown over a horse. "He went down pretty easy for a dark lord," Claudius said. "It makes me wonder. I'll be glad when the Sanuri has a look at him."

"Your attack was so fast and powerful he didn't have a chance," Raphael said with a grin.

Simon, Raul and five hundred men left Fort Salar within twenty minutes of the Enrops appearing in Sudfad's study.

They did not know when the Sanuri would reach the prison so they were riding hard and fast. The two young princes did not have a map; they followed the Enrops eastward.

King Mathas, Claudius and Fahron all had soldiers stationed at their castles, besides the soldiers who were stationed at the forts. Each of these castles had barracks, food, medical and supply facilities besides dungeons. The dungeons were housed in several large buildings that were away from the main castles. When Claudius and his group arrived at the castle of King Mathas, Claudius personally threw Deckor's unconscious body into a dirty cell and locked the door. Deckor was locked in an area where there were no other prisoners. Claudius assigned two soldiers to stand guard in front of Deckor's cell.

Rosa saw Claudius and his group walking towards the front door of the castle. The Queen ran out the door to meet them. "Rosa are you alright?" Claudius asked with concern.

"I just wanted to tell you that Deckor's wife came here moments before Matthew left to join the battle. She suspected her husband was involved with some murders so she stole some of his papers and brought them to Mathas. She showed Mathas, Matthew and the Sanuri a map that shows a prison with children in the Langa Woods. The Sanuri is leading troops there and Angelina is helping Mathas read the rest of the papers. Karin, that's Deckor's wife is still in the study. I wanted you to know before you went in there."

"Thanks because I just locked her husband in the dungeons. He sent his men after Ryan."

"Oh my! Is Ryan alright?" Rosa gasped.

"Yeah," Ryan said as he walked closer to Claudius and Queen Rosa.

"Well thank The Great Ruler," Rosa said. As she talked she realized that every one of the people appeared to be wounded. "I am sorry I didn't realize you were all hurt. Go inside I will get the physician and have a meal prepared for you."

Rosa led everyone but Claudius to the Great Hall. Claudius alone went to Mathas' study. Claudius opened the door and looked at Karin then at Mathas. "Mathas can I speak to you alone?" Claudius asked.

As Claudius and Mathas walked to the Great Hall, Claudius briefed Mathas on everything that had happened in Langer. Mathas and Claudius entered the hall and closed the door. "First I want to thank each and every one of you for what you have done. You will be rewarded for your service. Claudius just told me about Langer. Now let me tell you about what has happened here."

"This morning the Sanuri was meeting with Matthew and me about the christening when we heard a woman screaming and crying that she needed to see me and that lives were at risk. Deckor's wife Karin is in my study with Angelina now. Karin knew of her husband's many affairs. It was this morning that she heard that Linda Thurstand was missing and Geof Thurstand was dead. Karin believed Deckor to be involved so she went to his study inside of their home."

"Deckor has a secret safe that he told Karin to open if something happened to him. She opened it this morning and started to read some of the piles of paperwork that were hidden in the safe. Some of the things she read were so disturbing that she brought all of the papers here. There was a map with a location marked in the Langa Woods. The location had two words written next to it that none of us could translate."

"Karin said that Deckor is of Lithanize ancestry and that was the language of those words. The words were 'prison' and 'children'. The Sanuri is leading one thousand of our troops to that location. He sent word to Sudfad to have his troops assist us also. For those of you who don't know the Langa Woods it is a huge forest that is in both Lentz and Wetpr."

"As soon as the Sanuri left, Karin begged me to look at the rest of the paperwork. Although Karin is not fluent in the language of her husband's family she does know some words and is helping Angelina and me. My guess is that Deckor wrote some of his notes in this language as a code."

"Gabriel and Raphael after the physician has seen you I would like you to take a look at that paperwork."

"Of course," Raphael said. "But Michael has a talent for languages also, perhaps he should join us."

"Of course, actually any of you are welcome to help. Karin literally brought stacks of paperwork. I told her to stay here since it may not be safe for her to return home. Claudius just told me that Deckor is in the dungeons; this I have not yet told Karin."

"Mathas first could we speak to Karin and secondly what do you know of this woman?" Gabriel asked.

"Of course you can speak with her and I too wondered about a trap. If she is acting she is very good. Karin is known as a sweet, generous and charming woman. Her father was wealthy and owned a fleet of ships which Deckor now owns. Many believe that Deckor married Karin for her father's money," Mathas explained.

"While I would like to tell all of you that this mission is over, I will reserve that statement until after we have reviewed all of the paperwork," Mathas said.

At that moment there was a knock at the door and Rosa called out, "Mathas the physician and nurses are here."

"I will let the medical staff look at you now," Mathas said.

"Nana bandaged my wounds," Gabriel said as he stood up. "I would very much like to speak with Karin now."

"I would also," said Raphael.

Claudius opened the door and the Court Physician and five nurses entered the Great Hall as did three of the cooks who were carrying trays filled with pots of coffee and cups. "I will send something stronger in," Mathas said and left the room.

Like the army that Simon and Raul led, the Sanuri's army was riding hard and fast. A voice that the Sanuri often heard within his being told him of the urgency of the situation.

The Sanuri somehow understood that the lives of many were endangered. "Great Ruler give us speed and give me sight," the Sanuri prayed as he led over one thousand soldiers westward; their destination somewhat unknown. The Langa Woods was an ancient forest that covered many, many miles in two kingdoms.

The mark on Deckor's map was simply a circle around the name Langa Woods and the words prison and children were scribbled on the side of the map. If there was a prison it could be any place within that forest. While the Sanuri believed Deckor was a monstrous man he also believed Deckor to be intelligent and shrewd. The Sanuri understood that the prison they were looking for might not be in a form that they would immediately recognize.

As soon as the Sanuri prayed for sight his mind was filled with fast moving images; fragments of life. The Sanuri did not know if he was being shown glimpses of the past or future and he did not understand what he was seeing. But he did understand his overwhelming feeling that they had to move faster.

"Karin I am High Priest Gabriel and this is High Priest Raphael may we speak with you?" Gabriel asked in a soothing manner.

Karin started to cry again when she looked at Gabriel and Raphael. As she tried to compose herself, Karin did not speak but nodded. The three were in King Mathas' study, as were Mathas and Angelina.

"Would you like to go someplace in private?" asked Gabriel.

Karin appeared surprised by this question. She looked at Mathas then back at Gabriel and Raphael. "If you are going to ask me questions about my husband I believe the King should hear everything."

"Karin we don't want to upset you further but many items of dark magics were found in your husband's office. Would you allow us a test to determine if the darkness of these things have touched you?"

"Of course," Karin said then her voice became filled with fear. "What do those things look like?"

As Karin spoke, Raphael touched her arm with a few drops of blessed water; nothing happened. "Does that mean anything?" Karin asked as she watched the beads of water run off her arm.

"It is a good sign," Raphael said. "And we will show you what was found but first we have a few questions."

"Why did you bring those papers here today?" Gabriel asked.

Karin sat up straighter in her chair and wiped the tears from her face. "There are many in Langer who believe me to be a simple fool. My husband has been cheating on me since the first week of our marriage. He is not discreet about his affairs and they are a source of gossip always. Our marriage was a business arrangement between my father and Deckor. But as hard as it may be to believe he treats me well and we live a very comfortable life. I see the judgmental looks on your faces."

"We have been married for ten years. During that time he has never struck me or said an unkind word to me. He is thoughtful and caring and he showers me with gifts. We had no pretense of love when we married but as the years passed we have developed feelings for each other. But that is how he treats me. Since our marriage I have heard many rumors about his fits of rage. Of him attacking and threatening people. But I have never seen that side of him."

"I had met few politicians before I married Deckor. Some people feel that all politicians are liars and criminals who take advantage of people for personal gain. As I came to know my husband it is with great shame that I say that definition fits him like a glove. But about three years ago he changed and not for the better. He has secret meetings with dangerous looking men at all times of the night. He locks himself in his study and a room in our cellar and does not come out for hours at a time."

Karin's lips were quivering as she spoke. "While he has changed little towards me there is a presence about him now which scares me. I don't know how to describe it. It is sinister and evil."

405

"I have been telling myself that I was imagining it but somewhere deep inside of me I knew the truth. I have thought about leaving him but where would I go?"

"Then this morning I was on my way to the Ladies' Sewing Circle and my carriage driver had to change our route because of the smoke of the fire. This week's meeting was being held in the home of Tarla Grey. Because of the fire some of the other women were late also. The last women to enter was Betsy Sarbush. Her husband is a ship builder. Betsy was beside herself and told us that the body of Geof Thurstand was just found and that it was his ship that was burning. I exaggerate not when I say that every head in that room turned and looked at me. Then Tarla said that Linda had been missing for several days."

"I knew what they were all thinking because I was thinking the same thing; that Deckor was responsible. And it was as if a voice inside of me was screaming. It was telling me for the first time to do the right thing. I left the meeting and searched Deckor's study. As soon as I saw that map I threw all the papers in suitcase and came here." Karin paused. "I think you need to search our house. I saw strange drawings and statues in the study and now you tell me about black magic."

All the people in the room who were listening to Karin felt that she was sincere. "Karin, Raphael and I are demon hunters. From what you told us we agree that we should search your house if nothing else for your safety."

"Deckor won't be home until later; we could go there now," Karin said.

"Karin a great battle occurred in Langer today. Your husband had a private army and they attacked members of the ruling families. Deckor is in the dungeons now." Karin covered her mouth with both hands as the blood drained from her face.

"Were any members of the ruling families hurt?" Karin asked in a whisper.

"Only minor injuries but most of Deckor's men are dead."

"Did you get Ackley? He is a horrid man. I think that if anyone knows what Deckor is involved in it would be Ackley."

"We don't know if we have him in prison or if he is dead or has escaped," Gabriel said. The soldiers are still in Langer sorting everything out."

"If Ackley is unaccounted for, know he will try to help Deckor escape his prison. They have a bond that is, I don't know a good word perhaps abnormal. Come let's go to the house now. Take whatever you need and please get any black magic things out of there."

Gabriel, Raphael and Karin walked into the Great Hall. "This is Karin, Mayor Deckor's wife," Gabriel announced. "She is giving us permission to search their home. We have reason to believe there are items of black magic there besides evidence of crimes. We would like some of you to come with us and some of you to help Mathas and Angelina with the mountain of paperwork which Karin gave them. Edward since you can memorize everything you read, perhaps you should help Mathas."

Edward and Michael stayed at the castle to help Mathas sort through the paperwork. Everyone else went to Deckor's house. As one would imagine it was a mansion on the ocean. The house and lawn were well maintained. The carriage house held six carriages even though it was only Deckor and Karin living in the home.

Karin now seemed like a woman with a purpose instead of a victim. She led everyone into Deckor's study first since it was near the front door. "That safe that is open is the one the papers were in but I found another one that I couldn't open," Karin said and moved a large painting that was concealing a wall safe.

"Rachel," Gabriel called. "Give it a try."

"Natasha has been teaching me how to open safes," Rachel said excitedly. "I need a water glass." Risa saw a tray of empty glasses and handed one to Rachel. "Don't everyone watch me," Rachel said. "It will make me nervous."

407

"Dack and I will start on the bookshelves," said Joao.

"I've got the desk," Ralf said and started opening drawers and pouring the contents on top of the desk.

"Just take everything," Karin said. "God knows what he has in here. Do you need pouches?"

"We brought some," Luca said as he was examining a wall for hidden compartments.

"Every statue in here is for black magic," Raphael said. "Take them all."

"This is the drawing I was telling you about," Karin said and she reached behind a chair and pulled out a rolled up canvas which she handed to Gabriel. Both Raphael and Gabriel stared at the pen and ink drawing of a Plyogram. "Do you know what that is?" asked Karin.

"It's called a Plyogram. It is a series of pictures within pictures. They are used to hide things in plain sight," Raphael explained.

"What sort of things?" asked Adin as he walked across the room to look at this new discovery.

"Hidden messages," Raphael said and handed the drawing to Adin. "Put that in your pouch."

"I got it," Rachel was very excited as she opened the safe.

"Wait!" Gabriel yelled. "Don't put your hand in there it might be cursed."

Raphael and Gabriel stood in front of the open safe. They both prayed silently then Gabriel threw some blessed water into the safe. A popping sound was heard and smoke filled the safe. When the smoke cleared Gabriel reached in and started taking things out and placing them on a table. Calen opened ten pouches that were in the safe. "Karin this is all money I will put it over here," Calen said and moved the pouches to a smaller table.

"These small books appear to be ledgers," Kate said. "And they are in code."

"This is a book of spells," said Chaez.

"Will everyone move a second so we can pull up these carpets?" Dominic asked. Dominic and Lawrence rolled up the large carpet in the room and Karin gasped. A large area of the floor was brown with dried blood stains.

"We've got some books, not sure if they are spells or what but we are taking them," Dack said.

"Karin, we are taking just the books from this safe," Gabriel said. "We need to go to your cellar next."

Ralf and Enzo were standing guard at the front door of the house as the other team members followed Karin into the cellar. The group walked past storage areas and racks of wine bottles. "Here," Karin said and pointed to a door which was locked with a paddle lock.

Raphael felt the door for several seconds. "I don't feel and pulsing or hear anything. Karin can you step back behind the others?" Raphael busted the lock on the door while Gabriel grabbed more lit torches from the walls.

"Let us go in first," Gabriel said. After a few moments Gabriel and Raphael walked out of the room. "There is an unholy altar in there I would like our team members to see it but Karin you should stay out here."

"I don't understand what you are saying," Karin said fearfully.

"It is an altar for worshipping demons. And Deckor performed human sacrifices," Gabriel explained. Dominic caught Karin as her knees weakened.

Karin's voice was almost inaudible as she spoke, "Gabriel the King offered me a room in the castle. I believe I will take him up on the offer. Could some of your people help me pack?"

"We will," said Nana. Risa, Kate, Nana and Rachel walked Karin up the cellar steps. "I'll grab her money from the study," Nana said.

After Karin left, Raphael and Gabriel destroyed the physical elements of the unholy altar. Then they prayed to destroy the demonic powers within the room.

With the help of the team members Karin packed quickly. She gave a small pouch of gold coins to each of the cooks and servants and told them to take a month's vacation. As everyone walked outside Karin suddenly turned around. "I don't want to leave the horses can you use them?"

"Sure," Thor said.

"There are ten of them and they are in the back correl. The bridles and saddles are in the barn," Karin explained. Twenty minutes later Karin left her home with the members of Gabriel's team. "I would have thought I would cry but I just feel like running as fast as I can," Karin said with a numbness that only horror can bring.

Chapter XXXVI
Soulless

It took over three hours for the Sanuri and his men to reach the eastern outskirts of the Langa Woods. Because of the distance, the Sanuri had to slow the pace of the horses but he and the soldiers were filled with anxiety. Simon, Raul and the men they led were within a few miles of the western border of this ancient forest.

The Langa Woods had existed since time unknown. The enormous trees formed such a thick canopy that during the months when the leaves were full almost no sunlight reached the forest floor. Thus there was little undergrowth. This forest was filled with animals and birds which flourished because thus far they had eluded man's destructive nature.

By the time the Sanuri and his army arrived at the forest, a huge flock of Enrops had formed and were flying overhead. Speaking with his mind the Sanuri asked the birds to enter the forest first. All of the rescuers were vividly aware that if such a prison existed, Deckor's men might start murdering the children if they were aware of the rescue attempt.

A huge flock of Enrops also formed over the soldiers of Wetpr. These birds also heard the Sanuri's voice in their minds and flew ahead of the army and into the woods. One lone Enrop took the time to tell the Princes of Wetpr of the Sanuri's words. Raul and Simon stopped their men at the edge of the forest.

The Sanuri was filled with uneasiness as he and his men waited for the return of the giant birds. "Something is very wrong here," thought the Sanuri. "What am I not seeing?" "Old Friend is this a trap?" the Sanuri called out to the heavens.

"A better question would be to ask for help," said the voice of The Lion; the most powerful warrior Angel in heaven.

"Please help us," the Sanuri said. "Is there a prison of children here?"

For an instant time stopped in the World of Nunc. Neither the soldiers of the Army of Lentz nor the soldiers of the Army of Wetpr were aware of this miracle. Only the Sanuri, Simon and Raul heard the voice of the Angel.

"The prison is before you but your eyes cannot see it from your positions. You need to look down. The Enrops now know what they are looking for and the wind that is coming will blow the debris from the trap door so you can see it. Once again man has created a world of hell within the world given him by The Great Ruler."

"The vibrations of your horses will alert the monsters in that underground hell world. Have your men dismount and move forward. All of you can now see the location in your minds' eye. Prepare your hearts to weep."

Simultaneously Simon and the Sanuri ordered their armies to dismount. Some men were left behind to watch the horses and to keep watch for Deckor's men. "Lion is there only the one opening?" Raul called out.

"No. The wind will blow the second opening open allowing the Enrops to attack while your men enter the first opening."

The first opening to the prison was closer to the Wetpr side of the forest. Raul led the men of Wetpr to a clearing within the Langa Woods. In the middle of this clearing was a huge pile of rocks which looked quite unnatural in the setting. A wind of dynamic proportions blew through the forest. Dirt and debris formed small cyclones. The men covered their faces as debris pelted their bodies; but they did not turn back. As suddenly as the wind appeared it stopped and Raul and Simon saw two huge wooden doors on the floor of the forest.

Simon and Raul ran forward, followed by their men. The doors were heavy and it took the strength of several men to open these gates to hell. Raul descended the wooden ladder first. Simon was behind his brother when he heard a cry come out of Raul's throat that did not sound human. Consumed with rage at the sight before him, Raul killed the first two of Deckor's men before they realized they were being attacked.

412

The screeching of Enrops, the war cries of the soldiers, the screams of Deckor's men and the cries of the children created a roar underground that the Sanuri and his men heard as they ran through the forest.

Never had anyone attempted to enter this prison other than Deckor's men. All of the mercenaries were taken by surprise, some of them had been sleeping.

This man-made hell consisted of four underground caverns filled with cages and lit by torches on the walls. Each cage was filled with children of all ages. "Keep one alive!" yelled the Sanuri as he climbed down the ladder. The Sanuri was referring to one of Deckor's men. The caverns were not large enough to hold the soldiers of both armies. Horrified at the scene before them the soldiers of Wetpr showed no mercy to Deckor's men. The battle was swift and justice administered for the crimes committed.

Immediately the soldiers formed a line. As three soldiers broke the locks on the cages, others grabbed the children and handed them down the line and up the ladder to the arms of the soldiers of Lentz. Soldiers as well as the children were crying. Tears of joy as well as tears of horror.

Raul thrust his sword into the ground and stared upwards; his rage consuming him. "Lion why have you not come here before this?"

The Lion now appeared in front of Raul. "For all the love the families had for these children, not one mother or father called us in. No one prayed to The Great Ruler to help, no one! You called us in. This is a lesson none of you should forget." The Lion's voice carried throughout the caverns and throughout the forest. Every soldier heard the words of the Angel.

When the soldiers of Wetpr ascended from the caverns they saw the soldiers of Lentz feeding and hugging the children. Simon and Raul shook their heads as once again they were forced to see man's inhumanity for his own kind.

"Do all of these children have homes?" Simon asked as he walked up to a sergeant who was holding a little boy with blonde curly hair and huge eyes.

413

"We don't know. Some of these children are too upset to talk. They can't even tell us how long they have been held captive," the sergeant replied.

"If they need homes our people will welcome them also," Simon said.

Raul walked up to Simon and the sergeant. "When the Sanuri is done with that last killer we will escort your troops back to Langer. You can't fight with children in your arms."

Ten minutes later the Sanuri ascended the ladder, dragging one of Deckor's men behind him. The Sanuri threw the man onto the ground and said, "He is yours."

"Let us have one of those swine," said a soldier from Lentz who ran forward and ran his sword through the mercenary.

"What did you see?" asked Simon.

"I will tell you when we return to Mathas' castle. Our work here is done, let's get these children home," said the Sanuri.

Enrops flew ahead to the City of Langer, the castles of the ruling families and Fort Langer. The birds announced the success of the rescue mission. Screams of joy and laughter now filled the streets, still covered with blood. People ran to the homes of their neighbors to announce that the children were being brought home.

Small flocks of Enrops flew to the castle of King Sudfad and to the home of Gabriel to tell of the mission. The people in these homes were struck dumb by the horror that they heard.

"I can't stop hugging the children," Hannah said with tears in her eyes after the Enrops left the house.

"Now I wish I would have gone," Joshua said angrily and hit the top of the dining room table with his fist.

"Christopher come here," said Natalie.

"What's wrong?" Christopher asked as Natalie put him on her lap.

"Nothing Honey we just heard something sad," Natalie said and hugged Christopher.

"We hate having our loved ones gone," Vivian said to Natalie. "But then when you hear things like this I wish I was fighting with them."

"Are all of the missions like this?" Natalie asked incredulously.

"Unfortunately too many of them are," Misha replied somberly.

Annabelle cried as Sudfad told the family about the mission in Lentz. Vitomas kept hugging baby Miranda. Laurel and Alexander sat in shock and Renya flew into a rage.

"What kind of animals hurt children? Certainly they have no souls. Sometimes I think men are worse than the demons. Sudfad this has got to stop!"

Mathas sent a message to the armies returning with the children. All of the children were to be brought directly to the King's castle where physicians and nurses would attend to them. Mathas, Claudius and Fahron feared there could be more crimes committed against these children and wanted to verify that the people claiming the children were truly family members.

Bella and Isadore traveled to the castle of Mathas to help with the children. Mathas sent soldiers to the Nordes Tribe to tell them about the battle in Langer and the rescue of the children. As soon as the soldiers finished speaking, dozens of Nordes warriors mounted their horses and rode to the King's castle to help.

Karin was standing in the front courtyard of the King's castle with the members of the ruling families, the teams of Gabriel and Edward and the dozens of physicians and nurses who had traveled from the City of Langer.

415

There were both applause and gasps as the soldiers rode into the courtyard carrying the filthy and emaciated children. Karin started to shake uncontrollably. "Is my husband responsible for this?" she shrieked. No one answered. "King Mathas if you don't kill him I will!"

"Karin, he will pay for his crimes," Claudius said solemnly.

The Sanuri, Raul and Simon rode up to the ruling families. "Mathas your men acted admirably," the Sanuri said.

"Deckor is in the dungeons," Claudius said. "Sanuri question him now because he will not live through this day."

"I want to look upon the man responsible for this," Raul said angrily. I will go with you."

"I think we all will," Mathas said then looked up as Sorren led his warriors into the courtyard. Sorren was visibly enraged. "Sorren everything happened so fast that there was not time to get you," Mathas explained.

"That I understand," Sorren said. "This I cannot comprehend," Sorren said as he nodded towards the children. "If any children do not have homes to return to they will find homes in my village."

"Sanuri we found a variety of statues and things in Deckor's home and office," Raphael explained. "Would you like to look at them before you see Deckor?"

"Yes," the Sanuri said as he dismounted.

"They are in a shed in back," said Gabriel. "We didn't want to bring them into the castle."

"Where is Michael?" Simon asked. "Is he alright?"

"Simon and Raul, this is Karin, Deckor's wife," Mathas said. "She is the one who brought us information so you could find the children. She has given us full access to everything Deckor owns. Karin this is Prince Simon and Prince Raul of the Kingdom of Wetpr."

Karin curtsied before the Princes. "Under other circumstances I would be honored to meet you but this day I am filled with shame."

"Karin emptied one of her husband's safes and brought the paperwork here. Some of the papers appear to be coded. Edward, Michael and Angelina have been working on them. They are all in my study," Mathas explained.

Karin swung around and faced Mathas so quickly that the King jumped. "Mathas I know I can never repair all of the evil my husband was brought upon this kingdom but I will try. I have heard you are planning on building a hospital. Our house will no longer be my home. It is huge and very well built. Could it serve as the building for your hospital?"

Bella hugged Karin, "I think that is a lovely idea."

"So do I," said Mathas. "We will accept your gift."

"You probably want to search the entire house first," Karin said. "Gabriel and the others only took the time to search the rooms where we knew we would find things."

"Look its Ratri and Batina," Dack said. "I hope nothing is wrong."

A few moments later Ratri landed in front of the ruling families. "We came to help," he said. "What is going on?"

"What happened to these children?" Batina asked emotionally.

"We have a lot to tell you," said Gabriel. "Glad to have you here."

"We brought letters and gifts," Ratri said. "We can hand them out later."

"Why don't you come inside now and I will get you chambers so you can put your packs away," said Rosa.

The Sanuri was taken to a shed behind the castle. Luca and Calen had been posted as guards because no one understood the manner of the objects found in Deckor's possession.

"Be glad you are here and don't have to look at those children," Dagon said to his brothers as the small group stopped in front of the shed.

"Do we even want to hear?" Luca asked angrily.

"No!" Thor snarled. "All the girls are helping to feed and care for the children. In my entire life I have never seen Kate cry before. Let's get this over with so we can kill Deckor."

The Sanuri was carrying his staff, which started to glow as he entered the dark shed. "Everyone stay out here," he said. Five minutes later the Sanuri peeked his head out of the doorway. "It is safe for you to come in now. Can you tell me where these objects were found?" The shed was small so only a few people could enter at a time. Lawrence and Chaez went in first and organized some of the items into groupings.

"These are the things we took from his office in Langer," Lawrence said and he and Chaez walked out of the shed.

Gabriel and Raphael entered next and picked up two statues and a ceremonial knife. "We found these on his unholy altar," Gabriel said. "Everything else was found in the study in his home. This stack of books were found in a second safe that had a protection spell on it. The other books were found on bookshelves in his study."

"And Karin gave us this," Raphael said as he unrolled the plyogram. The Sanuri studied the objects in silence then walked outside where members of the ruling families had joined the team members.

"I find these things very interesting and a bit confusing," the Sanuri said. "As you know most dark lords either sell their souls or pay allegiance to a particular demon."

"Then they have things which represent the symbols or what they perceive to be likeness of that demon in certain areas. The dark lords believe these items give them power. That too is why Deckor had these things. But Deckor has items that pay tribute to different demons and demons I do not recognize. I don't believe he was worshipping demons attached to the World of Nunc."

"I have rendered these items harmless now. I would like to take them back to Wetpr. Perhaps Erebus can give us some insight," the Sanuri continued.

"We carried all of those things. Will any of us be affected?" asked Lawrence.

"Before we go any farther the voice in my mind said no," the Sanuri said. "You have been protected. Calen and Luca why don't you continue to guard this shed in case someone tries to retrieve these items. I am going to visit Deckor."

The group following the Sanuri grew as he walked to the dungeons. As large as the group was becoming they walked in silence.

"Dominic and Lawrence go in front of us," Gabriel said. "You need to see this; especially if you decide to lead a team."

"How about Edward?" asked Dominic.

"He has already witnessed such things," said the Sanuri.

When they walked up to the door of Deckor's cell they found him lying in the same position he had been when Claudius dumped his body on the floor.

"He is conscious," the Sanuri said. "He is pretending not to be."

Suddenly there was laughter in Deckor's cell and he jumped to his feet. The ropes that bound his wrists and ankles now fell to the floor.

"Sanuri I have waited to meet you," said Deckor.

"You aren't Deckor. Who am I talking to?" the Sanuri asked.

419

Deckor walked closer to the bars of his cell. "Why don't you come in and find out."

The Sanuri smiled. "Great Ruler engulf this creature with your white light," the Sanuri prayed. Instantly Deckor screamed as his body and the essence of the demon within him were imprisoned by holiness.

"Unlock the door," the Sanuri said to the guards. "And lock it behind me."

The Sanuri walked up to Deckor's body and placed the palms of his hands on either side of Deckor's head. Both the dark lord and the demon who were sharing the body screamed in pain because of the holiness of the Sanuri's touch.

The Sanuri stared into Deckor's eyes and saw the life and crimes of the man. The Sanuri also saw the gnarled and distorted face of a demon who was now trapped inside of Deckor's body. "Release me!" demanded the demon.

"What are you called?" the Sanuri asked.

"My name will fill you with terror," the demon snarled.

"All these damn demons are the same," Sorren said which caused others to laugh.

"Who dares to laugh at me!"

"Faithful men who do not fear you," the Sanuri replied. The Sanuri closed his eyes and started to hum while he maintained his hold on Deckor's body. The appearance of the Sanuri became lighter and transparent. The demon again screamed.

"You wretched creature of darkness I order you to tell me the truth," the Sanuri said with a voice of authority.

Deckor's body started to spasm. Green foam came out of his mouth and ran down the front of his expensive suit. Blood started to run from Deckor's eyes and nose as the powerful demon inside of him was fighting the order of a holy emissary.

"Again," demanded the Sanuri. "What is your name?"

"Daceron."

"What world do you come from?"

"Balterak."

"I don't know of that world. Where is it located?"

"In the Mensor Galaxy."

"How was Deckor strong enough to contact demons from another galaxy?"

Deckor's body started to laugh and blood now poured from Deckor's mouth. "The demons here are weak. They fall before the followers of The Great Ruler. We have offered our services."

"And who have you offered these services to?"

"Those who call upon us."

"The Insidiae."

"And others. The Insidiae are not the only humans who call to demons." Deckor's skin was smoking and blood and green foam where pouring out of his eyes, ears, nose and mouth.

"What is happening?" asked Lawrence.

"The holiness is destroying the demon," Raphael said.

"You have no idea of what is even happening in your world. Like all humans you focus only on what touches you personally. Soon you will find out how many enemies you have."

The Sanuri could see that the demon was deteriorating quickly. "Who in this world worships you and those from your world? Answer me!"

"Look to your neighbor."

"What do you mean?"

"Tansof," the demon said and Deckor's body burst into flames.

"What was he talking about?" Dominic asked.

"Tansof is the continent to the east of us on the other side of the Sea of Grevdt," Mathas said. "It is also the home of the Dura Tribe."

Chapter XXXVII
The Date

Except for Noah, Fennel, Seth, Jasmine and Lana who were at the castle of Fahron, the members of Gabriel's and Edwards' teams planned to spend the night at Mathas' castle. Raul, Simon and the Sanuri also planned to spend the night. These people were going through the mountains of paperwork and the books which once belonged to Deckor.

After dinner many took a break from work while Ratri and Batina handed out the letters and gifts they brought. "Some of these are from our household and some are from Sudfad's," Ratri explained.

Luca received a letter from Emeral, a letter from Natalie and a letter from Christopher. Luca opened the letter from Natalie first and as he read it he started to laugh. "Boy, Natalie must have some of Natasha in her," Luca said and handed the letter to Calen. "She is really pissed at me."

"Why?" Calen asked as he took the letter.

"I don't really know," Luca said. "Apparently I wrote something that offended her. Actually I am kind of surprised she has a temper."

Calen too laughed and handed the letter to Gabriel. "She does sound like our wives," Calen said to Gabriel.

Gabriel grinned as he read the letter. "I haven't met Natalie yet. All I have heard is that everyone likes her and that she is really nice." Gabriel handed the letter to Raphael but asked Luca, "You don't have any idea why she is mad?"

"I wrote her a short letter. It was late at night and I was really tired. Apparently I should have read it before I put it in the envelope," Luca said with a grin and opened the letter from Emeral. "Alright, I must have written something really bad because even Emeral is scolding me. And she says Maxwell read the letter too. I am going to have to see that letter when I get home."

"Emeral says that Natalie has been taking care of my chambers and my children and I should be more considerate of her feelings. Now I feel guilty and I don't even know why."

"Well, brother I would suggest you buy a few gifts before you go back into that house," Calen said. "And you better read my letter. Natasha says that Christopher is telling the other children that Natalie is going to be his mommy. I told you that you need to get your head on straight about this."

"Ok, what is going on?" Raphael asked. "Remember Gabriel and I left before Natalie and Kate came to the house."

"Iris and Joshua thought that Natalie and Luca would help each other heal if they had someone to talk to about losing their loved ones," Calen explained. "It was awkward for them at first but all of us could see the two of them coming back to life. Their relationship has been as friends because they both keep saying they aren't ready to get involved with anyone. Luca you explain the rest."

"Natalie is the sweetest person and as Emeral says a natural mother. You know she has a son. Without making this story really long, Natalie has been talking with Christopher and helping him with his nightmares. All of a sudden Christopher is getting upset and I have no idea why. Emeral and Maxwell said that Christopher is still healing from all of the awful things he has experienced and he wants a family again. They think Christopher has decided he wants Natalie as his mother and he is upset with her and me because we aren't becoming a family."

"Natalie adores Christopher and wants to help him," Luca continued. "She is staying in my chambers and taking care of Hunter, who is still a baby, Emma and Christopher. I wrote her a letter telling her that Calen and I would be here longer than I originally said. What I was trying to say was she should let the others help her with the kids but apparently that is not what the letter sounded like."

"Luca you certainly have improved," Gabriel said. "It was like you were walking but were dead inside for a long time. I am not saying you are completely healed but you appear to be thinking more clearly. What are your thoughts about Natalie?"

"She is beautiful and smart and sweet and funny and a great mother," Luca said.

"And sexy," Calen added with a grin.

"Yes she is," Luca said. "And I think at any other time in my life I would be jumping hurdles to be with her. Calen said that I shouldn't expect to get over Lila because she will always be in my heart and that is true. But you are priests; how long should someone mourn?"

"Before you answer that question what Luca didn't tell you is that Natalie is planning on going back to Ryed soon. She has no family. She is providing for her son by herself and she doesn't have a cent to her name. But you know that doesn't really matter in the Clan of Gesmal because they all take care of each other," Calen said.

"Luca I am speaking for every one of us here," Raphael said. "You have lived our nightmares and we can't even imagine the pain you have suffered. But too all four of us are fathers now and that changes your life. I am not saying you and Natalie should marry but whether you realize it or not you sound attracted to her. And you both have children to think of. I think you should ask her to stay longer and look at your relationship with new eyes. If it doesn't work out or you decide you aren't ready what really have you lost?"

"That's what Calen thinks too," Luca said then he turned to Gabriel. "What do you think?"

"Let me tell you what Hannah thinks first," Gabriel said with a warm smile. "She says that many people in the house think there is a connection between you and Natalie besides your pain. But both of you have been so lost you can't see it. I will be honest, when you came here it was like the old Luca was back and I was so happy to see that. I have to agree with Calen and Raphael. Give the relationship at the very least a consideration before she leaves."

Sorren and Shara walked into Mathas' parlor where everyone had gathered. "I didn't know you were still here," Rosa said and jumped up from her chair. "I will have dinner for you in a few moments."

"Thank you," Shara said. "We are starving and exhausted."

"We thought you left," said Mathas.

"Actually we did," Sorren said as he poured a glass of wine for Shara and a glass of whiskey for himself. "Now don't think I was stepping over your men but Shara and I came back to watch the children being reunited with their families. There are three children who are unclaimed and none of the other families recognized them. The children are not related so you probably have three families that were murdered. Some of the members of my tribe are taking the children into their homes and will care for them."

As Sorren spoke he walked up to Mathas and handed him a piece of paper. "Here are the names and descriptions of the children. If they are not claimed we already have families who will adopt them."

"I was so angry and disgusted I just wanted to cry," Shara said. "Those poor children. I hope you killed all those monsters."

"We did," Raul said. "And death seemed too good for them."

"Thank you for taking care of the children," Mathas said as Rosa entered the room.

"Shara, Sorren do you want to eat in here or in the dining room?" Rosa asked.

"We'll eat in here," Sorren said wearily. "Where are Angelina and Matthew?"

"They are in the study with Karin, Michael, Edward and Kate. The rest of us are taking a break because Ratri and Batina brought letters and gifts," Mathas explained.

"And we have things for you," Batina said and hugged first Shara then Sorren. Ratri handed letters and a couple of small packages to them."

"Where are Chaez, Dominic and Lawrence?" Sorren asked as he looked around the parlor. "They didn't get hurt did they?"

"No they went back to Fahron's castle to see Noah and Fennel," Simon said.

"I will say that Chaez's fighting sure has improved," Thor said with a grin. "No one should have to worry about him passing training anymore."

"Well, I'm going back to work," Gabriel said and stood up. "We won't really know if this mission is done until we get through that paperwork."

"Dinner's going to be a little late," Fahron said to Dominic, Chaez and Lawrence when they walked into the castle. "Don't ask me what they are up to but the girls are doing something?"

"Are they fixing dinner?" Dominic asked with a grin.

"I certainly hope not," Fahron said then looked towards the doorway to see if anyone heard him. The other men laughed.

"Dominic and Lawrence I assume you want whiskey," Fahron said as he was pouring drinks. "Chaez what would you like?"

"We've got him drinking whiskey with the rest of us," Lawrence said with a grin.

"Besides he deserves one," Dominic said. "Chaez fought well today. He doesn't have to worry anymore about passing training."

Fahron smiled proudly as he handed all of the men their glasses. But before anyone spoke again Sally walked into the parlor with a big grin.

"Your father says you are cooking dinner tonight," Lawrence said and smiled.

"Oh no, you would all die if I did," Sally said and laughed. "Chaez I need you to come with me. You can bring your drink."

"I hate to even ask," Chaez said and smiled.

"You will like it," said Sally.

"It must be important," Chaez teased. "You put the pup down."

Chaez followed Sally into one of the gardens surrounding the castle. She led him to a small candlelit table. The table had a white cloth and settings for two. "Sit down and I will be right back," Sally said and giggled. A few minutes later Sally led Lana to the table. Both Chaez and Lana laughed when they saw each other. "I am serving you and April is serving Jasmine and Seth," Sally said with a big grin. "I will be right back."

"Did you know anything about this?" Chaez asked Lana as he held her chair out for her.

"No but it is so cute."

April laughed at how deeply Seth blushed when she led him to a small candlelit table in one of the gardens. "What is this?" Seth asked.

"You'll find out in a minute," said April. "There is whiskey and wine on the table pour yourself a drink and I will be right back."

A big smile consumed Seth's face when he saw April leading Jasmine to the table. Seth stood up and held Jasmine's chair for her. "I will be serving you dinner tonight," April said with a huge grin. "And Sally is serving Chaez and Lana. They are in the garden over there." As April spoke she pointed to her right.

"Did you know about this?" Jasmine asked Seth in a whisper.

"No but I like it."

"Oh Fahron," Isadore said as she walked into the parlor. "You have to see what the girls are doing. They set up two romantic tables in the gardens. One for Chaez and Lana and the other for Jasmine and Seth and Sally and April are serving the dinners. It is so cute."

Chaez and Lana smiled as Isadore, Fahron, Dominic and Lawrence walked up to the table. "Our first date," Chaez said with a grin.

"This is so sweet," Lana said. "Isadore did you help them?"

"A little," Isadore said and smiled.

"Tell them what Sally said," Lana said to Chaez.

"I said this was our first date and Sally said there better be more," Chaez said and laughed.

"Your sister is quite the matchmaker," Dominic said as he grinned.

Jasmine and Seth were leaning across the small table and kissing when Dominic, Lawrence, Isadore and Fahron walked up to the table. Both Seth and Jasmine blushed.

"Your first date," Lawrence said teasingly.

"I didn't know what April and Sally were up to but now I owe them," Seth said. "This is very romantic."

"There isn't any reason you can't do this more often," Dominic said. "And there are great restaurants in the city." Jasmine and Seth looked at each other and smiled.

As Fahron, Dominic, Isadore and Lawrence walked inside of the castle Lawrence said to Dominic, "Our little boy is growing up."

Three days later Calen and Luca returned home in the middle of the afternoon. "We're home," Calen called out as they walked into the dining room.

"Calen," Natasha cried and ran out of the kitchen and flew into his arms. Hannah, Emeral and Casandra followed Natasha into the dining room.

"We are the only ones back," Luca said when he saw the look on Hannah's face. "The others may be back pretty soon too."

"They are trying to determine if they are still needed there. But we come bearing gifts."

"I am sorry. I didn't mean to look so disappointed," Hannah said and kissed Luca on the cheek then Calen.

"Well, we are glad to have you home," Emeral said. "Are you hungry?"

"Starving," Calen said. "We have so much to tell you. But first..." As Calen spoke he and Luca both took off the large packs they carried and emptied the contents on the dining room table. "Everyone there sent gifts and letters; we have to sort them out."

"Where are the children?" Luca asked.

"Vivian is giving them riding lessons on their ponies," Cassandra replied as she and Hannah were organizing the gifts and letters.

"We might be getting some more horses too," Calen said. "But we will explain all that later."

"Where is Natalie?" asked Luca.

"She is up a lot at night with the babies so after lunch she puts them down for a nap and tries to get a little sleep herself," Natasha said. "Luca she has been working really hard around here besides taking care of the children. I hope you appreciate that."

"I really have to see that letter I sent because everyone is mad at me," Luca said. "I was half asleep when I wrote it and I didn't mean to offend her or anyone else."

"I think you need to tell her that," Emeral said. "She hasn't said anything but I think you hurt her feelings."

"Calen and I have been talking," Luca said. "And our conversations have made me do a lot of thinking. Now Mother don't get too excited but I would like to take Natalie out to dinner tonight and ask her to stay so we can get to know each other better. Would you help watch the children?"

"First of all I think that is an absolutely wonderful idea," Emeral said. "And of course I will help with the children. In fact you two should have an entire night free of children. Take her dancing after dinner."

"Luca, we are all glad to hear this," Hannah said. "I don't know if you realize it but you are your old self again and that is because of Natalie. And Christopher absolutely adores her."

"Well, remember I said I have been doing a lot of thinking. That doesn't mean that Natalie has. She may not be willing to consider a relationship of any kind."

"We'll see," Emeral said with a smile. "I hope you thought to bring her a gift."

"Yes, but I didn't know what to get her so I bought jewelry," Luca said. "What do you think?" Before Emeral could answer Luca turned to Hannah. "Before we forget, Mathas has a building that he wants to turn into a hospital and he wants your advice on a lot of things." Luca took a large folder of papers out of the pocket of his robe and handed them to Hannah. "And Mathas said that if you know anyone who you think is capable of leading such a project he would like the name."

"Oh this is so exciting," Hannah gushed and quickly grabbed the papers.

"Luca I think this is perfect," Emeral said and handed the box to Natasha. "It is simple and elegant," Emeral continued. The box contained a golden chain necklace with tiny tear drop light blue sapphires hanging all around the chain. There were also matching earrings in the box.

"Oh I like it," Natasha said. "Luca this is really nice."

"Do you really like it or are you just saying that?" Calen asked with a grin.

"Calen you are awful," Natasha scolded. "I really do like it."

"Good because I got you the same thing but with rubies," as Calen spoke he handed a box to Natasha who squealed and hugged him.

431

"Hannah, Gabriel had this made for you," Luca said and handed her a small box. As Hannah opened it Luca said, "It has all your children's birthstones in it."

Hannah started to cry and put the ring on her finger then proudly showed it to the others.

"I am going up and talk to Natalie now," Luca said. "We will see if she throws this at me."

Luca entered his chambers and noticed how quiet it was. Although there were four bedrooms, Luca only had beds in the master bedroom and in Christopher's room. As Luca walked to the master bedroom he noticed that Natalie had cleaned his home.

Natalie was lying on top of the covers of the bed and Hunter and Emma were both sleeping in cradles. Luca sat down on the edge of the bed and Natalie instantly jumped up.

"I didn't mean to scare you," Luca said. "I am sorry and I am sorry for that letter I sent. I was so tired when I wrote it that I didn't mean for it to sound as it did. Are you still mad at me?"

"A little," Natalie said with a shy smile.

"I got this for you to make up for the letter," Luca said and handed Natalie the box.

She stared at the jewelry for a moment then said, "Luca I have never seen anything this beautiful before but I can't take it."

"Yes you can," he said. "Now, I have made arrangements for all our children to be taken care of tonight. I am taking you out to dinner and dancing and anything else you want to do."

"Luca that sounds like so much fun but things are very different here. What should I wear?"

"Did you move your clothes in here?"

"No. Why?"

"Well, I don't remember everything we bought you so wear the blue dress that Christopher picked out. That way you can wear your new jewelry."

"Luca will you stay here with the babies and I will run to my room and get some things. I will be right back," Natalie said excitedly.

"Natalie we have all night without children, you might want to change your clothes after dinner so why don't you bring several things."

"Why do I have a feeling like that sentence had more to it than I heard?" Natalie asked with a coy smile.

"Here I had planned this whole speech," Luca said with a grin. "Natalie I know both of us keep saying that we aren't ready for a relationship but I have been doing a lot of thinking. I really want you to stay so we can get to know each other better. Before you say anything Calen told me that he doesn't think you and I will ever really get over Lila and Troy. He said that because we loved them so much they will always be in our hearts. Calen said that you and I have to decide when we are willing to move forward. I really like you Natalie and I would like to see where this goes."

Natalie didn't speak but was searching Luca's eyes for answers. "Are you mad at me?" he asked.

"No," Natalie said in a whisper.

"You aren't ready to consider anything are you?"

"Luca I think you are a wonderful man and I really like you too but you have to understand that Troy was my first love. I never even had other boyfriends so this is kind of frightening for me."

"So you will stay?" Luca asked happily.

"Yes," Natalie said.

Luca leaned forward and kissed her on the lips. A tender kiss which she returned. They kissed several more times. "I am sorry I am nervous," Natalie said.

"That just means we have to kiss more," Luca said and putting his arms around Natalie he kissed her more intensely. She kissed him back and after a few moments Luca could feel her getting weak in his arms. "Can I talk you into anything else?" Luca asked with a grin.

"What do you mean?"

"Would you consider moving in these chambers with us?"

"Boy, once you make your mind up about something you don't waste any time do you?"

"All the men in my family are like that," Luca said. "Will you at least think about it?"

"Yes," Natalie said with a nervous smile.

"Natalie even if you decide not to have a relationship with me, I want to take care of you and Hunter." Luca expected Natalie to protest but instead she started to cry and put her arms around Luca's neck and hugged him.

Luca hugged Natalie back and said, "I don't really understand why you are crying."

"I have been so afraid that I wouldn't be able to provide for him or that I would be killed and he would be alone in the world. It just means a lot that you said that."

"I am very serious, I hope you understand that," said Luca. Natalie nodded. "Ok, we are going to have fun tonight. Why don't you go to your room and get your things. I will watch the babies."

Natalie returned to Luca's chambers twenty minutes later. Her arms were full of clothing and shoes. He smiled when he saw her. "Here let me show you were to put your things," Luca said and took some of the clothing out of Natalie's arms. Then he kissed her again.

"Which of these shoes can I dance in?" Natalie asked and held out the three pairs that Luca and Christopher had bought her.

"Try these," Luca said and put the other two pairs in the closet. "I'll watch the babies if you want to get ready."

"Luca I would really like to take a bath, I won't be long."

"Take your time," he said and kissed Natalie again. She giggled and took her clothes into the bathing room.

A few moments later the door to the chambers burst open and Christopher ran in. "Luca," Christopher yelled and jumped into Luca's arms. They hugged each other tightly then Luca sat down on the bed and put Christopher on his lap.

"There are presents for you on the dining room table but first we need to talk man to man," Luca said with a smile. "How did things go while I was gone?"

"Good. We had a lot of fun."

"Christopher what do you think about Natalie?"

"Luca I love her and I want her to live with us."

"You have spent more time with Natalie than I have and I need to get to know her too. Christopher, Natalie and I are going out on a date tonight so I made arrangements for you, Emma and Hunter to sleep in other chambers." Christopher's eyes grew wide as he listened to Luca.

"Grandma already told us that we can camp in the playroom tonight. Luca is Natalie going to live with us?" Christopher asked with a big grin.

"I asked her to think about it but there are a lot of things we have to talk about still."

"Where is she?"

"Taking a bath."

"Is that her clothes in your closet?"

"Yes, a few of her things."

"I've got to tell the others," Christopher said excitedly and jumped off from Luca's lap and ran towards the door then he stopped and ran back to Luca and hugged him.

"I'm watching the babies so go downstairs and open your gifts," Luca said and laughed as Christopher ran out of the door.

A few minutes later Natalie walked into Luca's bedroom. "Would you help me with the back of this dress?"

"You look absolutely beautiful," Luca said and kissed Natalie's shoulder. "Christopher was in here. He told me he loves you and wants you to live with us."

Natalie didn't say anything for a few moments. "Luca I care a great deal about Christopher and Emma too. Luca my village is a very different world than here. Troy and I started to date when we were very young and we married young. I guess I am trying to say that I don't know if I understand your customs. When you say things like consider a relationship what do you mean?"

Luca finished buttoning Natalie's dress and turned her around. He took her hand and they both sat down on the bed. "I guess I am using the word relationship for marriage. But our situations are complicated and we have so much to learn about each other. I would like us to spend time together and I mean a lot of time together to see if we want to marry. Now, that doesn't mean you have to move in here if you aren't ready. I know I am pushing things and I don't want to scare you off. But since we have children I don't know if regular dating is appropriate."

"What do you mean regular dating?"

"Well, here people can date more than one person at a time. For example you could date me and Dack and Joao at the same time. Then when two people get more serious about each other they decide to only date one person. In my culture that is when we ask someone to be our girl. That means you don't date other men and I don't date other women. Natalie I am not interested in dating other women. I like you and I know this is a lot to think about. I don't expect an answer right away."

"An answer to what?"

"Will you be my girl?"

"Yes, Luca I will and I am not interested in dating anyone else either but I am not sure I am ready to say yes to marriage yet."

"Honestly I am not sure I am ready to ask you to marry me yet but you have made me very happy," Luca said and kissed Natalie again. "Let me help you with your jewelry."

"Luca this was the most wonderful evening," Natalie said as they walked to the front door of Gabriel's house. "I have never been to such a fancy restaurant before and the dancing was so much fun."

"Perhaps we should do this again soon," Luca said and kissed her. They kissed passionately for several moments before they both stopped and started laughing. They turned and looked at the house and saw Christopher, Joey, Adrone, Nicholas and Paul standing in the window watching them and giggling. All the boys were in their night clothes.

"Maybe we should go in," Luca said and took Natalie's hand.

"Shouldn't you be sleeping?" Natalie asked when they walked into the house.

"We were but we heard something," Paul said with a grin.

"Well, we brought you some cookies from the restaurant," Luca said. "Maybe they will help you sleep."

Luca was handing each boy two cookies when Nicholas said sweetly, "You look really pretty Natalie."

"Thank you Nicholas."

"I picked out that dress," Christopher said as he was stuffing an entire cookie into his mouth.

"Ok hugs then you go to bed," Natalie said and hugged each boy and kissed them on their foreheads.

The boys started to run towards the playroom. "Natalie," Christopher yelled. "If Luca asks you anything say yes." All the boys started to giggle loudly as they ran.

Luca and Natalie were laughing and walking up the staircase to Luca's chambers when he said loudly, "Christopher she said yes to being my girl."

"Yippee!" yelled Christopher and the boys started to giggle again.

Luca lit candles and started a fire in the hearth all the while he was talking to Natalie who brought him a glass of whiskey. "Luca will you unbutton my dress?"

He kissed the back of Natalie's neck and shoulders as he unbuttoned her dress. She started to moan. When the dress was unbuttoned Luca turned her around and kissed Natalie passionately on the lips. In that instant all of their fears and loneliness were replaced with consuming passion.

Chapter XXXVIII
Crossroads

Luca and Natalie had just finished making love again when they heard the front door to the chambers open. Luca quickly rolled off of Natalie and they both pulled the bed covers up to their shoulders then laughed as they heard Christopher in the parlor.

"What a mess!" Christopher said and marched into the master bedroom. Christopher ran and jumped on the bed and hugged Natalie and Luca.

"Christopher, Natalie, Hunter and Emma are moving in with us today and we are going to live as a family," Luca explained.

Christopher hugged them both again and said excitedly, "Natalie I told everyone you were going to be my mommy now I have to tell them I was right." Christopher jumped off from the bed and ran out of the chambers.

When Luca and Natalie walked into the dining room for breakfast everyone was grinning at them. "I am sorry I didn't come down in time to help with breakfast," Natalie said as she walked over to Cassandra to get Hunter.

"That's alright," Vivian said and started to laugh.

"So, how did the date go?" asked Calen.

Koby started laughing and said, "Don't lie to us because Christopher already told us about your clothes thrown all over the parlor and the furniture moved around." Everyone in the room roared with laughter.

"Yeah, there's no secrets in this house," Calen said as he continued to laugh.

Both Natalie and Luca laughed although Natalie also turned red from embarrassment. Luca pulled Natalie's chair out for her but spoke to the family.

"Natalie and I have talked. While we both care about each other we really don't know if we are ready for a major commitment. But we both have children who need parents so we are moving fast to the first step. Natalie is my girl now. She, Hunter and Emma are moving into our chambers today. Now, Emeral please don't jump the gun and plan a wedding next week."

Everyone again laughed and Emeral said, "Me!" with feigned surprise.

"Natalie and I will most likely marry but considering our situations we need some time to work things out. Does that sound reasonable to all of you?"

"I think it sounds wonderful," Hannah said. "We all understand that you both are going through so much but you really are good for each other."

"I second that," said Joshua.

"And I believe we need to make a toast," Maxwell said with a big smile. "I will get the wine."

Both Vivian and Natasha jumped out of their seats and ran into the kitchen. Diana walked over to Natalie and hugged her then Luca.

"Iris we need to thank you for bringing us together," Luca said happily.

Rosa knocked on the door to Mathas' study as his morning meeting was being conducted. Many members of Gabriel's group were attending the meeting besides the members of the ruling families. "We are sorry to interrupt," Rosa said as she led Karin into the study. "But Karin needs to speak to you."

"Karin has something happened?" Claudius asked. "You look awful."

"Last night this horrible voice kept talking to me; I couldn't even tell if it was in my head or in the room," Karin said fearfully.

"After what you told me about Deckor I thought at first it was my imagination until it gave me a message for the Sanuri." As Karin spoke the Sanuri got out of his seat and walked towards her. "The voice said that the worlds are uniting and you are the trophy."

Karin started to cry. "I believe this is a demon speaking to me," Karin said and handed Mathas a piece of paper. "That lists all our properties, business and wealth that I am aware of. I have also listed the locations of the papers and money. If something happens to me I want you to take all of it and find ways to repay the kingdom for the damage my husband did."

"Karin this is most generous of you but we will protect you," Fahron said.

"I don't know if you can," Karin said fearfully.

"Karin may I look into your mind?" asked the Sanuri. "It will not hurt you." The Sanuri put the palms of his hands on either side of her head and stared into her eyes. Karin trembled with fear; fear of what the Sanuri would find. The people in the room looked on with horror as smoke slowly started to rise from Karin's body.

"Sanuri what is happening?" Karin cried. "Please help me."

"The Sanuri started to hum and to pray, while Karin's body started to jerk. The jerking became more and more intense then Karin collapsed. The Sanuri held her in his arms and continued to hum.

"What is happening to her?" Kate asked Raphael.

"I don't know but a demon has to have some kind of connection to her," Raphael replied.

Suddenly horrid shrieks were heard and Matthew quickly stood up and put his arms around his mother who was fearfully staring at the scene before her. When the shrieks stopped the Sanuri turned to Rosa and asked, "Where is her room?"

"This way; I will show you," Rosa said and quickly turned. The Sanuri carried Karin out of the study and up the stairs to her chambers.

He placed her on the bed then prayed to cleanse the evil from the chambers. Twenty minutes later the Sanuri returned to the study.

"Is she alright?" Mathas asked before the Sanuri could speak.

"She will be but..." the Sanuri paused. "I need to explain this from the beginning. While demons talk to humans all of the time they cannot invade a person's consciousness in the manner that happened to Karin without someone giving them the key to the door so to speak."

"Karin does not call to or worship demons. There were no spells on her jewelry or clothing but what I saw in her mind was even more heinous than that. Deckor offered his wife as a sacrifice to demons. She was drugged and placed upon the unholy altar. Karin has no memory of this. Deckor drew blood from her but did not kill her, which is the type of sacrifices that we are used to seeing."

"I believe this was done so Karin could be of use to the demons. But Karin was praying and fighting the voice in her head. I closed the door so the demon no longer has access. And I cleansed her but she will be horrified when she finds out what Deckor did to her."

"Can the door be reopened?" asked Edward.

"Not unless Karin herself worships the demon," the Sanuri replied. "And she has been cleansed with holiness so she no longer would be a desirable vessel for a demon."

"Do you think that demon was using Karin to spy on us?" Mathas asked.

"No. I saw Karin's spirit starting to fight with the monster as soon as he opened the door to her being."

"Did you see the demon?" asked Gabriel.

"No but I saw a symbol that should concern us all. We saw it in Ryed and on the bodies of the murdered Patronus priests at the monastery in Philiste. Four dots with swords underneath them."

"The first three swords are facing down and the last sword is facing up."

"Sanuri if Deckor was worshipping demons from other worlds could the codes in this paperwork be from other worlds too?" Michael asked. "We have been studying these papers for days and some of us think that Deckor made up that code."

"It certainly is possible," the Sanuri said. "I know you have divided into groups because of the volume of the paperwork. Let's give everything that is coded to one group and I will work with that group today."

"I know we are new members," Sol said. "But you keep saying demons from other worlds do you mean demon worlds or human worlds?"

"Both actually. There are the hell dimensions like the ones the Old Ones live in. Then there are hell worlds which are usually attached to human worlds. Demons are parasites; they feed off from the fears of humans."

"I may be the only one here who doesn't really understand all of this," Sol continued. But that demon in Deckor was from another galaxy. How did Deckor contact another galaxy to talk to anyone demon or human?"

"I don't know the answer to that question but apparently he was not the only one. In Ryed we stopped two of the Grand Masters from opening a portal to allow demons from other worlds into our world. And we know that some Masters of the Insidiae were trying to do business with demons from other worlds, now if that means other galaxies I don't know. But someone or something has opened a portal or a channel of communication. And I don't yet understand what is happening," the Sanuri explained.

"The Lion told me that Teivel was behind the murders of the Patronus priests in Philiste," Raphael said to the Sanuri. "And that is where we saw the same symbol you just saw. I believe we should assume that Emeric and Banaka were more successful than we thought with their treachery to this world."

"Are you sure they aren't making love or something?" Calen asked Natasha as the family gathered outside of the door to Luca's chambers.

"She just came down to get some cleaning rags and soap," Natasha said and giggled.

"You have company," Maxwell called out as he opened the door to Luca's chambers. "Can we come in?"

"Of course," Luca said as he and Natalie both came out of different rooms. "What is all of this?"

"We know you are expediting everything because of the children and we think that is wonderful," Maxwell said. "So we thought we would help."

"We bought everything you will need to fix up one of the rooms for Hunter and Emma when they get a little older," Emeral said with a proud smile. "Which room would you like us to put these things in?"

"Actually Natalie was just cleaning one of the rooms for that purpose," Luca said.

"I have to finish cleaning before you can put those things in there," Natalie said as she looked at the carpet, furniture and baskets of clothing. "I will work fast."

"We'll help you," Diana said as she and Vivian walked into the bedroom.

"I see you cleaned up the parlor," Koby said and laughed.

"Does anyone want a drink while we wait? I know it is a bit early," Luca asked.

"Sure," Calen said. "Just so you know there are more coming." And with Calen's words they heard voices in the hallway.

Joshua carried in an armload of bolts of fabric and set them in a chair, "Natalie, Iris will be here in a minute she wants you to look at this fabric."

Natasha walked into the bedroom and said, "Natalie go out there I will help clean."

"Actually we are almost done," said Vivian.

"We brought treats," Iris said as she and Ella carried trays of sweets into the chambers.

"I just can't believe all of this," Natalie said and it was clear to the others that she was overwhelmed.

"My dear you have a home now," Emeral said and hugged Natalie.

Adrone, Paul, Joey, Nicholas and Christopher pushed through the crowd and walked up to the table containing the treats. "Luca," Christopher said as he grabbed a sweet roll. "Joey said that Hunter is my brother now. Is that true?"

"Yes it is. What do you think about that?" asked Luca.

"It's good. When is he going to be big enough to play with us?"

Mid-afternoon Matthew walked into his father's study. "The Sanuri says he expects to be done with Deckor's men by dinner time. Do you want the executions open to the public?"

"Yes, those men terrorized our citizens. The people need to see their monsters destroyed. But considering the circumstances have extra security at the fort. Have Enrops and the Rualas flying overhead."

"Father you remember what happened in Wetpr," Matthew said. "I don't mean to be disrespectful but never once have you called to the Angels; don't you think now would be a good time? Because if you don't I will; I don't have a good feeling about this at all."

Mathas stared at his son in shock. Not so much at Matthew's words but at the idea; for Mathas had never considered personally asking the heavens for help or insight. When Mathas did not speak, Matthew continued.

"Father you are the ruler of one of the most powerful kingdoms in Opots. You have much to protect and you know how the Angels have saved us and helped us before. I can't tell you why but I feel strongly that you are at a crossroads and you need to make a decision this day."

"My son is now giving me advice," Mathas said warmly. "What is stunning my soul is that I realize I have never considered asking for help or advice. How do I pray? And do I pray to The Great Ruler or an Angel?"

"Praying is simply talking to The Great Ruler. It is my perception that there is a hierarchy of the Angels and The Lion seems to have more rank than Miranda, Daniel and Ruth. Since you are King and since you are asking, I would suggest you pray to The Great Ruler and ask Him to send you the messenger He deems appropriate. I am going to leave you now but I would suggest you do this soon."

As Matthew was walking out of the study Mathas said, "Son, you will make a great king someday."

"I don't know if I should speak out loud," Mathas thought to himself. "They can read my thoughts, I know that." Mathas got down on his knees and prayed, "Great Ruler while I believe in you I have never considered coming to you before. This is my weakness which I will correct. My faithful son just told me I am at a crossroads and I have no idea what he means but as he spoke I felt that the words were coming from you. Teach me how to talk to you and how to be a better king. And please send me a messenger for guidance and help. And this crossroads; help me to make the right decision."

"Mathas; Matthew and Angelina talk of the Angels as if they are family and friends, so close is their connection," said The Lion. "And your kingdom has been attacked again and again by the nightmares of mankind and yet you have never considered talking to the heavens. Why is that?"

Mathas began to tremble and his legs felt weak in the presence of The Lion. "I have no good answer for you," said Mathas.

"The answer is that for all you have witnessed you still put your faith in the frailties of mankind. Your adversaries are much more powerful than humans. Tell me King, would you lead your people to slaughter because that is the crossroads you are at?"

"Please tell me what I must do. I want you to lead," Mathas said sincerely.

"When we are done talking I want you to call together your leaders and tell them my words. Then I want you to write down what has been said and send it to Sudfad," said The Lion.

"Before we go any farther in this discussion I want to say to Mathas that I am pleased that you called to The Great Ruler and I hope you realize that you must do this often," the Sanuri said.

"Yes, as I said before, I know many of you have called to the Angles and I have witnessed Miranda and Daniel in the castle of Sudfad, but the experience still has me shaken," Mathas said.

"As it should," the Sanuri said. "You spoke to an emissary of The Great Ruler. But do you also realize the gift you have been given. You prayed for help and in an instant The Lion appeared before you. So many people believe their prayers go unanswered; they have no idea."

Edward stood up. "If I am changing the subject too quickly tell me to sit down, but my team are the newest players in all of this and we have some questions. But first I want to make sure I understand what Mathas just said. Demons can travel between other worlds and that means galaxies also. And that is how these other demons know about us here on Opots?"

"That is what The Lion said," Mathas replied. "He also said that the calls that some of the Grand Masters and Masters of the Insidiae have made resound in other worlds. And the main reason that demons from other worlds are paying attention to Nunc is because the people are standing up and saying no to the demons. And the people are winning."

"The Lion said that demons everywhere are terrified that humans will realize the power they possess. Because if the people reject the demons; the demons have nothing to feed off from and will be destroyed."

"So then basically you are telling us that demons from all other worlds can communicate with each other and unite and attack us?" Raphael asked.

"Yes," the Sanuri said and paused. "I am about to tell you something that your species may not be ready to hear. Mathas just said that demons need humans to feed off from and that there are demons in other worlds. So what does that lead you to believe?"

"That there are humans in those worlds," Sorren yelled excitedly.

"Yes or some species with similarities to humans," the Sanuri said. "Worlds and people differ but the fight between good and evil does not. Most worlds struggle but only a few have realized some truths and are standing up to the darkness as you are. And it is the same in every world; while some men battle the demons others dance with them. But you have to understand this realization among peoples is coming at a time when the demons hold incredible power. Do any of you believe that is a coincidence?"

"So the Angels are helping those other worlds also?" Matthew asked.

"The Angels watch over all of The Great Ruler's children and come when they are called in," the Sanuri replied.

"In between your meetings Mathas," Edward said. "I had a meeting with my team. Since our arrival here we have heard a great deal about the Dura Tribe and what monsters they are; can someone explain to us what they look like."

"In a way that is difficult," Claudius said. "Because words don't really describe them."

"They are almost shadows of humans and they all look exactly alike, just like the Amulth demons. They have the body shape of a human with a bald head. They have indentations in their faces where eyes and a nose would be but it appears that they can see and breathe. Their mouths look like round holes which are filled with pointed fangs. They are a color…" Claudius' eyes widened and he paused.

"We have never been able to explain the color that those monsters are but I just realized when we were in Baal's hell domain we saw that color. They are that strange brownish orange color of hell." Now everyone turned and looked at the Sanuri. "Sanuri, Miranda told us that demons do not want individuality among their slaves which is why the Amulth demons are identical. And the Dura Tribe is the color of hell. They are demons then?"

"Yes but not in the sense that you normally think," the Sanuri replied. "Think of the Rogetts. They once were human but they sold their souls to demons and after centuries the darkness took away their humanity giving them the features we see today. The Huta race too has changed greatly but the changes have been inside of them. If that race continues on the path it is on they will lose their physical appearance. That is what has happened to the Dura Tribe. You were able to kill them during that war because they are not true demons."

"Then I am confused," Gabriel said. "All of you told us that the sailors who survived the attacks on their ships said the Dura Tribe attacked them. But many of you were suspicious that was a hoax. It doesn't sound like anyone could confuse the Dura Tribe with other people."

"It has been over twenty years since anyone in Opots has seen a member of the Dura Tribe," Fahron explained. "I am told that the ships who trade in Tansof do not trade with the Dura Tribe or even see them. So most people really don't know what they look like. The stories of the sailors was so inconsistent with the known behavior of the tribe that we became suspicious."

"Gabriel remember what your team encountered in Taperia?" the Sanuri asked but did not wait for Gabriel to answer the question. "The Insidiae put out a call that the evil within men would answer. Remember how all manner of evil men flocked to that city?"

"Sanuri what are you really saying?" asked Claudius.

"If in truth the demon worlds are uniting in an effort to beat you into submission; do not underestimate them. They may send any manner of enemy after you. Don't let fear rule your lives but I believed The Lion warned you so you could fortify your cities."

Late that evening Luca walked into the master bedroom and saw Natalie sitting on the bed, feeding Emma. "Christopher is asleep," Luca said. "And you look so beautiful."

"It's the nightgown you bought me," Natalie said with a shy smile.

"No, it is everything," Luca said as he took his clothes off and sat down on the bed.

"Luca, please don't take this wrong but you seem so content with all of this and I have to admit that my head is still spinning," said Natalie.

"Honey in the last day you have inherited this huge, crazy family that you don't really know and became the mother of two more children. And you have become my wife; of course your head is spinning. Actually you are handling all of this very well."

"I love everyone in this house," Natalie said. "And I love the children; perhaps it is, oh I don't know. How can you seem so calm about everything?"

"I thought about us a lot while I was gone. I think I worked through more issues. You haven't really had time to think about all of this. Do you have any regrets?"

"No and that in itself surprises me. But Luca I thought about us too while you were gone and before that. You are so handsome and sweet it is hard not to be attracted to you. And well, Christopher isn't exactly subtle. He was asking me a lot of questions that really made me think. I don't know, maybe I am just a little scared."

"I will tell you a secret," Luca said with a smile and put his arm around Natalie's shoulders. "I am too. But for as crazy as this might seem I think we made the right decision. And I think it will all work out."

"I am glad you told me that; it makes me feel better," Natalie said and leaned forward and kissed Luca on the lips. "It was so nice waking up with you this morning that I found myself feeling guilty; like I was betraying Troy."

"I thought about Lila too," Luca said. "Calen said that he somehow knows for sure that Lila would want Christopher and me to move on and to be happy. And he said that although he never met Troy that if Troy loved you as much as you love him; that Troy would want you to be happy too."

"I think your brother is right," Natalie said. "But I still feel guilty."

Chapter XXXIX
Fears

Luca awoke early the following morning because he thought he heard talking. He rolled over and looked at Natalie who was sleeping then he got out of bed and grabbed his robe. It was then that Luca saw that Hunter wasn't in his cradle. Luca quickly walked into the parlor and smiled when he saw Hunter and Christopher sitting on the floor, surrounded with toys.

"Did you lift him out of his cradle?" Luca asked as he walked towards his sons.

"Yeah, he was awake and wanted to play," Christopher said. "Luca I just realized, I've never had a brother before."

Luca and Natalie laughed. Luca turned and saw her walking towards them. "Christopher I, we think it is great that you are getting to know your brother but I don't know if you should be carrying him," said Luca.

"Why not?" Christopher asked with a look of confusion.

"He might be too heavy for you and if you drop him you could hurt him. Natalie and I will gladly carry him for you."

"You were sleeping and he wasn't too heavy. You know I am pretty strong."

Luca looked at Natalie because he wasn't really sure what to say to Christopher. Natalie saw the look on Luca's face and said, "Christopher we know you are a strong boy but you will have to be extra careful when you pick up Hunter and Emma. Will you do that for us?"

"Sure," Christopher said with a smile.

"You know with both of you having blonde hair and blue eyes you really look like brothers," Luca said as he realized that for the first time.

"I know that's what Hannah said too. Nicholas has a brother and sister and so do Adrone and Paul; and now me. Joey needs to get a brother now."

452

"You tell that to Elan and Cassandra at breakfast," Luca said as he and Natalie laughed.

Natalie went downstairs before the rest of her new family so she could help prepare breakfast. Luca walked into the dining room thirty minutes later with his children.

"Here give Hunter to me," Joshua said since Luca was holding two babies.

"Now Luca?" Christopher asked and Luca grinned and nodded. Christopher marched across the room and took a deep breath and said, "Elan and Cassandra we all have brothers and sisters now except for Joey he needs a brother too."

"Did you put him up to that?" Maxwell asked Luca.

"Do you think I could put Christopher up to anything?" Luca asked and laughed.

Joey was standing next to Elan and nodding his head. "Joey do you want a little brother too?" Elan asked with a grin.

"Yes but can I help pick him?"

"Let me talk this over with your mother," said Elan.

"I don't know why we need to talk," Cassandra said. "You know we are both going to say yes."

"Can Christopher, Nicholas, Adrone and Paul come to the orphanage with us?" Joey asked excitedly.

"Yes, if they want to," Cassandra said.

Christopher looked across the dining room at Paul and Adrone and said, "I don't like that place its sad."

"Changing the subject a little," Misha said with a big grin. "Last night Diana and I were talking about hiring another nurse. Thor is going to live with us but we can't tell him he can't work on anymore missions. And Melinda never complains but she could use a day off once in a while."

"And look at this household now and we are all just starting our families. Emeral you need to get on the stick and hire some more nurses."

Everyone laughed at Misha's last comment. "Actually your mother and I have been talking about that," Maxwell said. "Not only do we agree but Emeral thinks we need to expand the nursery and playroom again."

"I think we all prefer to have those rooms in the location they are," Emeral said. "Calen will you take a look and see if we can expand on the back of those rooms; they both have exterior walls."

"I don't see why not," Calen said. "I will look after breakfast. But we should run this past Gabriel."

"He will think it is a good idea," Hannah said. "He certainly wants to have more children. Of course it would help if he was home once in a while."

"Emeral do the nurses have to be Ruala?" Bianca asked. "I know you want warriors to protect the children but there might be good candidates in my tribe and Micha's tribe too."

"I think we hire several nurses and also let them train for the teams," Vivian said. "But of course Gabriel and Raphael will have to approve that."

"I think these are all good ideas," Emeral said. "If Gabriel and Raphael approve Vivian's suggestion I propose that we send letters to the leaders of each tribe asking for volunteers then let those of you who know the people decide on the candidates."

After the Sanuri explained to Karin that Deckor had given her as an offering to a demon, she was despondent. The horror of what Deckor had done, compiled with her fear completely overwhelmed her. Every day the Sanuri, Raphael or Gabriel would go to Karin's chambers and pray with her. Although Karin believed the Sanuri when he said the demon could not touch or control her; she could not overcome her fears.

454

As Mathas' family and guests gathered in the Great Hall for breakfast they heard a blood curdling scream. Everyone bolted out of the hall and towards the screaming voice. "My Lord! My Lady!" one of the cooks shrieked over and over as she ran down the stairs.

"Margerie what is it?" Matthew asked as he was the first to meet the middle aged woman. Margerie did not speak but grabbed Matthew's hand and ran back up the stairs. Margerie stopped at the open door to Karin's chambers. Matthew led the group of people into Karin's chambers; as one they stopped when they saw her body on the floor of the parlor. The carpet was soaked with the blood that had drained from her slashed wrists.

The Sanuri walked up to the body and said a prayer then he bent down and examined Karin's body and wounds. Rosa started to sob after she pushed her way through the crowd and saw Karin's body.

"Was it suicide?" Mathas asked as he picked up a bloody knife from the floor.

"It certainly appears so," the Sanuri said. "You did not have any intruders in your home but I am not so sure that Karin didn't have intruders in her mind."

"I will be so glad when Gabriel gets home," Hannah said to Vivian as they were preparing the evening meal. "I miss him so and he has spent almost no time with Daniel."

"I feel the same way but after hearing about the children they rescued we have to be thankful that they went to Lentz," Vivian said. "Hannah I saw all of that paperwork that Mathas sent you. If you want to go to Lentz, I will watch the children. My family will help. Maybe you and Gabriel can spend a little time together and you can help them set up that hospital. It sure sounds like they need one."

"You know I had thought about that but Daniel is so young," Hannah said thoughtfully.

"Hannah look how many of us are nursing babies, we can take care of him. You have been so sad since Gabriel left again; we have all noticed it. I think the whole family will think it is a good idea for you to go. Why don't you bring it up at dinner?"

By time the entire household was seated for dinner, Hannah was so excited she could hardly contain herself. "I would like to discuss a suggestion that Vivian made," Hannah said. "And the more I think about it the more excited I am becoming. Vivian thinks I should do to Lentz to visit Gabriel and to help Mathas with the hospital. What do all of you think?"

"Honey, none of us have ever seen you sad before," Emeral said. "I think you need to spend some time with your husband and lord knows Mathas could use your help."

"Hannah we will take care of the children," Cassandra said. "Go. You work so hard and you never take any time off."

"Hannah, I am going with you," Joshua said. "I am still so damn mad after hearing about those kidnapped children."

"I was thinking the same thing," said Maxwell.

"Calen you go and watch over Hannah too," Natasha said. "You know where the lodge is."

"Emeral why don't you come too?" asked Hannah. "You are so good at organizing things you can help me with the hospital. They have a building that they want to remodel but Mathas has no idea as to what is needed. We could get that started for him."

"Thank you. I believe I will," Emeral said warmly. "When are we leaving?"

"How about after breakfast tomorrow," Maxwell said. "Of course we should send messages tonight."

"Misha you go too," Diana said. "I can tell you want to go."

"Thanks," Misha said and kissed her on the cheek.

Diana got a mischievous look on her face. "Hannah since both of my children will be in Lentz, I will take Nicholas and Cerey."

456

"Calen you should bring your drawing instruments," Emeral said. "We might need your help with that building."

"I was just thinking that same thing," Calen said. "Is anyone else coming with us?"

"I'm not leaving Natalie right now," said Luca.

"At least a couple of us need to stay here," said Koby. "I'm staying."

Joshua turned and looked at Thomas and Sasha and asked, "Are you ready to return to Lentz?"

"We've been talking about that and we are going to stay here for a while. For several reasons but one is that I just recently heard about the threat that Nada is to Diana's babies. With Misha and Thor gone..."

"I don't need a babysitter," Diana interrupted Thomas.

"Maybe he is right, I'll stay," said Misha.

"No, you are going and that is final," Diana said. "I'm not going to schedule my life around fear."

"Misha, there are enough of us staying here; go to Lentz," Micha said with a grin. "And keep our father out of trouble."

"Luca what are they talking about?" Natalie asked.

"I have no idea," Luca said to Natalie then he turned to Misha. "What is all of this about?"

"When we were in Ryed Diana started having visions and the Sanuri was having similar visions, so I was getting pretty worried. Diana can fill you in on all of the details but the Sanuri said that what Diana was seeing had two meanings. First it gave us information that we needed for the mission and it also was a warning to us about Nada. She is the wife of a powerful demon and someday she will have some kind of power and may come after our twins."

"What!" Vivian said loudly. "Why haven't you told us about this?"

"Because in the visions our sons were about five which gives us time and according to the Sanuri it will be some time before Nada has any power," Diana explained then she glanced at Misha and looked back at Vivian. "In the visions Misha and I were running away. I don't plan to run from that demon. I can't get to her where she is at and if she comes after my family it will be the last thing she does."

After dinner Luca and Natalie went to the chambers of Maxwell and Emeral. "We know you are getting ready for your trip but do you have time to talk for just a moment?" Luca asked.

"Certainly son, come in," Maxwell said. "Is anything wrong?"

"Not really we just want to head off any issues so we want some advice," Luca said as he and Natalie sat down on one of the sofas.

"I will pour us all a little wine," said Emeral.

"We weren't going to talk to you about this yet but since you are leaving I thought we should get your thoughts on the matter," Luca said as Emeral handed out the wine glasses.

"Go on," Emeral said as she sat down next to Maxwell.

"Well, you know how fast everything is going for Natalie and me and honestly we are both surprised that everything is going so well," Luca said then paused.

"Luca and I, well for my part I am falling in love with him and while this is wonderful it also makes me feel very guilty. I feel like I am betraying Troy."

"It's just not on your part," Luca said to Natalie and squeezed her hand then he turned to his parents. "I am having the same feelings. While we think this is probably normal we don't want it to fester and possibly become a real threat to our relationship."

Maxwell and Emeral looked at each other and smiled. "Well that is probably the easiest problem we can help you fix," Maxwell said. "You both are wonderful parents and you jumped into this relationship so you could provide a good home for your children."

"And before I go farther I want to tell you that all of us in this house saw the connection between you two even when you could not. If we would have thought you were bad for each other we would have told you."

"So much of your focus is on your children but you are both healing and need to get to know each other. You need to make time to focus on each other. I would suggest that you make time at least once a week to be alone. Go on a picnic, go shopping, anything but leave the children with us. Your children will be happy if their parents are happy."

"I agree with every word your father said. But this isn't something you should do once or twice. Make it a routine. For as many years as Maxwell and I have been together every night we have a glass of wine and make time to really talk. We believe that is very important in a relationship," said Emeral.

"And Luca tonight I was glad that you set your priorities and realized now is the time for you to stay home with your family," Maxwell said.

Luca put his arm around Natalie and asked, "Do you think you are ready to look at engagement rings? We could go shopping tomorrow." Natalie smiled and nodded.

The following morning about twenty minutes into the meeting in the study of King Mathas several Enrops flew into the room. Letters were handed to Mathas, Gabriel, Raphael and Sorren. "Hannah said to read them now," one of the birds said and flew out of the room. Fearing the worse, Gabriel and Raphael quickly tore their letters open and started to read them.

With a sigh of relief and a sound of excitement in his voice Gabriel said, "Hannah has been so sad that I am gone again that Vivian talked her into coming here to visit me and to help with the hospital you want to build."

"Excellent," Sorren said. "In my letter Hannah says that Emeral is coming to help also but that they want to meet with Shara and Angelina."

"Hannah believes that both Angelina and Shara are more than capable of completing the project but will need some advice."

"Angelina actually said something to me about that," Matthew said. "She will be happy that Hannah is coming."

"Well, I am very happy about this," Mathas said. "In my letter Hannah says that Calen is also coming with them to help draw up building plans for the hospital." Mathas put his letter down and looked at Gabriel. "This helps us greatly; of course we will pay your family for their service."

"I would really doubt if any of them would take money," Gabriel said. "Hannah says that by time we get these letters they will already be on their way. Maxwell, Misha and Joshua are also coming." Gabriel turned to Raphael and asked, "Did Vivian tell you about her idea?"

"Yes. What do you think about it?" asked Raphael.

"I think it is an excellent idea," Gabriel said. "Let's tell Sorren now."

"We are having an explosion of babies and the family has decided we need more than one nurse," Raphael explained. "But since the attacks on our children we want nurses who can protect them. Vivian's idea was to accept candidates from the Nordes Tribe, the Ruala Tribe and the Clan of Gesmal. We will hire several nurses and also train them for missions. Sorren if you think this is something that would appeal to your warriors would you get a lists of volunteers?"

"Of course we will pay them for their services and provide everything they need," Gabriel said. "They will live in our house so we will watch over them."

"I think you will have many who are interested," Sorren said. "I very much like this idea."

"Sorren we would also ask for your counsel on all decisions with your tribe," Raphael said.

Sorren looked at Fahron and winked. "Would you like to make a small wager on whether Lana volunteers for this so she can be closer to Chaez?"

Fahron laughed loudly. "I like the girl I hope she does volunteer for this. Because it may be the only way for them to work out a relationship."

"We don't want Toni," Edward quickly said.

"Why did I know that would be the case?" Sorren said with a big grin.

"Before this conversation goes any further," Claudius said. "You know we are going to have to let our wives know right away that Hannah and the others are coming. You know they will want to have at least one celebration."

"I know they will be welcomed in all of our homes," Mathas said. "But since they are going to be working on the hospital it might be more efficient if they stay here. Does anyone take issue with that?"

"Makes sense to me," Claudius said. "But Isadore and Bella will most likely plan some things for them while they are here."

Midmorning Luca and Natalie left the house and flew into the City of Salar. This was the first of their planned times to focus on their relationship. While they were both excited they found themselves not knowing what to talk about.

"Why does this suddenly seem awkward?" Luca asked as they landed in the city.

"I feel the same way and I think it is because we feel pressured somehow," Natalie said. "Instead of looking for a ring let's go someplace for coffee. You never finished telling me about your family and how they all came here. Let's start there."

"Good idea," Luca said and kissed her hand which he was already holding. They walked to The Dragon's Inn and took a seat in the always crowded restaurant.

Once Luca started talking about his family they both relaxed and the words came easily to them. One cup of coffee turned into lunch and lunch extended late into the afternoon.

"You know after Lila died I couldn't conceive of the idea that I would ever care for someone again," Luca said. "And now; Natalie everything just seems so natural being with you. I feel like we have known each other for years instead of a couple of months. But because this seems so right, well it just terrifies me."

"You mean that you can't trust your feelings?"

"I think it is more that now I will be terrified that something will happen to you."

Chapter XXXL
The Unexpected

"Did you get a ring?" Natasha asked excitedly when Luca and Natalie walked into the house early that evening.

Before either Luca or Natalie could answer Cassandra quickly walked up to them and said, "Let me see."

Natalie and Luca looked at each other and laughed. "For some reason we felt so awkward this morning that we went to The Dragons Inn and ate and talked all day instead of shopping," Natalie said then she looked at Luca and smiled.

"Then we got a hotel room and made love," Luca said.

"You didn't!" Natasha said then she started to laugh.

"It was so much fun," said Natalie.

"Did you hear that?" Cassandra asked Diana as she walked into the room laughing.

"Yes," Diana said. "Just for fun?"

"Wait until your babies are born, then you will understand," said Luca.

Hannah, Calen, Maxwell, Emeral, Misha and Joshua landed in the front courtyard of King Mathas' castle midmorning of the third day of their travels. Enrops had flown ahead of the Rualas and announced the arrival of the guests.

All of the members of the ruling families and some members of the Nordes Tribe were at the castle to greet Hannah and the others. All of the members of Gabriel's team and Edward's team were still at the castle trying to translate Deckor's papers. When Gabriel heard that Hannah had arrived he ran out of the castle and grabbed his wife and swung her in the air. Gabriel and Hannah, kissed and laughed.

"Joshua we are glad that you came," Raphael said as he hugged his father-in-law. "We need help with some translations. Would you mind taking a look?"

"Of course not; I came here to work."

After the greetings were completed Mathas announced that everyone should go to the Great Hall. After everyone was seated, Mathas said, "We are so very glad to have you come for a visit and so very honored that you came to help us with the hospital. Hannah we are at your beckon call. Shara, Angelina, Rosa, Bella and Isadore have volunteered to help you."

"We decided it would be more efficient for all of you to stay here, since this castle is the closest to the hospital. But all of our wives have made arrangements for entertainment during your stay. Is there anything you would like to say now?"

Hannah stood up, "King Sudfad had me combine the medicines of the Ruala Tribe and the Nordes Tribe with the traditional medical training that I have. I would suggest you consider this also. You are very lucky to have Shara and Angelina here already. Lakin came to Wetpr to help me; I am sure he would come here if you asked."

"I have prepared a list of some of the physicians who were in the top of my class in college. Unfortunately I have not kept in touch with these individuals to know of their current whereabouts. I put stars by the names of the physicians that I think you would be particularly pleased with."

As Hannah spoke she walked up to King Mathas and handed him the list of names. "Unless he has changed over the years my top consideration would be Jonathon Blackmoore. The last I heard he was accepting a job in the Kingdom of Ganz but I don't know which city. He is brilliant, a leader and a down to earth nice man."

"Thank you, we appreciate this," Mathas said. "Rosa is motioning to me that the food is ready, so I will finish up. Immediately after the meal we will have a meeting. I assume that the people here have been writing to you about our situation but I want all of you fully aware of what is going on. After the meeting Rosa will have you shown to your rooms. We are having a small celebration this evening starting at seven."

As soon as Mathas sat down Michael stood up, "We have been trying to translate a code. Although I can't read it I know I have seen something like it before. Before you go to your rooms would you mind looking at it?"

When the meeting at Mathas' castle ended, Michael and Edward started to push tables together while Thor, Kate and Sol placed stacks of Deckor's papers on top of the tables.

Gabriel and Raphael pushed three tables together on the far side of the room. These tables were for the people who were going to meet about the proposed hospital.

"Deckor was of Lithanize ancestry," Edward explained. "When his wife was alive she helped us translate some of the words. As you can see on the papers those words are underlined and the translations written next to them. But as you can see there appears to be a very different style to the Lithanize words and most of the other words that seem to be coded."

"The characters in this code or language or whatever it is," Michael said. "Are so unusual that we thought they might be symbols for something else; so we have been looking for patterns."

Joshua and Calen were each looking at sheets of paper then they looked at each other. "We recognize this," Joshua said. "This appears to be the same code that we found in the books that were taken from Berta's house."

"Shanksaw's?" Gabriel asked incredulously.

"It sure looks the same," Calen said. "While we were all in Ryed, Vivian asked the priests from the Patronus headquarters to help translate the code. Actually quite a few of them came out to the house. I don't know which one of them realized it but these characters represent numbers and the numbers stand for that letter in the alphabet. But the next problem they ran into is the code changed for half of the ledger; that's why only part of it is translated."

"Do you know the key for this code?" asked Raphael.

"No, because we were in Ryed at the time but I will bet that Maxwell and Emeral do and if not send a message to Vivian I know she has it written down," Joshua explained.

Thor quickly got out of his chair and walked across the large room to the tables where the meeting for the hospital was taking place. Within moments Thor and Maxwell joined the group who were trying to translate the papers.

"Both Emeral and I were fascinated with this entire thing," Maxwell said as he picked up a sheet of paper. "We didn't always get a chance to sit in with the priests when they were working but one night several of them stayed for dinner and explained it to us." Maxwell stopped talking as he reviewed a couple of sheets of paper. "These certainly look like the same characters. If you can get me some paper and a pen I will write down the meanings of these symbols."

Nana quickly walked up to Matthew who was talking with his father, Claudius and Fahron. Matthew left the hall and when he returned he had a huge stack of paper and a handful of pens. He joined the group who was working on the code.

"I wonder if this is a code that the Insidiae uses that both Deckor and Shanksaw would be using it," Gabriel said.

"Do demons use codes?" asked Michael.

"I really don't know," Raphael asked. "Are you thinking that some type of spell might be released because the Sanuri already examined these?"

"After what I have seen just since I've started working with all of you; well I expect anything these days," Michael said with a grin. "But I agree this is fascinating."

Maxwell looked up from his work and asked, "The Sanuri? Where is he? We haven't seen him yet." Now the people at the table looked at each other than around the room.

"Does anyone remember the last time they saw the Sanuri?" Gabriel called out.

466

Earlier that morning before Hannah and the other guests arrived at the castle of King Mathas the Sanuri decided to visit the chambers where Karin had killed herself. While no one had evidence that the death was more than a suicide, the Sanuri had been haunted by feelings he was unfamiliar with.

It had been several days since Karin's tragic death and the chambers had been thoroughly cleaned. New carpets and furniture now replaced the ones soiled with Karin's blood. The Sanuri carefully examined the room. While he did not experience any feelings of malevolence in the chambers something haunted him.

The sun was coming up and the birds were singing. These two simple acts of nature always brought the Sanuri happiness and a sense of peace. He walked over to the balcony doors to allow the morning air in and that is when he saw them.

Heavy red drapes hung on either side of the doors that led to the balcony. The drapes concealed the wooden frames of the double balcony doors. When the Sanuri moved the drapes so he could open the doors he saw four deep claw marks in the wood to the right of the doors. He quickly walked out onto the balcony where he found similar claw marks on the railing.

"What creature from hell entered here?" thought the Sanuri as he left the chambers and ran down the stairs and out into the courtyard. "And why would it disguise the death as a suicide and harm no other in the castle?"

The Sanuri examined the ground underneath the balcony to Karin's chambers. There was a small stone patio and thick bushes which gave no evidence of an intruder. The Sanuri widened his circle of search until he found a print that led into the forest.

The castle of King Mathas was surrounded by a thick old forest except on the east side where it faced the shore of the Sea of Grevdt. The balcony to Karin's chambers faced southwest. When the Sanuri first entered the forest he was following a trail towards Fort Langer.

The creature walked on two legs as a man. The prints were deep within the earth; telling the Sanuri that the creature was heavy. The prints were large and somewhat resembled a human foot except instead of toes there were strange markings in the earth. The Sanuri studied the prints for several minutes before he concluded that the strange markings were caused by long, possibly curly claws that extended eight to nine inches in front of the midfoot.

Karin's body had been found several days earlier yet these prints appeared to be relatively fresh. "If this creature did not kill Karin," thought the Sanuri. "Then why did it enter her chambers?" The morning birds had not stopped singing, which the Sanuri found curious since there was possibly at least one other intruder in the forest besides himself.

The Sanuri was also curious as to why the creature made no effort to hide its trail. The Sanuri considered the chance that he was walking into a trap when he suddenly felt the earth beneath his feet give way.

Maxwell made a list of the numbers that corresponded to the characters in the code. Everyone sitting at the table copied the list for their own reference and diligently set to work. Sorren had been sitting with the group who was planning the hospital and he now joined the group who was breaking the code.

Rosa had pots of coffee brought into the Great Hall as the people worked throughout the day. Mathas had been participating with the group who was planning the hospital. Now he stood up and addressed the room of people. "My wife tells me we need to prepare for the festivities this evening. We need to set up this room."

"We'll move this to my chambers," Edward announced as he stood up and grabbed a stack of papers. Gabriel did not join the others but walked over to Hannah. "I would like to spend a little time with my beautiful wife," he whispered into Hannah's ear. She smiled and picked up her things from the table.

"Forgive us," Gabriel said to the others who were seated at the table. "But Hannah and I have seen so little of each other over the past months that I want to take advantage of this opportunity."

"And I am glad to hear that," Emeral said. "I hope the two of you spend as much time together as you can while we are here."

"Would it be rude if we didn't attend the celebration and just worked?" Michael asked Edward and Raphael.

"Yes," Raphael said. "Besides Mathas' family is your family now. Have you taken any time to get to know them?" Michael did not answer. "Michael is something wrong? It seems like you have been spending a lot of time alone since this mission started."

"Well for one, I never feel comfortable at these big celebrations. Don't get me wrong, everyone is nice, I guess they just take some time to get used to. And I really don't have anything to talk about. I mean I don't relish telling everyone about my past."

"Michael in just the short time we have all known you; you have proven yourself over and over again. Everyone accepts you for the outstanding warrior and man that you are," Raphael said. "And everyone already knows about your past so you shouldn't have to talk about it."

"I don't," Kate said. "But it's none of my business." Michael looked uncomfortable.

Batina looked at Rachel then at Kate and said, "Perhaps we should get ready for the celebration. It takes a lot longer to dress in all that fancy clothes."

"That is fine," Kate said to Batina then she looked at Michael. "I didn't mean to put you on the spot I was just being honest."

"It's not that it is a secret," Michael said. "It is just difficult to talk about."

469

"Michael, I hope you don't mind the interference of an old man," Maxwell said with a warm smile. "I think what is really bothering you is that everyone here is like one big family and they are all so caring about each other that it is hard for you not to notice the contrast with your past. It somehow makes the horror more real to you." Michael stared at Maxwell in silence. "Michael you know that everyone here accepts you as family and cares about you. You have to learn to let us in."

An hour later all of the guests in Mathas' castle started to gather in the Great Hall. "Ladies you all look so beautiful," Edward said to Kate, Nana and Risa as his team gathered around him.

"We are just lucky that Emeral had dresses made for us," Risa said. "We never thought to bring such clothing on a mission."

"That includes us too," Adin said. "Perhaps after this mission we should go home and get more of our things."

"You certainly can," Edward said. "But Sudfad already told me to have complete wardrobes made for all of you. And I apologize but we didn't have time before we came here. Emeral and Maxwell told me they were having evening clothes made for you so I knew you had enough for this mission. Tell me, do all of you have just the one set of clothing?"

"No," Ralf said. "Maxwell brought us each three suits. I don't know what Nana and Risa have."

"We have three really fancy dresses each and Emeral loaned us some of her jewelry."

"This is a social event among friends," Edward said. "But there may be times when you need to dress like this for your roles. I will get you all jewelry and anything else that you need." Then Edward looked at Kate. "I know Natasha sent quite a few things along with you but when we have time I would like to see them. If you decide to stay on the team, you will need an extensive wardrobe."

Kate suddenly became angry and said through clenched teeth, "Edward why don't we dance."

Edward laughed and took Kate's hand and led her to the dance floor. As soon as they started to dance Edward asked, "Ok so why are you mad at me now?"

"Mad at you now," Kate repeated as she was becoming angrier. "First, I haven't been mad at you before this. And secondly why don't you think I am going to stay on the team. I have done everything you told me. If you have more issues with me you need to tell me. And will you stop grinning at me. Why are you grinning, I am serious?"

"I know you are serious. I am not laughing at you. I just enjoy the fire in you. And you are right, you have made all of the corrections that I asked. You are doing a fine job. But do you realize that at least for now you are the only human woman on the team which means you are going to be working a great deal and playing major roles? You have spent your life working alone do you really think you want to make such a drastic change?"

"Honestly I wasn't sure at first but now that I have a better idea of how the team works and the kind of missions you have I do want to be part of this. You know that Thor and I are old friends, well he told me he was skeptical about this life style at first too. Then he told me about some of the missions. About how they have helped people and how grateful the people were. Thor said he is dedicated to the teams now and he knew that I would be too. The more I listened to his stories the more I realized he was right."

"Kate, I am very glad to hear you say that. But know too that you can change your mind but I would hope you would give me advanced notice."

"So you are already thinking about my replacement? Seriously Edward I don't know how to take you sometimes."

"Kate, I know what an adjustment this lifestyle has been for Vivian, Diana and their families who are here. I am just saying that this is your first mission. You are allowed to change your mind."

"Edward I don't know why but what you are saying is making me angry. After I saw those children, the ones who had been kidnapped. I, I can't even tell you the last time I cried and now I start to cry every time I think of them," Kate paused for a moment. "Believe me when I tell you that I will be staying on the team."

"Good," Edward said. "And by the way you look very beautiful tonight." Kate was wearing a strapless emerald colored silk dress.

"See there you go again," she said. "You thoroughly confuse me. One minute I don't think you like me then the next you seem to be flirting with me."

"Oh, I like you," Edward said with a hearty laugh. "I just think you are dangerous."

"What do you mean?" Kate asked with a coy smile. Then she laughed. "Edward there is a woman staring at you and she looks really mad. I think it is Toni. Now she is coming this way."

"Edward heads up," Joao yelled then laughed.

"Edward who the hell is this woman and why haven't you contacted me?" Toni yelled loudly. The volume of her voice caused others to take notice of the situation.

Edward stopped dancing and said graciously, "Toni this is Kate, she is a member of my team and a Venator from the Clan of Gesmal. Kate this is Toni she is a warrior of the Nordes Tribe." Both women glared at each other.

Stephan and Thaos walked up to Sorren and Matthew. "We are taking wagers on this one. Want to place a bet?" Stephan asked.

"Yes," said Sorren. "Joao and Dack will want to get in on this too."

"Joao, Dack," Thaos called out and motioned for the two young men to join their group."

"Toni I have my own team now, like Gabriel does. And we are working on a mission that is why I haven't contacted you," Edward said as he watched the way Kate and Toni were staring at each other.

"What! You are going to have me on your team aren't you?" Toni almost yelled.

"Perhaps we should talk about that in private," said Edward.

"Why!" demanded Toni. "You better not be telling me you let her on the team and not me."

Joao's voice rang out in the now silent room, "Thor, want to place a bet?" This comment brought laughter from many but Kate and Toni were staring at each other so intently they paid little attention to the laugher.

"You're not on the team because you are a jealous bitch who can't stay focused on anything besides Edward. No one wanted you on the team," Kate said as she pushed past Edward.

"Ladies remember where you are," Edward scolded with a grin. Edward was still talking when Toni jumped forward and threw a right punch at Kate's face. Kate ducked and side stepped the punch at the same time. Kate grabbed Toni's right arm to restrain it and punched Toni in the kidneys three times. Kate jumped back and kicked off her shoes."

"Gabriel shouldn't we stop them?" Hannah gasped.

"We will," Gabriel said but he did not move.

Toni was wearing her warrior's dress so she had considerably more freedom of movement than Kate did in her gown. Toni was larger than Kate but both warriors were fast. Toni spun and did a round house kick to Kate's stomach. Kate saw the kick coming and went into a forward roll. She got behind Toni and kicked Toni behind the knee. Toni did not go down but screamed with rage and hit Kate with the back of her left hand. The blow landed on Kate's face causing her lip to bleed.

"Mathas are you going to stop this?" Rosa asked disapprovingly. Mathas was standing with Fahron and Claudius.

"He can't we've got bets going," Claudius said and laughed.

Kate punched Toni in the small of the back then kicked her in the side of her left knee. As Toni started to stumble she lunged to the side and grabbed the skirt of Kate's dress. Simultaneously Kate jumped back and the force tore the dress.

"Good, now I can kick," Kate said and ran towards Toni who had regained her balance and grabbed Kate's outstretched leg. Kate was in the process of a flying kick when Toni grabbed her leg and slammed Kate to the floor. Toni kicked Kate in the left side. Toni quickly bent forward and grabbed Kate's hair with her left fist and was about to punch Kate in the face with her right fist when Kate kicked Toni in the jaw. The big woman stumbled backwards but didn't fall.

Kate jumped to her feet and spun around and kicked Toni in the stomach, knocking the breath out of her. Toni bent forward and Kate hit her in the back of the head with double fists. Toni fell to the floor but she was still conscious. Kate did not go in for the attack but backed up and looked at Toni. "Are you done?" Kate growled. Toni nodded. "You can have Edward but don't you question my position on the team again," Kate said and the room erupted in laughter.

Edward bent down to help Toni up but she pushed him away, "Don't you touch me!" Toni said. "We are through!"

474

"Don't push me away," Sorren said as he helped Toni up. "It was a good fight. You did well."

"Wait!" Hannah yelled. "I want to check them both for injuries."

"I'm alright," Toni said angrily.

"Let her look at you," Sorren said and led Toni towards Hannah.

"I'm going to change my dress," Kate said to Edward and picked up the pieces of her torn skirt from the floor. As Kate started to walk out of the Great Hall, Edward walked with her. "You don't have to come with me," Kate growled.

"How are you going to unbutton the back of that dress?" Edward asked then laughed. "I wouldn't be surprised if you don't have a cracked rib after that kick."

Suddenly Kate started to laugh. "So Edward, do you have any more girlfriends at this celebration?"

"I don't know; what are you doing tonight?" Edward said and grinned as Kate quickly spun around and looked at him.

"Edward are you making fun of me or flirting with…" Kate stopped talking as Edward grabbed her and kissed her on the lips. Kate kissed him back.

"Still think I am making fun of you?" Edward asked as Kate stared at him. She stepped forward and as she reached her arms upwards to put around Edward's neck he bent down and they kissed again and again and again. It was Edward who broke the embrace. "I want Hannah to look at you then perhaps we can continue this later."

Chapter XLI
Attacked

"You're quiet," Edward said when he and Kate walked into her chambers. "Are you mad that I kissed you?"

"No, I liked it," Kate said with a smile.

"Are you in pain?"

"It's nothing," Kate said and turned her back so Edward could unbutton her dress. Now that her adrenaline was no longer pumping through her and her injuries were starting to swell, Kate felt great pain.

"Your side?"

"And my head. I am kind of dizzy."

"Let's get you into another dress then I am taking you to Hannah. Hold your dress in front because I am going to look at your side."

Kate held her dress against her body with her right hand and raised her left arm with obvious pain. "You are completely bruised," Edward said. "Are you having trouble breathing?"

"No."

"Well that is a good sign. What do you want to wear?" he asked as he opened the armoire in her bedroom.

"I don't really care, why don't you pick out something," Kate said then paused. "Edward I just realized that I left my shoes downstairs."

"We'll get them," Edward said as he was concentrating on the many dresses that hung in the armoire. "Here this is beautiful," Edward said and handed Kate a black lace dress. Kate didn't say anything. "Are you going to need help?"

"I think so, sorry."

"There is nothing to be sorry for and don't worry I won't look."

Kate laughed then winced in pain. "Don't make me laugh," she said and laughed again.

"Now Kate I am going to tell you the same thing I told Toni," Hannah said. "You need someone to watch you tonight. I think your ribs are just bruised but the injuries could be worse and you took a pretty bad blow to the head when you hit the floor."

"I'll watch over her," Edward said to Hannah then he turned to Kate. "You're staying in my chambers tonight."

"What?" Kate started to protest but Edward interrupted her.

"Kate, don't argue just let me take care of you, please," Edward said. Kate smiled and nodded.

"Well, I think I will leave the two of you alone," Hannah said with a smile. "Don't be afraid…"

"The door to the room that Hannah was using for an exam room flew open. "Hannah we need you now," Chaez said. "It's the Sanuri."

Hannah grabbed her medical bag and followed Chaez, as did Edward and Kate. "Where do you want him?" Gabriel asked as he and Raphael were carrying the Sanuri. "He's lost a lot of blood."

"Take him to that little exam room," Hannah said to her husband then she turned to the Queen. "Rosa I will need hot water, towels and bandages."

"Bella and Isadore are already getting those things," Claudius said to Hannah. Then he bellowed, "Boys this could be an attack, prepare the soldiers."

"Nana is getting her medical bag," Joao said as he handed Hannah a handful of crystal necklaces. "What do you need us to do?"

"Someone needs to search his chambers, we don't know where he was attacked," Raphael said.

"We've got that," Dack said and he and Chaez quickly left the room.

"Where did you find him?" asked Hannah.

"One of the servants saw him lying in the courtyard," Gabriel said. "Do you want him on top of this table?"

"Yes."

"Hannah, I have blankets and I got more of the supplies that we brought," Emeral said as she ran into the room. "I will help you."

"The blood trail leads into the forest," Dominic said. "Seth get us some torches."

"Found it!" Joshua yelled as he examined the Sanuri's footprints below Karin's balcony. "A couple of you fly up there and see if there is any sign of a fight." Enzo and Sol immediately flew to the balcony.

"There's some strange claw marks up here on the railing," Sol yelled down to the warriors on the ground. We will check out the chambers."

"Joshua you or Thor should go up there too. You are our demon experts," Michael said as he searched the thick shrubbery underneath the balcony.

"Which one?" asked Ralf.

"Take Joshua," Thor said as he was searching the ground.

Ralf picked Joshua up and flew to the balcony just as Enzo yelled out of the window, "Found more claw marks."

High priests Gabriel and Raphael prayed over the Sanuri as Hannah, Nana and Emeral washed and tended to his wounds. The Sanuri was in and out of consciousness. "Can you make out what he is saying?" Emeral asked Hannah.

"He keeps saying the forest," Hannah replied. "Look at these wounds; I don't know what made them."

Suddenly the Sanuri opened his eyes and grasped Hannah's hand. She bend down and listened as the Sanuri whispered into her ear. "Gabriel he says to get everyone out of the forest now," Hannah said urgently and Raphael and Gabriel ran out of the room.

"Nana I know that your medicine will be more effective on him than mine," Hannah said of the Sanuri. "Is there anything else we can do?" The women were cleaning the Sanuri's wounds and packing them with crystals.

"If Gabriel or Raphael have any blessed water we should give him some to drink," Nana replied.

"I'll find them," Emeral said and quickly left the room.

"Other than that, we continue to pray," said Nana.

"Out of the forest!" yelled both Gabriel and Raphael as they ran around opposite sides of the castle. "Tell everyone to get out of the forest!" Enrops now flew into the forest repeating the message.

"What are they saying?" Lawrence asked Dominic and Seth as the three of them were several hundred yards into the thick forest.

"I don't know," Dominic said and stopped walking so he could listen.

"Out of the forest! Everyone out of the forest quickly!" screeched a small flock of Enrops as they flew towards the light of the torches that Dominic, Seth and Lawrence held.

"What is going on?" Seth called to the birds.

"We don't know but you must get out now!"

The three men turned and ran towards the castle as the ground collapsed where they had been standing.

"Gabriel told me where it was," Emeral said as she ran back into the medical room. Emeral opened one of the small vials of blessed water and poured it into a glass then handed the glass to Hannah.

Hannah propped the Sanuri's head up with her right hand and poured a little of the liquid into his mouth. "Wait a moment before you give him more," said Nana.

Within seconds the Sanuri started to moan so Hannah poured a little more blessed water into his mouth. The liquid was cleansing and fortifying the Sanuri's body. By time the glass was empty the Sanuri had regained consciousness. He tried to sit up but he was too weak and fell back onto the table.

"Lie still," Hannah said. "Can you tell us what we can do to help you?"

"Do you need some of our life force?" asked Emeral.

"No," the Sanuri whispered and closed his eyes and began to hum. A few seconds later he opened his eyes. "There is something in my back that has poison in it. Don't take it out with your hands."

Nana and Emeral turned the Sanuri onto his right side as Hannah carefully examined his back. She removed two bandages and checked the crystals and the wounds. "All these crystals are black," Hannah said as she removed the bandages from a third wound. She carefully removed the crystals and saw a tiny dark sliver embedded in the wound.

Hannah removed the sliver with a forceps and put it into a dish. Then she poured another small vial of blessed water into the wound and packed it with new crystals. "That thing is moving," Emeral gasped.

"Pour some blessed water on it," the Sanuri said weakly.

Hannah and Nana rolled the Sanuri on his back then watched as Emeral poured some blessed water on the thing in the dish. Instantly it started to smoke then it burst into flames.

"Is everyone accounted for?" Matthew yelled as he and the men he was leading returned to the castle courtyard from the forest. "Where are Thaos and Stephan?"

"They came back a few minutes ago," Ratri said. "They are in Karin's room looking at the claw marks. And we don't know if everyone is back because we don't know who ran into the forest."

Dagon and Calen flew up to Matthew and Ratri. "We found these on the ground but we couldn't find who they belonged to. There wasn't any trail," Dagon said. "It's like they just disappeared."

"We're going back in," Calen said and the two brothers flew back into the forest.

Matthew examined the knife and the unsheathed sword that Dagon and Calen had found. Both weapons had the crest of the Military of Lentz on the hilts.

"Sanuri don't try to get up," Emeral said. "You are too weak. Gabriel and Raphael are bringing everyone back from the forest. Can you tell us what attacked you?"

"I am not sure what they are called," the Sanuri whispered. "Emeral will you go to my chambers. There is a very large book that contains pictures of demons; will you get it?"

"Of course. Where is it?"

"I believe on the desk. There are a lot of books and scrolls in there."

"I will get some others to help me then," Emeral said and left the room.

"Emeral bring him another robe also," Hannah called out.

"Already thought about that," Emeral yelled back.

"Sanuri would you be able to eat anything?" Hannah asked. "It might help you to feel better?"

"I don't know," he replied.

"I will see if I can get some soup," Nana said and left the room.

"Sanuri I have never seen marks like those on your body; what made them?" Hannah asked.

"The claws of the demons."

It was another hour and a half before everyone returned from the forest. Two soldiers of Lentz were unaccounted for. No one else had seen the danger that surrounded them.

The Sanuri remained in the medical room at his request because it was close to the Great Hall. After the Sanuri had eaten he did feel stronger and was able to sit up without assistance. He was searching his book for the name of the species of demons that attacked him when all of the warriors entered the castle. After reporting to Mathas, Stephan and Thaos went back outside to increase the guards around the castle.

Sorren and a group of warriors had searched the interior of the castle for intruders. No one was missing and the only evidence of invaders were the claw marks in Karin's room.

Claudius had sent Enrops to the soldiers at Fort Langer and at Claudius' and Fahron's castles with the message that there had been an attack and everyone should be on alert.

Fahron's group was the last to return from the forest. "Is the Sanuri conscious yet?" Fahron asked Mathas.

"Yes, I was in there a few minutes ago and Claudius is with him now. All I know so far is that he was attacked by some type of demons he had never seen before. He is searching a big book he has for information about those demons."

"So let me get this straight," Claudius said to the Sanuri. "You were following some strange footprints into the forest when all of a sudden the ground collapsed under your feet. What did you fall into; a hell world?"

"I don't really know," the Sanuri replied. "I didn't fall onto anything like a hard surface. It felt like I was in a net. I couldn't see because it was so dark but there was a strange smell. Not like the smell of the hell regions. As soon as I fell into the net or whatever it was I was attacked. It was a trap because there were multiple demons stabbing me at the same time."

"How did you get out?"

"I don't really know. I am sure the heavens helped me."

"I still don't understand why you were in Karin's chambers. They are far from yours so you wouldn't be able to hear an intruder, would you?"

"Ever since Karin killed herself I have had an overwhelming feeling that we missed something in those chambers. I have gone back in and searched those rooms a couple of times. Last night I woke up and that feeling was strong so I went to her chambers again and this time I found the claw marks."

"Since it appears to have been a trap do you think the demons woke you or gave you that feeling?" asked Claudius.

"They would have to be incredibly powerful to do that."

"I am alright," Kate said later that night as Edward walked her to his chambers.

"Hannah said you should be in bed. Now let's stop in your room and get some of your things then we will go to mine," Edward said. "Is it that you don't trust me?"

Kate laughed as she opened the door to her chambers. "Why wouldn't I trust you? No, it's that we don't know what attacked the Sanuri and we could have another attack coming."

"So you think you are needed to stand watch when this place is filled with warriors and soldiers?" Before Kate could answer he asked. "Now is this everything?" and picked up a pile of clothes.

"No, my hair brush," Kate said and grabbed her brush from a table. They walked out of her chambers and next door to Edward's rooms.

"You can have the bed," Edward said. "I will take the chair."

"Edward it's your room, take the bed."

"No, now turn around so I can unbutton you."

"We can both sleep in the bed," Kate said. "But I don't think I am in any shape for..."

"Kate I brought you in here so I could watch over you; we can always have sex later," Edward said and laughed heartedly. Which made Kate laugh. "Ok it's unbuttoned; are you going to need help changing into that nightgown." Kate didn't say anything. "You know you can just admit that you need help. I will hang onto you and just step out of the dress. And don't worry I won't look." Kate laughed again. "Honey, your back is all bruised too."

"I thought you said you weren't going to look," Kate said teasingly.

"I'm not looking at the important parts," Edward said and laughed again. "Ok, I am going to put the nightgown over your head."

"So Edward have you dressed a woman before?"

"Do you really want me to answer that? Now turn around and let me see if I got it on right." Edward looked at Kate admiringly. "You really are a beautiful woman. Now under the covers with you." After Kate was in bed Edward walked around to the other side of the bed and started to take his clothes off, after a moment he asked with a grin. "Are you watching me?"

484

"Don't worry I'm not looking at the important parts," Kate said teasingly. "You know I wouldn't mind a kiss now."

Edward slid under the covers and moved close to Kate, "Like I said you are dangerous." Edward put his arms around her and kissed her on the lips. She tried to put both of her arms around his neck then winced in pain. They stopped kissing. "We can stop if this is hurting you."

"No, I just can't move that arm," she said then pulled her head back so she could look into Edward's face. "You say I am dangerous at least I don't have a hundred boyfriends."

Edward kissed her again. "So how many do you have?" He asked and kissed Kate before she could answer.

"None; I hunt a lot."

"Wrong answer."

Kate gave Edward a confused look. "I don't understand what you are saying."

"Kate, I would like you to be my girl but you would have to understand that our relationship can't be a hardship on the team. I think now you understand the missions and you are dedicated to the team. But we will always have roles to play and some of them might make you angry."

"Are you afraid that I am going to act like Toni?"

"I just think we should talk about this and I notice you haven't said you don't want to be my girl."

"If I am your girl, does that mean I am your only girl?"

"Yes," Edward said with a grin.

"Do you think you would know how to handle only one girl?" Kate asked and giggled.

"I am certainly willing to give it a try," Edward said and kissed her again then he reached over her and extinguished the candle on the table next to the bed.

They kissed passionately for several minutes before they both froze. "Is that coming from my room?" Kate whispered. Suddenly they heard the door to Edward's chambers open and they both jumped out of bed.

There was no light in the room but the intruder was making some noise. Edward punched the figure then yelled as the intruder sliced his forearm open. Kate quickly lit a candle and grabbed one of Edward's knives from a table.

"Toni what the hell are you doing?" Edward yelled as she lunged at him again with the knife.

"You humiliated me; you and your tramp," screamed Toni. Edward side stepped her lunge and punched Toni again. Blood was running from his wound and covered them both.

"Toni stop I don't want to hurt you," yelled Edward.

"Well I want to kill you and that tramp of yours," Toni yelled as Michael and Dominic ran into the room. Toni turned when she heard the men enter and Edward grabbed the wrist of her hand that was holding the knife. He slammed her hand against the dresser twice and she dropped the weapon. "Let go of me," Toni shrieked. "I'll kill you. I'll kill you both." Dominic and Michael each grabbed one of Toni's arms as Kate grabbed a towel and ran to Edward.

"We need to get you to Hannah," Kate said as she wrapped the towel around Edward's bloody arm.

"You are mine!" Toni screamed as Michael and Dominic started to drag her out of the room.

"I was never yours," Edward said with disgust.

Edward's chambers were filling with people who heard the screaming. "Take her to the dungeons," Mathas said. "I'll let Sorren decide what he wants to do with her."

Nana pushed through the crowd with her medical bag. "I need water and towels," she yelled and Risa ran from the chambers to get the items.

"Sol is getting Hannah," Joshua said as he pushed his way into the bedroom and handed Kate another towel to absorb the blood from Edward's wound.

Joao, Dack and Thor entered the bedroom and Joao started to grin when he saw Kate in a nightgown and Edward naked. "Pay up Thor," Joao said and held out his hand.

Chapter XLII
Watching Over You

When Hannah and Gabriel ran into Edward's chambers they found Nana and Risa trying to stop the bleeding of his wound as Kate was trying to put Edward's pants on him. Batina and Rachel were changing the bloody bedding.

"Ladies I am truly sorry that I am in my natural," Edward said when he saw Hannah.

"I think we are all focusing on the blood," Nana said. "You tell us if you get faint."

Dack ran into the room again and said loudly, "Kate we looked in your chambers and she tore your pillows and mattress apart. She must have lost it when you weren't in your bed." Then Dack looked at Gabriel. "Mathas is having everyone else check all of the rooms to make sure Toni didn't hurt anyone else. Unless you need me I will go."

"Dack please stay," Hannah said. "If Edward passes out, Gabriel will need help carrying him."

Sorren marched into the room angrily. Dack turned to him, "Sorren she cut up Kate's bed before she came in here and attacked Edward."

"Edward, Kate if I would have known that Toni was capable of something like this I would have warned you," Sorren said remorsefully.

"Sorren no one knew," Edward said. "But I hope you plan on leaving her locked up until she cools down."

"Oh, she is going to be locked up for a long time," Sorren said. "Can I do anything?"

"No but thanks," Kate said to Sorren then she turned to Dack, "If she didn't cut up the quilts in my room would you get them? These are bloody."

"Sanuri you shouldn't be out of bed," Hannah scolded when she saw him walk into the room.

"I am doing much better, thanks to all of you. I wanted to see if you need my help," said the Sanuri as he walked up to Edward and placed his hand on Edward's still bleeding arm. As the Sanuri prayed over Edward the bleeding slowed down, then stopped. The people stood in awe as they watched the miracle.

"Thanks," Edward said gratefully.

As the Sanuri turned to leave Batina asked, "Sanuri those demons that attacked you, do you think they had any effect on Toni? I mean to make her act like this?"

"No, Toni was listening to her personal demons not the ones in the forest."

"Edward you need to go to bed," Hannah said as she and Gabriel were preparing to leave Edward's chambers. "That pain medicine will start working soon." Then Hannah turned to Kate, "That's about three days' worth of medicine on the table. Just follow my directions. Since it is so late, don't give him anymore until morning. Are you going to be staying with him after tonight because if you aren't I can watch him?"

"I'll be moving in here," Kate said. "And thank all of you so much."

"I will be back in the morning to check on him," said Hannah.

"And I am just down the hallway if you need anything," said Nana.

Kate walked everyone out of the chambers and returned to the bedroom to see Edward struggling as he tried to take his pants off. "I will help you," she said.

"Well this is certainly romantic," Edward said with embarrassment. "Kate, you are going to have to sleep on the other side of me now."

"Why?"

"So I can hold you."

Kate smiled warmly at this comment. "Now lay back and I will cover you."

"Honey, your nightgown is full of blood. We should go next door and..."

"You are not getting out of bed. I will just take it off," Kate said and slowly pealed the nightgown off. She had been so worried about Edward that Kate almost forgot about the pain of her own injuries. Edward started to laugh as the pain medicine affected him. "What is so funny?" she asked.

"We are both naked and can't do anything about it."

Kate slid under the covers and cuddled next to Edward. She stroked his hair and said, "There will be plenty of other nights."

"So you are going to be my girl then?"

"Yes, I am moving my things in here tomorrow."

"Good. You know I wouldn't mind a kiss now," Edward said with his natural grin. As Kate kissed Edward on the lips he fell asleep.

She kissed him on the forehead and whispered, "I am going to watch over you now." Kate got out of bed and locked both the doors leading to the balcony and the doors entering the chambers. Then she took some of Edwards' weapons and placed them on the tables near the bed. Kate did not extinguish the candles before she crawled under the covers.

Because of the attack on Edward, everyone in the castle was up. Angelina accompanied her father to the dungeons to talk with Toni. Although it had been almost an hour since the attack, Toni was still filled with rage. She was pacing back and forth in the cell and yelling. Toni stopped when she heard footsteps and the look on Sorren's face brought her shame.

"I want to hear your side of the story," Sorren said.

"They humiliated me!" Toni almost screamed.

"And how did they do that?" Sorren asked in a calming voice.

"Edward has a team now and he didn't even tell me much less choose me, then he chooses that little tramp," Toni paused.

"Go on," Sorren said. Toni didn't speak. "You are also mad because Kate beat you in the fight then told you that you could have Edward; isn't that true?"

"Yes and she said it like she was doing me a favor. He was mine from the beginning!"

"Toni did you and Edward ever make love?" asked Sorren.

"No."

"Did you ever kiss?"

Toni hesitated then said angrily, "No but what difference does that make?"

"Did he ever make a commitment to you or tell you he wanted to have a relationship with you?" Sorren asked.

"No," Toni said in a lowered voice.

"Toni, Edward was never yours. He told me that he thought of you as a friend," Sorren explained. "And what Kate told you is true although I will admit she could have said it better."

"What are you talking about?" asked Toni.

"All the members of both Gabriel's and Edward's teams could see that you were blinded by jealously. Every single member voted you down because they feared you would compromise the missions. That is why you didn't go to Ryed." Toni stared angrily at Sorren but she did not argue with him. "So tonight you went to Kate's room first; why?"

"To kill her."

"You would kill a wounded, sleeping person?" Sorren asked with disgust. "Those are not the actions of a warrior. Were you afraid that she would beat you in a fair fight again?" Toni didn't say anything. "Answer me!" Sorren yelled.

"All I could think of was that I wanted to kill her and when I realized she wasn't in her bed I knew she was with Edward and I knew I had to kill him too."

"So you would have murdered two innocent people because of something you made up in your mind," Sorren said. "Toni you have brought dishonor and shame upon your tribe. There is something seriously wrong with your thinking which makes me believe you are a threat to others. You will remain in this cell until I decide what to do with you."

"If I ban you from our tribe I am just unleashing a rabid animal onto others. I am going to ask the Sanuri to look into your mind to see if there is a way to correct the evil within you. Do not turn him away because he may be your only chance to get out of prison."

"But Sorren..." Toni started to say with disbelief but Sorren and Angelina had already turned their backs on her and were walking down the dimly lit corridor.

The following morning Adrone and Paul ran into the kitchen where Natasha, Ella, Iris, and Cassandra were cooking breakfast.

"Mother we need cookies," Adrone said breathlessly.

"After you eat breakfast," Iris said.

"No they aren't for us," said Adrone.

"And we need lots of them," Paul said.

"Is something wrong?" Natalie asked as she entered the kitchen from the dining room. Natalie saw Paul and Adrone run into the kitchen.

"The boys were just telling us," said Ella.

"Ok boys what is going on?" asked Iris.

"Yesterday we went to the orphanage with Cassandra and Elan and Christopher was right that place is awful," Paul said.

"Mother did you know that none of those kids have parents?" asked Adrone.

"Yes dear I did," Iris said. As Iris spoke Luca walked into the kitchen with Emma and Hunter. Natalie motioned for Luca to listen to the boys. "But I still don't understand what you are doing?"

"Well, we were all really sad when we left there," Paul said. "So we talked and we are going to give those kids some of our toys and cookies. That's why we need cookies."

"Christopher, Joey and Nicholas are getting bags and putting toys in them," Adrone said enthusiastically. "They told us to get the cookies." Everyone in the room smiled warmly at the two boys.

"I am so very proud of both of you," Iris said and hugged her sons.

"We all are," Natasha said. "As soon as we are done with breakfast I will start baking."

"Paul, Adrone I just saw the other boys and you don't have enough toys for all those children," Luca said. "How are you going to decide who gets toys?"

"Gee we didn't think about that," Paul said. "I don't know." Adrone suddenly looked like he was going to cry.

"I have an idea," Luca continued. "What do you say if after breakfast we go into Salar and buy some more toys?"

Both Paul and Adrone got excited. "Really?" Paul asked. "Come on Adrone we have to tell the others." Both boys ran out of the kitchen.

Natalie kissed Luca on the cheek. "Anyone want to come along?" Luca asked.

"All of you watched our children the other day; I will watch yours," Natalie said.

"Well then I will go," Natasha said. "This will be fun. Vivian and Diana are doing laundry; I will check with them too."

"I will wait to see who is going before I decide," Cassandra said. "We still have cookies to bake."

"I think someone should tell Zelda and Horace what we are doing," Ella said. "I will bet that they want to help too."

The next morning Edward awoke to the smell of food and the sound of voices. "Don't you get out of that bed," Kate scolded as she and Nana walked into the bedroom. "Nana was kind enough to carry your tray for me," Kate continued. "And Matthew told me Mathas is going to hold the morning meeting in here so you can be part of it. So I have to straighten up the room."

"What's to straighten up?" Edward asked with a grin as Kate put pillows behind his back and Nana set a tray on this lap. "Thank you ladies."

"How do you feel?" Nana asked as she checked his arm for swelling.

"Really tired and weak I guess, I don't know if my arm hurts more than the pounding in my head," Edward said. "But I can't complain. I've got two angels in here with me this morning and I could be dead."

"You lost a great deal of blood," said Nana. "I will ask Hannah to give you a different pain killer for at least this morning so you don't pass out during the meeting."

"I already cut your food," Kate said as she took the towels off from the plates of food." Edward laughed.

"Edward I am not sure what the Sanuri did to help you heal," Nana continued. "There is a possibility that whatever he did could make you feel different also."

"Guess I didn't think about that," Edward said to Nana then looked at Kate and asked. "What are you doing?"

"Rosa asked me if we needed a new carpet in here. I just realized we do. Nothing to bother yourself with; just eat your breakfast."

"Well, I can give you a little news while I am here," Nana said. "Not surprising the Sanuri is doing well this morning. Sorren asked him to look into Toni's mind to see if the evil in her can be healed."

"Last night after Sorren and Angelina left this room they went to the dungeons and Sorren asked Toni a lot of questions. Angelina said that Toni was filled with rage; she was yelling and pacing when Sorren and Angelina first saw her. Angelina didn't tell me everything that her father asked but he now believes that Toni has more problems than jealously. Sorren thinks Toni is insane and he doesn't want her released from prison."

"Will Sorren ban her from the village?" asked Kate.

"Apparently that is what they normally do for punishment but Angelina said that Sorren looks upon Toni as a rabid dog. He believes Toni will hurt others like Morgan, Bruno and Nada did when they were banned from the Ice Caves."

"I agree with Sorren," Edward said. "Toni can be a lot of fun but honestly I never even kissed her. There was something about her that would make the hair on the back of my neck rise."

"Then why did you spend time with her?" Kate asked.

"Well, she came to Wetpr a couple of times I couldn't be rude and I wasn't sure if I was imagining it. Besides she didn't seem that crazy all of the time or Sorren would have seen it."

"I'm not telling either of you anything you don't already know," Nana said. "But if they do release her she will come after you again."

495

Edward's chambers were filled with people for the King's morning meeting as anticipation was high that the Sanuri would tell of his attack.

"As much as I appreciate this I feel rather foolish," Edward said. "I could have come down for the meeting."

"Hannah says you have to stay in bed," Gabriel said. "This was no problem for us to move it in here."

The Sanuri was the last person to enter the meeting. He carried a large book and several scrolls.

"Sanuri why don't you go first," King Mathas said. "We are all curious about the demons that attacked you."

"For those of you who may not have heard the story," the Sanuri said. "I had been plagued with feelings that we missed something in Karin's chambers; something important. Night before last I awoke and that feeling was overwhelming so I went to her chambers and found the claw marks which you have all now seen."

"I found unusual tracks underneath her balcony and followed them into the forest. The trail was so clear and easy to follow that the moment I wondered if it was a trap the earth opened beneath my feet."

"I fell into total darkness," the Sanuri continued. "I felt like I fell into a net and instantly I could feel my skin being torn by multiple attackers. The next thing that I remember is being carried inside of this castle."

"I found an image in this book which I believe is the species of demon which attacked me. I will pass the book around." As the Sanuri spoke he handed the book to Mathas and pointed to a particular picture.

"The demons I encountered are called Daliosis. They are an ancient species that were prevalent in this world centuries ago. From my readings it appears that there have been other times when wars among the demons occurred. The Daliosis attacked Ahriman and lost the battle, they were never seen in the World of Nunc again."

"I have no information as to where the Daliosis went but I find it curious that they have returned at this time when we were told the demons are gathering against us."

"The Daliosis live underground like the Rogetts. I believe there is an infestation of them in the forest that surrounds this castle. Have you had any of your men disappear before the attack on me?"

"No," Mathas said. "At least no one we are aware of."

"Last night I spoke with The Lion," said the Sanuri. "As I suspected he removed me from the demons lair. He said the Daliosis have returned to this world because they are fighting in the demonic wars and want to claim a hell region. But they are also assassins for hire."

"Is Juleta behind this again?" Matthew asked with frustration.

"No," the Sanuri replied. "Although she did pay Deckor a fortune to bring her father to ruin. Deckor was relieved when Juleta was banished to The Abyss and kept the money with no intention of attacking the King until Hector came to Langer. Hector is now the Insidiae Master controlling the area of the Kingdoms of Marba and Ganz. This is the area once controlled by Dieter."

"Deckor was not corrupted by Juleta he had been a member of the Insidiae long before he met her. As of yet, I do not know about all of his business dealings other than he has communicated with demons from other worlds. I believe Hector is a threat to all of you and must be taken very seriously."

497

"Ok, I still don't understand how those demons in the forest enter in to all of the rest of this," Thaos said.

"I don't believe they have anything to do with Deckor or Hector. I believe they are after me and anyone they believe might be one of The Seven Sons. I plan to return to the forest today," said the Sanuri.

"Certainly you don't plan on going alone," said Claudius.

"I won't be alone," the Sanuri said. "But I want all of you to stay here until I return."

The Sanuri had not told the people in the meeting that the previous night he had a vision about the complex labyrinth the Daliosis demons had dug under the forest and grounds of King Mathas' castle. The complexity of the maze made the Sanuri wonder how long those demons had been in Lentz. And the Sanuri was fearful of a similar labyrinth near the castle of Sudfad. Mathas had promised to write a letter to Sudfad explaining all that had happened before the Sanuri walked out of the castle.

The Sanuri entered the dense forest carrying only his staff and a sheathed sword on his belt. He did not hear birds singing or any other of the usual noises of the forests. The creatures sensed a battle was at hand.

"Tell me the spot," the Sanuri whispered to the heavens.

"You will know it when you see it," the voice of The Lion said nothing more.

"Can I speak with the two of you a moment?" Sorren asked Edward and Kate when he returned to their chambers later that morning.

"Of course," Edward said. "Is this about Toni?"

"Yes, I didn't want to bring anything up at the meeting until I spoke with the two of you first," Sorren explained. "Earlier this morning I asked the Sanuri to go to the dungeons and look into Toni's mind. The reason I did this was after the attack Angelina and I went to Toni's cell and she acted like a mad woman."

"My tribe has never put to death any of our members. If the behavior is severe we have banished warriors from the tribe. But after seeing Toni last night I am afraid I would be unleashing a monster into the world."

"I told her to cooperate with the Sanuri or she would remain in prison," continued Sorren. "What he saw confirmed my fears. She has not called to demons like Timothy did. The Sanuri said she has been feeding her personal demons until they have taken control of her. She can choose to fight them and to conquer them but I will be honest I don't think she is going to."

"I told her she will remain in the dungeons until I can decide what to do with her. I can give her a chance to change, execute her or leave her in prison because I will not set her free as she is. Since she want's both of you dead I thought I would ask for your opinions."

"Sorren I am not going to tell you to kill her," Edward said. "Yet I agree with everything you have said. The monster that was in this room last night was not the woman I have spent time with. Can the Sanuri help her?"

"Since Toni is consumed with her personal demons he cannot cast them out. She has to make her own choices in that matter but he can give her guidance. This morning she allowed him to look into her mind but she would not listen to what he had to say."

"Maybe she will listen to him after she has spent some time in the dungeons. She may try anything to get out of there," Kate said. "And I feel the same as Edward; I will not ask you to execute her."

"I am glad to hear you both say that because if you would have asked I probably would have complied with your request," Sorren said. "This is a very difficult matter for me. My people have such integrity and pride as warriors that they police themselves in a way. And from my conversation with Toni she has lost her sense of integrity and her identity as a warrior. She knew Kate was injured and she planned to kill Kate in her sleep. Only true cowards act in such a manner. Toni no longer has a place within our tribe."

"But you are afraid that if you free her she will turn into a criminal like Bruno, Morgan and Nada did," said Edward.

"That is exactly my fear," Sorren said. "I don't think it would take much for Toni to become a murderer. So unless you have objections I will keep her in prison."

"For how long?" Kate asked. "Because if you release her we would like a warning."

"I don't see how I can ever release her unless she conquers her demons," Sorren said sadly.

The Sanuri walked almost a mile into the forest when he had an overwhelming sense to stop. He looked around and the ground did not appear to be disturbed nor did anything seem unusual in this area. The trees were old forming a thick canopy which prevented sunlight from reaching the floor of the forest. Because of this there were few smaller plants or trees in this site.

The Sanuri grabbed the hilt of his sword with his left hand and pulled it from the sheath. He grasped his staff with his right hand and held both weapons high into the air. The Sanuri began to pray and as he prayed he began to glow with Holy Light. First his body, then his staff and lastly his sword were all consumed with glowing, pulsating Light.

In his mind's eye the Sanuri saw one word, *Now*. With all of his might the Sanuri plunged the staff and the sword into the ground simultaneously and yelled, "I claim these grounds for The Great Ruler. Demons be gone!"

The earth began to shake violently, trees started to fall; yet the Sanuri held his positon. He could feel the holy energy flowing through him as he acted as a conduit between the worlds.

Horses and people screamed as the quaking of the earth terrified many. People fled to Fort Langer for protection.

"I certainly hope that is the Sanuri doing that," Claudius said as he climbed to the top of the stone wall that surrounded the King's castle; where Stephan was keeping watch.

"Thaos and Matthew and I have been doing constant rounds and no one has caught sight of a demon," Stephan said. "Do you want us to look for the Sanuri?"

"No I mean yes I would, but he told us to stay here."

"Edward what do you think you are doing?" Kate yelled as she entered the bedroom and saw him getting out of bed.

"Are we being attacked?" Edward asked.

"The Sanuri went into the forest and told everyone not to follow him," Kate explained as she covered him up. "That is all I know but I can't find out any information if you get out of bed every time I turn my back."

"Kate sit down," Edward said and took her hand. "You haven't stopped moving all morning. Are you nervous about our relationship and moving in here?"

"No Edward, I'm not."

"Then what is it? You are acting different."

Tears started to well in Kate's eyes, "Last night I got so scared when she hurt you. Edward I mean really scared. I don't want anything to happen to you."

"Come here," Edward said with a warm smile as he pulled Kate onto his lap with his left arm. "I like this side of you my beautiful little warrior." Edward kissed her passionately.

They embraced until they were both breathless and sweating. "I will be so glad when I can make love to you."

Kate giggled and said with a grin, "Now what should I call you? How about my big teddy bear?" Then she kissed Edward again. "Now, teddy bear you are just going to have to get used to me watching over you. And that's all there is to it."

Small explosions were heard as the holy energy engulfed the nest of demons in their lair. The demons were running, trying to escape the Light but they had no place to go for the Sanuri was standing on the one entrance into the labyrinth.

The Sanuri's body was in stasis as he acted as a conduit for the Light. What the Sanuri did not know was that the Light was engulfing more darkness than that one nest of Daliosis demons. The thunderous quakes and the explosions were happening throughout the Continent of Opots.

The Sanuri had no sense of time, or anything else for that matter. His role was not that of a normal human on this cold morning and he played his part well.

"What the hell!" barked Fahron. "Chaez get Mathas and Claudius; they have to see this."

"How long has that been there?" Chaez asked as he walked closer to the bloody writing on the wall of the castle.

"It just appeared. Better get Gabriel and Raphael too. They are going to want to see this," said Fahron. "I will stand watch incase this is a trick."

Fahron and Chaez were walking around the exterior of the castle, checking the doors and windows when the bloody writing suddenly appeared. "I don't know if this is the only place that it showed up," Fahron said as Claudius and Mathas ran to him. "Chaez is getting Gabriel and Raphael."

The three men stood in silence and stared at the words *We are watching.*

Chapter XLIII
Tears of the Heart

High Priest Othnial wept and prayed before the altar in the monastery in Rubar Ryed. It had been several months since the murderous dictator Teivel was destroyed. But these months had been filled with terror and bloodshed as the peasants of Ryed battled the armies of two different men who would replace Teivel.

Villages were attacked and burned and the villagers executed as power hungry killers sought to control the kingdom. Fortunately for the peasants the thousands of weapons that King Sudfad and King Mathas sent to Ryed had been distributed by Dominic and his men before they left the kingdom.

The Angel Ruth had come to Erebus in a dream and told him of the plight of the peasants in Ryed. Erebus told the Angel to take his castle which was filled with weapons and provisions. Erebus also told Ruth to take the castle of the sorcerer Malus who had been killed in Taperia while helping Erebus with a job. Malus had no family. Erebus was the closest person that Malus could call a friend so Erebus took it upon himself to assume responsibility for Malus' possessions which Erebus gave to Ruth.

The following morning when Erebus awoke from his dream he was healed from the devastating burns that had crippled him. A gift to him for the choices he had made. Erebus would learn later that Ruth had distributed the wealth of the two sorcerers among the peasants. Not only did these riches feed and clothe people but they helped the peasants to purchase weapons to fight the troops who sought to murder them.

The armies of General Astar and General Geobel knew how terrified the peasants were of the dark lords and sorcerers. So as the armies burned much of Ryed they never went near the castles of Erebus and Malus where thousands of people had taken refuge.

The armies of these two powerful generals not only fought with the peasants but they fought each other. While at times the battles between these armies seemed to benefit the peasants; innocent people were still dying.

The one gift that the peasants of Ryed were given was hope. When Gabriel's team and the armies of Wetpr and Lentz killed Teivel and his demons the people of Ryed realized that monsters can be destroyed. A handful of people had entered the world of Ryed and turned it upside down. Now the citizens of Ryed knew it was up to them to stand up to their monsters.

The Clan of Gesmal had been told not to leave their village to join the civil war. The Angel Daniel told them to defend their homes if the battle came to them. Duncan and his sons had battles of their own as Sampson had reappeared in Ryed. The demon Visterle had released Sampson into the worlds to hunt for Hecate. But as the demon wars raged for territory in the World of Nunc, Visterle's focus on Hecate was moved to other issues. Visterle was fighting to become the leader of a hell region.

The demon Ale, who had turned Sampson into a low level demon had been defeated in the wars. But no sooner had Ale been destroyed than three of his lieutenants fought each other for control of Ale's territory. Without the voices of Ale and Visterle in Sampson's head, his memories slowly came back to him. Sampson was frustrated because he had been hunting Hecate for months. When the voices stopped, he returned to Ryed and moved into Hecate's lair. But his hatred for his tribe did not diminish. Sampson stalked and terrorized the Clan of Gesmal.

Two hours later the Sanuri returned to the castle of King Mathas. He was completely exhausted and simply told the King, "You are safe now." The Sanuri returned to his chambers and went to bed. It was then in a vision when the Sanuri was told the extent of the miracle which had occurred. The Sanuri saw an image of the Continent of Opots with hundreds of dark lines in the image.

Suddenly these lines were filled with light. "Thank you for using me in such a manner," the Sanuri said to the heavens.

When news that the dictator Teivel had been killed came to the people of Ryed an amazing phenomena occurred. As if one collective thought was shared by hundreds of thousands of minds, music was reborn in that kingdom. The hearts of people sang as they created words and melodies that told of their lives, their hardships and spurred them in battle.

Music fueled the fires within them and gave them strength and hope. Music was an expression, a weapon and a miracle for these prisoners of demons. Instruments were literally made out of everything and for the first time in centuries amidst the horrors of war; the people danced.

The Sanuri spent two days in bed to heal from his ordeal. During those days the members of Gabriel's and Edward's teams along with members of the ruling families of Lentz worked diligently on plans for the new hospital and on translating Deckor's papers.

While these groups were working, Matthew hired crews to clean out Deckor's house and property. It was one of the members of the cleaning crew who found things in the attic that he could not explain. The foreman of the crew contacted Matthew. After Matthew saw the attic he returned to his father's castle and brought most of the team members and the Sanuri to the home. The King, Claudius and Fahron were attending a military celebration at Fort Langer.

"Let me go first in case there are spells," the Sanuri said as he carried one of the lit torches into the attic. "It's safe," he called out after a few moments. The group walked around the huge attic and stared at the drawings.

"Sanuri do you know what these are?" asked Gabriel. "Yes, they are groupings of other worlds. See how they travel around the suns. I am not familiar with them. The question is what did Deckor do to obtain this information?"

"Sanuri, Rachel, Jasmine and Joao are going to draw these images is it safe for them to do so?" Dagon asked.

"Yes and when they return to the castle they should make many copies of what we see here," said the Sanuri.

"Is the building safe to become a hospital?" asked Matthew.

"Yes it has been cleansed," the Sanuri said to Matthew then he turned to Dagon. "Have the artists indicate the positions these images are on the walls and ceiling; that might be significant. And Matthew after all of the copies have been made, paint over these images. While there is no evil attached to them, we don't know their purpose here."

"The following day Rosa, Isadore and Bella took all of the female guests on a shopping trip and out to lunch.

"Are you supposed to be out of bed?" Gabriel asked when Edward entered the Great Hall.

"Kate watches me like a hawk; I have to take advantage of the situation," Edward said and laughed.

"And he loves every minute of it," said Dack.

"Actually I do enjoy it," Edward said with a grin. "But it is time to get to work. Actually I misspoke. Kate brought some of the papers to our room and we have been working on them. This is what we have completed." As Edward spoke he handed the papers to Raphael who was sitting to his right.

"Let's get you up to snuff," Michael said. "The more we work on these papers the more we believe they are important because Deckor is using several codes to hide the information."

"You know about the words that were written in Lithanize. But the majority of words were written in this code of numbers. As we have been translating the words we realize that the sentences don't make sense."

"Joshua started looking at these pages like a puzzle. He realized there are tiny marks on the edges of the papers. When we line those marks up with others of their kind and read across the pages we see a pattern develop. Go to the table where Joshua and Thor are sitting and you will see."

"Are you kidding me?" Edward asked loudly when he looked at the numerous sheets of paper that were spread out over several large tables. "They form pictures. Do you know what these pictures are?"

"We are working on that," Joshua said. "But you have to wonder what is so important to go to such extremes."

"Another thing," Gabriel said. "These are the papers that Deckor told Karin to take out of the safe if something happened to him. Except for a few pages she had no idea what they said or what she was supposed to do with them. We are wondering if that is why Deckor gave her as an offering to a demon; so she could be used as some sort of tool. Unfortunately we may be here a lot longer than I had planned; we can't leave until these are translated."

"What has the Sanuri said?" Edward asked.

"He was in bed for two days after he returned from the forest and since then he has been in Deckor's house. I hope to have him join us soon," Gabriel replied.

It was after midnight when the Sanuri returned to Mathas' castle. Instead of going to his chambers, the Sanuri went to the Great Hall were the coded papers were spread out on top of several tables.

"Oh My Lord, I thought I heard a noise," said Margerie one of the cooks as she walked into the Great Hall. "Can I bring you anything?"

"Thank you Margerie; I believe I will need a pot of coffee," the Sanuri replied.

Hannah and Gabriel were both catching their breath after making love. "Honey I believe I will be able to go home after next week will you be coming with me?" asked Hannah hopefully.

Gabriel rolled onto his side and propped his head up in his hand so he could look at his beloved wife. "At this point I just can't say. I want to go home but the more we work on those papers the more we are convinced they hide something of great importance. I am hoping the Sanuri will be able to help us. You know you could always stay longer."

"I had thought about that but Vivian has Daniel so she is getting up at night and feeding two babies. I feel guilty leaving her with so much work and I do miss the children."

"So do I," Gabriel said and sat up in bed. "I am very pleased with how Edward is doing with his team. He is a natural at this and will be able to work independently soon. Dominic has not made a commitment to lead a team yet. He is so disturbed by the letters he receives from High Priest Othnial that he is considering returning to Ryed. Both Raphael and I have been trying to talk him out of it."

"No he can't," Hannah said as she too sat up. "That would be a death sentence for him. He and Fennel and the others are finally having lives and aren't being hunted like animals. Would you mind if I talk to him?"

"Be my guest. I would love it if you could get through to him. Besides that he is our friend and I don't want to see him going back to that nightmare, it will help greatly to have another team."

"Have you thought of any others who could lead teams?"

"There are several members of the Patronus priests who Raphael and I have considered. We have also discussed having one of the Rualas leading a team since they know the operations but they would still have to recruit humans to play the parts."

"While I agree with what you are saying the only Rualas with that kind of experience are members of our family and team. The idea was to give us all a break, so that rather defeats the purpose."

"Lakin could easily lead a team."

"You know who I think would be a natural is Thaos. I mean the life he led before seems to fit into covert missions."

"Raphael and I have thought about that also. Stephan would also be another idea. But both are well known in Lentz so they would have to work in other areas. And honestly they are in the same boat we are; they have been in battles or on missions constantly for the last two years."

"I think you should still ask them. If you get enough teams then they should be able to rotate missions. Have you thought about Sorren, Archetenus and Jared?"

"Of those three I think that Sorren has more of the mindset but he also has many responsibilities and he too is well known in Lentz."

"Gabriel so many of the people who have worked on missions have been honored to have been chosen. I think you should bring up the idea of leading teams to several of the people we have talked about. They are all intelligent men and if they want it bad enough they will do what it takes."

"Dominic have you talked to Fennel and the others about this?" Raphael asked.

"Not yet."

"You know they will follow you back into hell and you will all be killed," Raphael said. "You can do so much good in this world please don't go on this suicide mission."

"I showed you the letters," Dominic said as he choked on his words. "They are murdering my people."

"I have an idea," said Raphael. "You know that Ruth has not abandoned those in Ryed. Let's call her together and see what she says. Will you agree to that?"

Matthew awoke and rolled over but Angelina was not in bed. He found her in the kitchen rocking baby Mathas. "Did I wake you?" Angelina asked.

"No, I don't know what woke me. I just came to see where you were. Do you want me to take him for a while?"

Stephan sat up in bed so quickly that he woke up Ingr. "Stephan what is wrong? Did you have a dream?"

"It wasn't a dream. But something is wrong I can feel it. Ingr get dressed I am going to wake the others."

"Thaos what are you doing?" asked Nikki groggily as she saw that he was out of bed and getting dressed.

"Nikki get dressed. I don't know what it is but something is wrong."

"The Angels," Nikki gasped and jumped out of bed.

"What!" Sorren yelled and sat up in bed. He looked around the room trying to figure out what woke him. "Shara where are you?" Soren asked and jumped out of bed.

Shara came running into the bedroom. "Sorren something is happening. I woke up and went into the kitchen and Sorren the entire village is awake."

"Claudius," Thaos called as he knocked on the bedroom door. "Claudius."

"What is going on?" asked Bella as she sat up in bed.

"Claudius something is wrong. Nikki thinks it's the Angels warning us," Thaos said as soon as Claudius opened the door. "Stephan is alerting the troops." Without speaking Claudius got dressed and ran out of the bedroom.

"Great Ruler be with us," the Sanuri prayed and jumped up from the table in the Great Hall. "Margerie, Margerie!" yelled the Sanuri.

"Yes My Lord," said Margerie as she ran into the hallway.

"Wake the King and tell him we are being attacked. I am going to ready the troops," the Sanuri said and ran down the long hallway.

"I know why you called me," the Angel Ruth said as she materialized in the chambers of Raphael. "Do not speak but listen. It is not Ryed that should worry you this night but your own shores. The war has started."

They wanted to be soldiers

Politicians and kings

They were never prepared

For what the darkness of man can bring

When horror becomes routine

And we no longer listen to the screams in the night

What does this say about humanity

What does this say about man's plight

Walking With Angels © 2009

By

Sandra J Yearman

Glossary of Characters

Aaron: an escaped prisoner from Wetpr

Aaryan: a male Grand Master of the Insidiae

Abaddon: an ancient demon/one of the Old Ones

Abella: daughter of Prince Lakin and Princess Zada/Ruala

Abigail: sister of Marie/ nurse for grandchildren of King Sudfad

Ackley: hired fighter for Mayor Deckor of Langer

Ackly: an arms dealer in Ryed

Adi: son of Elen and Batya/ Ruala

Adin: male Ruala warrior

Adrone: youngest son of Joshua and Iris/younger brother of Vivian/Clan of Gesmal

Adwell: Prince/ son of King Zachariah and Queen Noella of New Samona/husband of Nada/father of Misha/ Adwell was killed in battle leaving Nada to raise ten children/Ruala/

Ael: an ancient demon/ one of the Old Ones

Aetes: Shettee warrior

Ahriman: an ancient demon/ one of the Old Ones

Aiden: five year old Ruala boy/son of Artis and Jenna/nephew of Ratri

Akasha: former king of Ryed/grandfather of Nehmota

Alexander: former servant of King Roch's parents/ father of Annabelle

Alexander: one of the twin sons of Simon and Annabelle

Alexandras: King of Wetpr/brother of Jaretta/uncle of Sudfad and Roch

Alexas Rose: daughter of Matthew and Angelina

Alexis: son of Usman, the leader of the Valdore tribe

Alice: and her husband find Jorge near death in Nora

Aloeus: Shettee warrior

Amiee: sister of Marie/ nurse for grandchildren of King Sudfad

Amundsen: Commanding General of Fort Friada in the Kingdom of Ganz

Amy: a young girl who was kidnapped by Sal

Ana: eleven year old Nordes girl/daughter of Edgar and Cora/younger sister of Batina

Ana: Princess/daughter of Zeman and Oda/niece of King Manu of New Samona/Ruala

Anda: one of Chief Romogi's three wives/Huta

Andrea: female Ruala warrior/ sister of Bekka

Andres: Princess of Ryed/daughter of Oren and Astrel/ has twin sister Jorga

Andrew: jeweler in Salar

Andrus: father of Rabi/Ruala

Angelina: daughter of Sorren, Chief of the Nordes tribe/female warrior

Annabar: daughter of King Sharonne

Annabelle: handmaid and best friend to Queen Vitomas of the Kingdom of Stordt

Anthony: one of the twin sons of Simon and Annabelle

April: a young girl who was kidnapped by Sal

Arca: Enrop leader who protects King Mathas' family

Arches: a Patronus priest

Archetenus The Brave: Captain in the Taperian Army

Arianna: daughter of Simon and Annabelle

Ariel: daughter of Raul and Vitomas

Arlene: housekeeper and cook for Erebus/wife of Theodore

Armstrong: soldier and scout in the army of Wetpr

Arthur Marcus: father of Hannah

Artis: male Ruala warrior/oldest brother of Ratri/husband of Jenna

Asher: male Ruala warrior

Asher: youngest of three brothers who formed the Libertas in Ryed

Asmodeus: an ancient demon/ one of the Old Ones

Astar: General in the Military of Ryed who tries to take over the kingdom after the fall of Teivel

Astrel: former princess of Ryed/daughter of Akasha and Norah

Atomos: Elder of the Centras and Keeper of the Box of Itifer

Augustus Endleson: a wealthy businessman who owned part of the City of Nora

Ava: twin of Benjamin/daughter of Archetenus and Delilah

Baal: an ancient demon/ one of the Old Ones

Babu: Enrop

Bac: male Ruala warrior

Bachnenus: warrior guarding refugees/Shettee

Bali: Enrop leader of the flock that does battle at Juleta's castle

Balin: Prince of Norkv/son of Thaddius and Omara/grandson of Benjeman and Esther

Balius: Shettee warrior/brother of King Neputa

Banacus: General in the army of King Tobias of Puntd

Banaka: a female Grand Master of the Insidiae

Barak: Prince of Norkv/grandson of Benjeman and Esther

Barak: Prince/son of King Neputa and Queen Tiara/Shettee

Barid: Prince of Ogg

Barid: Prince of Ryed/son of Nehmota and Vasart

Barnabas: a member of the wealthy and elite in Ryed

Bart: male Ruala warrior/ married to Bekka's sister Andrea

515

Bartholomew: alias used by Raphael in Ryed

Barush: a major in the Military of Ryed

Bastra: Huta captain

Batina: young female Nordes warrior

Batya: wife of Elen/Ruala

Beatrice Endleson: wife of Augustus

Becca: Princess of Norkv/daughter of Thaddius and Omara/granddaughter of Benjeman and Esther

Behtay: Princess/daughter of Segal and Cahina/niece of King Manu of New Samona/Ruala

Bekka: female Ruala warrior

Bella: wife of Claudius and mother of Stephan

Benedict: Prince of Norkv/son of Benjeman and Esther

Benjamin: twin of Ava/son of Archetenus and Delilah

Benjeman: vicious rebel leader who overthrew the government of Samona

Benson: a Private in the Wetprian military

Bentra: an ancient demon/ one of the Old Ones

Berta: cook at Racing Horse Tavern

Berta: Queen of Stordt/wife of Micha/grandmother of Roch and Sudfad

Bertha: an elderly woman from Nora

Betsy Sarbush: wealthy socialite in the City of Langer in the Kingdom of Lentz

Betty: a woman from Nora

Betu: male Ruala warrior

Bianca: young female Nordes warrior

Black Jack: a regular patron at the Ghost Ship Tavern in Port Friada

Bode: Shettee warrior

Boris: a general in the Military of Ryed

Botis: a demon

Bremmer: an arms dealer in Ryed

Brent: a soldier from Lentz who fights in the Gefrey Games in Ryed

Brik: son of Prince Lakin and Princess Zada /Ruala

Brina: Princess of Norkv/daughter of Valor and Cai/granddaughter of Benjeman and Esther

Bruce: male Nordes warrior/eldest son of Edgar and Cora/older brother of Batina

Bryce: male Ruala warrior

Cabal: son of Karzman and Nadia

Cacu: Enrop leader that joined Raul and Simon on a mission

Cade: son of King Pergo and Queen Vinus/ Kingdom of Gandt

Cadi: daughter of Prince Hadar and Princess Paj/ granddaughter of Manu/Ruala

Cael: Shettee boy who is adopted by Thedes and Ibula

Cage: male Ruala warrior

Cahina: Princess/ married to Segal son of King Zachariah and Queen Noella of New Samona/Ruala

Cai: Princess of Norkv/wife of Valor who was the son of Benjeman and Esther

Calen: male Ruala warrior/cousin of Luca/son of Maxwell and Emeral/

Calla: female Ruala warrior

Calvin: a desk clerk at The Captain's Retreat Hotel in Port Friada

Campbell: one of the spies at the Castle at Wetpr

Canton: Cisero's second in command

Cara: Princess of Ogg

Carlsman: a Lieutenant in the Army of Lentz

Carlton: alias used by Archetenus in Ryed

Carson Dormors: a wealthy landowner in the Kingdom of Ganz

Carston: member of the governing body of Nora

Casey: male Ruala warrior/father of Melanie/husband of Tasha

Cassandra: female Ruala warrior

Cassandra: daughter of King Friada and Queen Marla of the Kingdom of Ganz

Cates: alias used by Sorren in Ryed

Cedrick Teivel: a ruthless, powerful man in the Kingdom of Ryed

Celo: Prince of Ryed/son of Oren and Astrel

Cere: daughter of Tristt/Shettee

Cerephus: General in the Taperian Army

Cerey: orphan girl/sister of Nicholas/adopted daughter of Gabriel and Hannah

Ceria: Princess/daughter of Gunnel and Uma/niece of King Manu of New Samona/ sister of Elan/Ruala

Chaez: son of Fahron

Chaladrone: an ancient demon/ one of the Old Ones

Chalice: hired fighter for Dieter

Chalta: daughter of King Pergo and Queen Vinus/ Kingdom of Gandt

Chance: works with the Patronus

Chara: three year old Ruala girl/ daughter of Orin and Rene/niece of Ratri

Charlene: a woman from Nora

Charles: Father of Cassandra, Joao and Melinda

Charles: hired farmhand of Arthur Marcus

Charter: Colonel in the Military of Ryed

Chief Romogi: leader of the Hutas/ Kingdom of Marba

Christopher: six year old boy who Luca saves from the Hutas/brother of Lila

Ciao: female Ruala warrior

Cicely: adopted daughter of Elan and Cassandra

Cisero: a member of the Insidiae

Clair: a woman from Nora

Clair: female Ruala warrior/mother of Ratri/wife of Joseph

Claudius: General in the Army of Lentz

Clay: the manager of the Teivel Manor Hotel in Ryed

Cleo: a man who works for Cicero/a vessel

Cleta: female Ruala warrior who fought in Ryed

Clifford: a general in the Military of Ryed

Cobren: Prince of Norkv/son of Grace and Makalo/Grandson of Benjeman and Esther

Compro: Taperian soldier injured at Wall of Dorath

Conrad: father of Jasmine/husband of Leta/Nordes Tribe

Cora: mother of Batina/wife of Edgar/Nordes warrior

Corina: young female Nordes warrior

Corwin: son of King Fahra and Queen Sitha of Zorta

Crater: a Sergeant in the Wetprian army

Crater: a soldier in the army of Wetpr

Crispus: a guard at King Roch's castle

Crocell: a demon

Cronn: a demon

Cronos: Shettee warrior

Curtis: male Ruala warrior who fought in Ryed

Daceron: a demon from the world of Balterak in the Mensor Galaxy

Dack: male Ruala warrior

Dacron: former prince of Ryed/is murdered by his younger brother Nehmota for the throne

Dael: an ancient demon/ one of the Old Ones

Dagon: a male Ruala warrior

Dagor: son of King Fahra and Queen Sitha of Zorta

Dai: son of Gael, grandson of Manu/Ruala

Daisy: nine year old Nordes girl/ daughter of Edgar and Cora/younger sister of Batina

Damas: an ancient demon/ one of the Old Ones

Danar: a man created to be a vessel for demons

Daniel: an emissary of The Great Ruler who takes on the disguise of a human man

Danilla: mother of King Mathas

Dano: seven year old Nordes boy/son of Edgar and Cora/youngest brother of Batina

Darius: Prince of Samona/son of Thomas and Rewel/brother of Varden

Darla: young female Nordes warrior

Darlah: sister of Marie/ nurse for grandchildren of King Sudfad

Deckor: mayor of Langer, the capital city of the Kingdom of Lentz

Delilah: wife of Dieter

Delilia: Queen of New Samona/mother of Ibula, Lakin, Gael and Hadar/ wife of King Manu/Ruala

Demanko: a demon

Demetries: a demon

Denise Froush: wife of Martin who is a wealthy ship builder in Port Friada

Denks: a soldier in the army of Wetpr

Denton: one of the spies at the Castle in Wetpr

Derek: friend of Thaos

Derlock: Huta warrior

Diana: a Venator/sister of Thor

Dieter: member of the Insidiae

Dion: Princess of Samona/wife of Yorggi who was the son of Thomas and Rewel/brother of Varden

Dixon: a Taperian soldier

Dominic Petlov: was the senior High Priest at the monastery at Malga before he was murdered

Dominic: oldest of three brothers who formed the Libertas in Ryed

Dorme: Prince of Ogg

Doros: works for High Priest Meekos

Douma: King of Ogg

Dresden: a Sergeant in the Wetprian army

Duncan: Chief of the Clan of Gesmal in Ryed/ husband of Liza

Duran: father of Nikki/Nordes tribe

Dymas: Shettee warrior

Eachann: Shettee warrior

Edgar: father of Batina/husband of Cora/Nordes warrior

Edith: wife of Lloyd a banker in Nora

Eilig: male Ruala warrior

Elan: male Ruala warrior/son of Gunnel and Uma/

Eldridge: works with the Patronus

Elen: son of Andrus and Naomi/ brother of Rabi/ Ruala

Elexas: a female Nordes warrior

Ella: female Ruala warrior/mother of Bekka/wife of Sam

Eloise: a store clerk in Salar

Eloise: female Ruala warrior/oldest sister of Bekka/wife of Tony

Elsa: female Ruala warrior/mother of Mia/wife of Tyron

Emeral: mother of Calen/Ruala

Emeric: a male Grand Master of the Insidiae

Emma: daughter of Luca and Lila

Emmet: worker for Gabriel

Emon: a male Grand Master of the Insidiae

Enzo: male Ruala warrior

Erebus: sorcerer from Ryed

Erwat: a member of the Half-Man's Tribe who helps the Clan of Gesmal

Esser: Prince/son of Segal and Cahina/nephew of King Manu of New Samona/Ruala

Esteban: a member of the Insidiae

Esther: Queen of New Norkv/wife of rebel leader Benjeman

Fabron: Prince of Ogg

Fadil: a male Grand Master of the Insidiae

Fahra: King of Zorta

Fahron: General in the Army of Lentz

Fairoot: demon/ lieutenant for Salzar

Fala: female Ruala warrior

Farnsworth: General in charge of building Fort Serpha in Wetpr

Fatima: Prince of Ryed/ son of Oren and Astrel

Fatronas: an ancient demon/one of the Old Ones

Felistine: a member of the wealthy and elite in Ryed

Fengu: Enrop leader who helps Gabriel and his group against Omnibus

Fennel: one of three brothers who formed the Libertas in Ryed

Ferguson: a Sergeant in the Army of Lentz

Fiona: mother of Nadia/grandmother of Michael

Fraisier: a businessman and member of the Insidiae in Nora

Frank: a villager in Telmark

Fred Stapleton: a farmer in Wetpr

Friada: King of the Kingdom of Ganz

Gabriella: sister of Marie/nurse to grandchildren of King Sudfad

Gad: male Ruala warrior

Gael: Prince/son of King Maru and Queen Delilia/Ruala

Gala: a healer from the Kingdom of Stordt

Galen: male Nordes warrior

Geobel: General in the Military of Ryed who tries to take over the kingdom after the fall of Teivel

Geof Thurstand: ship owner/husband of Linda

Geoff: Prince of Lentz/son of Princess Isabella and Captain Josef

Geoff: Prince of Norkv/son of Benedict and Sasaha/grandson of Benjeman and Esther

Georganson: an arms dealer in Ryed

George: an advisor for King Fahra of Zorta

George: middle son of Chief Duncan and Liza of the Clan of Gesmal in Ryed

Giles: hired fighter for Mayor Deckor of Langer

Giovani: Rachel's older half-brother

523

Gita: wife of Hadi/ Ruala

Gladys: member of Nordes tribe/ mother of Nikki

Glenda: great, great, great grandmother of Gala/ a healer from the Kingdom of Stordt

Grace: Princess of New Norkv/daughter of Benjeman and Esther

Gracie: cook for the Arthur Marcus family

Grady: worker for Gabriel

Great Ruler: God

Gregory Bancar: a wealthy landowner in the Kingdom of Wetpr and member of the Insidiae

Greta: older Ruala woman/friend of Emeral's

Greta: wife of Hugo/mother of Sasha/ sister-in-law of Sorren

Gunnel: Prince/ son of King Zachariah and Queen Noella of New Samona/husband of Uma/father of Elan/Ruala

Gus: owner of Racing Horse Tavern

Haas: a Lieutenant in the Wetprian military

Hadar: Prince/son of King Manu and Queen Delilia/Ruala

Hadi: son of Andrus and Naomi/ brother of Rabi/ Ruala

Hadi: son of Andrus and Naomi/brother of Rabi/Ruala

Hadu: female Ruala warrior

Halsal: Sergeant in the Military of Lentz

Hamon: one of the members of the Nordes Tribe who was injured in an attack at Snakes Crossing

Hamond: General of the Taperian Army who declares himself king

Hanger: one of the spies at the Castle at Wetpr

Hangered: Wetprian soldier

Hannah: physician in Nora/ Roch murdered her sister

Harold: husband of Berta/part owner of the Racing Horse Tavern

Harold: owner of the general store in Nora

Harriet Marcus: mother of Hannah and Laurabelle/wife of Arthur

Harris: male Ruala warrior who fought in Ryed

Harrison: Lieutenant in the Military of Lentz

Hatus: General in the Army of Lentz/on loan to Sudfad

Hector: fighter hired by Juleta

Hector: Prince of Samona/son of Varden

Henry: and his wife Alice find Jorge in Nora

Henry: husband of Noreen/father of Jacob

Hermanas: second in command to Archetenus at Wall of Dorath

High Priest Aaron: member of the Patronus

High Priest Alfonso: a member of the Patronus

High Priest Amos: a member of the Patronus

High Priest Barnabas: most Senior High Priest of the monastery at Leven

High Priest Caleb: member of the Patronus

High Priest Ephraim: a member of the Patronus

High Priest Gabriel: member of the Patronus/demon hunter

High Priest Gideon: a member of the Patronus

High Priest Gregory: member of the Patronus

High Priest Joseph: member of the Patronus, in charge of the Cicero Headquarters

High Priest Josiah: member of the Patronus

High Priest Meekos: priest at the monastery at Malga

High Priest Nicholas: most Senior High Priest of the monastery at Philiste and most Senior High Priest of the Patronus

High Priest Othnial: Senior High Priest of the monastery in Rubar in the Kingdom of Ryed

High Priest Paulas: member of the Patronus

High Priest Phanuel: member of the Patronus

High Priest Philetus: member of the Patronus in charge of Malga Headquarters

High Priest Pravis: priest at the monastery at Malga

High Priest Raphael: a leader of the Patronus

High Priest Rueben: member of the Patronus in charge of Nora Headquarters

High Priest Silas: a member of the Patronus

High Priest Tenebrae: priest at the monastery at Malga

High Priest Timothy: was murdered by Meekos, Pravis and Tenebrae

High Priest Tyrus: a member of the Patronus

High Priest Uriel: member of the Patronus

High Priest Vincent: assigned to the monastery at Malga before he was murdered

High Priest Zophar: priest at monastery at Malga/ trained as a healer

Hobart: a man who works for demons

Horace: father of Rachel and Zach/husband of Zelda/freedom fighter in Ryed

Hores: son of Chief Romogi and Anda, Kingdom of Marba/Huta

Horta: Prince/son of Gunnel and Uma/nephew of King Manu of New Samona/brother of Elan/Ruala

Hugo: younger brother of Sorren/father of Sasha/husband of Greta

Hunter: Prince of Samona/son of Varden

Hunter: son of Natalie and Troy/Clan of Gesmal

Ian Maxwell Luca: son of Koby and Bekka

Ian: husband of Mia/ brother in law of Calen/ Ruala

Ibula: warrior princess and healer of the Ruala tribe/daughter of King Manu and Queen Delilia/

Iden: warrior guarding refugees/Shettee

Igor: brother of King Sharonne

Ike Ferguson: elderly neighbor of Gabriel and Hannah

Imad: a male Grand Master of the Insidiae

Ina: daughter of Mia and Ian/ Ruala

Ingr: female warrior of Nordes tribe

Inon: one of Cisero's men/a vessel

Ipos: an ancient demon/ one of the Old Ones

Iris: mother of Vivian/wife of Joshua/Clan of Gesmal in Ryed

Irit: daughter of Hadi and Gita/ Ruala

Isabella: Princes of Lentz, sister of Mathas, Renya and Tasha, married to Captain Josef

Isadore: wife of Fahron

Isla: daughter of Prince Lakin and Princess Zada/Ruala

Isla: female warrior of Nordes tribe

Ivan: youngest son of Chief Duncan and Liza of the Clan of Gesmal in Ryed

Jace: husband of Oda/ brother in law of Calen/Ruala

Jack: member of governing body of Nora

Jackson: a private in the Army of Lentz

Jackson: an escaped prisoner from Wetpr

Jacob: boy who Angelina found in the woods

Jacot: son of Prince Lakin and Princess Zada/ grandson of King Manu/Ruala

Jaden: Sergeant in the Army of Lentz

Jago: son of Elen and Batya/ Ruala

Jake: hired fighter for Mayor Deckor of Langer

Jake: works for Talverson Transport Company in Port Friada

Jakiv: Prince/son of Segal and Cahina/nephew of King Manu of New Samona/Ruala

Jama: Enrop leader who protects Chief Sorren's family

James: Taperian soldier

Jana: female Ruala warrior

Janja: Princess/daughter of Gunnel and Uma/niece of King Manu of New Samona/ sister of Elan/Ruala

Janson: Wetprian soldier

Jared: hired fighter

Jaretta: King of Stordt/husband of Queen Lillian/ father of Roch and Sudfad

Jarrod: works for Pravis/leads attack on castle in Wetpr

Jarvis: a farmer who is killed by escaped prisoners

Jasmine: young female Nordes warrior

Jasper: a large white dog that Gabriel brings home

Jasper: Prince of Lentz/son of Princess Isabella and Captain Josef

Jatu: Enrop leader who protects Fahron's family

Jeb: friend of Thaos

Jeb: one of Cisero's men

Jela: Queen of Samona/wife of Varden

Jenna: female Ruala warrior/married to Ratri's oldest brother Artis

Jenny: secretary of Mayor Deckor

Jeremy: cousin of Andrew the jeweler in Salar

Jerik: a male Grand Master of the Insidiae

Jess: a soldier of Wetpr

Jillian: Queen of Ogg/wife of King Douma

Jinn: an ancient demon/ one of the Old Ones

Joao: male Ruala warrior

Joey: adopted son of Elan and Cassandra

Jonas: Captain in the Taperian Army

Jonathan Gabriel Maxwell: son of Calen and Natasha

Jonathon Blackmoore: a physician who attended college with Hannah

Jonathon: a waiter at the Calla Lily Restaurant in Teivel Ryed

Jorga: Princess of Ryed/daughter of Oren and Astrel/ has twin sister Andres

Jorge: a cook who is kidnapped from Endleson Hotel in Nora

Josef: Captain in the Lentz military/ married to Princess Isabella, sister of King Mathas

Joseph: male Ruala warrior/father of Ratri/husband of Clair

Joseph: nine year old Ruala boy/son of Artis and Jenna/nephew of Ratri

Joshua: father of Vivian/husband of Iris/Clan of Gesmal in Ryed

Josie: an escaped prisoner from Wetpr

Juleta: cousin to Raul and Simon/daughter and oldest child of King Mathas and Queen Rosa

Kadin: a member of Valdore tribe

Kagen: a man who kidnaps and exploits children

Kalee: female Ruala warrior/married to Ratri's older brother Quinn

Karin: wife of Mayor Deckor of Langer

Karl: two year old Ruala boy/son of Artis and Jenna/nephew of Ratri

Karta: male Ruala warrior

Karzman: leader of Kozach tribe/ stepfather of Michael

Kasper: Prince/son of Zeman and Oda/nephew of King Manu of New Samona/Ruala

Kata: Princess/daughter of Gunnel and Uma/niece of King Manu of New Samona/ sister of Elan/Ruala

Kate: a Venator from the Clan of Gesmal

Khryriss: an ancient demon/ one of the Old Ones

Kiana: Princess/daughter of Gunnel and Uma/niece of King Manu of New Samona/ sister of Elan/Ruala

Klass: Lieutenant in the Wetprian Army

Koby: male Ruala warrior

Koh: son of Prince Gael and Princess Mada/grandson of King Manu/Ruala

Kora: Princess/ married to Raphael son of King Zachariah and Queen Noella of New Samona/ mother of Luca/ Raphael and Kora were killed in battle when Luca was a small boy/Ruala

Korth: son of Tristt/Shettee

Kraus: hired fighter and intended vessel, works for Dieter

Kretcher: Commanding General of Fort Polta in Wetpr

Krister: Princess of Samoan/daughter of Thomas and Rewel

Kyra: young sister of Marie/ friend of Petra

Laban: Prince of Samona/son of Yorggi and Dion/grandson of Thomas and Rewel

Lael: daughter of Nina and Rhea/ Ruala

Lakin: Prince/son of King Manu and Queen Delilia/husband of Zada/Ruala

Lala: Princess/daughter of Adwell and Nada/niece of King Manu of New Samona/ sister of Misha/Ruala

Lana: female Nordes warrior

Lana: female warrior of the Nordes tribe

Lana: Princess/daughter of Segal and Cahina/niece of King Manu of New Samona/Ruala

Lani: daughter of Mia and Iar./Ruala

Lara: one of Usman's wives

Larson: a fighter hired by Juleta

Laurabelle: Hannah's sister who was murdered by Roch

Laurel: Annabelle's mother and former servant of King Roch's parents

Lawrence: a member of the Libertas

Lazo: fighter hired by Juleta

Lea: Princess/daughter of Adwell and Nada/niece of King Manu of New Samona/ sister of Misha/Ruala

Leith: four year old Ruala boy/son of Quin and Kalee/nephew of Ratri

Leo: Prince of Samona/son of Darius and Rebek/grandson of Thomas and Rewel

Leon: Captain in the Military of Ryed/ a member of Teivel's inner circle

Leta: mother of Jasmine/wife of Conrad/Nordes Tribe

Lieutenant Tarp: Lieutenant in the Wetprian Army

Lila: seventeen year old girl who Luca saves from the Hutas/sister of Christopher

Lilian: female warrior of the Nordes tribe

Lillian: Queen of Stordt/wife of Jaretta/ mother of Roch and Sudfad

Lily: daughter of Calen and Natasha/Ruala and human

Linda Thurstand: wife of Geof/lover of Mayor Deckor

Liza: wife of Duncan the Chief of the Clan of Gesmal in Ryed

Lloyd: banker in Nora

Loftus: Commanding General of Fort Styls

Loni: daughter of King Frieda and Queen Marla of the Kingdom of Ganz

Louie: works for Talverson Transport Company in Port Friada

Luca: male Ruala warrior

Lucene: male Nordes warrior/oldest son of Hugo and Greta/older brother of Sasha

Lucifer: an ancient demon/ one of the Old Ones

Lucile: a member of the wealthy and elite in Ryed

Lucky: Sally's puppy

Luque: Prince/son of Segal and Cahina/nephew of King Manu of New Samona/Ruala

Mab: a female Grand Master of the Insidiae

Mable: a servant in the castle of King Nehmota of Ryed

Mabon: warrior guarding refugees/Shettee

Mada: Princess /wife of Prince Gael/Ruala

Madam Bular: owner of a dress shop in Port Friada

Madix: General in the Army of Ryed/member of Teivel's first inner circle

Maggie: elderly store owner in Salar

Mahon: son of King Neputa

Makalo: Prince of Norkv/husband of Grace who was the daughter of Benjeman and Esther

Malana: daughter of King Neputa

Malard: Captain in the military of Wetpr

Mali: Princess of Norkv/daughter of Makalo and Grace/granddaughter of Benjeman and Esther

Maligma: an ancient demon/ one of the Old Ones

Malik: member of the Insidiae

Malus: sorcerer from Ryed

Mandrake: Taperian soldier

Manu: King of New Samona/The Chief of the Grand Council made up of Rualas and Shettees/ father of Ibula, Lakin, Gael and Hadar/husband of Delilia

Manutu: King of the Gants

Marcia: friend of Hannah's/ Roch's men murdered her family

Marcus Stephan: son of Stephan and Ingr

Margarit: daughter of King Mathas and Queen Rosa of the Kingdom of Lentz/ cousin of Raul and Simon

Margerie: female cook of King Mathas and Queen Rosa

Margo: a young girl who was kidnapped by Sal

Margolia: girl from Nora who was sacrificed to a demon

Marie: a cook for King Sudfad and Queen Renya

Markus: a soldier in the Army of Wetpr

Marla: High Priest Meekos' housekeeper

Marla: Queen of the Kingdom of Ganz

Marsha Jarvis: a sixteen year old girl who is raped and killed by Timothy

Martha: a cook for Cerephus

Martha: hotel owner in Telmark

Martin Froush: wealthy ship builder in Port Friada/husband of Denise

Martin: a member of the Libertas

Mary: Jared's young wife who was brutally murdered by Hutas

Mata: Igor's wife

Mateo: Chief Healer of the Ruala tribe

Mathas Sorren: son of Matthew and Angelina

Mathas: King of Lentz/ brother to Queen Renya

Matilda: one of Usman's wives

Matthew: son of King Mathas and Queen Rosa of the Kingdom of Lentz/ cousin of Raul and Simon

Matty T: son of Stephan and Ingr

Maximus Bartholomew Joshua: twin son of Misha and Diana/brother of Thor Adwell Gabriel

Maxwell: father of Calen/ Ruala

Maxwell: infant son of Nina and Rhea/grandson of elder Maxwell/Ruala

Melanie: female Ruala warrior/daughter of Casey and Tasha

Melina: mother of Thaos

Melinda: grandmother of Misha

Melinda: older sister of Cassandra and Joao

Mia: daughter of Maxwell and Emeral/ Ruala

Mia: female Ruala warrior/daughter of Tyron and Elsa

Mica: Princess of Norkv/daughter of Benedict and Sasaha/granddaughter of Benjeman and Esther

Micha: oldest son of Joshua and Iris/older brother of Vivian/Clan of Gesmal

Micha: son of King Sharonne/ grandfather of Sudfad and Roch

Michael: ancient king of Wetpr/father of Queen Sumona

Michael: son of Sudfad and Nadia

Milo: male Ruala warrior

Miranda: daughter of Raul and Vitomas

Miranda: emissary of The Great Ruler who takes on the disguise of a human seer

Miriam: a friend of Hannah's/works at Endleson Hotel in Nora

Misha: male Ruala warrior/lieutenant

Molach: a member of the Insidiae

Moloch: an ancient demon/one of the Old Ones

Morris: member of governing body of Nora

Morton: Cedrick Teivel's original name

Muhar: Shettee warrior

Myla: wife of the owner of the Dragons Inn in Salar

Naal: warrior guarding refugees/Shettee

Nabi: male Ruala warrior

Nada: Princess/ married to Adwell son of King Zachariah and Queen Noella of New Samona/ mother of Misha/ Adwell was killed in battle leaving Nada to raise ten children/Ruala

Nadene: a member of the wealthy and elite in Ryed

Nadia: wife of Karzman/mother of Michael

Nana: female Ruala warrior

Naomi: mother of Rabi/ Ruala

Napo: Enrop leader who protects Claudius' family

Natalie: female Venator/wife of Troy/mother of Hunter

Natasha: sister of High Priest Gabriel

Nathaniel: Sorren's oldest son/ Nordes tribe

Nebula: son of Chief Romogi and Anda/ Kingdom of Marba/Huta

Nehmota: King of Ryed

Nelpus: Shettee warrior

Neputa: leader of the Shettee tribe when it was conquered by the Hutas

Nestor: a demon that specializes in procuring things for a price

Nica: Enrop leader who protects Sudfad's family

Nicholas: orphan boy /brother of Cerey

Nicolas: Prince of Puntd/son of King Tobias and Queen Tasha

Nieatzae: an ancient demon/ one of the Old Ones

Nikki: female warrior of Nordes tribe

Nina: daughter of Maxwell and Emeral/Ruala

Nina: youngest daughter of Karzman and Nadia

Nita: Princess/daughter of Adwell and Nada/niece of King Manu of New Samona/ sister of Misha/has twin brother Waed/Ruala

Noah: a member of the Libertas

Nobel: former prince of Ryed/son of Akasha and Norah/father of Nehmota

Noel: a cook at the Teivel Manor Hotel

Noella: the first Queen of New Samona/wife of King Zachariah/mother of seven sons/Ruala

Norah: former queen of Ryed/grandmother of Nehmota

Noreen: mother of Jacob/ wife of Henry

Norris: hired fighter and intended vessel, works for Dieter

Nyla: oldest daughter of Karzman and Nadia

Oda: daughter of Maxwell and Emeral/ Ruala

Oda: Princess/ married to Zeman son of King Zachariah and Queen Noella of New Samona/Ruala

Odam: male Ruala warrior

Odell: one of the spies at the Castle at Wetpr

Oliver: a member of the Libertas

Omar: Prince/son of Zeman and Oda/nephew of King Manu of New Samona/Ruala

Omara: Queen of Norkv/wife of Thaddius who was son of Benjeman and Esther

Omnibus: an ancient demon/ one of the Old Ones

Omoria: former queen of Ryed/wife of Nobel/mother of Nehmota

Opago: an ancient demon/ one of the Old Ones

Orcus: Shettee warrior/brother of King Neputa

Oren: former prince of Gandt who marries princess Astrel of Ryed

Oriah: name used by the Grand Master Banaka

Orin: male Ruala warrior/older brother of Ratri/husband of Rene

Ottillia: Princess of Lenz/daughter of Princess Isabella and Captain Josef

Otu: son of Hecate and Sampson

Padre Augustus: a member of the Patronus

Padre Bartholomew: survives the massacre at the monastery at Avaide

Padre Cornelius: a member of the Patronus

Padre Darius: a member of the Patronus

Padre Dibon: a priest at the monastery at Malga

Padre Dominick: priest at monastery at Malga

Padre Edgar: member of the Patronus

Padre Edward: a member of the Patronus

Padre Finn: Patronus priest assigned to the Cicero HQ

Padre Francis: priest at monastery at Malga

Padre Joram: member of the Patronus

Padre Lucas: a member of the Patronus

Padre Markle: a Patronus priest

Padre Nebat: alias for Dominic leader of the Libertas

Padre Octavos: runs orphanage in Salar

Padre Philip: a member of the Patronus

Padre Philip: a priest at the monastery at Malga

Padre Simpson: priest at the monastery at Malga

Padre Sorben: a member of the Patronus

Padre Sornce: Patronus priest assigned to the Cicero HQ

Padre Stephens: priest at monastery at Malga

Padre Thomas: priest at the monastery at Malga

Padre Tobias: a member of the Patronus

Padre Xavier: priest at monastery at Malga

Paj: Princess/wife of Prince Hadar/Ruala

Pallas: Shettee warrior

Pata: daughter of Chief Romogi and Trina/Huta

Paterson: a Private in the Wetprian military

Patrick: owns a company of mercenaries/ a member of the wealthy and elite in Ryed

Patris: six year old Nordes girl/daughter of Hugo and Greta/younger sister of Sasha

Paul: third son of Joshua and Iris/younger brother of Vivian/Clan of Gesmal

Paulas: a man who works for Cicero/a vessel

Paulas: Sergeant under Archetenus in Taperian Army

Paullo: works for High Priest Meekos

Pearl: eldest daughter of King Tobias and Queen Tasha of Puntd

Pergo: King of the Kingdom of Gandt

Peter: Sorren's second son/Nordes tribe

Peters: member of the governing body of Nora

Petorus: an ancient demon/one of the Old Ones

Petra: peasant boy from Ort who saves Padre Bartholomew

Phifer: nine year old Nordes boy/ son of Hugo and Greta/younger brother of Sasha

Philip: Prince of Puntd/ son of King Tobias and Queen Tasha

Phillip: Court Physician to the Royal Family of Wetpr

Polgate: one of the men who kidnapped Petra

Potomas: warrior guarding refugees/Shettee

Powell: a lieutenant in the Military of Lentz/stationed at Fahron's castle.

Prescott: a hired killer

Quin: male Ruala warrior/older brother of Ratri/husband of Kalee

Rabi: male Ruala warrior

Rachel: member of the freedom fighters in Ryed

Radnor: a male Grand Master of the Insidiae

Rael: Prince of old Samona/husband of Krister who was the daughter of Thomas and Rewel

Rahi: a female Grand Master of the Insidiae

Rakio: Prince/son of Adwell and Nada/nephew of King Manu of New Samona/brother of Misha/Ruala

Rako: a male Ruala warrior

Ralf: male Ruala warrior

Raphael: Prince/ son of King Zachariah and Queen Noella of New Samona/husband of Kora/Ruala/father of Luca/ Raphael and Kora were killed in battle when Luca was a small boy/Ruala

Ratri: male Ruala warrior

Raul: Prince/son of King Sudfad and Queen Renya of the Kingdom of Wetpr

Raum: an ancient demon/ one of the Old Ones

Rebek: Princess of Samona/wife of Darius, who was the son of Thomas and Rewel

Rebke: six year old Ruala girl/ daughter of Orin and Rene/niece of Ratri

Remi: an Enrop

Rene: female Ruala warrior/married to Ratri's older brother Orin

Renya: Queen of Wetpr/ wife of Sudfad

Rewel: Queen of Samona/wife of Thomas/mother of Varden

Rex: a notorious pick pocket in Port Friada

Rhea: husband of Nina/ brother in law of Calen/ Ruala

Ridon: General in the military of Wetpr

Riftca: male Ruala warrior

Riker: a scout in the Wetprian military

Riley: an abused dog that Luca saves

Risa: female Ruala warrior

Risha: a witch who deals with potions

Roch: King of the Kingdom of Stordt/brother of King Sudfad

Rogers: one of the men who kidnapped Petra

Rolif: son of Chief Romogi and Silva/ Kingdom of Marba/Huta

Romale: member of the Insidiae

Romos: an elder of the Centras

Rosa: Queen of Lentz/wife of King Mathas

Rosalie: a dressmaker in Nora/wife of Peters

Ruth: emissary of The Great Ruler who takes on the guise of a frail old woman

Ryan: grandson of Jeb/friend of Thaos

Rybkin: Warlock who worked for the dictator Teivel

Sabot: member of the Insidiae

Sahil: a male Ruala warrior

Sal: a murderous pedophile/also goes by the name Tyrone

Sally: a young girl who was kidnapped by Sal

Salzar: powerful demon on Sidus

Sam: male Ruala warrior/father of Bekka/husband of Ella

Samael: a demon as powerful as Ahriman who rules the hell world Xibalba

Samara: wife of Tristt/Shettee

Samat: son of Chief Romogi and Silva/ Kingdom of Marba/Huta

Samos: Prince of Norkv/son of Thaddius

Sampson: oldest son of Chief Duncan and Liza of the Clan of Gesmal in Ryed

Sampson: Sergeant in the Taperian Army

Samuel: a high priest at the monastery at Malga who was murdered

Samuel: Prince of the original Samona/grandson of Thomas and Rewel

Samuel: second son of Raul and Vitomas

Sanuri: a holy man/emissary of The Great Ruler/warrior

Sar: an Enrop

Sar: male Ruala warrior

Sara: daughter of Usman

Sarah: baby granddaughter of Mathas and Rosa

Sarah: housekeeper for Claudius and Bella

Saran: daughter of Karzman and Nadia

Sasaha: Princess of the original Samona/granddaughter of Thomas and Rewel

Sasha: young female Nordes warrior

Sasha: female warrior of the Nordes tribe/wife of Galen

Satan: an ancient demon/ one of the Old Ones

Satter: male Ruala warrior

Sattleman: a Sergeant in the Wetprian army

Sauer: male Ruala warrior

Saunders: a Taperian soldier

Saxton: powerful lieutenant who works for Teivel the dictator of Ryed

Schroeder: man who works for Insidiae leader Dieter

Schuester: Commander of a special unit of Teivel's government/identifies betrayers

Segal: Prince/ son of King Zachariah and Queen Noella of New Samona/husband of Cahina/Ruala

Seguna: former princess of Ryed/daughter of Akasha and Norah/ committed suicide

Selen: house keeper for Juleta

Seth: a member of the Libertas

Shanksaw: mercenary

Shara: wife of Sorren/Nordes tribe

Shard: Captain in the Military of Ryed/ a member of Teivel's inner circle

Sharon: one of Mayor Deckor's lovers

Sharonne: King of Stordt; great, great, grandfather of King Roch and King Sudfad

Shon: son of King Fahra and Queen Sitha

Shone: Princess/daughter of Zeman and Oda/niece of King Manu of New Samona/Ruala

Sicily Bella: daughter of Stephan and Ingr

Sila: Princess of Ogg

Silva: one of Chief Romogi's three wives/Huta

Simmons: Commanding General of Fort Nir

Simon: adopted son of King Sudfad and Queen Renya of the Kingdom of Wetpr

Sinclair: King of Lentz/father of King Mathas

Sirius: works for High Priest Meekos

Sitha: Queen of Zorta

Smoking Joe: a regular patron at the Ghost Ship Tavern

Sol: male Ruala warrior

Sonja: female warrior of the Nordes tribe

Sophie: cook and servant of King Roch

Sorren: leader of the Nordes tribe

Soto: male Ruala warrior who leads first death squad for criminals

Sporos: priest turned demon

Stephan: Captain in Army of Lentz/son of Claudius and Bella

Stiller: a fighter hired by Juleta

Stolas: an ancient demon/one of the Old Ones

Stone: an alias used by Dominic during the mission in Ryed with Gabriel's team

Stone: hired fighter and intended vessel, works for Dieter

Sudfad: King of the Kingdom of Wetpr and brother to King Roch of Stordt

Sudfad: little Sudfad is grandson of King Sudfad

Sumona: Queen of Wetpr/wife of Alexandras/aunt of Roch and Sudfad

Swenson: one of Shanksaw's hired men

Syrius: a Bakken hired by Juleta

Tabeth: daughter of Fahron

Tabith: son of Tristt/Shettee

Tabitha: Princess of Lentz/daughter of Princess Isabella and Captain Josef of Lentz

Tadeo: Prince/son of Adwell and Nada/nephew of King Manu of New Samona/brother of Misha/Ruala

Tafer: a warlord who drove the Hutas out of the Kingdom of Norkv after years of wars and rebellions

Tahira: a female Grand Master of the Insidiae

Tahira: Princess of Samona/granddaughter of Thomas and Rewel

Tal: son of Oda and Jace/ Ruala

Talmai: Shettee boy who Thedes and Ibula adopt

Tambor: male Ruala warrior

Tamour: General in the Army of Lentz/on loan to Sudfad

Tanner: a Lieutenant in the Wetprian army

Tanner: a Sergeant in the Army of Lentz

Tapster: a demon who works for Meekos

Tarig: a lieutenant in the Huta army

Tarin: son of King Neputa and Queen Tiara/Shettee

Tarla Grey: wealthy socialite in the City of Langer in the Kingdom of Lentz

Taron: Prince/son of Adwell and Nada/nephew of King Manu of New Samona/brother of Misha/Ruala

Tasha: female Ruala warrior/mother of Melanie/wife of Casey

Tasha: Queen of Puntd/ married to Tobias/ sister of Renya and Mathas

Tate: a Lieutenant in the Wetprian Army

Tatterd: a Sergeant in the Wetprian military

Tavin: son of Prince Lakin and Princess Zada/Ruala

Teddy: male Nordes warrior/son of Edgar and Cora/ older brother of Batina

Tega: housekeeper for the cabins of the captains of the Taperian Army

Tegman: soldier of Wetpr

Tehtfote: a Lieutenant for Dieter

Temark: villager of Neva

Tetly: a mayoral candidate in Langer/ Kingdom of Lentz

Tetro: Huta warrior who was a captive in Ogg

Thadddius: Prince of the new Kingdom of Norkv/son of Benjeman

Thaddies: member of Nordes tribe/ father of Ingr

Thanatoes: an ancient demon/ one of the Old Ones

Thaos: a hired fighter

Thatcher: Prince/son of Zeman and Oda/nephew of King Manu of New Samona/Ruala

Thatus: Taperian soldier

The Lion: emissary of The Great Ruler who takes on the appearance of a lion when he is in the world of man

Thedes: warrior guarding refugees/Shettee

Theodore: handyman for Erebus/husband of Arlene

Theodore: the physician at Fort Stanus in the Kingdom of Wetpr

Thomas: King of the original Kingdom of Samona/father of Varden

Thomas: second son of Joshua and Iris/older brother of Vivian/Clan of Gesmal

Thomas: the young husband of Zoya who was murdered in Taperia

Thompson: Wetprian soldier

Thor Adwell Gabriel: twin son of Misha and Diana/brother of Maximus Bartholomew Joshua

Thor: a Venator/brother of Diana

Thronson: one of Meekos hired killers

Tiara: Queen of Shettee tribe when it was conquered by Hutas/wife of Neputa

Timothy: son of Fahron

Tina: Mother of Cassandra, Joao and Melinda

Tito: member of Valdore tribe

Titus Derek: son of Thaos and Nikki

Titus: a lieutenant in the Taperian Army

Tobart: a member of the Nordes tribe

Tobey: a carriage driver in Ryed who helps Gabriel's team

Tobias: King of Puntd.

Tomas: works for High Priest Pravis

Tome: a businessman and member of the Insidiae in Nora

Tomi: son of Usman the leader of the Valdore tribe

Toni: young female Nordes warrior

Tony: male Ruala warrior/ married to Bekka's oldest sister Eloise

Toomback: Huta warrior

Torance: father of Thaos

Torin: oldest son of Karzman and Nadia

Trace: male Ruala warrior

Tratz: one of the men who kidnapped Petra

Travor: Taperian warrior who was injured at the Wall of Dorath

Tresdore: son of King Sharonne

Trevor: Prince/son of Zeman and Oda/nephew of King Manu of New Samona/Ruala

Tria: daughter of Oda and Jace/Ruala

Trina: one of Chief Romogi's three wives/Huta

Trina: Princess/daughter of Zeman and Oda/niece of King Manu of New Samona/Ruala

Trist: a male Ruala warrior

Tristt the Horrible: Shettee warrior

Tritor: a powerful demon of Sidus and ex-lover of Hecate

Troy: male Venator/husband of Natalie/father of Hunter

Tye: Prince of Norkv/son of Princess Grace and Prince Makalo

Tyron: male Ruala warrior/father of Mia/husband of Elsa

Tyson: Wetprian soldier

Ulger: a demon

Uma: Princess/ married to Gunnel son of King Zachariah and Queen Noella of New Samona/mother of Elan/Ruala

Umar: Prince/son of Adwell and Nada/nephew of King Manu of New Samona/brother of Misha/Ruala

Uri: an Enrop

Uri: son of Nina and Rhea/ Ruala

Usman: leader of the Valdore tribe

Valdus: name used by the Grand Master Emeric

Valerie: young female Nordes warrior

Valor: Prince of the new Kingdom of Norkv/son of Benjeman and Esther

Vandrew: Petra's male tutor

Vania: Princess of Samona/daughter of Yorggi and Dion/granddaughter of Thomas and Rewel

Varden: last king of Samona/he and his family were murdered by rebels

Vardin: one of the men who kidnapped Petra

Vasart: Queen of Ryed/ wife of Nehmota

Viktor: an ancient priest in Ryed who tried to stop the Insidiae

Vinca: Queen of Stordt, wife of Sharonne

Vincent: Prince of Ryed/son of Nehmota and Vasart

Vinus: Queen of the Kingdom of Gandt

Visterle: a powerful demon

Vitomas: Queen of Stordt

Vivian: a demon hunter from the Clan of Gesmal

Voltar: Prince of Samona/son of Darius and Rebek/grandson of Thomas and Rewel/later becomes King of Wetpr

Vuall: a demon

547

Waed: Prince/son of Adwell and Nada/nephew of King Manu of New Samona/brother of Misha/has twin sister Nita/Ruala

Wallis: member of governing body of Nora

Wanda Ferguson: elderly neighbor of Gabriel and Hannah

Wickfield: editor of the most powerful newspaper in the Kingdom of Lentz

Wilard: Captain at Fort Polta

William: son of Jared and Zoya

Willis: son of King Pergo and Queen Vinus/ Kingdom of Gandt

Xeni: a female Grand Master of the Insidiae

Yara: daughter of Nina and Rhea/Ruala

Yorggi: Prince of Samona/son of Thomas and Rewel/brother of Varden

Yori: son of Usman the leader of the Valdore tribe

Yuri: Prince/son of Adwell and Nada/nephew of King Manu of New Samona/brother of Misha/Ruala

Zac: one of the men who kidnapped Petra

Zachariah: first King of New Samona/husband of Queen Noella/father of seven sons/Ruala

Zack: eight year old brother of Rachel

Zada: Princess/wife of Prince Lakin/Ruala

Zadok: a male Grand Master of the Insidiae

Zede: an ancient demon/ one of the Old Ones

Zehmann: an ancient demon/ one of the Old Ones

Zelda: mother of Rachel and Zack

Zeman: Prince/ son of King Zachariah and Queen Noella of New Samona/husband of Oda/Ruala

Zieman: a demon

Zorda: Taperian soldier injured in battle at the Wall of Dorath

Zortus: demon/lieutenant of Visterle

Zoya: a seer from Taperia

Glossary of Terms

Aboultis: the calling cards of demons

Abrax: the planet that orbits closest to the three suns/ uninhabited

Abyss: a vast void used to imprison demons

Acura: the whispering shadows/are in the inner circle of demons that directly serve the Old Ones

Adros: one of five solar systems in the Mensor Galaxy

Alferto: a type of grain that is common in Opots

Amark: ancient language of the Great Ruler

Amulth: means filth in the language of demons/these monsters are made out of the waste of tortured souls from the hell dimensions

Anewa: one of seven continents in the world of Nunc

Aplewort: an herb when mixed with water purges poisons from a body

Asherane: ancient tribe that lived in the northern regions of the Kingdom of Lentz

Ashta: a common herb/when the dried leaves are boiled they give off a pleasant scent

Astras: the ancient underground city of the Centras

Astrum: the solar system that consists of three suns that form a triangle and seven planets

Backor: one of the eight worlds in the Naz Solar System in the Mensor Galaxy

Balterak: one of the eight worlds in the Naz Solar System in the Mensor Galaxy

Beltrad: a species of lower level demons

Blood rings: Large red rubies set in silver with markings of the Old Ones

Boca: a covered wagon pulled by horses

Box of Itifer: a gift to the world of man from the Great Ruler; this gift affects the balance of creation

Bozie: a game of skill played by the Nordes tribe

Cava plant: a poisonous plant that grows freely near bodies of water

Centras: ancient race of creatures who have the responsibility of protecting the Holy Box of Itifer

Cerfic: an ancient language widely spoken among many kingdoms/a language of the masses not royalty

Chalice of Ascension: a gift from the Great Ruler, this gift contains unimaginable powers

Cicero College: in Wetpr, outside of Salar, where Raul, Simon and Hannah attended college

Clan of Gesmal: a tribe of demon hunters who live in the southern region of the Kingdom of Ryed

Crystal pillars: in the Ice Caves of Mordv/are blessed by the Great Ruler and filled with spiritual life force

Czarsta: one of seven continents in the world of Nunc

Daliosis Demons: an ancient species of demon that lives underground in lairs

Demalogs: an inferior species of demons

Demosa: a slow acting poison from the cava plant

Diamond of Cazo: a gift from the Great Ruler, this gift can unleash powers from the center of the world

Dirtx: one of the eight worlds in the Naz Solar System in the Mensor Galaxy

Durisks: large demonic birds/their elongated beaks contain rows of fangs

Ekel Beast: similar to a deer

Engas: a wild cat that inhabits the Vandrew Mountains

Engor: a small pack animal that lives in trees

Enrop: a large species of bird that can speak many human languages

Epocos: one of the original tribes in the Kingdom of Ryed

Farduth: a Shettee necklace that symbolizes a male has completed his rite of passage to become a warrior

Filsum: the sixth planet in the Astrum Solar System/ two moons

Frebre: one of five solar systems in the Mensor Galaxy

Fuln: one of the eight worlds in the Naz Solar System in the Mensor Galaxy

Gafet: an ancient Shettee weapon

Gants: large apelike creatures/Watchers of the Caves of Muldun

Gate of Isula: the only opening in the great Wall of Dorath

Gefrey Games: games of sport where men fight each other and great beasts to the death

Grand Masters: the first people to call to the demons and invite them into this world

Great Ruler: God

Half-Mans: a tribe of creatures that are partially human and partially nature. They are three feet tall and walk on two legs but can change their coloring to match their environment.

Hall of Antiquities: a giant hall located in the monastery at Malga/ a sanctuary for holy items and manuscripts

Hall of Light: the Great Hall in the Ice Caves of Mordv

Hengers: giant blue eagles/ birds of war

Highland Pass: the only passage through the Rosu Mountain Range

Holy Scrolls: gifts given to each kingdom by the Great Ruler, these gifts contain powers, wisdom and immortality

Holy Vault: a secret vault under the King's study in the castle in Wetpr designed to protect holy objects

Horn of Asher: a horn used by the Patronus warrior priests to signal each other

Horn of Cass: a horn used by the Wetprian soldiers to signal each other

Horn of Cornwell: a horn used by Dieter's men to signal each other

Horn of Eel: a horn used by the Ruala warriors to communicate with each other

Horn of Esker: a horn used by the Valdore Tribe to communicate with each other

Horn of Ire: a horn carried by the Taperian soldiers to communicate with each other

Horn of Shana: a horn carried by the soldiers of Lentz to communicate with each other

Horn of Tula: a horn used by the members of the Nordes Tribe for communication

Horn of Vamont: a horn used by the Kozach Tribe for communication

Horn of Xepoltr: a horn used by the Shettee warriors to communicate

Huta: a race of humans that is driven by hatred and ideas of racial superiority who live in the Kingdom of Marba

Insidiae: means conspirators/a highly organized secret group of humans who have sold their souls to demons

Irtma: one of the eight worlds in the Naz Solar System in the Mensor Galaxy

Jacar: giant leech-like creatures

Jacept Plant: a plant that a powerful poison is made from

Jaze: one of the eight worlds in the Naz Solar System in the Mensor Galaxy

Kafer: a small crescent shaped knife carried by the Beltrad

Keepers of the Scrolls: the Royal Family of the Kingdom of Wetpr entered into a covenant with the Great Ruler to protect his gifts until a time when they can be safely given back to the world of man

Kier: one of five solar systems in the Mensor Galaxy

Kozach: a tribe that lives in the far north central regions of the Kingdom of Wetpr

Lafz: one of five solar systems in the Mensor Galaxy

Lamsman: an ankle bracelet worn by Venatores/stones in the bracelet signify great feats they had to accomplish to become a demon hunter

Learning Center: the first of its kind/a complex educational facility that is open to multiple peoples and guards the students and staff from terrorists

Leaves of the Talamar plant: used for food and medicine but also used in black magics to alter people's senses and to create illusions of the mind-in small quantities/ in large quantities can effect time/

Libertas: the name of a group of freedom fighters in northern Ryed

Linges plant: a plant that grows in damp, swampy regions in Opots/the white berries are used to make the drug Melanwhop

Lithanize: an ancient language common to the southern kingdoms of Opots.

Lynswood: an herb that reveals tracks that are concealed by black magic

Mark of Satan: a coiled red snake with green eyes and a yellow tongue

Matu potage: a food staple of the Shettee tribe

Mayka: one of seven continents in the world of Nunc

Melanwhop: a drug made from the linges plant, causes lethargy and apathy

Mensor Galaxy: is 20,000 light years from the Astrum Solar System/this galaxy contains five solar systems: Adros, Kier, Lafz, Frebre and Naz

Mordov: the special place in hell for hypocrites

Motfer: the land of the dead

Naz: one of five solar systems in the Mensor Galaxy/this solar system has eight worlds: Balterak, Nords, Jaze, Fuln, Backor, Dirtx, Irtma and Puner

Nefandus: a secret sect within the Insidiae

Nordes: a tribe of fiercely trained warriors who live in the northern region of the Kingdom of Lentz

Nords: one of the eight worlds in the Naz Solar System in the Mensor Galaxy

Nunc: the world where this story takes place/third planet from the three suns

Old Ones: the original demons that came to the world of Nunc

Opatu bread: a food staple of the Shettee tribe

Opots: one of seven continents in the world of Nunc/the continent where this story takes place

Oran: a tobisk that is filled with a mixture of ramni oil, buruto powder and meno salts, designed to explode on impact

Orantho: the seventh planet in the Astrum Solar System/inhabited/four moons/ large planet/many hell worlds

Patronus: an elite group of men who serve as the protectors of the church

Pfison screen: a type of demonic cloaking devise/it is sensitive and has to be calibrated for the specific individuals it is intended for

Planteen: the fourth planet in the Astrum Solar System/inhabited/two moons

Plyogram: a drawing containing pictures within pictures to hide secret messages.

Porto: one of seven continents in the world of Nunc

Prophesy of the Blood Moon: a demonic prophesy that predicts the doors to hell being opened.

Prophesy of Izera: Predicts the downfall of the Teivel regime

Propilatry: a powerful form of demonic curse

Prostras: an ancient tribe that once inhabited the Ice Caves of Mordv

Puner: one of the eight worlds in the Naz Solar System in the Mensor Galaxy

Raftifa: ancient bat-like creatures that devour human flesh

Ravens: messengers used by the dark lords

Recupero: a sect within the Insidiae that worships the demon Omnibus

Rogetts: a tribe of humans that have digressed into murderous mutant monsters

Rualas: an ancient tribe of warriors said to be half human and half bird

Salszar: one of seven continents in the world of Nunc

Salts of Envoy: a sleeping potion

Schumack roots: used for food and medicine but also used in black magics to alter people's senses and to create illusions of the mind-in small quantities/ in large quantities can effect time/

Scio: a crystal ball

Scroll of Imari: a gift of the Great Ruler, a scroll that unleashes the power of The Box of Itifer

Seal of Natun: a gift from the Holy Ruler that can open doors to other worlds

Serpents of Satan: can only be called forth by dark lords and demons, large red snakes with green eyes and yellow tongues

Seven Sons Prophesy: an ancient prophesy about seven sons who stand up against the demons and dark lords

Shesone: an ancient fighting style of the Shettee tribe

Shettee: an ancient tribe of warriors said to be half human and half lion

Sidus: the fifth planet in the Astrum Solar System/inhabited/red fog surrounds the planet

Solv: a specific prison within the Abyss

Song of the Second Son: an ancient prophesy about an evil that is passed between second sons of a family resulting in a monster that brings terror and darkness to the world of man

Sundra Templer: a gift from the Great Ruler that was stolen by dark lords/an orb with extraordinary powers that can be used in multiple ways such as transporting humans through other worlds

Tabutu: an ancient form of fighting developed by the Asherane tribe of the Kingdom of Lentz

Talisman: an object with magical or supernatural meaning

Talmuth: giant red dragon-like creatures

Taluth: a light weight metal used to make the ancient Shettee weapons called the Gafets

Tameric: the place where Karzman claims he came from although it does not exist on any map of Opots

Tangers: large wild, grazing animals that travel in herds

Tansof: one of seven continents in the world of Nunc

Tarus demon: huge, power creatures that walk on two legs but have the head, neck and shoulders of an ox

Telgras: a hell beast that looks like it is half wolf and half panther

Teragon: death terror/a monster created as a result of diabolical acts

Terbot bear: a bear that roams in the northern regions of the continent of Opots

Tervator: fourteen foot monster that walks like a man with long dark hair over its entire body and bull   like horns protruding from its head

Texts of Semalia: ancient texts about demonic language and rituals

The Book of Horror: a book that is worshipped by demons/contains prophesies

The Celebration of Days: an annual celebration of the Centras

The Hall of Understanding: the building in Astras where the history of the Centras is documented in drawings

The Hunters: another name for the Shettee Tribe

The Lion: a very powerful messenger of the Great Ruler assumes the form of a lion when he walks in the worlds of man

The Thirteenth Color: not seen in the world of man it is the color of horror/hell

Timbar: ghost dragons/ demons that can fly

Tinchure water: an herbal pain remedy used by the Nordes tribe

Tincture of the Redeti Plant: Hutas dip the tips of their weapons in this insect infested liquid. The insects lay eggs inside of the victim. When the eggs are mature and hatch, two inch worm-like creatures are produced and will eat the organs of the victim causing a long and painful death

Tobisks: sphere shaped objects, metal and hollow inside that are designed to be launched from a Trebuchet

Traxsor: the second planet in the Astrum Solar System

Trebuchets: wooden machines used to catapult objects

Trimoth: a game of skill, strength and speed

Triolie: a Nordes gambling game

Tygrus: a ship that docked in Port Friada

Unholy altar: altar used to worship demons

Valdees: the tribe that lives in the underwater Kingdom of Ogg

Valdore: a tribe of merciless separatists who live in the extreme northern regions of the Kingdom of Lentz

Venator: means hunter in the old language

Venom of the Atha serpent: one of the poisons that Hutas put on their arrows

Vessel of Darkness: a human created from darkness to hold the essence of a powerful demon

Wall of Dorath: a giant wall that separates the Kingdoms of Norkv and Xepoltr from the Kingdom of Marba

Willimonns: small furry creatures that are hunted for food and sport

Xelope: the oneness of spirit with all that lives

Yellow Jay: a bird native to Opots

Yellow Mandeze: a song bird common to Opots

Zehno demon: thin, creature with long red and blue plumes on the back of its head with large eyes and round mouths

Zendoti: demons that are distinguished by the geometrically shaped tuffs of hair that protrude from their heads

Glossary of Maps

The maps are displayed in order of relevance

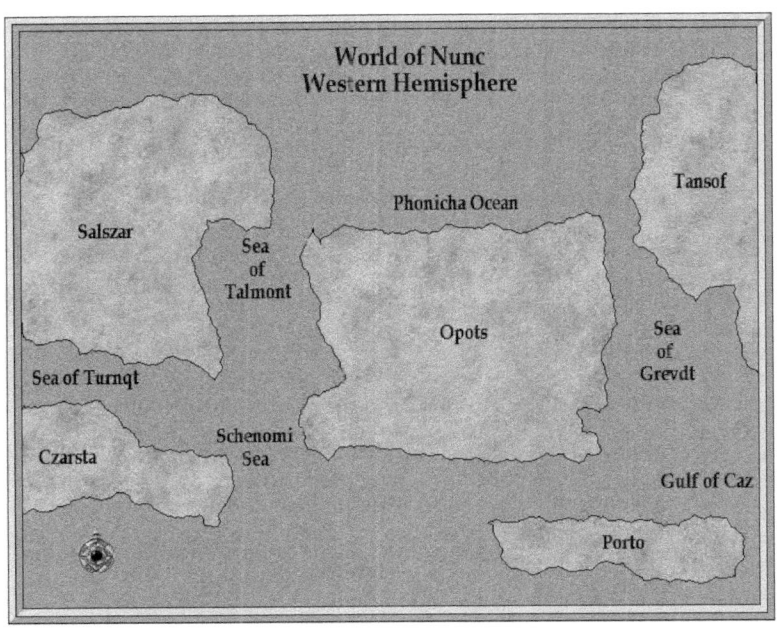

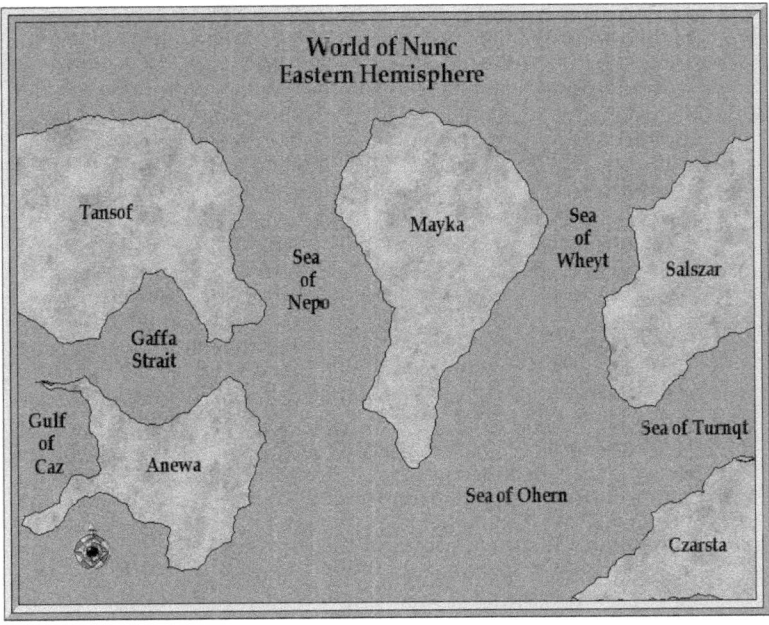

Continent of Opots
With new forts

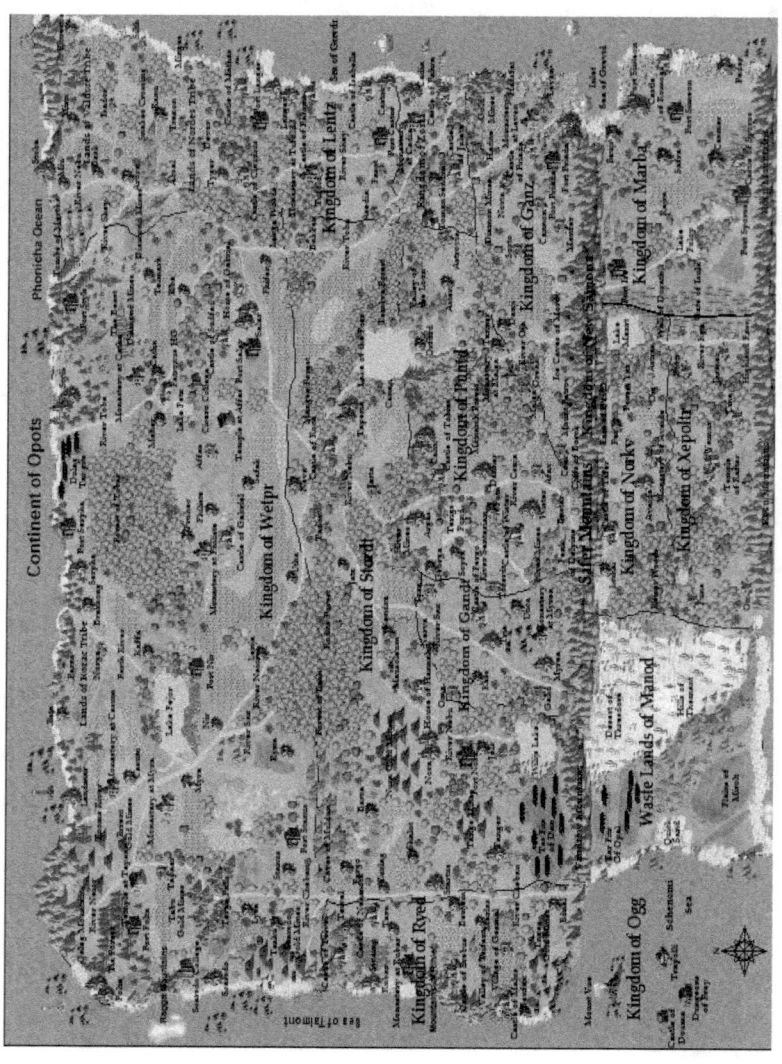

Western Stordt
With Fort Nora

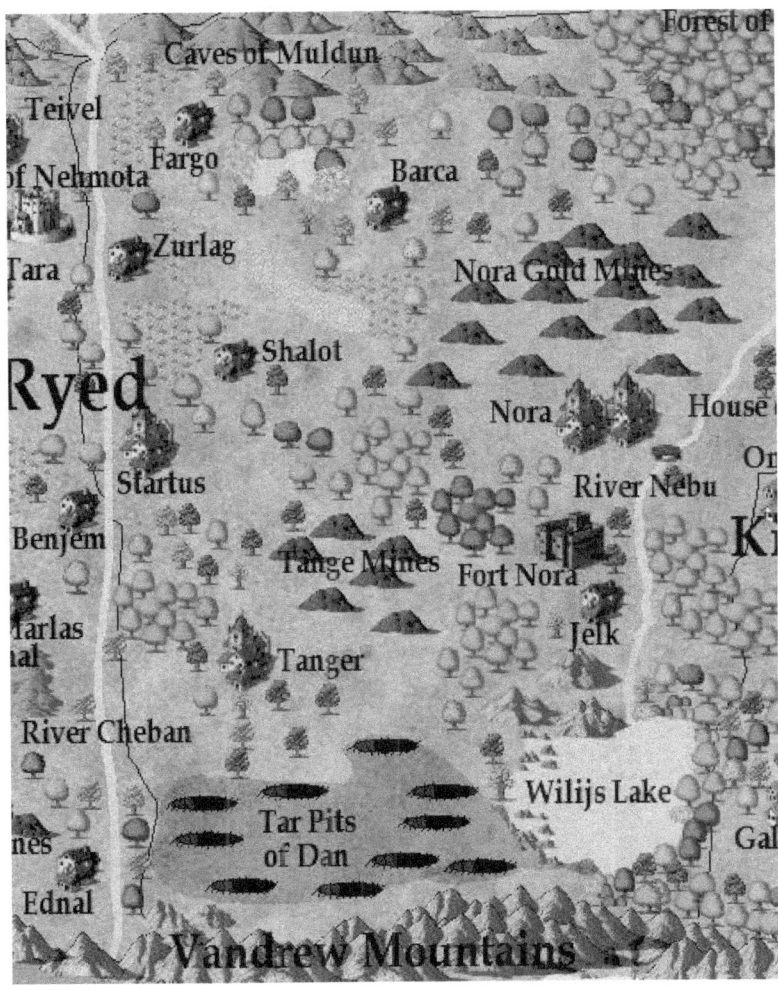

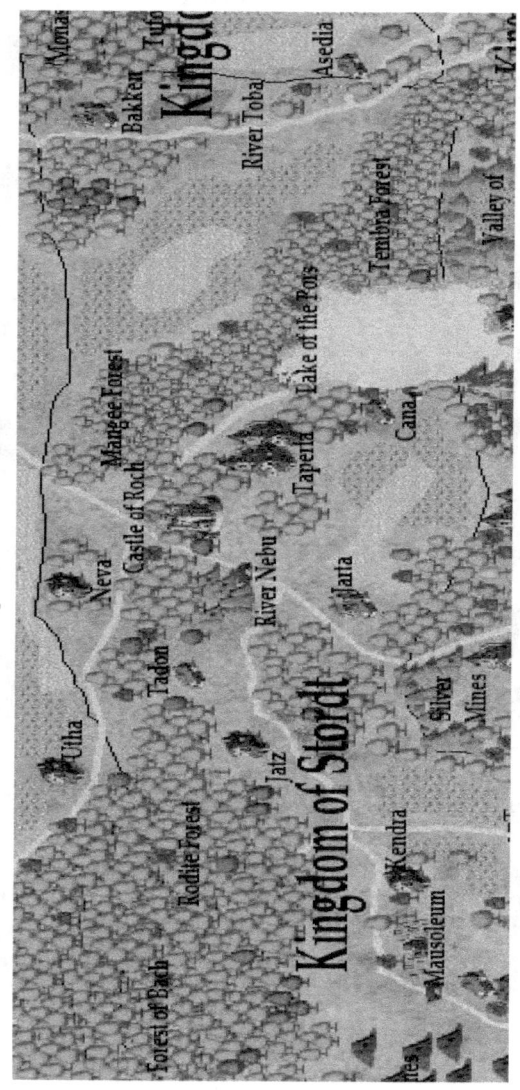

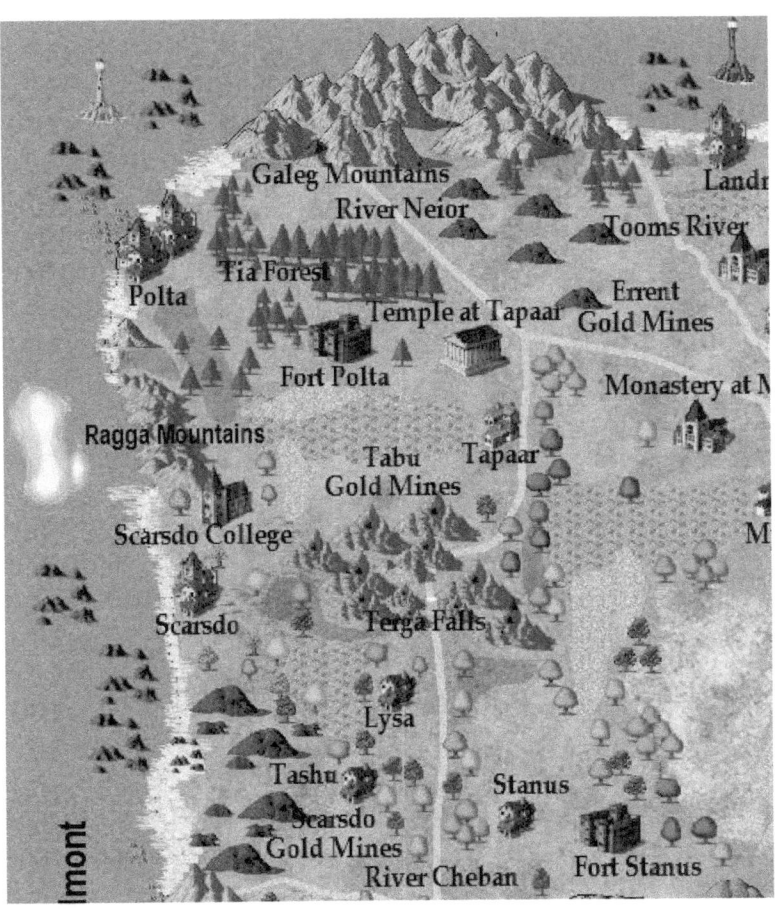

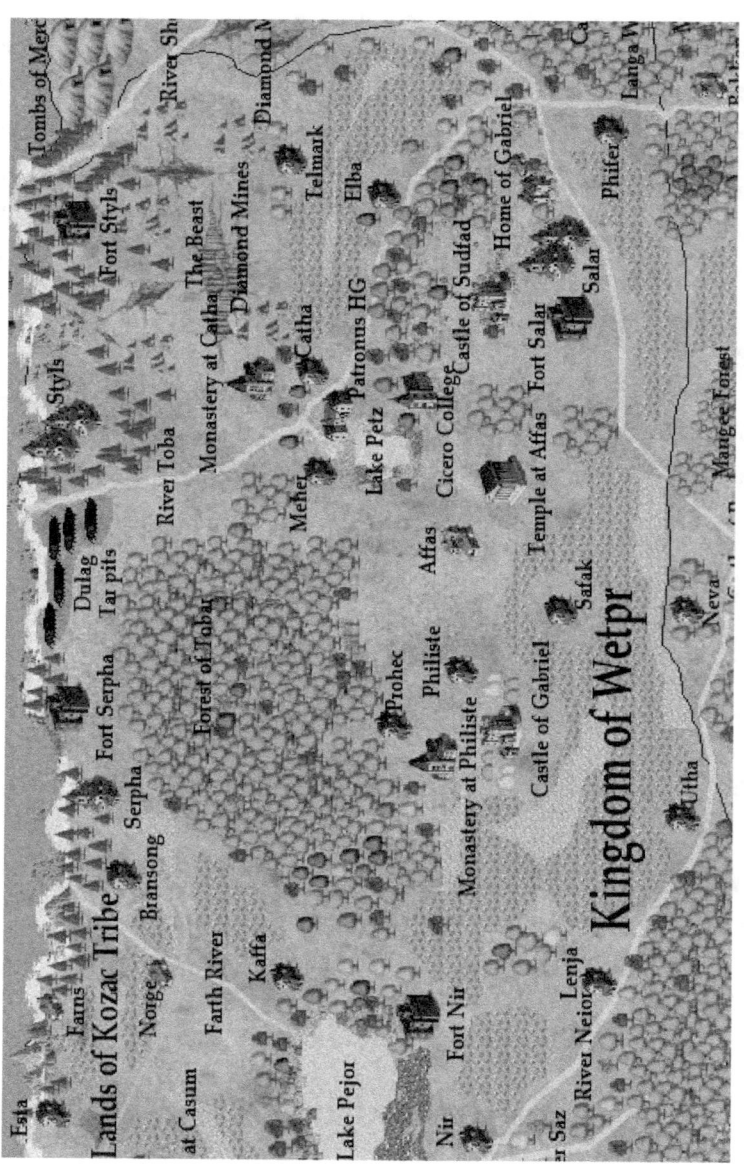

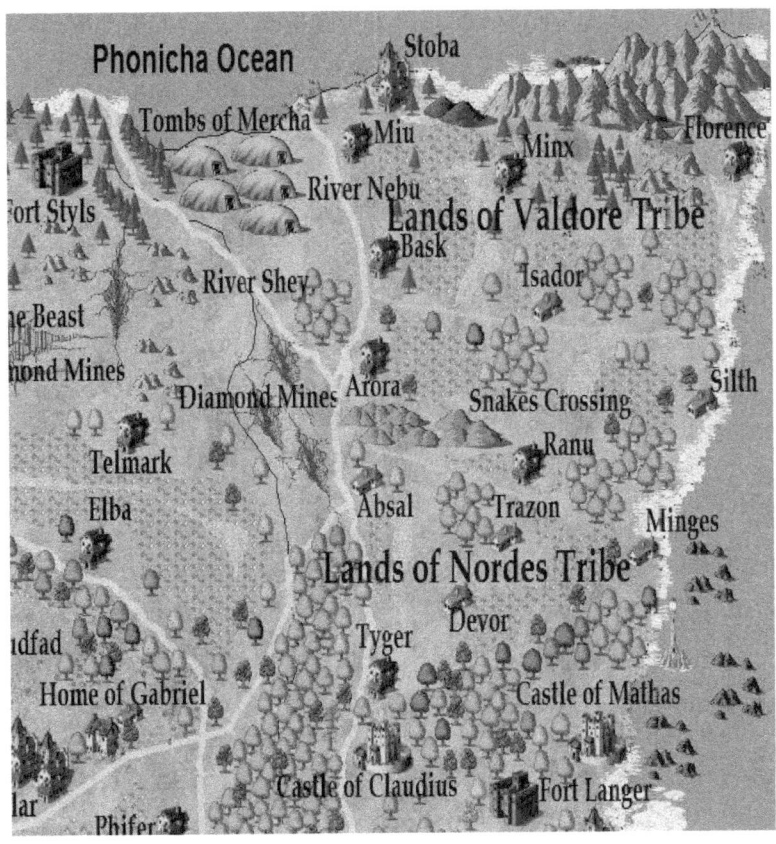

Marba

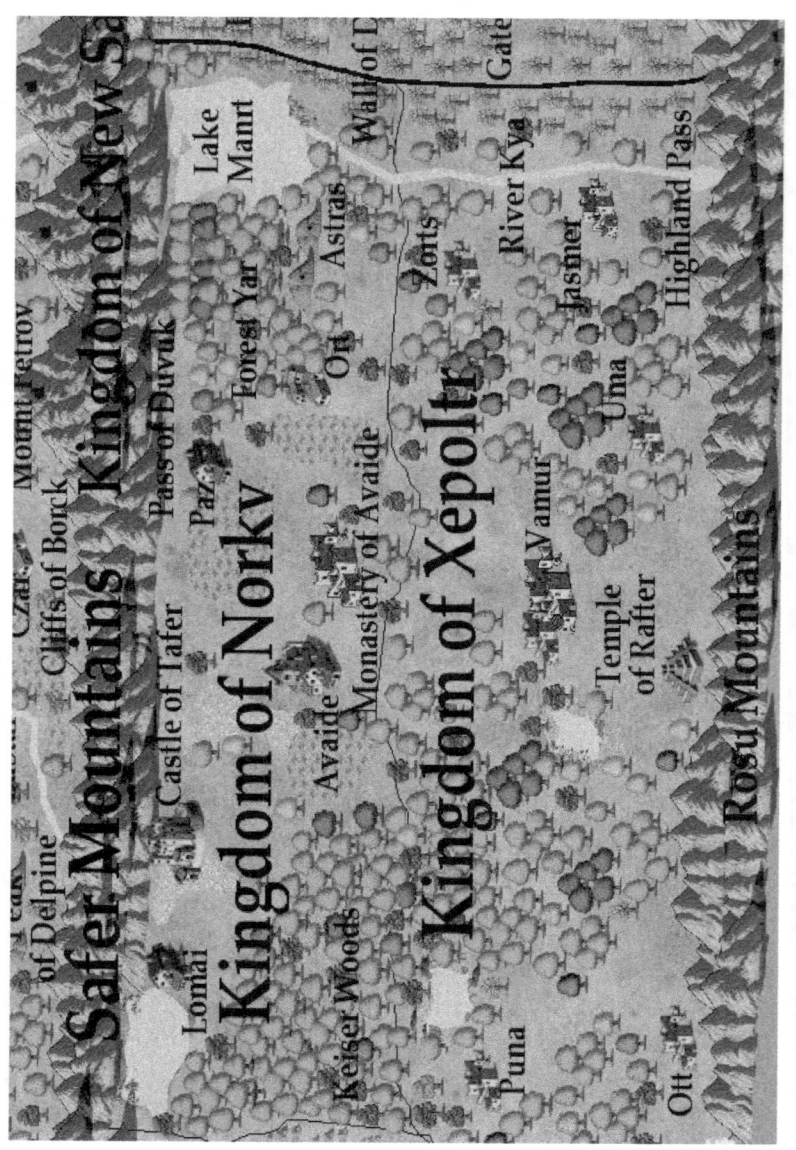

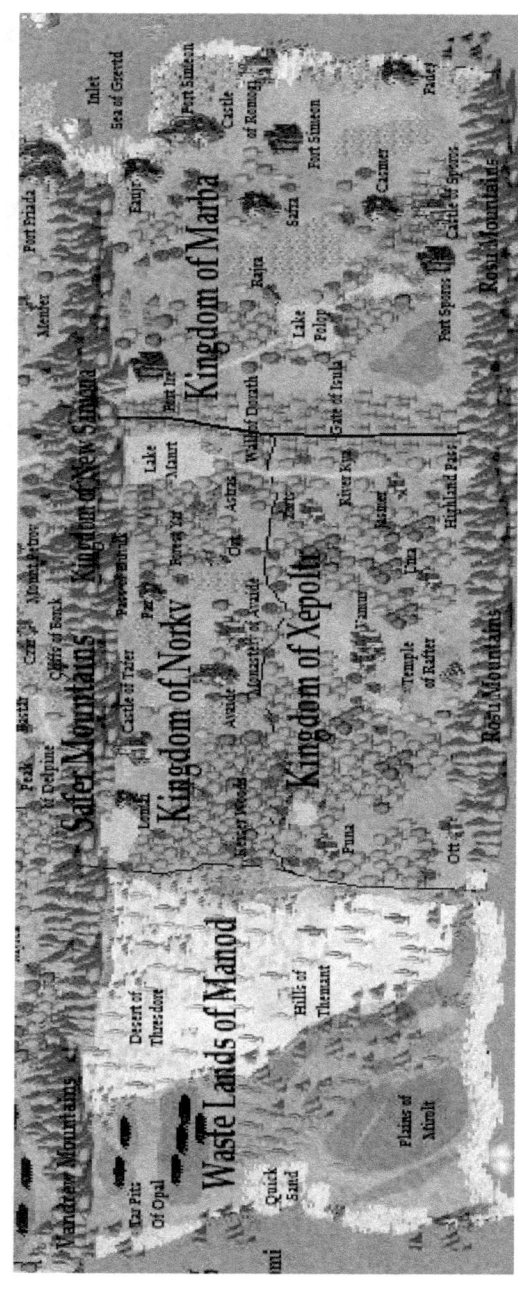

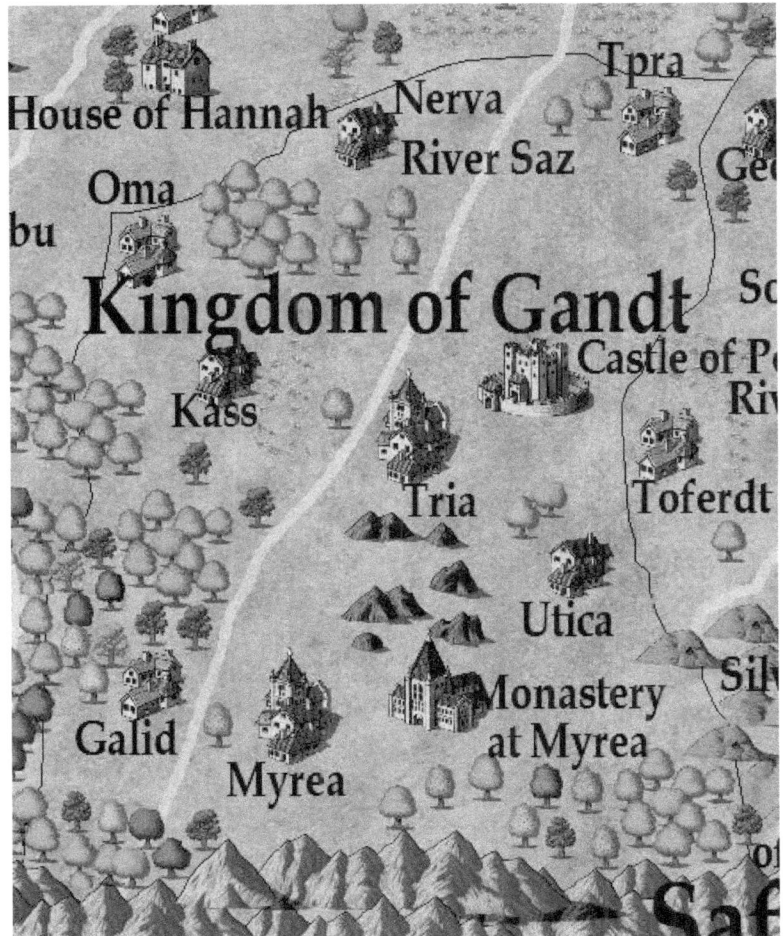